The Remaining
Refugees

ALSO BY D.J. MOLLES

The Remaining

The Remaining
The Remaining: Aftermath
The Remaining: Refugees
The Remaining: Fractured

The Remaining: Book 5 — Coming Spring 2015

The Remaining Short Fiction

"The Remaining: Trust"
"The Remaining: An Empty Soul"

The Remaining
REFUGEES

Book 3

D.J. Molles

www.orbitbooks.net
www.orbitshortfiction.com

Copyright © 2012 by D.J. Molles
Excerpt from *The Remaining: Fractured* copyright © 2013 by D.J. Molles
Cover design by Lauren Panepinto, cover photo by Arcangel Images. Cover copyright © 2014 by Orbit Books.

Orbit
Hachette Book Group
1290 Avenue of the Americas
New York, NY 10104
www.orbitbooks.net
www.orbitshortfiction.com

Originally self-published by the author: November 2012
First published by Orbit as e-book: January 2014
First Orbit print edition: July 2014

Orbit is an imprint of Hachette Book Group. The Orbit name and logo are trademarks of Little, Brown Book Group Limited.

The publisher is not responsible for websites (or their content) that are not owned by the publisher.

ISBN: 978-0-316-40420-4

Printed in the United States of America

10 9 8 7 6 5 4

*Thanks for everything—from proofreading
to trucks to demolitions training:
C. Adkins, Chris, Ed Herro,
and of course Dad.*

ONE

KILLBOX

THE TWO MEN WORKED QUIETLY.

In the cold morning light, diffused through a thin veil of clouds, their breath came out of them in bone-white plumes. Thick beards covered both of their faces. The shorter, balding man crouched over a single-burner camp stove and attached the small green propane tank. As the shorter man worked, the taller man held his tan-coated M4 rifle at a low-ready and scanned the derelict streets around them.

The concrete surrounding them sparkled with a thin sheen of frost. Squat buildings stared down over them like empty and plundered tombs. Their windows were either boarded up with graying plywood or smashed through, leaving only jagged glass teeth protruding from the window frames. Directly behind where the two men worked stood a two-story brick building, and as the tall man scanned, he could see dark figures atop the roof, silhouetted against the sky. The figures peered over the side and watched intensely.

The two men worked in the center of a four-lane street. Along the edges, trash had gathered at the base of the buildings and the gutters, where wind and rain had swept them. All of it was old and sun-bleached and melded into anonymous heaps. From these mounds of trash, hastily disguised, small green rectangles poked up. Wires ran off of them and trailed up the side of the building to where they dangled from the rooftop.

A lighter clicked.

Lee looked down to see Harper setting the lighter's tiny butane flame to the gas grill and slowly turning on the propane. There was a shallow hiss, and then blue flames jumped from the burner, sending up a wave of heat that felt pleasant on Lee's face. Harper adjusted the flames so they quivered low and then set a grungy-looking aluminum pan atop the grill.

"Your turn." Harper stood, his knees popping.

Lee took one last look at his surroundings and bent to the ground, where he had laid a small canvas satchel. He opened the top and retrieved the only item it contained: a gallon bag full of deer guts, the pale coils of intestines steeping in a marinade of blackening blood. His nose wrinkled as he bent over the grill and dumped the bag into the heating pan. The air smelled immediately of a stagnant slaughterhouse.

Harper growled low in his throat and shook his head. "Disgusting."

Lee nodded in agreement and gingerly zipped the plastic bag closed, stuffing it back into the canvas satchel. Letting his rifle rest on its sling, Lee pointed to the building where all the thin black wires trailed up to the roof. "Let's go."

Harper snatched his own M4 off the ground and they headed for the open door at the base of the building. Lee matched his pace, just barely showing the limp in his left leg. The ankle had never healed properly from his fall down the elevator shaft three months ago. His back hadn't been the same either, and it had become quite a process to get mobile in the morning.

They picked their way through the ransacked interior of the building—an old mom-and-pop pharmacy. The shelves had been tipped over, everything emptied and looted. Refugees and scavengers had taken what they needed, leaving behind the pill bottles and packages. At the back of the pharmacy, where a sign that read COLD REMEDIES hung over empty white shelves, a door opened into a stairwell that led up to the second level, and from there to the roof. The door was in splinters from when Lee had kicked it in earlier that night. The place still smelled of death. They had not moved the bodies of the pharmacist and his wife. They remained huddled in the dark corner of this shit-stained storage area.

The only light in the upstairs area came from an open skylight with a pull-down ladder to provide roof access and from the three glow sticks lying on the dark floor like a strewn-out constellation leading to the ladder and creating an eerie green glow across the floor.

Harper went up first and Lee followed.

On the roof, he found the other eight members of his team with their backs against the brick abutment of the roof and their rifles lying across their laps. Seven men and Julia, Marie's sister from Smithfield. She had insisted on being a part of the team and working as their medic. After she had explained her background as an EMT, Lee welcomed her to the team.

He crossed the tar-paper roof and sidled down between Julia and LaRouche. The sergeant's old tactical vest was worn and grimed to a grayish tan, and some of the edges were frayed from the constant hard use. His light brown hair was about as overgrown as Lee's, but he kept his reddish beard hacked shorter with his knife. As Lee sat down next to him, LaRouche dug a packet of Red Man out of his cargo pocket and stuffed his cheek with a giant chaw. He'd found a box of the stuff squirreled away in a house earlier that week and had been so overjoyed that Lee thought he might shed a tear.

LaRouche offered Lee the pouch, but he declined.

Lee turned his attention to his right, where Julia sat. Her skin was pale to the point of looking green and her lips were seized down to a short, flat line across her face. She avoided eye contact with Lee.

"You gonna be all right?" he asked.

She nodded but didn't speak.

He leaned back and stared up at the granite skies. "It has to be done."

She closed her eyes and shook her head. "I just can't find a way to make it right, Lee. I'm sorry, but I don't think I'm ever going to be comfortable with it like you are."

Lee didn't respond for a moment, just watched his breath drift up into the air. *It's going to be a cold winter*, he thought. *Not usually this cold by November*. He moistened his lips. "Just because I do it doesn't mean I'm comfortable with it."

"They're people."

"I don't know."

"They're people," she repeated.

Lee looked at her again, and this time she met his gaze.

He nodded. "Okay."

The smell of burning innards began to drift up to them from where the bloody mass boiled and smoked on the pan below them. He turned to his left where LaRouche, Harper, Father Jim, and the rest of the group were lined up, their hands resting on the grips of their rifles.

"Everybody locked and loaded?"

Thumbs-up from everybody.

Silence and grim faces.

Lee rose to his knees and peered over the abutment to the street below.

The downtown area of Lillington was spread out over a few small blocks. The building they were perched on stood at the southwest corner of Main Street and Front Street, where they had set up the small burner, letting the smells of dreadful cooking waft across the small town. Opposite them was a collection of small businesses: a barbershop, a diner, the Lillington Chamber of Commerce, and a few boutiques. Everything stood gray and dead and falling apart.

Still, there could be some salvage there.

Lee rested his bearded chin on his hand as he knelt. He watched and waited and remained silent along with his group as the minutes dragged themselves by like wounded animals, slow and painful. One of the group checked the chamber of his rifle, and then snicked the bolt back into place. LaRouche spit out a stream of tobacco juice that hit the tar paper with a sharp *splat*. Somewhere the lilting voice of a winter bird called out from a barren tree.

"Cap," someone whispered.

Lee looked over and saw Jeriah Wilson, the stocky black kid fresh out of the Air Force academy. He'd been a running back throughout high school, and his build showed it. His face bore only patchy wisps of hair across his chin, but his once-regulation crew cut had now become shaggy.

He tapped his ear and pointed out to the east toward Main Street.

Lee strained to hear, and for a brief moment as the steady cold breeze lulled, he could hear the patter of numerous feet coming from the streets below them. He looked at Jeriah again and nodded, then leaned up slightly over the abutment so he could see Main Street. Everything looked empty and devoid of life, and yet Lee could hear their soft footfalls just around the corner.

They were coming.

He shifted slightly and his hand came down slowly to touch the comforting grip of his rifle. His eyes stayed locked on the intersection.

The footfalls were louder now and interspersed with short, breathy snorts that could have been mistaken for some other noise from nature, if Lee were not so familiar with it. It was the noise they made when they were tracking something. Especially when they were tracking by smell.

The first one came around the corner quickly and then slowed.

Seeing it made every muscle in Lee's body stiffen.

Staring at it from his concealed vantage point, Lee thought it was a young boy, dark-haired and short of stature. He wore a stained pair of jeans and what had once been a white T-shirt, now tattered and darkened with gore. Steam rolled off the boy's shoulders, his body still hot from whatever wretched hovel he and his hundreds of den mates had packed themselves into for warmth. They liked low places, like basements and cellars, and they all huddled together during the night in one giant, twitching mass.

The thought of it made Lee's skin crawl.

"Eyes on," Lee whispered.

"Eyes on," LaRouche repeated down the line.

In the street below, the boy trotted out cautiously, now hunching down, now standing erect. His squinted eyes surveyed the scene but always came back to what had drawn him to this intersection: the scent of the deer guts, steaming atop that single-burner grill.

Marie had been right. The smell of cooking drew them in quickly. It tickled some tiny memories in their violently rearranged brains that promised food. It worked better than anything else.

The boy sniffed the air and eyed the grill again, then began to move closer. Behind him, his den mates appeared, a bedraggled horde of them. They began to chitter back and forth to each other excitedly. As they drew closer, their calling got louder, and they began to bark and screech and growl. They worked their hands reflexively and snapped at the air with their jaws. Lee counted as they moved onto Front Street, measuring them in segments of twenty-five, up until he reached approximately a hundred and fifty. The old and the weak and the nearly dead straggled in, taking up the rear of the column.

Lee crouched there on the abutment and breathed very slowly so that the fog of his breath would not give him away. His pulse was strong and quick, and he could feel the tightness in his stomach and in his throat.

He lowered himself very slowly and touched LaRouche on the shoulder. The sergeant looked up and Lee whispered, "You ready?"

LaRouche moved his chaw around in his mouth and nodded, his lips stained brown. He reached down to his side and held up a little green box with a wire running off of it.

Looking out onto the street again, Lee watched as the horde gathered around the boy. Now others were on the scent, and they were less cautious and quicker to move in on a possible source of food. This was a herd, not a pack. There was no leader, only the instinct to stay together, to move together. The stink of the burning entrails began to mix with the pungent living odor of the infected and it lifted up on the breeze and made bile rise in the back of Lee's throat.

"Little closer," he whispered to no one in particular, his lips barely moving.

Now the tip of the crowd had reached the bubbling pan of guts. They stood back perhaps three feet away or so and circled around, wary of the heat but certain there was food there. They were all on the verge of starvation, their skin stretched taut over their bones and their ribs standing out like the rungs on a ladder. The rest of the horde bunched up behind them, fanning out and filling the street.

Almost there, he thought.

The sweat on his palms chilled in the air.

The first of the infected leaned forward and took a swipe at the pan, knocking it off the grill and spilling the hot, bloody contents into the street. They screeched and jumped forward, their clawlike fingers rasping across the concrete as they grabbed chunks of organs and long strings of intestines. The horde pressed in, compacted, became one blob of flailing, grasping limbs, and the screeches became desperate as the feeding frenzy began.

"Now," Lee said.

LaRouche counted out the three clicks from the detonator: "One, two, *away*."

Lee watched as the four daisy-chained claymore mines exploded from where they were hidden in the piles of trash, scattering tatters of white paper that billowed out into the crowd like some violent confetti cannon.

The outside of the horde appeared to wilt as the hundreds of steel balls shooting out of the four simultaneous detonations cut them down. With the dust and smoke still hanging in the air and the horde of infected still unsteady on their feet, as their eardrums bled and their animal minds attempted to comprehend this thunder that had struck down their den mates, the rest of Lee's team crested the abutment with their rifles at the ready and barrages of withering fire erupted along the rooftop.

The creatures below howled in rage and pain. They turned in mad circles, striking out at each other in the smoke, biting and slashing at anything before them. They began to scatter, but then they bunched up again as their instinct took over, and they ran this way and that as the rifle fire echoed off the storefronts and confused them.

Their screeching began to lessen as more and more of them fell. The horde became a few stragglers trying to cling to life, and then only a dozen or so wounded that crawled and moaned and growled. The rifle fire became sporadic until there was only one infected left.

It was the same small boy who had come around the corner. His left arm was sheared off at the shoulder and he clutched his belly with the hand he had left and made a hideous noise.

Calmly, LaRouche raised his rifle while all the others ported theirs, smoke rising from the barrels. The boy writhed and moaned as LaRouche squinted through his sight and fired. Then there was silence.

LaRouche spat. "That's the last one."

The group looked down at their handiwork.

In the street lay the sprawled remains of what was left of Lillington's populace. Some of them stared up into the sky with glassy eyes while others lay facedown in their own muck. The spaces between their bodies glistened darkly as thin streams of red meandered away from the road and toward the trash-clogged drains.

LaRouche slapped Harper's shoulder and pointed. "Shit, Harper. I think your grill is still going."

Harper nodded slowly and looked slightly nauseated. "Yeah."

LaRouche was clearly impressed. "Damn thing's indestructible."

Lee grabbed his pack up from the floor and slung his arms into it. "Everyone refresh your mags."

Those who had not done so already put fresh magazines in their rifles and stowed the half-full ones in the pockets of their field jackets. They stooped and gathered their empty magazines and put them in a different pocket.

Julia remained still during this.

She hadn't fired a shot.

"Wilson." Lee pointed to the Air Force cadet. "Get your guys and pull the Humvees around. Let's start setting up shop."

Wilson nodded and headed for the ladder down, his three companions falling in behind him.

The two Humvees that Lee had repossessed from Milo were parked around the corner. The block of buildings that they stood in created a perfect square around an empty parking lot. With some measures to fortify the doors and windows of these buildings, the interior parking lot could be used as a base and the buildings as a wall. A little concertina wire and some barricades, and Outpost Lillington would be secure.

Wilson and his team slid quickly down the ladder and disappeared into the empty pharmacy below. Lee thought about telling them to be cautious—there would be others lurking in the city. But it was unnecessary. Everyone was already cautious. They all jumped at shadows and slept lightly, always anticipating the next round of misfortune.

"Let's go down there and check it out." Lee put a hand on LaRouche's shoulder. "You mind keeping overwatch again?"

The sergeant shook his head. "Nope. I got it."

They went down and emerged from the pharmacy onto Front Street. It was Lee, Harper, Julia, and Father Jim. They were a good team, Lee had to admit. Though Julia refused to take part in the traps they set to clear the small towns of infected, she still did the training and pulled her weight along with everyone else. Plus, her medical knowledge made her invaluable. Lee had spent a lot of time training his team, and they were practiced and tested almost every day. They were still a far cry from professional soldiers, but they were fluid, most of them were decent shots, and they got the job done.

Standing on the sidewalk in front of the shop, they stared at the carnage in the streets.

"Jim, Harper..." Lee pointed to the front of the shop. "Post up here. We'll strip the pharmacy."

The two men nodded. Julia followed Lee back into the building. The interior already looked ransacked, but most things did these days. There wasn't much left, but they managed to pull a few large bottles of medications that Lee was unfamiliar with, along with some prescription pain relievers and some over-the-counter items such as antidiarrheal medicines, ibuprofen, acetaminophen, and antibacterial ointments. Julia piled these items into her pack just as the Humvees rumbled into the back parking lot.

Lee called out to Jim and Harper and they all headed for the back lot.

The two Humvees sat in the interior parking lot, one behind the other. The lead Humvee had been outfitted with a dozer blade that now sat angled up so as not to impede the vehicle's ground clearance—a bit of creative welding. Wilson and his three teammates were already offloading spools of barbed wire, some of which they had taken from the barricades in Smithfield and some they had found in various farm equipment stores.

The back lot was half paved and half dusty gravel. Two small sedans and a pickup truck sat abandoned, parked along the rear of the buildings. There were two entrances into the back lot, one from the south and one from the west. The western entrance was only wide enough for one vehicle to pass through at a time, while the southern entrance was much bigger. For this reason, Lee made the decision to block the southern entrance. The materials to barricade it would be harvested from the refuse around them, including the cars already parked in the back lot, Dumpsters, and any other heavy objects they could haul into place.

While the rest of the team finished offloading the Humvees, Lee sat in the passenger seat of the lead vehicle and grabbed the handset to the SINCGARS—Single Channel Ground and Airborne Radio System—mounted inside. He dispensed with proper radio protocols and used plain English when he spoke.

"Captain Harden to Camp Ryder. How do you copy me?"

A hiss of static.

A gravelly voice answered. "Yeah, I got you, Captain."

Lee smiled. "Morning, Bus. Haven't had your coffee?"

"Don't remind me. Haven't had coffee in months." Bus cleared his throat. "Did you get Lillington cleared?"

"Yeah, it's clear."

"Anybody hurt?"

"Nope." Lee looked out at his team, now in the process of breaking into the abandoned cars in the back lot so they could be moved and used as barricades. "They're just getting everything set up right now."

"Sounds good. I know Old Man Hughes won't tell you, but everyone from Dunn really appreciates what you're doing out there. It's been cramped quarters over here."

Lee nodded. Old Man Hughes was the leader of nineteen other survivors from the town of Dunn to the southeast. He was a crotchety old bastard, but for some reason the Dunn survivors loved him. Due to overcrowding at Camp Ryder, the twenty from Dunn were slated to move to Lillington and establish an outpost there, along with another twelve from Fuquay-Varina.

"Not a problem," Lee said simply.

"I'll let Old Man Hughes know. They'll be on their way shortly. Any trouble on the roads?"

"No, the road was clear. Make sure they stick to the route we planned."

"Will do. What time should we expect you back?"

Lee thought out loud. "I think we'll leave most of the scavenging for the new residents. My guys need some sleep and I need to restock some of our ordnance. So we'll probably head out shortly after they get here." He clucked his tongue. "I'd say around noon at the latest."

"Sounds good. See you at noon."

"Roger. Out." Lee put the handset back on its cradle.

As he stood from the Humvee, he watched Harper exit the back door of the pharmacy. The older man's face was clouded, and he approached Lee with a purposeful walk, avoiding eye contact until he was standing right in front of him.

Lee felt that old familiar certainty of the worst-case scenario creeping up on him. "What's wrong?"

Harper squinted one eye. "Not really sure."

Lee stared at him blankly.

"Take a look at something." Harper began walking back toward the pharmacy, and Lee followed. "Jim just pointed it out to me. I hadn't noticed it before but...Well, just come look."

They made their way through the pharmacy to the open front door and out onto Front Street.

In the middle of the road, mired by bodies lying two deep in places and surrounded by the overwhelming stench, Jim stood and looked around at the corpses, a finger pressed thoughtfully to his lips. Lee turned to catch a glimpse of the rooftop behind and above him and saw LaRouche resting his elbows there on the abutment. The sergeant met Lee's eyes and gave a minimal shrug, as though Father Jim's actions mystified him as well.

Lee stood at the edge of the bloodbath. "Jim?"

The man in the tortoiseshell glasses looked up and nodded by way of greeting.

Harper put his hands on his hips. "Tell him."

Jim looked around hesitantly, as though he were in the process of some complicated calculation, confident that his math was correct but somehow coming up with the wrong answer every time. Finally he gestured to the bodies around him. "There are no females."

Lee's brow narrowed.

He looked around as though he might prove Jim wrong. He stared down at the pale limbs covered in dried and fresh blood. Their clothing barely clung to them in tatters. It was difficult to determine gender by a glance—malnutrition robbed them of most of their distinctions so that all that remained were bony sacks of flesh. Lee had to look at their faces and see the grizzled, mangy beards, clumped together by clots of blood. Some of them were too young to have beards, but they were male as well. He searched and searched but could not find a single female to discount what Jim had said.

"That's weird." Lee spoke slowly. "But..."

"There were none in the last two traps we set in Smithfield either." Father Jim looked at him with fevered eyes. "Or at the university. Or at Dunn. In fact, when was the last time you saw an infected female, Captain?"

Lee didn't respond.

He had no answer.

"What do you think happened to them?" Harper asked quietly.

Jim began carefully stepping between the bodies, making his way toward Lee and Harper. "Not sure," he said simply. "Could be that they aren't as strong, so the male infected feed on them."

Lee thought back to the young girl, the first infected he'd encountered as he stepped out of his house and into this new reality so long ago. She had been a scrawny thing but shockingly powerful. "I don't know about strength being the issue," Lee said. "Besides, if that were the case, why not kill and eat the young ones too?"

Jim shrugged. "I have no idea. I'm just making an observation."

Lee stared down at the bodies for a moment more. He could find nothing further to say on the subject, so he nodded back toward the buildings. "Let's get rid of these bodies. I don't want to give the assholes from Fuquay-Varina anything else to bitch about."

They drove the Humvee with the dozer attachment out to Front Street and lowered the blade so that it was only an inch off the ground. Lee watched from the sidewalk as Harper moved the vehicle in slow, broad strokes, the blade gathering up a tumble of pale bodies and pushing them toward a vacant lot at the northeastern corner of the intersection. Then Harper put the vehicle in reverse and backed slowly through the thickening blood, the tires slinging droplets of it down the sides of the vehicle. The thought of all that infected blood still gave Lee cause to worry, but over the last few months, several survivors—including Lee—had come into contact with infected blood and had not contracted the plague. They'd determined that simple blood-on-skin contact didn't contribute to infection.

After nearly an hour of back and forth, Harper had managed to clear Front Street of most of the bodies. The ones he couldn't get to—the ones that were huddled behind trees and in the corners of buildings—were picked up by hand and placed in the path of the dozer so he could push them into the growing pile. They mixed in pallets and pieces of wood and doused it all with diesel fuel and set it on fire with a road flare. Lee stood back from the blaze and watched the acrid black smoke curl into the sky as Harper drove the Humvee-turned-dozer back into the parking lot behind the buildings.

The use of fuel was a shame, but they didn't have the equipment to dig mass graves, and leaving rotting bodies out in the open was not only offensive to the senses but a serious health hazard, even if they were uninfected. An expired human body became a petri dish for diseases of all types. On top of that, the rotting meat had been known to draw other infected into the area. It was best to dispose of them quickly.

Beside him, Father Jim looked down Main Street. "They'll see the smoke, you know."

Lee shrugged. "Nothing I can do about it, Jim."

"I know." He put a hand on Lee's shoulder. "But you know that asshole White is going to say something."

Lee smiled and looked shocked. "Father . . . such language."

Jim waved him off. "To call Professor White anything but an asshole would be to lie. And lying lips are an abomination to the Lord."

LaRouche joined them in the middle of the street, his cheek still bulging from tobacco.

Lee nodded to him. "How long you keep that shit in your mouth?"

LaRouche spat. "Gotta conserve."

Both Jim and Lee shrugged and nodded. It was a valid point.

From the north end of Main Street they could hear the rumble of a bus downshifting, muted by distance. Main Street dipped down into a slight grade and leveled out as it crossed over the Cape Fear River. Lee could see clearly in the winter air, and from the other side of the bridge, he watched the big white bus come into view, led by a blue sixteen-passenger van. Those two vehicles would contain all that was left of Dunn and Fuquay-Varina, along with all the worldly possessions they had managed to carry out with them. Which wasn't much.

Lee remained standing in the intersection as the vehicles approached, his hands folded and resting on the buttstock of his slung rifle. The gray skies washed the windshields out to a pale reflection of nothing, and he could not see who was driving either vehicle. He supposed the Fuquay-Varina group would be in the van, as there were only twelve of them compared to Dunn's twenty.

LaRouche smiled at Lee. "Can't wait to hear what the great Professor White has to say to you this time."

Lee smiled wanly but didn't feel much humor in it.

The van crested the hill and began to slow, the brakes on it squealing as it pulled to a stop in the middle of the intersection with the driver's side window rolled down. Sitting in the driver's seat was an aging man with longish salt-and-pepper hair, pulled back into a ponytail. He looked over the rims of thick glasses as though Lee were one of his pupils who had spoken out of turn in class.

Lee met his gaze and fought to keep his face neutral. "Mr. White."

Professor Tommy White of the once-prestigious Chapel Hill University pursed his lips. The rumbling of the engines at idle filled the silence between the two men. Lee watched as the professor's eyes flicked to the burning pile of bodies. They stayed there and the man's face seemed to wilt. Then he just looked straight ahead again. Someone in the van began to weep loudly.

Lee sniffed and smelled charred flesh.

He pointed down Front Street. "Take your first left onto Eighth Street. Entrance is on the left."

A teary-eyed girl, perhaps twenty years old,

appeared in the front of the van. She stared accusingly at Lee and bawled at him. "Why? Why'd you do it?"

"So you can be safe," Lee responded with thinly veiled annoyance.

The girl began to speak but Professor White held up his hand and shook his head. "It's pointless, Natalie. You won't convince him." White looked at Lee again. "We'll be going now."

Lee nodded. "Please do."

The van lurched forward quickly and made the right-hand turn onto Front Street, followed by the quick left turn onto Eighth Street. Lee watched them go with a small shake of his head and kept telling himself, *You don't get to choose who you rescue. You don't get to choose...*

The bus lumbered after the van. From the driver's window, Lee could see Old Man Hughes standing in the center aisle while a younger survivor from Dunn piloted the bus. The old man tossed Lee a salute and a nod of thanks.

"Hey." LaRouche put a hand on his shoulder. "At least someone appreciates us."

Lee made a chuckling sound that was born of frustration and anger. "It just never ends with these fuckers, does it?"

LaRouche flicked his hand dismissively. "Those fuckers have been living off of guys like me and you for centuries. They love their safety and security, but they'll never stop bitching about how we accomplish it." The sergeant shrugged. "Ain't nothin' you can do about it."

Lee nodded. Without further words, they began

to walk toward the newly created Outpost Lillington. They had nearly reached the door to the pharmacy when Jeriah Wilson burst through. His eyes found Lee and he raised his hand to flag him down.

"What's up, Wilson?"

"Hey, Captain." Wilson looked confused, maybe a little curious. "Just got a call from Camp Ryder. Outpost Benson made contact with a guy, some survivor, and they're bringing him into Camp Ryder right now."

Lee's eyes narrowed. "Okay. And why are they calling for us?"

"Well, they're calling for you," Wilson corrected.

"Did they say why?"

"The guy says he's from Virginia." Wilson met Lee's gaze. "And he asked for you by name."

TWO

THE HUB

LEE STALKED TO THE Humvee as quickly as he could without showing his limp, ignoring the young college kids from Fuquay-Varina who sided with their old professor and grumbled about him as he passed. A few of the middle-aged survivors from Fuquay-Varina murmured their appreciation to Lee, and he nodded to them politely but distractedly. Not everyone from Fuquay-Varina was opposed to him, but as a whole they went along with whatever Professor White said. Jeriah Wilson had been the one major exception.

At the big green truck, Lee ripped open the passenger door and snatched the handset from the cradle, keying it up before he even had it to his ear. "Captain Harden to Camp Ryder."

A click. Someone whose voice he didn't recognize came on. "This is Camp Ryder. Go ahead, Captain."

"Is there someone asking for me?"

"Uh…" Shuffling, and then the radio clicked off for a brief moment. "Yeah, let me get Bus."

Lee waited quietly, leaning his elbow on the frame of the Humvee and chewing at the inside of his lip.

"Bus here."

Lee looked at the radio as though he might see Bus through it. "Is there some guy looking for me?"

"Yeah, two of our guys from Outpost Benson are bringing him to Camp Ryder." Bus sounded bewildered. "From what they described, the guy's at death's door. Dehydrated, starving, but they say he's wearing a vest, like a military one. Says his name is Jacob."

Lee racked his brain. "I don't know a Jacob."

"Well, he knows you."

"Was he armed?" Lee pinched the bridge of his nose and squeezed his eyes shut.

"When they first found him, yes," Bus said. "But they said he wasn't hostile. Surrendered immediately and laid down his weapon. They said it was an M4, but they're also saying this guy doesn't seem like military at all."

Lee could think of plenty of people he knew in the military who didn't look the part. Not everyone was a lean, mean fighting machine. Many of them worked behind the lines and would never see a day of combat in their entire career.

Lee opened his eyes again. "Did he say why he's looking for me?"

"Um...damn, Lee." Bus huffed into the microphone. "I haven't talked to the guy yet. I just have secondhand information. I think they said he claimed to have information for you or something. Something about Virginia."

"Virginia?" Lee said incredulously. "What the hell do I need to know about Virginia?"

Bus keyed up again. "Look, I have no idea what this guy is about. We'll get him cleaned up and tended to. You just get back here so you can talk to him and figure out what's going on."

Lee licked his lips and felt them getting chapped in the cold, dry air. "Okay. We'll be en route here shortly."

He hung up the handset, grabbed a bottle of water from the floorboard, and drank from it. The cold water ached as it filtered through the empty slot in his gums where he'd lost his right canine tooth to a flying cafeteria chair. If the memory of it didn't make him cringe, it might have been humorous.

He turned outward and regarded the parking lot, encircled by brick buildings. It was now crowded, the two Humvees, the van, and the bus taking up much of the space, but also with more than thirty survivors carrying their personal items from the vehicles and placing them to the sides of the building. Everything they owned, wrapped up in a tattered old blanket or stuffed in a ragged pack of some sort.

Looking out at all these people, he caught their sidelong glances at him, and the expressions behind those brief moments of eye contact varied greatly. The survivors from Dunn revered him as some sort of war hero. He and his team had rescued them after a hard-fought battle, and their appreciation showed. Then there were those from Fuquay-Varina, whom Lee had simply stumbled across, and their perceptions of him were much less generous.

He resented them, though he tried hard not to let it bother him.

He resented their looks and their whispers.

He resented their simplistic worldview.

But most of all, he resented being judged. He resented that every action was worthy of intense scrutiny and that some Monday-morning quarterback would always have an astounding hindsight solution for him that somehow, he should have already known. "Weren't you trained for this?" they would ask him. And he would bite his tongue and try not to think about kicking their teeth in.

This was the war he was destined to fight.

A war where victory would be measured in how many he could save, regardless of their opinions. And though he may be weak in patience and politics, he was gifted in fighting and winning. And if winning meant putting up with some assholes who thought they knew how shit should be run, then so be it. That was just a pill he would have to swallow.

He finished what was left in the water bottle and dropped it in the front seat so he could refill it later. His thoughts turned back to the stranger from Virginia who somehow knew him. From across the parking lot, he saw Harper and Jim standing together near the pharmacy entrance and eyeing him with open curiosity. He waved them over.

"What's going on?" Harper asked as he approached.

Lee adjusted his rifle sling so it was more comfortable across his shoulders. "I don't know. Some guy from Virginia is asking for me. By name, apparently. I don't know the guy, though." He craned his neck to survey all around him. "Where's LaRouche?"

Jim threw a thumb over his shoulder in the general direction of Front Street. "He and Jake are helping secure the doors and windows on the outside."

"Alright." Lee rubbed some warmth back into his bearded face. "Jim, go get LaRouche and let him know we're leaving in five. Jake can stay. Harper, relay to Wilson and his team that we'll be leaving. I want them to stay here and help for the time being. I'll radio them if I need them back over at Camp Ryder. I'm going to, uh…" Lee trailed off. "I'll be ready in a minute."

Harper and Jim nodded discreetly.

Lee turned away from them and headed into the crowd.

He found Julia making her way down the line of refugees, checking everyone for illness before they let them cram together in tight spaces and get the whole outpost sick. Cold, flu, and the ensuing pneumonia promised to be a problem for them this year. People simply couldn't sanitize like they used to. There was now a full generation of people who had been addicted to sanitizing gels and wipes, whose immune systems were not quite as robust as they should be for this type of lifestyle.

Julia was easy to spot by her tawny hair, pulled back into some practical arrangement Lee didn't know the name of. It was darkened now with sweat and oil and smoke from three days in the field, and it was plastered back to her skull because she constantly worried at it with her dirty hands.

He fell in step behind her as she worked her way through the thirty or so refugees.

"How are you?" she asked one of them, an older woman.

"I'm fine, just tired."

"Any persistent cough, runny nose, or soreness in your throat?"

"No."

"Any aches or chills?"

"No."

"Can you breathe through your nose?"

The woman demonstrated.

Julia held up a penlight. "Open your mouth and say 'ah.'"

"Aaahhh."

Julia shone her light around, decided everything was good except for a case of bad breath—not so uncommon nowadays—and smiled. "Thank you."

Lee nodded to the older woman as they passed to the next person. "We're heading out in five. Wilson and his team are staying. You staying here or coming with us?"

She looked at him and Lee didn't see any of the reproach from earlier.

She nodded quickly. "I'll be ready to go in just a few. I'm finishing up now."

"Okay." Lee turned partially away but felt the need to reiterate the time frame. "Five minutes."

Her eyebrows went up slightly. "Yup. I'll be ready, Captain."

He decided not to say anything else.

In four minutes they were rolling. A thin layer of clouds ranged across the horizon, showing sterling in the thickest parts, shot through with ribbons of bright sunlight like gold and silver smelted together.

The Humvee with the dozer attachment growled out of the parking lot, bristling with weapons as it exited the outpost and left the town and its new residents behind them. Harper drove with Lee in the passenger seat. Jim and Julia sat in the back, and LaRouche was crammed in the middle with the .50-caliber M2 machine gun mounted on top.

Lee turned to look out the driver's side of the vehicle and found LaRouche's dirty boots once again resting atop the radio console—a natural footrest for whoever was sitting in the turret. Lee elbowed them off.

"Keep your fucking feet off the radio, LaRouche," Lee griped for the umpteenth time.

"My bad," LaRouche mumbled from up top.

All the windows were down, letting the cold wind blow through the vehicle so that they could all rest their weapons in the window frames, pointing out into a world that had grown dangerous and alien.

"Well, I'm very pleased with Outpost Lillington," Father Jim offered up brightly. "It seems like a very secure location."

Lee looked out the passenger-side window at the passing terrain. He nodded slowly and remained introspective.

"Should lock down this section of highway," Jim continued. "Extend the patrols out a bit... Make movement a little safer..." He seemed to

realize that no one else was in the mood for conversation and let his words trail off. He turned
back to his own window.

Lee's mind poked cautiously at the questions
that nagged him, like you might poke a stick into
a dark hole in the forest floor, unsure of what lay
inside. Who was the man from Virginia, and what
did he want? What news did he bring? Lee wanted
to believe that it could be good news but felt in
his gut that it was not. Good news didn't come
with a single man, sick and exhausted from miles
on the road.

Underneath all of that, a question remained
that seemed so inconspicuous in its simplicity but
that Lee felt was just the tip of something vast and
unseen, and it whispered foul omens:

Where have all the females gone?

They passed over the Cape Fear River. The
water looked cold and dark, the same color as the
woods that surrounded it. The weather had only
been this cold for the past week, and a few trees
along the banks still clung stubbornly to their
brown and wilted leaves, but for the most part
the forests were bare. Just a tangle of empty limbs
and gray bark, splashes of emerald here and there
where a lonesome evergreen stood.

Clattering over the four-lane bridge, Lee wondered when was the last time the bridge had been
refurbished. Infrastructure was just another one of
the many concerns constantly vying for attention
in the back of his mind. Survivors were integral to
the success of his mission. He had to rely on them
to assist in rebuilding.

But there were so few.

Far fewer than he had ever imagined.

Engineers were at the top of his list: civil engineers, electrical engineers, mechanical engineers... the list went on. At this point, he'd take any kind of engineer he could get his hands on. But it seemed that they were lucky to find survivors at all, let alone someone with a specific skill set.

"Heads up," Jim said suddenly from behind him.

Lee's eyes snapped into focus and he looked out the passenger side of the vehicle. The grade of the earth coming off the road sloped down into a deep ravine that cut toward the Cape Fear River and ran parallel to the roadway. On the other side of that ravine, the ground rose up in a steep incline, and it was there, about midway up the face of that hill, that Lee could see what had drawn Jim's attention.

"Movement! Right side!" Lee called.

"I don't think..." Jim pushed his glasses up on his face and squinted to see farther.

There were four of them in all. Two large ones and two small. They were strange and bulky in their appearance, and it took a moment for Lee to realize that all of them were heaped with heavy coats and blankets to keep them warm.

LaRouche swiveled in the turret, bringing the fifty about.

Jim slapped at LaRouche's legs. "Don't shoot! I don't think they're infected!"

"Relax!" LaRouche dodged his legs about. "I'm not gonna waste 'em..."

"Stop here!" Jim spoke with urgency.

Harper looked back incredulously. "I'm not stopping here."

The sound of Jim's door unlatching.

"Close your fucking door!" Harper barked at him.

"Hey!" Jim leaned out the window, his door still hanging partially open. "Hello!"

Lee reached across and slapped Harper's shoulder. "Stop before he falls out."

The Humvee screeched to a halt, causing everyone inside to lurch forward and LaRouche to slap the top of the roof, trying to gain his balance again.

"It's okay!" Jim yelled again.

The figures were now almost to the top of the hill. One turned and Lee could see the face peering at them with dark, suspicious eyes, his jawline shadowed by the scraggly beginnings of a beard. It was a younger man with a tan complexion, possibly Hispanic, but difficult to tell from this distance. The unknown man turned back around and pushed the others ahead of him—they appeared to be a dark-haired woman and two small children.

"What are you doing, Jim?" Lee said with a note of caution.

From behind him, Lee heard the loud creak of the dry, rusted door hinges as the ex-priest flung his door open. Lee twisted in his seat and tried to reach through to the back and grab a fistful of his jacket, but Jim was already out the door.

"Hey!" Lee growled. "Get the fuck back in here!"

Father Jim completely ignored Lee, even left his rifle in his seat and stood outside the Humvee with both arms raised above his head. "It's okay, we're here to help! You don't have to be afraid. We won't hurt you!"

They continued to clamber up the steep embankment.

Lee kicked his door open with force and slid out of his seat, bringing his rifle to his shoulder. He resisted the urge to simply grab the other man and stuff him back in the Humvee. Warning Klaxons were blaring in his head and he could feel heat rising up the back of his neck. He reached out and put a hand on Jim's shoulder. "What are you doing? Leave it..."

Jim shrugged the hand off and continued waving his arms. His voice took on a desperate quality. "We're here to help you. It's okay! You don't have to be afraid!"

The four strangers reached the top of the hillock and dipped over to the other side, the man pushing the woman and the two children over before disappearing himself. Just before vanishing onto the other side, he turned and looked at them again, and this time his eyes locked onto Lee. He appeared to hesitate for the briefest of moments, but then ducked down over the top of the hill.

Jim stood in the street with his hands still raised.

The look on his face was one of complete confusion.

The breath came out of him in a long blast of steam.

Finally he let his arms drop to his sides.

"What the heck?" he said indignantly.

He turned back around and found the rest of his squad looking at him. From the driver's seat of the

Humvee, Harper shook his head just slightly and then studiously avoided eye contact. Julia held his gaze a bit longer, showing a measure of concern. Lee looked at him severely and grabbed his shoulder again, this time more firmly.

"What the hell was that?" Lee demanded.

Jim looked over his shoulder toward the hill, but they could see nothing. "I dunno...I just thought that...I thought..."

"Come on." Lee pulled him toward the Humvee again. "Let's go."

"I thought they needed help."

"They probably did. But we're an armed vehicle—would you have stopped?"

"No," Jim mumbled.

LaRouche sighed and let the barrel of the fifty rise up and point at the tops of the trees. He leaned over and spat. "Maybe I shouldn't have pointed the Ma Deuce at 'em."

Lee looked back into the woods. Faintly, he thought he could hear them crashing through the forest, just barely audible above the grumbling Humvee at idle. He ushered Jim back into the Humvee, the ex-priest seeming deflated and limp. He closed the door and then got back into the front passenger's seat and pointed on down the road.

"Let's keep moving."

There was a moment of silence, thick and uncomfortable.

Then Harper put the vehicle in gear and they continued on.

From the backseat, barely audible over the

sound of the engine and the wind rushing by the open windows, Father Jim murmured, "I'm sorry. I thought we could help."

They arrived at Camp Ryder before noon.

In the span of a few months, Camp Ryder had undergone some extreme changes. Some of the ramshackle huts were gone, and "The Square" had graduated from an empty area with a fire pit in the center to a noisy open-air market. Those who scavenged would set up spots inside the Square to barter items they had found—anything from dental floss to batteries or canned food. While everything Lee and his group gathered in their scavenging operations went into a pool to be distributed evenly through the group, scavenging had quickly become a livelihood for those with the impetus to go outside the gates.

The influx of Lee's rifles and ammunition had played a large role in making scavenging possible. Since accessing Bunker #4 three months ago, Lee had emptied it in the course of several trips to and from. The outposts they had set up at several key locations in the area ran patrols along the major roads, keeping them mostly clear of raiders and their roadblocks. He had distributed a rifle and five hundred rounds of ammunition to every member of the community who wanted them, provided they were over the age of sixteen. This was a defensive measure. If the community came under attack from infected hordes or from a human threat, Lee wanted each and every adult man and woman to be able to join the fight.

While the area was safer now than it had been after the initial collapse, it was still dangerous and they'd taken some losses. Infected were a constant threat, and the patrolling of the roads did very little to limit them. The previous week, two scavengers had been killed before they could make it back to their vehicles and flee. The infected had them almost completely surrounded by the time the scavengers knew what was happening.

Last month alone they'd lost five.

The month before that, seven.

But even with the constant danger, the scavengers had successfully created a thriving trade economy right there in the heart of Camp Ryder. They traded among themselves frequently, but people came in from the other communities that had been incorporated into the collection of towns and neighborhoods that was being called the "Camp Ryder Hub," and every so often they got visitors from the two groups of survivors that had decided to remain independent of Camp Ryder: Newton Grove to the southeast and Broadway to the west.

Speak of the devil...Lee thought as he noticed the red Isuzu Rodeo pulling in just past the gate.

The driver would be Kip Greene from Broadway. He came to Camp Ryder for two reasons: to talk with Bus and to trade with the scavengers. The Broadway survivors were almost all farming families, and they had continued to tend their crops as best they could after the collapse. They used what they could spare of their harvest to trade at the Square.

Harper pulled the Humvee up to the gate,

where a group of three scavengers was preparing to leave and receiving white armbands from the sentries posted there. Every day had a randomly assigned color. An appropriately colored strip of cloth would be given to the scavengers as they left so they could quickly identify themselves as friends when they approached the gate later.

The three scavengers hustled out of the way as the sentry pulled the gate open for the Humvee as they rolled into camp. Harper pulled their Humvee to the right and parked it out of the way. Behind them, Lee could hear the chain-link fence rolling shut. Recently reinforced with scrap metal and hanging heavy on its hinges, it rattled and clanked noisily as it closed.

Lee eased his way out of his seat and took a moment to work some blood back into his stiff ankle. Feeling a little more limber, he walked to the rear of the vehicle and hauled his heavy pack onto one shoulder. As he stood up, the hollow feeling of hunger seeped into his midsection and his stomach growled noisily. He glanced across the dusty parking area and could see Angela standing there with Sam by her side. They both waved to him when he looked in their direction.

Inwardly, he could not shake how strange this made him feel, still the impostor living another man's life. But outwardly he smiled, waved back, and made his way over to them.

Angela looked at him brightly, her pale skin flushed at the nose and cheeks against the chilling wind. She pulled her jacket closer around her. "Good to see you back, Lee."

She reached one hand out, and Lee took it. Not a handshake, but a quick and heartfelt squeeze. What there was between them was a mystery to Lee, but he had long ago decided to go with it, because despite his reservations, it was something real. It was something he could come back to. Something to ground him so that his entire existence was not an unending slough of death and conflict.

"Where's Abby?" Lee asked.

"She's learning how to sew with some of the other kids."

Abby hadn't warmed up to him, and it didn't seem like she was going to.

"Did you hear about the guy who's asking for you?" Sam broke in, peering up at Lee with one eye squinted against the sun.

"Yeah, I heard," Lee said and glanced at Angela, who returned a quizzical look. To Sam again, Lee said, "Did you learn anything new the last few days?"

"Mr. Keith taught me how to shoot his .22 rifle," Sam nodded with a smile. "We went out and got a couple rabbits. He said I was a natural. Showed me how to skin them and cook them and everything."

"Wow." Lee's eyes went up. "He took you outside the fence?"

"Is that okay? We didn't go very far."

"Yeah." He pictured the old man and Sam running through a field with wild-eyed and shit-covered crazies sprinting after them, screeching and howling. Then he saw blood and entrails smeared across the grassy earth. He swallowed. "I'm sure Mr. Keith was smart about it."

Angela spoke up. "Where're you off to now?"

Lee pointed a thumb toward the Camp Ryder building. "I gotta get up with Bus and figure out what's going on with this guy from Virginia. You hear anything about it?"

She shook her head. "Last I heard he was in the medical trailer, passed out. He was in pretty bad shape."

"How so?"

"Jenny mentioned dehydration, dysentery, mal-nutrition..."

"He must've been on the road for weeks."

"Yeah." Angela nodded.

Lee craned his neck toward the medical trailer. "I should probably see what's going on with him."

"Of course. See you at dinner?"

"Yeah," Lee said, slightly distracted. "I'll be there."

Harper met with him as he made his way toward the Camp Ryder building.

Ahead of them, people gathered at the entrance to the medical trailer to peer in curiously at the man from Virginia. While the novelty of newcomers had faded somewhat as contact was made with more and more survivors, this particular newcomer had caused a stir. A man who showed up out of the blue and asked for Captain Harden by name was an immediate subject of interest, if not downright suspicion.

Lee and Harper stopped there in front of the medical trailer, and the passersby watched as though they believed there would be some great reunion between Lee and the stranger. Inside the trailer, a nearly shapeless form of skin and bones lay crumpled like a discarded piece of paper upon one of the cots, a white bedsheet draped over him like a body in a morgue.

Lee could smell the man from outside the trailer. Most of the people managed to bathe regularly now, but they all still smelled of hard work and body odor, Lee probably being the most offending of them, since he'd been in the field for the past few days. That Lee could smell the stranger over his own stink was a feat in and of itself.

"You recognize him?" Harper asked.

Lee shook his head. "Don't know him."

They didn't linger. The man was clearly passed out from exhaustion, and they could not expect to have a lucid conversation with him until he was rested.

They continued on to the Camp Ryder building.

A short series of cement steps led up to a pair of steel double doors kept closed to block out the cold air. Pushing them open, the pair was immediately inundated with the overwhelming smell of the place and the noisy clamor from inside. The building had once been a service bay for Ryder trucks, and the smell of oils and car parts was forever steeped into the concrete floors and walls. However, it was now home to several families and Marie's kitchen. There was always a slight haze of smoke in the place, and it bore with it the heavy scents of people and cooking food.

Immediately upon entering the building, they could see a metal staircase to their right that rose up to a second level that overlooked the floor below, with a series of metal catwalks that led to a roof access point, a few utility closets, and what used to serve as a foreman's office—a twelve-by-twenty-foot room that housed a desk, a filing cabinet, a few folding chairs, and a large corkboard with a map of North Carolina pinned to it.

In the office they found Bus and Kip Greene standing in front of the map. Bus wore the same OD green jacket as Lee and Harper—actually a Gore-Tex parka—and a pair of jeans with the beginnings of holes in the knees, twice patched and twice ripped. Stress had drawn some of his size from him, but he was still an imposing figure, especially next to Kip Greene, who stood all of 5'8", with wiry arms and a thin neck.

"Captain…Harper…" Bus greeted them as they walked in.

Lee clasped hands with him. "Good to see you, Bus."

"How was Lillington?" Bus ventured cautiously.

Lee dropped his pack to the floor. "Nothing worse than usual."

"Glad everyone came out all right." Bus nodded.

Lee turned his attention to the man from Broadway. "Kip…how are ya?"

"Decent. You?" Kip nodded, his hands planted deep in the pockets of his tattered old Dickies coveralls.

"Good. But we could still use some help." Lee looked pointedly at him.

Kip smiled grimly. "Funny enough, that's what I came to talk about."

"Oh?" Lee perked up a bit. He took a seat at the edge of the desk. "I sense there's a caveat."

Kip nodded.

Bus folded his arms across his chest. "I've been trying to explain to Kip that we need to use Broadway as a launch point for Sanford—"

"My people aren't interested in being a base for you guys," Kip said steadily.

"It's not just about us, you know." Lee pointed to the map. "You guys have been catching all the shit leaking out of Sanford since this started. You're doing an admirable job, but if you let us go in and clean house, you'll be able to focus more on your farming and less on watching your back."

Kip shook his head. "Not an option at this point."

Lee let his hands drop to his lap. "Okay. Why don't you explain what you want with us, then?"

Kip looked up at Lee from underneath his eyebrows. "We've been taking a lot of heat from Sanford. More and more lately, in fact. I'm not sure why, but they're coming out of that place in droves. I don't know, maybe they're running out of food in there. They all look pretty lean." He adjusted the brim of his cap. "Anyway, we've been getting them as they try to go down 421, but..."

Lee waited.

Kip seemed a little abashed. "But we're running out of ammunition."

Lee folded his hands. "Ah."

"That's why I'm here. To set up a trade."

"And what are we trading?"

"Food for ammunition. We've got corn, wheat,

peanuts, and tobacco. We'll trade any of them, in any combination, as long as the deal is fair."

Silence blanketed the room.

Lee was the first one to speak. "Kip, you mind if I talk with Bus and Harper for a moment?"

Kip shook his head. He stepped out and closed the door behind him as the three men from Camp Ryder gathered in close so they could speak in hushed tones.

Lee spoke first. "I think this is a good opportunity to build up some goodwill by making a generous trade with them. Keep in mind, they'll probably need rifles as well, since most of what we can give them is 5.56mm and I doubt they have many rifles that are chambered for that."

"We could play hardball," Bus suggested. "If they need the ammo badly enough we might be able to break him down and let us use Broadway to get into Sanford."

Harper made an ugly face. "I don't know if playing hardball is a good idea. That might just piss them off, and then Broadway is out as a source of food *and* as a base."

Bus rubbed his eyebrows. "I just want to avoid a repeat of Smithfield. I sure as hell don't want you guys camping in the woods outside of Sanford while you clear it. We need them."

Lee spread his palms. "Ammunition is a finite resource. We can have the best of both worlds. Let's make a small but generous deal with him now so he's forced to come back soon. Then we can play hardball. If we have some goodwill built up with him and his group, we're less likely to scare him off when we do. Plus we'll get a little fresh food out of it."

"We need the wheat," Harper nodded. "Cornmeal would be good too."

"Any value to tobacco?" Bus questioned.

Harper and Lee both shrugged.

"As a trade item, yes," Lee said. "But I wouldn't worry about it for now."

Harper grinned. "Don't tell LaRouche."

Lee stretched his arms. "So what's the offer?"

"You're in charge of guns and ammo," Bus pointed out. "You tell us what we can afford."

Lee considered it for a short moment. "How about we trade five rifles and six hundred rounds total. That'll be six mags per rifle. Depending on their level of contact, that could last them one or two weeks."

"That's a good time frame for us," Harper noted.

"Alright. Everyone agree?"

"Agreed."

"Yup."

Lee headed for the door.

He was about to reach for the handle when he heard shouting and the sound of footsteps pounding rapidly up the metal staircase. Someone cried out in alarm. The steps thundered as they drew closer. He didn't recall grabbing it, but Lee's rifle was suddenly in his hands and addressed toward the door.

The door burst open and a madman with sunken eyes and sallow skin tumbled in. The strange creature's eyes landed on Lee and the captain's finger went to the trigger. The thing reached forward and sank down to its knees and seemed about to scramble at Lee on all fours.

Lee was about to pull the trigger when it spoke.

"You're Captain Harden!" the man said and clasped a hand over his face. "I found you...I finally found you!"

THREE

BAD NEWS

LaRouche hit the top of the stairs, breathing hard, with his old Beretta M9 thrust out before him, aiming it at the back of the stranger's head. His eyes worked quickly between the man kneeling on the ground and Lee, who stood looking shocked. "You okay, Captain?"

Lee's eyes were wide as he stared down at the man. "Yeah, I'm fine." He lowered his rifle so the barrel was not pointing at the man's chest. Gaunt, sickly, emaciated—the dirty look of someone who has been on the road for a long time. "You must be Jacob."

The man clasped his hands together. The fingers were long, almost spiderlike. Black dirt encrusted the underside of the ragged fingernails. The skin appeared browned, like leather. Deep-set eyes and a hawkish nose. Wiry dark hair. The man nodded, clearly expending much effort on maintaining a handle on his emotions and just as clearly on the verge of failing.

"Yes. I'm Jacob. I'm from Virginia." His eyelids closed tightly as he fought for control of himself. "You have no idea what I've had to do to get here.

I thought...for a while there...I thought I just wasn't going to find you. I thought maybe you were dead." He opened his eyes and they glistened with tears. "Then I found this place and I fell asleep and I thought maybe I'd dreamed the whole thing up, and you weren't really here at all. But here you are!"

Lee glanced up at LaRouche, who had ported his gun. Lee gave him a nod, and the sergeant holstered up. Lee set his own weapon to the side and then knelt down and hefted the slender man up to his feet, grimacing at how horribly light he felt.

"Jesus, there's nothing left to you!" Lee exclaimed.

Jacob laughed weakly and let himself be led to one of the folding chairs. Harper and Bus were still standing in a sort of daze, looking like they weren't sure what the hell was going on. For that matter, Lee wasn't sure either. Jacob didn't seem entirely sane, but then again, God only knew what he'd been through to get there.

"You came all the way here from Virginia?" Harper asked in amazement.

Jacob nodded. "From Petersburg. I've been on the road since..." He looked at a scratched and worn watch that clung to his wrist. He regarded it with some confusion. "Shit. It's busted. When did it break? Damn...I don't know how long I've been on the road. A few weeks, I think. Last time I checked my watch, I'd been on the road for fifteen days, and that was at least a week ago. Maybe two." Jacob looked up and realized he was rambling. "Sorry. I've gotten into the bad habit of speaking to myself. Passes the time. Makes things seem less..." He didn't finish the thought.

Lee took a seat across from the man. "Do you need anything? Food or water?"

"Oh, no. Thank you, Captain. I've just..." He swallowed and for a moment seemed to be lost in an unpleasant memory. "I've just been looking for you."

"Yeah." Lee shifted. "I'm sorry...I don't..."

"No. You don't know me." Jacob smiled. "Captain Mitchell sent me here."

Lee jerked like a lightning bolt had touched him. "Captain Mitchell sent you here?"

"Yes."

"Why? What's wrong? Does he need help?"

Jacob's smile grew brittle, and then it shattered and fell away. He looked to the floor, and Lee felt his stomach knot up, reading that expression as clearly as if it were a billboard and knowing that something had happened...something bad.

Jacob cleared his throat. "Captain Mitchell is dead."

LaRouche and Harper and Bus stood with incredible stillness, watching Lee and gauging his response. Lee looked right back at them, caught in some indecisive loop as his brain whittled away at those words and tried to carve from them some other meaning, though there was no other meaning to be had.

When he did speak, it was subdued. "He's dead?"

Jacob nodded.

The question burned in Lee's mind, and he spit it out suddenly. "How did he die?"

Jacob avoided eye contact. "I had to kill him."

Everyone stiffened. Lee felt a tingling sensation in his fingertips, and he glanced at his rifle, leaning against the wall. But after a moment of thought, Lee realized what Jacob must have meant.

"Because he was infected."

Jacob nodded again. "I tried to do it quickly, I did. But I couldn't use the gun because they were all around us and in the trees and I knew they'd come running. So I used a knife. And he made me promise! He put the knife in my hand and he made me promise! I didn't want to, but I did...I did."

Lee stared. "Jesus Christ..." He rubbed his face rapidly. "So what about the people he rescued? Who's with them now? What about the Coordinators from Delaware and Maryland and West Virginia? Are they helping? I mean, shit...Captain Connors from Maryland should be right there across the water..."

"They're all dead."

There was a sudden humming sound in Lee's ears. "What?" His voice sounded muted, as though he were hearing himself from a different room in a large house.

"They're all dead," Jacob murmured.

Lee stared, his hands planted on his knees and his fingers digging into the fabric of his pants and the flesh underneath. The humming noise rose to a high-pitched ringing sound, and then throbbed in time with his heartbeat. He wanted to speak, and though he wasn't struck speechless, nothing came to mind but curses. He closed his mouth and the words and anger and indignation sat back in his throat and curdled there.

The thin man's eyes watered and grew red. He was on the verge of breaking down. "There's nothing left, Captain. There's nothing left up there. There's nothing left anywhere north of here."

That ringing in his ears, the sound of a teakettle in another room, it seemed to grow louder, to fill the vacuum created by the lack of words being spoken. He could feel his heart beating in his chest, sharp and rapid taps like a snare drum, and he could feel his palms beginning to sweat. But there was a numbness there, like the point of a pin being pressed against a thick callus so that you could feel the pressure but not the pain.

Lee waited for it in silence, for the moment to become real and for that deep wringing feeling in his gut to come back again. He was familiar with it now, like a frequently visiting but unwanted guest. But the longer he waited, the more certain he was that it was not going to happen. He felt little more than hollow disappointment.

He leaned forward in his chair until he was sitting on the edge and he steepled his fingertips in front of his face and rested his chin on his protruding thumbs. He closed his eyes and breathed deeply through his nose so the air whistled past his fingernails.

He could smell his hands.

Like musty earth and sweat.

"Excuse me," Lee said quietly. "This is a lot to take in right now."

He opened his eyes again and looked at the

pathetic form huddled in the chair before him, his skinny limbs like thin branches shoved into pant legs and shirtsleeves, like a scarecrow.

Lee spoke very slowly, choosing his words. "I think we need to stop and have you explain some things so that we're all on the same page. I understand that Captain Mitchell is dead. I understand that you allege the other captains are also dead. Please explain, and let's start with your relationship with Captain Mitchell. Who are you, and how did you come to know him?"

Jacob took a quick swipe at his eyes, then raked his fingers through his dirty hair. "My name is Jacob Weber. I'm a microbiologist with the CDC, or I suppose I was until a few months back." He had a strange way of speaking. Oddly formal in its wording but somehow disjointed and meandering, as though nothing he said was planned, but rather a simple verbalization of his own train of thought. "I was visiting the Level Four facility at Fort Detrick in Maryland when all of this happened. I was requested to stay and gather as much information as possible, and by the time anyone knew what was happening, travel had become very unsafe."

His eyes wandered. "Actually, that's just what I tell myself—I don't really know why they left me at Fort Detrick." He pursed his lips. "Seems like they could have sent a helicopter for me. Or something...but they didn't. So I continued to work there, locked down in the bowels of Fort Detrick until everything collapsed. It was just me and another scientist, an epidemiologist named Lori, and a skeleton crew of army security personnel.

"After a while we decided to leave. I'd already gathered what data I could, made some interesting discoveries, but the...uh...samples...they became nonviable. Anyway, it was out of the question to try to get more samples and there was no reason for us to stay where we were, so we left. The army personnel came with us." He swallowed hard. "It was very bad. Much worse than I expected. I mean, I watched the news up until they stopped broadcasting, but I guess things just got exponentially worse when the power grid failed." He looked thoughtful. "That's my guess, anyway. I don't suppose it was the reactors that went out. They'll go on forever by themselves, I think. But maybe it was just the grid itself. With no one there to repair and maintain it. Maybe it was just that fragile."

He directed his gaze to Lee, his face becoming abruptly blank and detached. "So...Lori died first. She was eaten. Then some of the personnel began to get sick with flu-like symptoms. I told them it didn't necessarily mean they were infected with FURY. It could've just been a cold. But I think it got into their heads that they had been infected. Three of them committed suicide, and then it was just two others and me. After the first few days outside we realized we weren't going to get through it, so we holed up in an office building and we waited."

He paused there. "I'm not sure what we were waiting for. We knew that if we tried to continue on that we would die or be killed or be eaten. But I think we didn't want to give up just yet. We wanted to stretch out our last bit of time, maybe. Eke a little more out of our pathetic existence."

Jacob smiled sadly. "Lucky for us, we saw Captain Mitchell and a little gathering of refugees getting the hell out of the city, so we came running to catch up with them. Almost got ourselves shot for it, they were so jumpy. And that's how I met Captain Mitchell."

Lee waited a few beats after Jacob had finished talking. "So why did Captain Mitchell send you down here? And what happened to everyone?"

"Captain Mitchell sent me because I know about FURY." The scientist held up his hands. "That's not to say I know *everything*. But I have what information we were able to get from studies prior to the collapse. I may be the only person in the country, maybe even the world, who knows what I know."

"The samples..." Lee said.

"Infected subjects," Jacob stated flatly. "We were able to capture several of them in the beginning and observe them for an extended period of time. Studied their blood and their biochemistry. Very...intriguing."

"What have you learned?"

Jacob considered this with faraway eyes and Lee imagined that the scientist's thoughts took the shape of spectrograph analyses and microscope slides and vials filled with tainted blood. "Let's see...the FURY bacterium is a very interesting little life-form. It adapts and mutates incredibly quickly. In fact, it underwent some very extreme changes, even just in the time we were able to observe it at Fort Detrick.

"During its first stages of existence, the bacterium was much smaller, which accounted for the extremely high infection rates. You see, the smaller and lighter the bacterium is, the more likely it is to be aerosolized, which means it can attach to globules of mucus or spit coming from a person sneezing or coughing…even laughing or talking. So it acts almost like an airborne virus, at least in close proximity. In addition to its aerosolized mode of infection during most of the first thirty days of the outbreak, the bacterium could remain alive on a dry surface for upward of twenty-four hours.

"Of course, without the proper investigations, we'll never know, but I think this explains the huge spike in infectivity we saw. I'm sure you can imagine the havoc that could be created by a single host individual, contagious in an airport, sneezing, coughing, wiping his nose, and leaving a trail of bacteria behind him for others to touch, which would remain infectious for a whole day."

Lee narrowed his eyes. "We come into contact with infected subjects all the time. Very close contact sometimes. We've touched them, even got fluids on ourselves, but we've never been infected."

Jacob wiped the corners of his mouth. "That goes back to the mutations that the bacteria went through. During the first month of the initial outbreak, the onset of symptoms was a little slower. It took almost a week for the infection to advance into its final stages—lack of reasoning, loss of language skills, hyperaggression, et cetera, et cetera…What we see now from an infected host is nearly *complete* infection in the course of a few days." He faltered. "Captain Mitchell took just about seventy-two hours. I believe this is due to the size of the bacterium. Over the course of the first month, June going into July, it mutated and grew much larger.

"From the last study I conducted, I observed the bacterium mutate into its larger form as it reached the end stages of infection, and then it continued to multiply until it inundated the host's entire body." For a moment, Jacob's eyes looked feverish. "It does some very strange things to people at that point…But going back to your question about infection, after the bacterium mutates to its larger form, not only is it too cumbersome to be aerosolized, but it becomes hydrophilic, which means it cannot stay alive on a dry surface for more than a few moments. About a minute, actually.

"So the reason you've gotten the infected fluids on you and you haven't been infected is partially because the bacterium is too large to absorb through your dermis, but also that the active bacteria in that infected fluid die within a minute of landing on you. At the current stage, or what I guess is the current stage unless it has mutated again, there are only four different methods of infection that I'm aware of: blood to blood, blood to mucus, mucus to blood, and mucus to mucus. Generally speaking, mucus to mucus is the least likely mode of infection, requiring a gross exposure to infected materials. But anytime it involves blood, the chances skyrocket. It seems the FURY bacterium has grown to prefer that as a method of transference."

"Which is why the bites infect so fast," Lee said thoughtfully.

Jacob nodded. "Now, it stands to reason that if the infected host bites you in a place where your flesh does not have as many capillaries, such as in the hand or foot, and the bite is quick, there's a chance the infection might not take hold. I personally haven't seen an instance of a bite *not* turning into an infection, but it is possible."

"So what about the rest?" Lee asked cautiously. "What did you mean when you said there's nothing left north of here?"

Jacob looked down. "An unfortunate side effect of the infection. The infected hosts operate with very high core temperatures, and it affects their metabolism in a way I don't quite understand. I'm no nutritionist, but I would venture to say that the infected hosts are burning through four thousand to five thousand calories in a day, if you combine the physiological stress that the infection places on their bodies and their increased activity levels. Others hypothesized that the bacteria were eating through the parts of the brain responsible for hunger and thirst signals, but if that were the case I believe the infected subjects would be eating themselves to death. Instead, you see them able to eat almost nonstop, and yet they suffer no physical consequences, which can only mean that the body is using every bit of what they eat."

Jacob leaned forward, close to Lee, and looked disgusted. "I kept one of our captured subjects on a three-thousand-calorie diet for two weeks. At the end of those two weeks he'd lost thirteen pounds of body weight." Jacob shook his head. "It's incredible, really. But it's also causing our biggest problem. The insatiable hunger combined with hyperaggression and lack of reasoning skills is why we're seeing the subjects turn cannibalistic. Furthermore, their digestive tracts are still the same as ours, and we are not made for digesting raw meats. This means that the infected host can eat pounds and pounds of raw meat in a day and still not be satisfied because his body cannot process it and get the right nutrition out of it.

"The problem with all of this"—Jacob began to pick nervously at his fingernails—"is the population density of the northeastern states. You see, with cities like DC, Baltimore, Boston, Philly, New York... back when people lived there... there were millions and millions of mouths to feed on a daily basis. But the food doesn't come from those cities; it comes from the surrounding countryside. They ship it in. So what happened when everything collapsed? Everyone went out and looted the supermarkets and the grocers. In addition to that, the infection hit these places the hardest. Everyone all jam-packed in like that... it was just a waiting game. So now, that high-population density has become a high population of infected subjects. And there's no food for them to find, because by the time the infection even got its momentum up, every bag of potato chips had been looted. And there's no food for them to kill, because there's very little wildlife, and all the normal people like you and me have either been infected, or they've fled or died. So what do these hordes of infected subjects do?"

"They push out into the countryside?" Lee asked dazedly.

Jacob nodded. "Yes. But there are millions of them, Captain. They roll through like locusts, and they consume everything that can be consumed, plant and animal alike. They don't leave anything behind. They just keep driving forward, stuck in an endless hunger loop."

Finally, someone besides Lee spoke up.

Harper raised his hand like a kid in class and spoke hesitantly. "Why don't we just wait for them to starve themselves out?"

Jacob smiled, but it was defeated. "Do locusts simply starve to death after they ravage a farmer's field?"

"No."

"No." Jacob shook his head. "Because they move onto the next field."

"What if they move west?" Harper asked.

"They won't move west," Jacob said firmly. "The Appalachian mountains are a barrier for them. They'll follow the path of least resistance, which is south."

"Can we back up a second?" Lee sounded irritable. He rose from his chair. "How do you know the other captains are dead?"

Jacob met Lee's gaze. "Captain Mitchell was in contact with them from his bunker. He spoke with Captain Connors several times. Connors was on the run from Maryland. Baltimore had pretty much made the entire state a danger zone. So he headed south and managed to link up with us. I actually... saw him die." Jacob took a deep breath.

"Captain Roberts from Delaware—we never made contact with him. But Captain Connors had brief contact with him before he got out of Maryland, and he was firmly set in his opinion that Captain Roberts didn't make it."

"So why did he send you?" Lee grated out, feeling queasy now.

"When things went bad in Virginia, Captain Mitchell put everything he had into protecting me . . . because of what I knew." Jacob's eyelids fluttered. "When he realized he wasn't going to make it out, he left it up to me. He believed that if you had enough forewarning, you might be able to hold the line here at North Carolina and prevent a mass migration into the other southeastern states."

Lee nodded slowly.

"So . . . what do we do now?" Bus began, but he stopped when Lee planted both of his hands on the map of North Carolina and hung his head.

"Jesus Christ," Lee breathed. "This is a clusterfuck."

"No shit," LaRouche murmured and leaned up against the wall, hands in his pockets.

Lee raised his head and looked at the map, inches from his face. Roads with funny names, spiderwebbing their way across the thin paper to small blobs of urban areas scattered about the state. Blots and splotches of blue for lakes, thin lines for rivers. The state was full of rivers and lakes . . .

Jacob began to look physically uncomfortable, and he leaned back in his chair, holding a hand to his stomach. A greasy-looking sweat broke out over his face. When he realized the others were looking at him, he smiled wanly. "Still dealing with this…stomach bug…Think I drank some bad water."

Lee spoke into the map, his own breath hot as it swam back at him. "What you did was incredible, Jacob. You put yourself in harm's way to come down here. But you shouldn't be stressing your body right now. There will be plenty of work in the coming days, but now you need to rest."

Jacob stood up silently and prepared to leave.

Lee turned around fully and stepped up to the man, placing both of his hands on his shoulders. "You did a damn fine job. Captain Mitchell would have been proud."

Jacob smiled weakly. "Thank you."

"Go rest." Lee looked up at LaRouche. "Make sure he gets back okay."

"Will do," LaRouche said.

The two men left. As they walked through the door, Lee could see that Kip Greene was still standing outside. Lee blinked and felt his eyes moving sluggishly, burning with a need for sleep. The exhaustion of the last few days was catching up to him quickly now, even overpowering the aching hunger in his stomach.

Lee waved the man inside. "Mr. Greene, come in here for a moment."

The man entered the room and Lee stepped back to the map, placing his finger on a dot called Sanford. "This is Sanford. I need to clear Sanford, because I need to access what's on the other side of Sanford. It's not an option at this time. It just became a necessity. Is that clear?"

Kip nodded slowly.

"We didn't want to hardball you, but the situation has changed. We'll give you a fair trade for your food. But I'm not gonna beat around the bush." He looked the man in the eyes. "If you're not going to at least let us operate out of your town while we retake Sanford, then I think we're done talking."

Kip didn't respond directly. He considered this for a long time and through several noisy sighs, and then said, "Everything that guy said...is it true?"

"He has no reason to lie."

"What are you gonna do about it?"

Lee looked at Harper and Bus. "Right now we're going to gather our leaders together so we can figure that out. You're welcome to stay if you'd like. Our committees can get interesting."

FOUR

GRAY AREAS

HARPER LEFT THE ROOM as Lee, Bus, and Kip struggled to come to an agreement over the exchange rates between food and ammunition. In fleeting moments like this, Harper saw himself very clearly, as though the real him were still asleep in his comfortable king-size bed in his nice three-thousand-square-foot house in a pleasant little neighborhood, just dreaming a strange dream where he was no longer brokering million-dollar contracts between banking firms, but instead finagling over the price of corn versus 5.56mm cartridges.

But no...

This was his life now. This was his reality, however unreal it was. No more king-size bed. No more lawn service. No more three-piece suits and conference calls. His wife, Annette, was dead, and that hurt the most. His brother, Milo, was dead, and that was just a blank spot in his memory that he refused to think about. There were others he had known who had died. Miller, not least among them. And at times he would wake up at night crying, but he wouldn't remember what his dream had been, only the residual feeling of a great loss.

In a way, the suddenness of the collapse was a blessing. It had acted as a severance between his old life and his new, so that it seemed to him at times that he had simply ceased to exist in that alternate universe and had appeared here in this one. Had the collapse dragged out over months and years, it would have been an invisible thread that forever tied him unmercifully to all the things from that aching hole in his subconsciousness that left him confused and teary-eyed in the early morning hours.

He was much the same man, though without the frills. His suits had been replaced with a military-issue green parka and a pair of old jeans. His Italian leather shoes had turned into old work boots. No more trips to the barber to keep him looking presentable—his nose hair was ridiculous, and Annette would have screamed if she saw the overgrowth of his back hair. He didn't carry a briefcase anymore, just a rifle. He didn't worry about interest rates; he worried about how much rain they were going to get this week, and whether he was going to get eaten by a pack of starving cannibals.

Yes, many things had changed, but for the most part, Bill Harper was still Bill Harper. The partner. The adviser. The go-to guy. But not the leader. Never the tip-top. Because he wasn't comfortable there, and he wasn't good at it. He couldn't think clearly or objectively when he was in control of everything and everyone. Second-tier suited him just fine.

He exited the Camp Ryder building and headed

down what they had dubbed "Main Street," the wide, open dirt path that ran through the length of the camp, with the shanties crowding in on either side. There were nearly twice the people in Camp Ryder that there had been when Harper had first arrived. There were stragglers from other towns, people who had escaped the larger cities, refugees who never got evacuated. Most came in pairs, but a few were in small groups or family units. Some of them had skills and knowledge that contributed to the effort, but most of them had to be taught something to keep them occupied and useful. Jerry had a fucking hissy fit every time they let someone into the camp, whether that person had a useful skill set or not. But Jerry was smartly steering clear of Harper after he'd knocked him out.

A day after Harper had punched him, Jerry called for a public apology.

Harper told him to go fuck himself.

So, that was one bridge burned.

He reached the Humvee and yanked open the passenger's side door, then he sat down and palmed the handset. "Camp Ryder to Wilson or anyone at Outpost Lillington."

A crackle. "Go-ahead for Wilson."

"Hey, relay this message to Wilson from Captain Harden: You guys need to hold down the fort while Old Man Hughes and Professor White come in for a meeting. We just got some bad news and Captain Harden needs all the group leaders back at Camp Ryder so they can, you know...talk about shit forever."

"Yeah. All right." A pause. "So, how bad is bad?"

"Bad," Harper said to the handset. "Real bad."

Nearly an hour had passed by behind the closed door of the foreman's office when Lee, Bus, and Kip Greene finally exited with an arrangement made. Five rifles and nine hundred rounds of 5.56mm ammunition in exchange for ten pounds of wheat flour, ten pounds of cornmeal, and thirty large mason jars of home-canned corn.

Kip Greene agreed to let Lee and his team use Broadway as a stepping-stone to Sanford, but they refused to fall underneath the purveyance of the Camp Ryder Hub. He didn't like the idea of being told how to run things by "outsiders," but he relented that it would be a relief when Lee had cleaned out Sanford of infected.

Throughout the process, sleep deprivation and distracting thoughts wormed their way through Lee's mind and caused flickers of brief, nightmarish images behind his eyes, as though his brain were a television set picking up some hijacked broadcast.

When they finally left the office, Lee turned back inside and went to his pack. He took from it an old red cloth, the kind used as a mechanic's towel. Inside the folded cloth was the remainder of a bar of soap Lee had steadily been using for the last month. It was amazing how long you could stretch a single bar of soap when you only bathed every few days.

He took his cloth and soap and his rifle and

made his way downstairs. Outside, near the rain catches, there was a collection of buckets in various sizes and colors. Lee took one and filled it with water from one of the rain catches, feeling the bitter coldness of it as it splashed on his hands and woke him up a bit.

Feeling slightly less dead on his feet, he took his bucket around the other side of the Camp Ryder building where something of a "bathing area" had been set up using some tent poles and tarps to create privacy screens. He shrugged against a gust of wind that pestered at his clothing. Between the cold water and the cold wind, it promised to be an unpleasant experience.

The stalls of blue tarps had been erected over a cement sidewalk that ran parallel to the fence so that everyone could stand on the hard surface, rather than in the grass and dirt. It was early afternoon and the warmest part of the day, therefore the best time to bathe, so Lee only found one open stall. He entered and put the tarp back over the opening like a shower curtain. He stripped down all of his dirty and bloodstained clothing, placing his rifle atop these, and, out of habit, he checked himself thoroughly for bites and scrapes.

A few purplish bruises here and there, but no broken skin.

He stood over the bucket of cold water with his little sliver of soap and steeled himself. Then he plunged in and scrubbed himself down as quickly as he could. A moment later he was done and shivering. He swiped the excess water from his body and dabbed the rest of it up with the red towel he'd taken from his pack. He pulled on the same dirty pair of trousers and stomped into his old Bates M-6 boots, still trustily holding together.

That was when the screaming started.

"Shoot it!"

"Oh my God!"

"Get away from the fence!"

In a flash, Lee was standing outside of the stall, his rifle in his hand, cold wind scouring his back dry. In front of him, five people filled the twenty-foot space between the showering area and the chain-link fence that bordered the camp. Three of them were backing away quickly from the fence, while the other two were shouldering their rifles.

Lee's first thought was, *Shit! There's a breach in the fence!*

"What's wrong?" Lee yelled, scanning the fence.

One of the men pointed and looked back at Lee. "You see it? Right there!"

Lee focused into the woods and saw it almost immediately. The glassy, vacant eyes. The slack jaw. The withered torso, ribs standing out grossly. A moving sack of tissue and organs. For some reason, the small gathering on Lee's side of the fence fell abruptly silent, and Lee could swear he could hear the thing's breathing; heavy, labored, and raspy.

"What the fuck's it doing?" one of the men whispered.

Lee raised his rifle and took a step forward, feeling soft grass beneath his feet instead of hard concrete. The creature in the woods had that wild-eyed look of the infected, but it did not charge them, did not show any clear aggression. It stood in a small clearing between two trees, just a few yards from the fence line, and watched them with eerie curiosity. Its head tilted to one side, and then the other, like a perplexed dog listening to a confusing sound.

After a few steady steps, Lee was between the other two men, all three pointing their rifles at the creature on the other side, but still it made no movement toward them.

"What's wrong with it?" one of the men asked.

The infected—an emaciated male—turned in the direction of the man who spoke.

"Holy shit!" the man gasped. "It's fucking looking at me!"

"Are you gonna shoot it?" another asked.

Lee's finger touched the cold trigger.

"Captain?"

Lee glanced to his left at the man who had spoken, but he could not keep his eyes from wandering back to the creature who stood on the other side of the fence, mere yards away. He remembered the infected woman and her dead infant, kneeling out in the middle of that tilled field, his first day out of the bunker. Was this one of the same? One of the rare nonviolent infected?

"Is it infected, Captain?"

Lee watched as the infected tracked the flight of a bird through the trees, his head moving slowly and lazily, eyes squinting in the sun. He seemed childlike.

"He's gotta be infected," Lee said absently, and he raised his rifle marginally.

A voice called out, thin and reedy. "Wait! Don't shoot him! Don't shoot him!"

Lee turned and found Jacob hobbling quickly toward them, his feet bare, his right hand clutching at his gut. His face was scribbled with the effects of pain, and he was still sweating, despite the cold.

Lee's own body prickled in gooseflesh as he remembered how cold it was.

Jacob came abreast of them, panting and shaking his head rapidly back and forth. "Don't... don't shoot him."

Lee regarded the man with a doubtful look. "Why not?"

Jacob took a gulp of air. "Because I can use him."

"The fuck is this crazy guy talking about?" one of the two men grumbled.

Lee raised an eyebrow. "You mean capture him?"

Jacob nodded vehemently.

"Absolutely fucking not." Lee turned back toward the fence.

"Wait!" Jacob hissed and pawed at Lee's elbow. "I've got to get samples from somewhere! Clearly he's a nonaggressive infected, which means he's the safest one to get them from!"

"What the fuck are you gonna do with samples, even if you get them?" Lee said. "You've got no lab; you've got no equipment..."

"No, Jenny told me about Smithfield and the hospital. I can do research there. I have so much left to learn! Things that can help us not only understand them, but possibly develop some sort of cure! Please!"

Lee sighed through his nose, felt the warm air brush across his bare chest. "This is ridiculous."

"It's not ridiculous. It's science."

"Where the hell you gonna keep him?"

"Wherever."

"Wherever?" Lee felt himself shivering again. "We're completely unprepared for this. What are you gonna do when the damn thing gets loose and fucking bites one of the kids?"

"He's nonaggressive!"

"He's unpredictable."

"Fine." Jacob drew himself up. "I'll do it myself."

The scientist turned and began to limp away.

"Jacob, don't leave that gate."

But Jacob continued on, calling over his shoulder with bitter resolve, "Captain Mitchell would never have kept me from my research!"

Lee stared at the scarecrow of a man striding determinedly toward the front gates. What were they going to do, hold him prisoner? Restrain him for his own safety? Lee looked back toward the fence and swore under his breath. The infected was staring up at the sky, his mouth agape. He didn't look dangerous at all...

Lee felt a welling of pity for him, rather than fear.

He raised his rifle and fired.

The thing rocked back and collapsed.

Even as the echo of the shot died, Lee turned and found Jacob staring wide-eyed at the fallen body out beyond the fence. He rushed forward with his arms outstretched toward the thing, as though he might cradle him and coax him back to life, a beloved child.

"What did you do?" Jacob screamed as he came forward.

Behind him, people ran out of their shacks to see what the gunshot had been. They filled Main Street and craned their necks to see. As Jacob tried to run past, Lee took two steps and intercepted him, grabbing a firm hold on his jacket and pulling the man close so that Lee could smell the stink of his skin and the warm staleness of the man's breath.

In the narrow space between them, Lee spoke with force, but quietly so no one else could hear. "What were you going to do, Jacob? Were you going to go all the way around the fucking fence by yourself? What if that thing's friends came out of the woods after you? Were you gonna make it back to the gate before they got you? Did you even fucking think about that?"

The people were beginning to stare and murmur.

Lee released the man's jacket, causing him to stumble back a bit. Looking with grim resolve out at the gathering crowd, he slung into his rifle and felt the nylon strap rasp across his skin. Jacob stood, slope-shouldered and dejected, and Lee kept his voice low when he spoke again. "When and if it's safe for us to do so, we'll capture one of them for your goddamned sampling. But only if it's *safe*." He jammed a thumb into his chest. "And I'm the one who determines whether it's safe."

Jacob didn't reply.

The crowd looked at Lee, and Lee at them. He

struggled to determine what he should say in that moment, and eventually he decided to say nothing at all. Disgusted, though unsure whom he was disgusted with, Lee turned and marched briskly back to the shower stall, where he snatched up his belongings and headed back to the foreman's office.

Bus followed him into the Camp Ryder building. "What the hell was that?" he said with exasperation.

Lee tossed him a sidelong glance. "That was Jacob trying to get himself killed and me stopping him."

"Lee." Bus held up a hand for him to stop.

The two men halted at the base of the staircase to the foreman's office and faced each other.

"What do you want, Bus?"

"We're on the same side here." Bus lowered his head and looked at Lee from under his bushy eyebrows. "I'm with you. I get it. I understand. But some of these other people don't. And every time you do something like that, they use it against you and they use it against me."

"Every time?" Lee leaned on the railing. "Because I do things like that so often?"

Bus put a hand to his temple. "No..."

"No, I don't." Lee nodded. "Look...I have a job to do, and I don't give a fuck about some wannabe commandos trying to second-guess every goddamn decision I make. They can say what they want, as long as they're not standing in the way of me doing my job. Right now, I need Jacob; it's that simple. I need his information, and I need his knowledge. If anyone puts that in jeopardy, including him, then they force my hand." Lee began climbing the stairs. "Trust me, Bus, I don't want to be the bad guy. But I'm also not going to play games with people."

Bus stormed after him. "I'm not asking you to play games. I'm asking you to think about the backlash from people like Jerry and Professor White. They already have enough people backing them—they don't need a rallying cry."

Lee made a derogatory noise. "What are they gonna do? Picket me?" He could feel himself going on the defensive, and he didn't like it. He took a deep breath and stopped halfway up the stairs. "I understand that my actions sometimes put you in a shitty situation. There are hundreds of situations where I've avoided taking action, because I knew it would put you in that situation." He leaned against the railing. "But you gotta look at things from my perspective. What was I going to do there, Bus? If I let Jacob leave the gate, I let him put himself in unnecessary danger. And if I restrain him from leaving the gate, I turn him into a prisoner." Lee tossed up his hands. "Yes, it's a shitty fucking situation. But the alternatives were worse."

Bus hung his head. "We just can't win, can we?"

"Maybe we're just not winning the way we want to win."

Lee turned and continued up the stairs, not waiting to see if Bus would follow. When he reached the door to the office, Bus was no longer on the stairs. Gone off to conduct damage control, perhaps. Why? Because Lee was a loose cannon? Because Lee was someone who needed a spin doctor to defend his actions?

Lee shut the office door behind him and dropped his things next to his pack. He knelt down there and placed his hand on the tan nylon and became still. For a long moment his eyes were unfocused, unseeing, and he sat silent and unmoving for the better part of a minute. There were no conscious thoughts that went through his mind in those moments, just the overwhelming sensation of being absolutely and completely exhausted.

Moving again, but slowly, he pulled a pair of trousers from his pack. They were identical to the ones he was wearing but not quite as filthy. Before dressing himself, Lee looked at his dim reflection in the office window. His body showed the signs of long days of hard work and not quite enough calories to fuel them. His torso looked etched, and he'd lost what little body fat he'd had and, along with it, a lot of his musculature.

When he had on relatively clean clothes, he leaned his rifle against the desk, opened the door to the office, and then went to the map on the wall. He crossed his arms over his chest and sat on the edge of the desk.

The map was large and displayed the entire state of North Carolina. With a black marker, Lee had split the state into three zones: East Zone, Central Zone, and West Zone. Camp Ryder was positioned in the Central Zone. Inside this zone, Lee had used a red marker to shade in the urban areas of the larger cities to designate them as "nonviable," meaning he could not safely clear them with his current resources. These "nonviable" areas included the Fayetteville and Fort Bragg areas and the Raleigh-Durham area.

For a long time Lee stared at the map. His eyes tracked across distances and terrain features, roads and rivers and lakes. He visualized the endless hordes, vast and wretched and stretching from horizon to horizon.

How do you defeat a superior force? Lee rubbed his forehead. *You minimize their numbers. You force them to bottleneck.*

He looked at the map and shook his head. The state of North Carolina was a very wide state, its northern border working in from the coast all the way to the Appalachians. It would be nearly impossible to force a bottleneck in such a huge area.

Use the terrain to your advantage.

Lee leaned in and looked closer.

Every elevation, every rise, every valley, every riverbed.

The wheels turning, feeling slow and rusted with fatigue.

He planted the tip of his index finger on the North Carolina coast, directly on top of the words SWAN BAY, and then traced a meandering course northwest, then west, all the way across the top of the map, and ended on a little town called Eden.

Lee tapped it. "Eden."

"Do what?"

Lee turned to find LaRouche entering through the door, Julia, Harper, and Jim close behind. Still halfway lost in thought, Lee repeated himself.

"Eden. It's a little town northwest of here. Near the border."

"Sounds like a nice place." LaRouche sighed and sat in one of the folding chairs. "We should go there sometime."

Julia remained standing and leaned against the back wall. "What's going on, Cap?"

Lee realized he was still holding his finger to the map. God, he was tired. His arm dropped down to his side. "I'm assuming you all heard?"

There was a round of grim nods, hesitant, as though if they simply didn't admit to knowing it, they could make it untrue. Just a bad dream that could be dispelled by hiding their heads under the covers.

Lee planted his hands on the desk and leaned on it. He looked at each of them in turn. "You guys are my team," he said with quiet resolve. "You know that I would never ask you to do something I didn't think we could accomplish."

LaRouche hung his head. "This is gonna be bad, isn't it?"

Harper nodded solemnly. "What do you need us to do?"

Lee took a deep breath. "LaRouche is right. It's gonna be bad."

FIVE

DISSENSION

THE "COMMITTEE" LASTED ABOUT five minutes into Jacob's methodical retelling of events before it began to fall apart.

As always, everyone met in the middle of the Square, with the fire pit glowing with hot coals that mimicked the color of the setting sun. At first, the crowd was attentive, interested, even excited to hear what this knowledgeable newcomer from Virginia had to tell them. But then, as he began to tell them of the deaths of the captains from Maryland, Delaware, and Virginia, his words became like an electrical current, and the still and somber crowd began to stir uncomfortably and to murmur back and forth. As he continued to speak, the murmur grew louder, until Jacob was sweating profusely again and holding his stomach as he stammered out a few words at a time.

Lee stood quietly beside and slightly behind Bus, with his team flanking him to his right. He rested his weight casually on his good leg and his hands were folded and resting on the buttstock of his slung rifle. As the crowd became louder, Lee cast a sideways glance that Julia caught. She blew out a breath and shook her head very slightly, communicating what Lee already knew: This was not going to be easy.

The dam broke when Jacob began speaking about the infected.

Jerry was the first to shout over the rest of the crowd, forcing his voice to be heard above everyone else's. "How many are there? Surely you have some sort of estimate!"

Jacob glanced back at Bus, who gave him a reassuring nod. "Yes. We did actually run some numbers when we were initially determining the probabilities of a widespread outbreak. But you have to keep in mind those numbers are outdated at this point in time. You also have to factor in such things as infected attrition due to starvation and a myriad of other factors."

Jerry raised both eyebrows. "So? What are the numbers?"

Someone else shouted, "Would you just tell us a fucking number?"

Jacob wiped a bead of sweat from his eye and blinked a few times. "Uh…millions? Several. Million."

There was a collective gasp of shock and disbelief as everyone wrapped their heads around such a large number. Lee could see people doing the math, comparing "millions" to what they had seen already. In Smithfield, some of them had seen a few thousand. They must have been visualizing what a thousand times as many infected looked like.

"The numbers vary," Jacob said defensively. "I think we can safely say there are at least two to three million of them. It's possible there are more."

"How many is more?" Another faceless voice.

Jacob coughed into his hand. Then: "Some estimate as high as ten."

"Ten million?"

"Are you fucking kidding?"

"We can't survive that!"

Bus held up a hand and spoke calmly. "Folks, that's why we're here—to talk about our options. Right now, this is just the news. There's no reason to panic right now."

"Bullshit!" A man from Camp Ryder pointed at Bus. "That's what they said when this whole thing started!"

Jerry seized the moment to wrest control away from Bus. "There's a reason everyone is scared right now, Bus. I think this is a major problem." He turned to the crowd. "But we need to clear up some things, and we can't ask questions if we're all yelling at the same time."

Lee could almost feel Bus tensing. The anger rolled off of him like a burning fever.

This time it was Professor White who stepped forward. "Excuse me, Jerry."

Jerry yielded graciously. The two men were as thick as thieves. Nauseating, like a pair of Washington politicians. Lee wondered absently how many of those politicians were now running wild and naked through the small towns and forests of Virginia, eating unspeakable things and growling to each other.

"I'm Professor Thomas White," he introduced

himself grandly. "Now, you've established that there are somewhere between two and ten million plague victims north of us," White said, with one hand in his pocket and the other gesticulating mildly at his side, as though this were another lecture. "My first question is, how big of a group have you actually seen with your own eyes?"

Jacob looked uncomfortable. "Maybe a thousand? I don't know. I was running."

Professor White smiled, but it was unpleasant. "So it's safe to say you haven't seen the…What does our friend Captain Harden call them?" White put up a pair of very sarcastic air quotes. "Hordes? At least not in the numbers that you postulate, correct?"

Someone growled, "Speak English, you stuffy fuck."

A few people cleared their throats to disguise a chuckle. Lee restrained a smirk.

White looked at the crowd with a sneer, then turned back to Jacob. "So you haven't seen a million plague victims all in one spot? Not even close to that number, correct?"

"No, but…"

White held up a hand. "Isn't it possible they're breaking off into smaller, and I would say more manageable and less threatening groups? Once again, I think our revered captain calls them 'packs'?"

Jacob spoke loudly, a little irritation showing in his voice. "First, I should remind you that I'm not one of your students, Professor, and I've probably written more textbooks on the subject matter of my expertise than you have taught from in your entire career." Jacob swallowed, glared, let the moment hang. "Secondly, the grouping together of infected subjects, at least as it pertains to establishing a pack mentality, appears to be a primarily rural anomaly. The vast majority of infected subjects originating from large urban areas tend to stay cohesive in large crowds. There are packs up north, just as there are here, but since the majority of the infected are coming from those urban areas, the majority will be in hordes."

Looking somewhat miffed, White hesitated to speak again, and Old Man Hughes overtook him.

The grizzled, white-haired man from Dunn spoke in a low, growling voice that spoke of a lifetime addiction to tobacco, only recently and unwillingly overcome. "These big groups, or herds, or hordes, or whatever...will one join up with another?"

Jacob shrugged. "I don't know, to be honest. But it's a definite possibility."

Hughes nodded once. "Any idea how long it'll take them to get down this way?"

Lee had not thought it possible, but Jacob's face grew even more drawn. "By my best estimate, they'll be crossing into North Carolina before the year is out."

The crowd buzzed like a live wire.

"That's not enough time!"

"Where are we gonna go?"

Jerry stepped forward again. He fixed Lee with a weasel-eyed look and Lee knew exactly what was coming. He raised one hand for quiet and pointed the other right at Lee. "I want to know what Captain Harden has planned for this. Surely you have some...contingency in place?"

Professor White snorted loudly. "Or are you just going to wade in with your guns blazing and hope for the best? Kill everything in sight, right? It's simpler that way."

Lee pictured two quick shots: one to cap his knee and bring him down and the other to bust his head open. Yes, violence *was* simpler.

Steeling himself with a deep breath, Lee stepped forward. "Yes, we have a plan." His lips stretched wide in a smile that lacked humor. "And it involves as little shooting as possible."

Jerry spread his arms, the ringmaster inviting the participant into his circus.

"Roanoke River," Lee said simply.

Jerry and White both stared blankly.

He turned his attention to the crowd, made up of the group leaders and several residents of Camp Ryder who just wanted to watch. Most of the faces he recognized. "The Roanoke River is an unbroken waterway that cuts across most of the top of our state's northern border. It terminates into the coast. Further inland, near a little town called Eden, it's known as the Dan River. That waterway can be a natural barricade."

"Can't they just go around that town, then?" Jerry's eyes narrowed to dark little slits.

Lee nodded. "Yes. That's the point. The town is about forty miles from the Appalachians. Jacob has already established that the infected won't cross into the mountains because they naturally follow the path of least resistance. So between the mountains and the river, we create a bottleneck." Lee looked directly at Professor White. "So we can thin the herd."

"This is ridiculous." Jerry raised his hands and looked to the crowd for support. "What about all the bridges? They'll just cross there! This plan holds water like chicken wire!"

There was a mumble of concurrence from the crowd and it peaked out, sounding hostile. Everyone was scared and angry, but they weren't sure whom to be angry with. Jerry was trying his damnedest to make them angry at Lee, but the vast majority owed Lee their lives, even if they didn't agree with him all the time. The exceptions were those who had sided with Jerry from the start, the people who had been here before Lee.

Lee waited for the grumbling to pass and then spoke. "We'll blow the bridges."

Jerry's eyes went wide.

Professor White held up his hands. "You're gonna blow the bridges? What the—"

Old Man Hughes's voice boomed over White's. He wasn't shouting, but his voice carried when he wanted it to and immediately stole the attention from the two men who appeared to be in the beginnings of a fit.

"You asked the man a question," Hughes said and gestured to Lee. "At least have the decency to let him answer it before you get your knickers all twisted up."

A welcome quiet fell over the crowd as everyone listened instead of yammering back and forth.

Lee took the opportunity to continue. "I'm setting up two teams. The first will be responsible for spearheading out east to where the Roanoke River ends in Swan Bay. They will then work their way back west, dealing with the bridges as they go. Obviously, we won't be able to blow every bridge. But there will be groups of survivors that live near these bridges, and we will attempt to make contact with them, to enlist them to guard the bridges near them. If there is no one to guard the bridge, then we'll destroy it. If we can't destroy it, we'll mine it and barricade it as best we can."

"What about the Followers?" someone yelled.

Lee shook his head. "There's no reason to believe there's any truth to those rumors."

A middle-age man stepped forward, his eyes wide with fear. "I talked to a man who came from out east. He said the Followers burned his camp to the ground. He said they cannibalize the children, rape the women, and hang the men from a cross if you refuse to join them."

The crowd stirred.

Lee held up a hand. "I don't know about the rest of you, but I think it seems a little far-fetched."

Bus jumped in before anyone else could revive the topic. "Let's focus on what we know, folks. Let's get back on track here and listen to the rest of this plan." He nodded to Lee. "Go ahead, Captain."

Lee shifted his weight. "The second team will head northwest toward the town of Eden. They will establish a secured route between Camp Ryder and Eden, and we will use this route to run supplies and to ferry refugees away."

Jerry's eyebrows shot up. "Refugees?"

Lee nodded tiredly. "Yes, refugees. If there are hordes as large as Jacob suggests there are, and they are migrating south, I anticipate there will be refugees fleeing from these hordes. If they can fight, we'll arm them and use them, but if they're unable or unwilling to fight, we need a safe place to send them. The Camp Ryder Hub is the safest place I can think of."

Old Man Hughes tossed his gray head up. "Excuse me. But how do we know that they will be migrating south? From what we've seen around here, the infected hordes are pretty much sticking to where they're from. Why would the ones from up north be any different?"

Jacob nodded to Lee and politely fielded the question. "It's about food supply. I've actually seen it. You asked me earlier whether I'd seen these massive hordes, and I haven't, but I've seen what they can do. I've been through cities they've left behind. They've picked them clean of every edible thing. Even the canned goods—I've seen them bash them against a curb to get at what's inside. They won't sit around and starve to death, you understand."

He looked around the crowd, gauging how many people were actually comprehending him. "The FURY bacterium eats away at your reasoning abilities, the mental safeties we've put in place over generations of living in civilization, which help us to be nonaggressive and productive citizens. All that's gone, but they still have the instinct to survive. In fact, that instinct is even stronger in them than it is in us, because they're incapable of shame or morality. They don't have limits on what they will do to survive. And the primary survival mechanism that drives them is hunger. They'll go to where the food is . . . and that's south."

Lee looked at Professor White and saw the unbidden shock rise on his features, as though he simply couldn't believe what he'd seen with his own eyes for the past few months, and he was only believing it now because someone with a PhD was telling him about it. *Yes, we're the food, Professor*, Lee thought. *Do you still want to save them all? Are they still "plague victims"?*

"Okay," Jerry said, his voice more subdued. "Let's talk a little about your plan, Captain."

Lee tensed slightly, knowing this would be the hard part. "We have the equipment to get the job done." He looked around. "We just don't have the manpower."

"Ah." Jerry smiled viciously. "So now you need us, huh? Things aren't so one-sided, are they?"

Lee tried hard to remain placid. "They never were. I can't do my work without survivors, and without me, the survivors don't survive."

This angered Jerry. "We were doing just fine before you came!"

Keith Jenkins, the man who had loaned Lee his pickup truck to make that first fateful run to Bunker #4, stepped forward, and Lee watched Jerry bristle like a dog with its hackles up. It was a well-known fact that the two men despised each other.

The old man adjusted his dirty old ball cap on his balding head and spat on the ground. "I know

I'm gettin' old, but I'm pretty sure my memory is still good. And as I recall, we was pretty much starving before Captain Harden came along. Didn't have no guns, didn't have no medicine, and we never left the damn gates." He raised his head so he was peering at Jerry from underneath the shade of his cap bill. "Seems like you're one ungrateful motherfucker."

The crowd stirred, and everyone started shouting, some in support of Jerry and some against him. Keith Jenkins just shook his head and stepped over to Lee while Jerry looked around, seeming unsure of what to do or say in that moment. Keith smiled and nodded at Julia, then planted himself firmly beside her, clearly on Lee's side, as though he'd drawn a line in the sand.

He raised a hand and hollered, "I don't know about y'all, but I'm with Captain Harden." He turned to Lee. "Anything you need, Cap. You let me know."

Another, younger man stepped out of the crowd and over toward Lee. "I'm with you, too."

"Wait!" Professor White wailed, holding up his hands. "Wait! There's no need for a military force! We don't need a goddamned draft right now. This isn't Vietnam, Captain!" He spoke with such vehemence that spittle flew from his mouth in sprays. "Stop looking at everything through the eyes of a warlord and try to see it through the eyes of the peaceful people you're supposed to be protecting. We're trying to rebuild a civilization, not fight a war! Why do you want us to keep fighting when we don't get anything out of it?" His eyes were beginning to water and his voice cracked with emotion. "It's like you're living out your childhood fantasies, playing war in your backyard! But it's not a game anymore, Captain. These are real lives you're taking. You're sending real people to die when there are other options!"

Lee bit his tongue hard enough to draw blood. The pain cleared the buzzing in his ears and the rising, prickling heat that washed over his head. A few more deep breaths. "If there is another, better option, please let me know."

The professor's emotion was like a radio transmitter, and the group of his students from Fuquay-Varina that had come along with him were all picking it up; they were beginning to shout and to cry along with him, their forms hunched over and pleading, desperate.

Lee thought they looked pathetic, but he tried to clear the anger from his head and detach himself from them. What were they, really? They were scared sheep. Scared of the shepherd, scared of the sheepdog, and scared of the wolf. Their only capability for problem solving was to stampede away. He couldn't fault them for it. It was who they were.

White drew closer to Lee and his posture was both furious and supplicating. "We run. We leave this behind. You said that they don't go over the mountains, so we should go over the mountains where they can't get us! The mountains are rich with wildlife. We can live there in communities until the infected die out. They must eventually die out. We can wait it out rather than fight! At least we'll be alive!"

Lee shook his head pityingly. "And what about the rest of North Carolina? What about South Carolina and Georgia? We just leave them to figure it out on their own? Better them than us, right?"

"They can run too! They can go over the mountains..."

Lee's control was like a wet rope slipping through his fingers. "The mountains only go so far. Why don't you take some fucking responsibility for something instead of shoving it on down the line? This is *our* problem now. *We* need to solve it."

White opened his mouth to protest, but Lee cut him off and pointed a finger in his face.

"You talk all these high ideals about society, but you're not willing to do shit for it. And you know what? That's fine! That's why there're people like me, and Julia, and LaRouche, and Father Jim, and Harper. People who are willing to fight. If you're not willing, that's okay. But don't hold back those who are."

White was shaking his head, tears beginning to stream down his face. "You're going to ruin us. He's going to ruin us! He's going to send everyone off to die in a war for no other reason than his personal 'warrior's code.'" White stepped backward into his crowd of weeping students. "We had the chance to create something better, Captain. All you want to do is send us right back to where we were!"

"Guys!" Bus stepped between them. "I think there's been enough shouting for one meeting."

But White was done. He kept shaking his head and then he brought up his finger and waved it toward Lee. "This man is a criminal. He's a warlord. All he wants is power, and he'll spend your lives to get it!" White turned before anyone else could speak. "We're done with this meeting. Clearly no one here is going to listen to reason."

Professor White and the others from Fuquay-Varina gathered around him and slowly began to edge away. The young people looked accusingly across at Lee as they crowded around their beloved leader and comforted him, as though Lee had physically hurt the man. The older ones followed the crowd, but they avoided looking up at Lee or anyone else from Camp Ryder. Their faces were full of shame.

Lee watched them go, grinding his teeth.

Jerry remained standing with his arms crossed. He shook his head slowly, looking between Lee and Bus. "Bus, I think your judgment has been clouded. In fact, I think your judgment has been clouded since Captain Harden arrived here. This isn't something we can fight. Sometimes you have to cut your losses and run."

"It's not something you can run from either," Lee said, taking a step toward the man but keeping his voice as level as he could manage. "What happens when the infected reach Georgia? There are no more mountains to hold them in. They'll just keep spreading. Are you going to live on top of a mountain for the rest of your life, scared to death to go down into the rest of the country? Is that the future you want?"

Jerry shook his head. "This is all gonna blow over."

"You don't know that."

Jerry sighed smugly, as though he knew something Lee did not, and that he was unable to explain it to Lee because the captain was so simple-minded he wouldn't be able to understand. "Where does your plan start, Captain? What's your first order of business?"

"Sanford," Lee said. "Sanford to recover what military equipment was left over from the evacuation attempt. Then to Bunker Two on the other side of Sanford. We haven't tapped that bunker yet, so it's got everything we need. Once we have the equipment we need to begin, we'll split up. One team east, one team north."

"You still don't have the manpower."

"Yeah." Lee nodded. "I had hoped to ask for that during the meeting. It kinda got derailed."

Jerry held up both of his hands and backed away. "You can count me out of your crusades, Captain. Me and my people have no desire to get ourselves killed for nothing."

Lee spat in the dirt. "I only ask that if you're not willing to help, you get out of the way of those who are."

Jerry's supporters, about a dozen from the original Camp Ryder group, bolstered up behind him as he looked directly at Lee and shook his head. All he said, loud and clear, was, "Madman."

SIX

A LONG NIGHT

WITH JERRY AND WHITE and their groups of supporters gone from the meeting, there still remained about sixty people from Camp Ryder and Smithfield, unsure of what to do and where to go.

The winter sky had turned a deep blue in the waning twilight, and the horizon behind Lee was a pastel-colored smudge that would soon disappear. As the last sliver of sunlight glowed dimly across their faces, they began to huddle closer in the cold, pulling their jackets tighter around themselves as their collective breath took vaporous form and hovered over them. Many of them wore the OD green parkas that Lee had brought from his bunker, while others wore jackets that had been pilfered during scavenging operations.

In the last bit of light, Lee met as many of them in the eye as he could. "I know I'm asking a lot. I'm asking for you to possibly leave your loved ones and definitely to put yourself in harm's way. But I would not ask for you to do so if I didn't think we could accomplish the mission. I need help, folks. I need as much help as I can get."

Lee held up a hand. "This isn't an altar call. You

don't have to step forward now. Go get some food. Talk to the people you need to talk to. Sleep on it. Come see me in the morning if you think you are willing and able to help. Thank you."

With that, Lee turned, and his team went with him. They made their way toward the Camp Ryder building, and behind them they could hear Bus thanking everyone for showing up. Kip Greene was still standing there next to Bus, probably confused, or dismayed, or scared shitless. God only knew what the man was thinking, whether it be about the near-violent disunion among the members of the Camp Ryder Hub or about the impending threat that loomed over everyone.

As they entered the building, the smell of Marie's cooking filled the place. Rather than ration food out to each family and individual, Marie cooked community meals from a combination of Lee's supplies, foodstuffs that had been scavenged, and meat from the hunters—most commonly venison, but sometimes squirrel or rabbit. Even with Lee supplementing from his bunkers, there wasn't a lot to go around. With the population of Camp Ryder growing, feeding everyone was always a challenging prospect. More and more people had to turn to scavenging to feed themselves and their families, but eventually that too would run out.

Still, every evening, Marie would have a meal prepared, however meager.

The group headed for the line that was beginning to form at Marie's little kitchen area, but Julia remained by Lee's side. He approached the metal staircase and turned to climb it.

"You not hungry?" she asked.

Lee rubbed the back of his neck. "I'll come down in a minute...once the line's died down."

She regarded him dubiously.

"Just give me a minute."

She shrugged. "Suit yourself."

Lee clomped up the stairs. In the office, he placed his rifle against the far wall, beside the bed-roll that he kept there. He would sleep in the office tonight, as he would most of his first nights back. He hated waking in the middle of the night, cold with sweat and his heart pounding, to find Angela and Abby and Sam staring at him because he had shouted them awake in his sleep. It was always worst the first night back.

Most survivors had the dreams, but almost everyone on Lee's team had them with disturbing frequency. They were dreams of helplessness, mostly, and they often shared similar ones. The most common was their weapons not firing, or the bullets dribbling out of the barrel or simply being ineffective. Some dreamed that the claymore mines would not go off, or that the infected had found them and swarmed the building they were atop.

Lee's own personal nightmare was something less tangible. In the dream he knew he was asleep and that his eyes were closed, but he would see the room where he slept in vivid detail. And always at his feet was something, some dark figure crouched there, formless and black and inexplicable. Its presence filled him with dread, and he would try to shake himself awake and to move, but his body would be paralyzed under the weight of sleep, as though he were encased in concrete.

Lee had no explanation for the dream, save that it was some fetid mental by-product of the things he had witnessed while awake.

Every day was full of fear. Not only fear for oneself but for the people you cared for and loved. There was no safe haven, no place of peace. The dangers were constant and inescapable. Worst of all, there was no light at the end of the tunnel, no date that one could point to and say, "Yes, I'll be back home at this time; I'll be out of danger if I can last just a few more months." And no one, not even Lee, could escape the effect that this had on the subconscious.

Lee shook his head to open his drooping eyes. He blinked a few times and then stepped over behind the desk to where they had installed the base station for their radios. The base station and all the digital repeaters that Lee and his team had installed around the Camp Ryder Hub were fed from small but powerful solar panels.

He changed the channel on the base station to a prearranged frequency, used for the Coordinators to communicate with each other. Captain Mitchell had easily made contact with the others because he still had use of the secure connections in his original bunker. Establishing contact with the other Coordinators had become a problem for Lee when his original bunker had been buried underneath the burning ruins of his house.

Lee picked up the handset and made the same transmission he always made: "This is Captain Lee

Harden, Project Hometown, North Carolina, to any other Coordinator who can copy this transmission...please respond."

He released the transmit button and sat on the desk and stared at the radio. It hissed and crackled a bit after he ended his transmission, and then became silent. He sat and waited for the radio to speak up and perhaps catch something from another Coordinator, some stray radio wave bouncing across the atmosphere.

As he stared at the silent box, everything around him grew gray and monochromatic as his eyes lost focus and his mind slipped into a haze of sleepiness. He felt his head falling forward and jerked awake, and then tried to shake the sleep away, but the wakefulness would only last for another minute or so.

A rap on the doorframe caused him to turn.

Julia entered, holding a bowl and a spoon. It was laden with a stew that Marie had prepared and tendrils of steam lifted off of it. She walked over to the desk where Lee sat, placed the bowl next to him, and stuck the spoon in it.

"Brought you some dinner."

Lee smiled. "Thank you."

She stepped back and waited.

"Just give me a few minutes..."

"You need to eat," she said sternly.

"I will."

"Eat."

"Okay. You win. I'll eat."

"What's the matter? You don't like my sister's food?"

Lee took the bowl and shoveled a spoonful in his mouth. "I love your sister's food." He took another mouthful without swallowing the first so that his cheeks bulged out with it. He mumbled around the food, "See? Love it."

She smiled and sat beside him on the desk. She motioned to the bedroll. "You sleeping up here tonight?"

Lee nodded while he ate. The stew was actually very good. He really would have gone down and gotten himself some in a little bit…or fallen asleep. The hot food took the edge off his hunger and relaxed him even more, so that his whole body felt warm and heavy.

"Trouble in paradise?" she asked.

Lee looked at her, confused for a moment, then realized she was speaking about Angela. He shook his head and looked back to his bowl. "No, it's not like that with us."

"Hmm." She pondered this for a moment. "What is it, then?"

Lee shrugged. "I dunno. Friends, maybe?"

"More than that," she said quietly.

"Yeah. More than that." He finished his bowl in silence, and then felt the need to clarify. "But never…you know…"

"Really?"

"No."

"I would've thought so."

"Nope."

"Weird."

He bobbled his head. "It's good."

"So you're sleeping up here because…?"

"Oh." Lee set the bowl down on the desk. "I don't want to wake up her and Sam and Abby at night. From the dreams."

"Yeah."

Lee looked at Julia as she stared at the ground absently. "How are they for you?" he asked.

"I hate going to sleep at night. Especially by myself."

"I thought you were staying with Marie?"

Julia smiled. "Well, Marie's been staying with Harmon."

Really? Lee thought. *Good for Harmon.*

It was getting late and Lee decided it was time to roll out the bed. The talk of going to sleep was doing him in.

"You can sleep up here with me if you like." The words came out before Lee's tired mind could really put much effort into vetting them. Immediately after the last word left his mouth his mind began to race. He hadn't meant it quite like it had sounded. When they were out beyond the wire, they all slept together anyway, and it didn't seem odd to him in that moment to offer it up.

"What I meant was..." He tried to correct himself.

"Okay," she said.

Lee glanced at her. "Okay."

"I just don't wanna sleep alone," she said quietly.

"Yeah. Me neither."

"You have any extra blankets?"

"Yes."

Before rolling out his bed, he switched the radio

back to the main channel and took the lantern from the desk. Then he pulled the extra blankets from his pack and gave them to Julia. He extended his own bedroll and laid the blankets across, and Julia situated herself to his left. In an odd and yet somehow comfortable silence, they lay down on the bedroll, not touching, but close enough if one were to reach out. Lee turned off the LED lantern that glowed brightly and then, exhausted and secure in the comfort of human company, fell asleep almost instantly.

He was with his father in this dream, as he was in many other dreams of late. A presence that imparted quiet encouragement in the face of a deep and para-lyzing dread that Lee could only feel when he was asleep, lost in the twists and turns of his subcon-sciousness. Gene Harden had always been a quiet man, and in these dreams he never spoke a word.

They were on the front porch of a house that Lee had never lived in, some house drawn from memories of his father's old Western movies. They stared out at a barren, windswept landscape and it filled Lee's soul with an empty fear, like the howling of wind in a canyon. When he looked to his right, he could see his father, as young as he'd looked when Lee was a boy, perhaps seven or eight years old, and his father in his late thirties. His father stared out at the wasteland before them and he smiled and nodded.

Lee turned away from the scene, hoping to escape into the house, but instead found himself in Lill-ington or some poor facsimile of it, manufactured from disjointed bits and pieces from his subconsciousness. He was standing outside, in the middle of the street, and all around him were the corpses of the dead infected he had killed. Across from him he could see Father Jim, and the man wept violently and beat at his chest.

"What's wrong?" Lee asked.

And Father Jim gestured all around them, at the bodies that littered the streets, and his tears ran bitter down his face. "Where are the females, Lee? Where are all the females?"

Lee looked down at the bodies, pale flesh smeared with dirt and dried blood and shit. All of them were naked, and they were all females, and they all bore Lee's old girlfriend Deana's face, in all the different grotesque attitudes of death. In some of them Deana's tongue lolled out, in others her eyes were open, gazing at the sky or at some invisible fixed point beyond reckoning. In the dream, the sight of Deana's face had very little effect on him. It was a face from another life, another time.

Someone he could barely remember.

He tried to comfort Jim by pointing to all the dead bodies. "No, Jim! We got 'em all! They're right here!"

But Jim was inconsolable, and he only continued to ask, "Where are all the females?"

"Lee."

He opened his eyes to darkness, staring at the ceiling above his head.

"Lee."

He leaned forward and could see the dark shape

of Julia, wrapped in a blanket and standing at the door to the office. The Camp Ryder building had grown cold in the night and Lee could see her breath, fogging in the black air. Julia looked at him and made a little waving motion from underneath her blanket.

"There's someone at the gate," she whispered.

Lee leaned up onto his elbows, sweeping a layer of dust from his slumbering mind and trying to remind himself why he should care if someone was at the gate. The sound of it was faint when he heard it. Someone was yelling outside, and another was raising his voice. Two men in disagreement.

Lee threw his blanket off of himself and the cold air bit at him mercilessly. He grabbed his jacket and his rifle and fumbled them on as he headed for the door. Julia had dropped her blanket and was donning her jacket as well. Lee thought about telling her to stay put, but there really was no purpose to it. Besides, they might need a medic.

He took the metal stairs as quietly as he could, not wanting to wake anyone sleeping inside the building, but the sounds of the disturbance outside were already beginning to cause people to stir. In the small quarters constructed in the middle of the building, lanterns and flashlights were beginning to flicker and glow.

"What time is it?" he asked Julia as she followed him.

"Almost three."

Damn. Lee gritted his teeth. *You can't pay for a good night's sleep nowadays.*

They reached the bottom of the steps, turned

through the short hall to the front doors, and slipped out of the Camp Ryder building. From the elevated entryway, Lee could see clear to the gate. A flashlight illuminated a small bubble of existence there and it consisted of two men and the chain-link fence that divided them. All through the shantytown of Camp Ryder, more lights were coming on and people were poking their heads out of their little shacks, trying to see what the yelling was about.

Lee began to run for the gate. Sleep and cold stiffened his joints now, particularly his left ankle, and he couldn't hide his limp as he ran. Ahead of him, Lee could see that the sentry was stepping away from the gate, pointing his rifle at a man on the other side, some strange, bulky-looking bear-man, with wild eyes and a wiry beard stained with blood. The crazed man on the outside had his fingers woven through the chain link and he was shaking it and yelling.

For a moment, Lee slowed his pace and raised his rifle, wondering why the sentry was not taking out this infected. Then he heard Julia's voice huffing alongside him. "Is that the guy from the woods?"

"What?" Lee asked, but then realized whom she was talking about. The man and the woman and the two children, with their blankets and coats draped heavy and thick over their shoulders. The ones Jim had tried to make contact with, but who had run away.

The bear-man shook the gate again. "Get out here! I know you can help! You said. You said you could help! Get the fuck out here and help me, goddammit!"

Lee stopped at the gate, rifle ported. "What the hell is this?"

The man on the other side looked at Lee. "You were there! You were with that guy who said he would help! Where is he? It's my wife and kids... we need help!"

Lee leaned closer and hissed through his teeth. "Would you shut the fuck up? I'm going to help you, but you gotta be quiet!"

The man lowered his voice. "Please..."

Lee nodded to the sentry.

"You sure?" The sentry looked shocked.

Lee skewered him with a glare. "Yes, I'm sure. Open the damn gate."

The sentry hopped to, and Lee leveled his rifle at the strange man who stood outside the gate, wringing his hands and looking about nervously. "Put your hands up and don't make any sudden movements. I'll help you, but you need to cooperate with me first, or you're not getting shit. Understand?"

The man's wild and desperate eyes locked onto Lee. Then he nodded and raised two dirty, blood-stained hands.

Lee turned to Julia. Her matted blond hair was bulging out in odd directions and there were dark rings under her wide eyes. "Go grab the team and tell them to suit up. Better grab your medic pack too."

She nodded rapidly and ran for the Camp Ryder building.

Lee turned and found that there was no longer a fence between him and the bear-man, and only about ten feet of open space separated them. The man's arms were still raised up, but now his head had leaned back and his eyes were staring at the sky and they looked hopeless.

"Are you listening to me?" Lee asked.

The man didn't look, but he said, "Yes."

Lee spoke slowly and clearly. "Kneel down, and put your hands on top of your head, interlacing your fingers."

The man complied, going to his knees with a sudden collapse, like a wounded beast.

"Do not move; just answer my questions. Do you have any weapons?"

"Crowbar," the man said. "In my belt. Knife in my pocket. Look, man...we gotta hurry..."

Lee made eye contact with the sentry and nodded. As the sentry moved toward the stranger, Lee spoke again. "The sentry is going to take your weapons. If you move, I will kill you. Do you understand?"

"Yes."

The sentry riffled through the man's thick layers of clothing, then paused and looked at his own hands, which were dark and glistening. "Jesus!" the sentry exclaimed. "He's fucking covered in blood!"

"Keep going," Lee said steadily.

The kneeling man looked at the sentry. "I had to kill two of them to get here," he said, but he did not elaborate.

As the sentry extracted the crowbar and knife,

Lee stepped closer to the man. "You can stand up now. What happened?"

The man reached out for Lee as he drew closer and his eyes were sharp and dark as obsidian, chipped to some primitive arrowhead. "Please! We don't have time...they're in the truck. They're in the back of the truck, and they're surrounded!"

"Slow down." Lee helped the man to his feet. "Explain."

The man's eyes flashed back and forth. "They tracked us, the crazies. We ran from our camp and we made it to this big truck and we hid in the back, but they tracked us down." The man breathed rapidly and pointed out into the dark dirt road that led away from Camp Ryder. "I was able to fight my way out and run to you guys. Please, you gotta help!"

"Where's the truck?"

"It's maybe a mile from the end of this dirt road. I...I don't know." The man made a miserable noise and his hand went to his head and raked through his hair. "It's dark. I was disoriented."

The sentry leaned into Lee. "There's an overturned tractor trailer out on Highway 27, near Outpost Benson."

Lee took the man by the shoulder to get his attention. "Are you talking about infected?"

"Yes, the crazy people!"

"Not real people with guns?"

"No...the ones who try to eat you."

"How many of them were there?" Lee asked.

"I don't know. Maybe ten? I killed a few. Or maybe I just wounded them." He began to breathe heavily again. "Shit, I don't know..."

"Alright, calm down." Lee turned and saw Harper jogging toward them down the dark Main Street of Camp Ryder. He held his rifle in one hand and was in the process of pulling on his parka with the other. Lee looked over to the Humvee, parked just a few yards from them. He didn't want to just rush out into the darkness. He didn't know this guy, didn't know his family, didn't know what the threat was. Was it a pack? Was it a horde? How many were there? Ten? Fifty? A hundred?

Maybe there were no infected at all.

Maybe this was just a trap to draw Lee and his team out of Camp Ryder.

But a decision had to be made.

"Alright," Lee said with finality. As Harper pulled up next to him, breathing hard and rubbing sleep from his eyes, Lee pointed to the Humvee. "Get that thing ready to roll. We're headin' out as soon as the others get here."

"Okay." The man slapped his hands together. "But we gotta go fast!"

Lee looked at him, tight-lipped. "We'll go as fast as we can safely go."

"Uh, Lee..." Harper said quietly.

The two men made eye contact.

Harper jerked his head over toward the Humvee.

Lee stepped to the side with Harper, already knowing what was coming.

"What the fuck is this about?"

"Look, his wife and kids are trapped in the back of a truck. Surrounded by infected. It's the guy from the road earlier."

Harper peered over Lee's shoulder at the man,

as though to confirm that it was the same person who had run away frightened when Jim had tried to make contact with him only hours ago. "It doesn't matter. Are you thinking clearly right now?"

Lee rubbed his hands together for warmth. "Yes, I'm thinking clearly. The guy's been banging and yelling at our gate for the last five minutes. If we refuse, he's going to keep freaking out at our gate and draw infected in and we'll have to fight them anyway. At least this way, we can keep the guy quiet and maybe save his family."

Harper made a leery face. "I dunno..."

"Me neither. But it's happening." Lee opened the driver's door and waved Harper in like a chauffeur.

Harper growled but complied.

SEVEN

STRANGERS

As the Humvee rumbled to life, Julia, LaRouche, and Father Jim all came jogging up, rifles in hand. Lee pointed to the bearded man in the rags and waved him over. To save time and arguments, Lee wanted the man standing there when he told the group what they were doing.

Jim stared, perplexed. "Hey . . . is that the guy . . . ?"

Lee nodded toward the bearded man. "This guy's wife and two little kids are stuck in the back of a truck about a mile from here. Pack of infected around them. We're going to go bring them back."

There was a moment of uncomfortable silence.

Julia broke it. "Is he coming with us?"

Lee nodded. "He's gotta point out where he's talking about." Lee turned and faced the stranger with a hard look. "And I swear to God, if this turns out to be anything but what you say it is, I will put a bullet in your brain. You understand me?"

The man held up his hands but looked angry. "Jesus! Fuck, let's go! I swear to God, it's not like that!"

Julia looked pissed. "Alright. Get in the damn truck. Let's go."

The tired crew scrambled aboard the vehicle, the bearded man sitting in Father Jim's normal spot, with Jim crammed in the cargo area and Julia regarding the filthy, stinking man who took his place with a scowl and a curled nose. The man didn't seem to notice. He was on the edge of his seat, poking his head between Harper and Lee and staring anxiously out the windshield.

The Humvee spewed gravel as it lurched out of Camp Ryder and into the darkness. They kept the headlights off because the moon gave enough illumination to see by, and all their eyes were adjusted to the dark.

"Take it out to Highway 27 and make a right." Lee turned partially to face the man. "What's your name, stranger?"

"What?" The man looked at Lee as though he had spoken a foreign language. It took him a moment to understand the question. "Oh. Eddie...Ramirez."

"Where are you from?"

"From Winston." The man's voice grew heavy. "We were headed to the coast. Heard things weren't as bad there."

"Things are bad everywhere," Harper griped.

"What did you do for a living?" Lee asked.

"Diesel mechanic."

Lee and Harper exchanged a quick glance. Any type of mechanic could have proven himself incredibly useful, but a diesel mechanic in particular seemed to be a rare stroke of good luck. Between the tractor that trailed their tanker of diesel fuel, the diesel generators that kept the hospital running in Smithfield, and the Humvees, in terms of immediate value, only a doctor rivaled a diesel mechanic.

The rescue mission had just quickly gone from an act of kindness to an absolute imperative: If they failed to rescue this man's family, it was doubtful he would help them with anything.

Everyone in the Humvee seemed to realize this without Lee having to spell it out.

They all hunkered down a little more seriously over their rifles.

They reached Highway 27 and Eddie leaned forward even farther and thrust his hand out. "Turn here! Turn right! It's less than a mile from this turn."

As Harper made the turn, Lee twisted and looked at his crew behind him. "Everyone, check your weapons. Make sure you're locked and loaded. We're gonna do this fast. Take out the threat, pull Eddie's wife and kids out of the truck, and then we're fucking gone, okay? Remember that they're inside the truck, so watch your backdrop. Those bullets will punch straight through that sheet metal."

Everyone nodded silently.

Eddie looked terrified.

"Hey." Lee grabbed the man by the shoulder. "Don't fucking move until I say so. You got that? Do not. Get out. Of the car."

"Yeah. Don't get out."

"That's it right there." Harper slowed the Humvee.

Up ahead, the bulk of an overturned tractor

trailer and a pileup of cars around it gleamed like bleached bones in the moonlight. Some sort of mechanical elephant graveyard.

Harper came to a stop in the road. "I don't see any infected."

"Keep an eye out," Lee called. "Three-sixty."

Eddie began jabbing his finger in the air. "They're right there! They're right there!"

Lee thought about smacking him but restrained himself. "Calm down. Where are the infected?"

"I don't know!" Eddie was breathing rapidly. "You gotta go get my family!"

Lee leaned forward in his seat. The tractor trailer was lying parallel to the roadway, the dark windshield staring straight up the asphalt at Lee, the tires oriented toward the shoulder so that they were looking at the top of the rig. It was there, just beyond the front bumper, that Lee could see something odd.

He pointed. "Hey, Harper...you see that?"

Harper squinted. "Yeah. Steam."

"Breath," Lee said quietly.

Just behind the cab, Lee and Harper could see the faint rising clouds of steam coming from something huffing its hot lungfuls into the frosty night air. They billowed out from behind the bumper with force and then drifted lazily up into the air where they dissipated into blackness.

"We should—" Lee began, but was interrupted by the sound of the door behind him opening.

"Hey!" Julia shouted.

Lee turned in his seat to find that Eddie was no longer behind him but had bailed from the vehicle and was now running for the back end of the trailer. Almost in the same instant that Lee comprehended what had happened, a wiry shape lurched from around the tractor trailer, scrambling on all fours, then coming upright into a full sprint.

"Shit!" was all Lee could get out. He threw open his door and stepped out, not feeling the pain in his ankle, though he could feel the wobbling weakness in it. He ran forward about three steps and then planted his feet wide and pulled the rifle snug into his shoulder. As he sighted through the Aimpoint scope, he realized there was nothing there. He'd either forgotten to turn the damn thing on or the batteries had finally crapped out.

Lee lowered the rifle for the slimmest of seconds and gained himself the whole panorama of what was happening, fighting against tunnel vision.

Far off to the left, a few more ghostly shapes had appeared out of nowhere. About thirty yards ahead of him, the first infected was heading straight for Eddie, who was trying desperately to juke right. The infected was quick, and if Lee waited too long, it would be on top of Eddie, and Lee would not be able to take the shot without his sights.

He snapped the rifle up and fired off three rounds. He couldn't tell if they connected, but the infected hesitated in its run and turned its head toward Lee for a split second, and Lee pulled the trigger again. He didn't count the rounds— it could have been two; it could have been ten. He just fired until he saw the infected jerk back, and then crumple to the ground where it began twitching and pawing at the concrete.

"Eddie!" Lee yelled, but the man was off and running again.

Behind him, the 50-cal thundered into action, each shot illuminating the night around them like a lightning flash. The long burst of automatic fire ripped chunks of concrete into the air and then tracked up the shoulder of the road to the other three or four shapes that Lee had seen.

Lee sprinted toward Eddie but looked to his left and watched the huge bullets find two of the four infected. Entire limbs and great pieces of anatomy flew off of them, like they were delicate and poorly assembled mannequins.

Eddie reached the back end of the trailer and Lee watched him stutter-step as though he couldn't decide which direction to go from there. Then he began to backpedal quickly.

Swearing, Lee reached down and engaged the backup iron sights on his rifle.

"Get back!" Lee yelled and squared himself toward the trailer.

Eddie kept backing away, but he wouldn't turn and run.

From around the corner came two more figures. Lee began firing immediately. He could hardly see the iron sights in the darkness, but he approximated his aim and kept pulling that trigger. One of them went down, but the other was going for Eddie and was in too close for Lee to take the shot. Eddie tried to rear back and kick the thing in the chest as it closed in, but it deftly swatted his leg out of the way and leaped onto the man.

The two figures tumbled to the ground. At first,

the infected was on top, biting viciously at Eddie but only catching great mouthfuls of dirty clothing. It fixated upon a thick lapel and began rending at it, shaking its head back and forth with the piece of cloth in its teeth and snarling like a dog. Eddie clamped both hands around the thing's throat and pushed it away from him with a cry of terror. Then he rolled the thing and managed to gain the top position.

Underneath him now, the creature scrambled and gnashed its teeth, strangely silent as Eddie bore all his weight down on the thing's throat so that it couldn't make a sound.

"Shoot it!" he screamed at Lee.

Lee extended his rifle out, holding it with one hand as though it were a giant pistol, and pushed the muzzle against the infected's eye. Both men cringed and turned their faces away. The head seemed to explode as the gases from the barrel entered through the ocular cavity and exited out the nose and ears. One hand flailed out, sightless and aimless, and slapped against Eddie's face a few times before it lay still.

Lee brought the muzzle of his rifle up and scanned for other threats, the blood steaming off the hot barrel.

Julia and Harper ran up to them.

"What the fuck was that, asshole?" Julia yelled at Eddie.

"Is that all of them?" Harper looked around.

Without giving heed to either of them, Eddie scrambled up from the dead body he was seated on and stumbled like he was drunk toward the trailer once more. "It's okay... they're in there... They're in there..."

Lee jogged after him. "Watch my back," he called over his shoulder.

Motherfucker! Lee wanted to break this guy's ankles so he couldn't run away anymore. In the two seconds it took to reach the back of the trailer, Lee thought of a dozen scathing remarks he wanted to give the mechanic.

But when Lee reached him, the man was frantically opening the locks and levers that held the trailer doors closed, and Lee knew that whatever he said now would be wasted breath. This man's brain was on a single track, and it was the welfare of his family. For that, Lee could not fault him, though it did nothing to ease his anger, and he still wanted to break the guy's ankles.

Eddie flung the door open and pulled two squirming bundles of clothing and blankets out, followed by a woman in similar dress who stared at him with something that was a mixture of rage and relief. Tears glistened at the bottoms of her eyes and her mouth worked as though she were trying to find the right words.

"You left us!" she cried, and smacked him hard across the face. "Don't you ever fucking do that again!" She hit him again and again and finally seemed to dissolve as he grabbed hold of her and pulled her in tight so she couldn't move. Her strained voice was muffled into the shoulder of his coat. "Don't you ever! Don't you ever!"

"I'm sorry. I'm sorry."

Beneath the two adults, the kids, a girl and a

boy, wailed and clung desperately to each other and their mother.

Lee gritted his teeth and felt the rising of something in the back of his throat, but it wasn't from disgust. It was that clenched, acidic feeling of sympathy, and it threatened to eat away at the hard edge Lee had honed over the last few months, like a fine blade drawn ceaselessly across a strop. He looked away.

Speaking into the darkness, Lee said, "Alright, come on. You guys can do this in the Humvee. We gotta move."

With Julia, Harper, and Lee surrounding them like the points of a triangle, the family of four quieted down and began moving toward the Humvee.

"Thank God," the woman kept whispering. "Thank God."

Harper drove fast for Camp Ryder. In the back, everyone bumped around and jostled as he dodged or simply ran over debris in the road. Most of it was tree branches from the past storm season that had ripped through the Carolinas. Some of it was debris from traffic accidents, and some of it was abandoned cars that forced Harper to take the shoulder.

While they drove, Julia knelt in the back cargo area, crammed in next to Jim and LaRouche, and dealt with the family of four that now took up the two backseats and the floor space where LaRouche would normally stand and man the gun.

Lee was turned in his seat, and he watched her work quickly and calmly. She looked natural in this element. Crouched in the back of the Humvee, tending to patients. She pulled the dirty clothes off the whimpering children, calming them with a smile and a friendly question while she checked arms and legs for bite marks. The girl's name was Elise and the boy's name was Anton. Julia shone her little penlight in their eyes and looked into their mouths. She asked them their ages and if they knew how to sing certain songs, and gradually they stopped crying.

As she worked, Lee fiddled with the sight on his rifle and discovered that it had been turned on, but that the batteries had finally run out. He thought he had scavenged some double-A batteries, but he would have to check. Batteries of any kind tended to be a luxury to find nowadays. They were one of those staple items that disappeared quickly along with canned food, bottled water, and ammunition.

He felt someone touch his arm and looked back to find Eddie looking at him and rubbing his red nose with the sleeve of his jacket, leaving glistening snot trails behind. "Thank you. I...I don't even know who you people are. Thank you."

Lee nodded and extended his hand. "Captain Harden."

Eddie shook his hand and looked bewildered. "Where...I mean...How did you get all this stuff? Are you with the military?"

"Yes and no." Lee decided to skip the lengthy explanations. Eddie would work that out on his own. "We're part of a larger group. You mentioned you were going east."

Eddie nodded. "Yeah. We heard it wasn't as bad out by the coast."

"Hmm."

"Where'd you hear that from?" Harper looked back momentarily.

"Just…" Eddie shrugged. "From other people."

"Look." Lee pulled out his nearly empty magazine and replaced it with a fresh one. "I'm not trying to deter you from chasing your dreams. I'm just telling you how I believe it is. I haven't heard anything to suggest that things are any better in other regions."

"In fact," Harper said, "we've heard the opposite. According to people coming out of the coastal region, there's a group called the Followers…"

Julia threw him a sharp look. "Don't fill their heads with that crap, Harper." Looking back to the family, she shook her head. "It's nothing but unsubstantiated rumors. Bogeyman stories."

Lee cleared his throat and continued. "Regardless, if you're determined to continue looking out east, we won't hold you back. I'd like for you and your family to at least stay a few days in the camp before you head out." Lee looked at him. "I was also hoping you might look at some things for us. We have several diesel machines. It'd be great if you could make sure they're in good working order before you go. I don't know when I'm gonna come across another diesel mechanic."

Eddie nodded emphatically. "Right. Yes. Of course."

Julia interjected. "Excuse me. I need to check you too, sir."

Eddie showed her his arms. "I haven't been bitten. I swear."

Julia smiled, but Lee could see it was strained. "We just have to check. Look straight ahead, please." She flashed the light in both eyes, watching the pupil dilation. "Open your mouth and say, 'Ah.'"

He complied. Julia shot Lee a little look but nodded that he was good to go.

"You say you guys came from the Winston-Salem area?" Lee started again.

"Yeah."

"How are things there?"

"Bad. Winston-Salem and Greensboro...man, there's just not much left."

"How about the infected? Are the groups large?"

"It's the surrounding countryside. Man, those little groups of 'em, the wolf packs, they're all over the place outside the city. Inside the city, it's mostly regular people who do the most damage. More like gangs. They're not really friendly toward anyone." Eddie reached across and took his wife's hand. "They pretty much looted and burned our neighborhood to the ground. We barely made it out."

"How long have you been on the road?"

"About two weeks now." Eddie looked at his kids. "It's been slow going with the little ones."

"I'm surprised you made it this far," Lee said frankly.

"Me too."

Harper pulled the Humvee up to the front gate of Camp Ryder and the sentry took a moment to shine his flashlight inside the windshield and see who it was. Harper squinted against the light and waved his hand. The sentry pulled the gate open and they drove through, back in the same spot they had left from. A few people hung around the main drag, curious about the goings-on, and a few more shacks glowed as people lit their lanterns and flashlights and poked their heads out to see what the hubbub was about.

Harper made a rude noise and flung his door open. "I'm going back to bed."

LaRouche opened up the back hatch and climbed out, his rifle clattering across the tailgate. "Yeah, Cap. If you don't have anything for me, I'll be catching some Zs."

Lee nodded as he got out of the car. "Yes. Thank you. You guys can all go grab some sleep. We'll talk in the morning."

Beside the Humvee, Eddie and his family huddled in a tight unit.

Julia nodded toward them. "I'll try to get them a little food and some water. Probably have to sleep in the medical trailer tonight. I don't know if we have room for them anywhere else."

Lee nodded. He could feel his body crashing underneath him. He felt worse now than he had when he'd turned in for the night. But he didn't want to leave Julia by herself to take care of the newcomers. "Yeah. I'll grab the water and food if you want to get them settled into some bunks."

Father Jim laid a hand on his shoulder. "Let me handle it, Captain. You look dead on your feet, and I'm not gonna be able to sleep anyway." He smiled. "Some people crash after a fight. I tend to lie awake."

"You sure?"

But Jim and Julia were already escorting the family toward the medical trailer. Lee was too tired to argue, and frankly, he lacked the concern. He needed to sleep. Maybe he would actually give a shit in the morning.

Harper and LaRouche both threw up their hands and yawned, one after the other.

Harper smacked his lips. "Guess that means we're good. Don't wake me up again."

Lee smiled and turned toward the Camp Ryder building, where he could see the tall frame of Bus making his way toward him, looking half asleep and very confused, holding on to his M4 by the carrying handle.

"What happened?" Bus looked at the family being escorted into the medical trailer.

Lee motioned toward them but kept walking. "Newcomers."

"Oh." Bus watched them for a second longer, but then turned and fell in with Lee. "Did you leave? I thought I heard the gate opening."

"Yeah. The guy was banging on the gate. We went out and grabbed his family from the back of an overturned tractor trailer. They were holed up in there, surrounded by a pack of infected."

"What? Damn." Bus rubbed his curly hair. "I can't believe I missed all of that. I must've really been out of it."

"He's a mechanic," Lee added. "Diesel mechanic."

"Really?"

Lee stopped at the front steps to the Camp Ryder building and looked back over his shoulder. "Yeah . . . I dunno."

"Don't know what?"

"I don't know about him."

Bus followed Lee's gaze, but they could only see the glow of the lantern inside the medical trailer. A few people stood around outside, rubbernecking, before they hurried back to their shacks, rubbing their arms in the cold.

"You get a bad vibe from him?" Bus asked.

"No." Lee shook his head. "I really haven't had a chance to think about it."

"We rescue people all the time," Bus pointed out. "What's different about him?"

Lee couldn't really put his finger on it. It wasn't Eddie so much that Lee had an issue with, but how Lee hadn't been able to control the situation. It had been such a rush to get out and bring them back in. With other refugees, Lee usually had a chance to speak with them at length and develop a good sense of whether they were decent people or not.

"Just indulge me," he said, concluding his thoughts. "Get the sentries on shift to keep an eye on them. They should be able to see the medical trailer from their post. I just don't want to give him free rein of the camp until I've had a chance to make up my mind about him."

"He's a diesel mechanic." Bus smiled.

Lee couldn't help but smile back. A mechanic was such a stroke of good luck that Eddie could have been a raging lunatic and they might have welcomed him anyway. "I'm sure everything will be fine. Just wanna be careful."

Bus stretched his neck. "I'll talk to the sentries."

They parted ways and Lee continued up to the foreman's office, where he dropped his gear at the foot of his bedroll and collapsed into it. Groggily, he recalled his dead Aimpoint sight and he took a moment to scrounge a spare AA battery from his pack and replace the one in the sight. With his eyes drooping closed on him, he laid the rifle beside him, still loaded and ready. He barely had time to take off his boots and pull the blankets over himself before he was fast asleep once more.

Lee slept for three more hours and could have slept longer, but Camp Ryder was waking up below him and the smells of something on the cook fires made him realize that he was painfully hungry again. He could hear the clamor and talking of the people on the main level, everyone getting ready for their day and whatever it held. Some would go off and scavenge a bit, some would set up their little trading posts. Everyone had a job to do, and it took a lot of work to keep everything running smoothly.

With the scavengers finding their own sources of food to barter with, some of the people in the camp were able to provide for themselves, though it was usually only one meal out of the day. Generally speaking, most who could feed themselves did so for their midday meals, while breakfast and dinner remained largely communal.

Lee sat up in his bedroll and looked to his left. Nothing of Julia's was in the room. She had not come back after last night's excursion. She had probably spent the last few hours caring for the Ramirez family.

He twisted a few times to get the kinks out of his back and began drawing circles in the air with his foot, working some blood into the joint and loosening up the tendons. When he felt it was ready for him to stand on, he got up and pulled on his boots. He shuffled over to the radio unit, taking a look out the office window to see the world bathed in bright sunlight. The solar panels would get a good charge.

He checked to make sure he was on the right channel as he took the handset and keyed it. "Captain Harden to Wilson, or anyone at Outpost Lillington."

Wilson must have been in the truck, because his answer was almost immediate. "Yeah, this is Wilson. Go ahead."

"Everything go all right last night?"

"Yeah. I don't know what the meeting was about, but the professor came back fucking pissed about something. No one would even speak to us. Is everything okay?"

"Yeah." Lee rolled his eyes. "Everything will be fine. Do a check and make sure they have everything set up before you leave, okay? Come straight back here and do nothing."

"Do nothing?"

"Yeah. R and R."

"Oh." Strangely, it was only until Lee heard the surprise in Wilson's voice that he realized how much they ran themselves ragged. Every day they were running to this place or that, putting out fires, making contact with and escorting bands of survivors, debriefing people, scavenging, and fighting. They were all beyond exhaustion now. They had entered that rut where they were so used to running themselves into the ground that they didn't even think twice about it anymore.

Lee keyed his mike. "We'll see you when you get here. Be safe."

"Thanks. We will."

Lee set the handset back on the cradle.

They needed a day to get everything in order.

Sanford might be a tough nut to crack.

EIGHT

A DELICATE MATTER

LEE WENT DOWNSTAIRS AND discovered that the line for breakfast was almost gone. People stood around and talked, holding the battered plastic plates that had once been considered "disposable" but were now rinsed and reused for as long as they would hold together. A quick glance at a few of the plates revealed that breakfast today was some sort of scramble consisting of dehydrated eggs, some bits of dehydrated vegetables, and little chunks of meat, most likely what was left of the venison.

Marie was leaning against the wall, having a small plate to herself. She smiled and waved her plastic fork at him as he approached.

"Well, hey there, Captain!" She set her plate down. "How've you been?"

Lee smiled and nodded. "Got some sleep, so I'm feeling pretty good."

Marie looked about as tired as he felt, though her demeanor was cheery. She worked hard to feed a lot of mouths, and though things weren't as tight as they had been when she'd been forced to give everyone only a half scoop of rice and beans at dinner, it was a daily battle for her to scrape up enough to feed seventy-some-odd people. The worries of an inevitably lean winter tugged at the corners of her mouth and gave her smile a downward slant.

She took a plate and gave him a wink as she began piling on a larger-than-normal portion for him. "I heard about last night," she said quietly. "Everything go okay?"

"Yeah." Lee put his hands on the table and leaned on it to take the weight off his ankle for a moment. "No one got hurt, and I think the family is all going to be okay. Julia checked them out last night, and I haven't heard any bad news, so I'm assuming they're all okay."

Marie nodded. "Where you think I get all my intel from? Yes, the family is okay."

Lee chuckled. "Of course. Did she tell you he was a diesel mechanic?"

"I heard." She handed the plate to Lee. "That's great news."

Lee regarded his portions. "Wow. That's a lot of food."

She gave him a critical look up and down and waved the serving ladle at him. "Yeah, I'm putting you on double portions, mister. You're looking a bit thin."

Lee patted his stomach. "I'm solid as a rock."

"A very skinny rock."

"Is it really that noticeable?"

"Look at your pants."

Lee looked down. His jacket was open so he could see the front belt line of his pants. The belt was tightened down so that the loose-fitting waist was bunched up. He shook his head. "No, the pants have just stretched out a little."

"Go eat your food before your pants fall off."

Lee grabbed a fork. "Thanks, Marie."

"Hey there, Lee." Angela appeared beside him and put a lingering hand on his arm. "Breakfast was delicious," she complimented Marie.

"Thanks." Marie smiled back, and Lee noticed her eyes flick to him, as though gauging his response to Angela's presence. "How's Abby?"

"She's good." Angela sighed. "Much better, thank you."

Ever since Lee had rescued Angela and Abby—after gunning down their infected husband and father right in front of them—Angela had worried about Abby's increasing withdrawal. She spoke very little over the following months, acted out around Lee, and often refused meals. Just recently, inside the relative safety of Camp Ryder, she'd begun to open up a bit more. Now she was playing with some of the other children, and Angela said she was acting more like her old self.

Her attitude toward Lee had not changed, but Lee could not blame her for that. She was young, and her understanding of things was limited. It would be a long time before she was able to wrap her brain around why Lee had killed her father.

Lee wasn't sure what had happened inside Angela's mind, but she had never held any animosity toward Lee for what he had done, and he had never seen her grieve for her late husband. It was too much of a sensitive and uncomfortable subject for Lee to broach, so he stayed the hell away from it.

Throughout the last few months, they had grown closer, though it was the closeness of two survivors who had made it to the other side of some wretched crucible together. Though their trials were far from over, that common thread still bound them, and the comfort they took from each other had grown.

Whether there was a name for this type of relationship, or whether it was some strange psychological syndrome that they were suffering from as a result of what they had been through together, Lee hadn't the slightest idea. Nor did he care to ruminate on it.

"Glad to hear it," Marie said, breaking into Lee's thoughts. "Captain, you eat your food. Angela, make sure he eats it all."

"You are looking a little thin," Angela pointed out.

"Great." He looked at the two women. "Gettin' it from all sides now."

Lee took his plate of food and headed for the door.

Angela walked beside him. "Little crowded in here. You wanna eat outside?"

"Yeah, that's fine."

Outside, the shade was chilly, but the sun was warm. It would be more pleasant today than it had been in several days. Perhaps the last week had just been a cold snap. In Lee's experience, the temperatures during a North Carolina November fluctuated greatly. It might be forty degrees out one day and seventy the next. Typically, though, Lee noticed that it would begin to chill toward the end of November. Then there would be one last little heat wave of sixty- or seventy-degree temperatures, as though summer was attempting to get one last kick in, and then the climate would fall into winter.

They chose a place in the sun where a few plastic crates had been set up around a small fire pit that no one appeared to be using. Lumps of ashes were all that remained of the fuel that had burned the night before. There was still some mild warmth coming from underneath the blanket of gray.

Angela sat beside him on another crate and clasped her hands between her knees, facing the sun and seeming to enjoy the warmth. She looked content.

Lee chewed a few bites and swallowed. "Where's Sam today?"

"He went out with Keith again. They left really early this morning."

"Oh." Lee nodded. "Hunting?"

"Yeah. Rabbits and squirrels."

"Okay."

Angela looked at him, one blue eye regarding him, while the other squinted shut against the morning sun. "I think he knows that you're very busy," she said. "I don't think he holds it against you."

"Well, I wasn't planning on doing anything today." Lee picked at a bit of venison in his teeth and wondered why he felt so responsible for the damn kid. Guilty that he was gone all the time, like Sam was his own son and Lee was missing his baseball games to go on business trips. "It's not like that," Lee murmured to his own thoughts.

"Like what?" Angela asked.

Lee tapped the fork against the plate. "I'm not his father."

Angela hesitated for a moment. "I know that. I'm sure he knows that too."

Lee sighed and leaned back on his crate a bit, slouching his shoulders. "I feel like I should be."

She turned partially toward him and rested her head on her hand. "Why?"

"I guess I feel partially responsible for his father's death. I didn't stop it, and I saved Sam. That makes me the de facto caretaker."

Angela shook her head. "Sam likes you, Lee. You're like a hero to him. But I think he views you as more of a ... big brother. Or maybe an uncle."

"Hmm." Lee considered this.

"You can't really replace a child's parents, Lee."

"I wasn't trying to replace—"

"At his age, that's a hole that's never going to get filled. All you can do now is be a friend."

Lee set his empty plate down on the ground beside him. "Yeah, I suppose so."

Angela reached out and put a hand on his shoulder. "You do good."

He smiled guardedly. "Thanks."

They passed another ten minutes, just sitting in the sun and enjoying the warmth. Angela sat with her elbows leaning against her knees and her hands clasped in front of her, a contemplative pose, and he sensed that she was taking her time, considering her words.

When she spoke, it was delicately. "I want to ask you something, but I don't want you to be angry at me. I just...need to know something."

Lee tensed, a bowstring being drawn back.

"How do you feel about Julia?"

There it is, Lee thought. *You knew it was coming.*

"Julia," Lee said with a deep breath. "Why do you ask?"

Angela laughed, but it sounded sad. "We're not married, Lee. Stop putting responsibilities on yourself that don't exist."

"Yeah, I know." Lee turned slightly so he was looking at Angela. She was shading one side of her face with a hand. Her smile was enigmatic. "Julia...is a good teammate."

The smile remained, but Angela looked away from Lee. "Old Captain Harden. Always such a secretive creature."

Lee scratched underneath his chin where his beard itched. "Well...what do you want me to say?"

"I don't *want* you to say anything."

A moment of silence passed between them and they both just looked out at the barren woods beyond the barbwire-topped fences.

"I don't know what we are," Lee stated.

"Who?"

"Me and you."

Angela considered this at length. Lee was surprised that she did not have a ready answer for him. He had always kind of figured that he was the only one confused about things, and that she would have a better idea of what was going on.

Apparently the mystery of them was just as elusive to her.

"I don't know," she said, as though coming to a decision. "But I think we trust each other. I think we lean on each other. Maybe because we don't think there is anyone else to lean on."

A gust of wind blew a bit of hair into her face and she hooked it with a finger and drew it back. "Maybe there would be more between us if we didn't both realize just how fucked up that would be."

They both laughed suddenly.

"Right?" She looked at him sheepishly.

"Yeah." Lee smiled at the ground. "I guess it would be kind of fucked up."

Another long silence.

"It's sad, actually," she said.

"How so?"

"It's sad that we still think like that, when obviously things have changed." Angela looked at her hands and the stubborn dirt under her fingernails that she picked at incessantly. "Otherwise..."

Lee waited for her to finish, but she did not.

She sniffed and Lee thought it sounded wet, but when he looked, she had turned her face away from him. Her voice was solid when she spoke. "You don't have to sleep up in the office, you know."

"All right."

He didn't want to leave her question unanswered.

"Julia is a good friend," he said. "A good teammate."

"You can tell me if you like her."

"I do in some ways," Lee said earnestly. "In other ways she pisses me off."

Angela smiled. "And you can tell me if you have feelings for her."

Lee shook his head. "I'll let you know if that happens."

"Okay."

"Okay."

"Captain Harden," a voice said from behind them.

Lee turned and found a man of about thirty years that he recognized from Camp Ryder. He'd never had much reason to speak with the man, but they'd been friendly in passing. He was one of those who gave Lee a respectful nod when he saw him but never approached, and the extent of any conversations they had were one-word greetings.

"What can I do for you?" Lee's expression was cautious.

The man glanced quickly between Lee and Angela, but whatever he was thinking remained a mystery. He pointed in a general direction toward the Camp Ryder building. "Could I get you to come with me for a moment? It won't take long."

Lee looked at Angela and she nodded graciously. He stood and motioned the man forward. "Lead the way."

The man turned and began walking, his rifle slung diagonally across his back from shoulder to hip, the barrel pointing down. It swung slightly as he made his way, not into the Camp Ryder building, but around the side of it, toward the rain catches. Lee followed a few paces behind and became suddenly and acutely aware that he was unarmed.

His whole body tensed when he turned the corner.

Facing him were almost twenty armed men.

NINE

FIGHTERS

UNCONSCIOUSLY, LEE'S FEET SPREAD, and the tension pulled the muscles in his legs taut. He was only about ten feet from the corner of the building, and he estimated he might be able to leap back into cover before they began firing. They were only about twenty feet from him, so he would have to move quickly, as each one of their shots was unlikely to miss at this range.

Then he realized that none of them was pointing a rifle at Lee, and in fact only a few of them were even holding their rifles. The others had them slung on their backs. And they were not standing in any sort of firing line, but rather jumbled together in a mixed-up circle.

"What is this?" Lee growled, not quite sure what he was looking at.

The man who had led him around the corner turned to face the captain. He clasped his hands in front of him. "We've all talked it over and slept on it. And we want to help."

Lee tried not to let it show when the breath came out of him in a long blast. His heart knocked on the inside of his chest hard enough to make his vision jump with each pulse. He folded his arms across his chest and said, "I see."

One of the men stepped forward from the group. He was younger than the others, perhaps in his early twenties. His head was a shaggy mop of brown curls. His face was covered in patchy scruff. "We're with you, Captain."

The twenty before him were not all men, but a few women as well. Some of them stood beside their husbands, determined to accompany them into the fight, while others stood alone, having made the decision on their own. But the thing that struck Lee the most was that there were so many of them. This was nearly a fourth of the camp. The very same people who ran scavenging operations into abandoned apartment complexes and neighborhoods, who bartered over cans of tuna and rejoiced when they found something as simple as a bottle of aspirin or a toothbrush. These were people who worked hard for the group, who gave what they could for the group. These were people who had virtually nothing to their name but ramshackle huts and the clothes on their backs. And yet, here they stood, ready to give even more so that the group might survive.

He took two steps toward the group and stopped, his expression forthright and cautious. "You understand what I'm asking you to do?"

There was a chorus of affirmative sounds.

Lee nodded. "You understand that I'll be asking half of you to go toward the east coast, which we have virtually no intelligence on? And the other half will be going northwest, past one of the biggest urban areas in the state? You understand that even with all of your help, we're going to be incredibly outnumbered, our supplies are going to be stretched thin, you'll be far from your loved ones and possibly never see them again?"

"Sir." The thirty-something man who had retrieved Lee took a step forward. "Believe me, we've talked about all of this. Not only with our families, for those of us who have them, but also amongst ourselves. We understand the risks involved. But we believe this is the best chance we have at survival, even if it is a slim one. We want to help fight for it."

One of the women stepped forward, not much more than a girl. "We're not running into the mountains, Captain. We've busted our asses to build what we have here, and we're not giving that up. We're tired of being on the run all the time."

The shaggy-headed guy nodded fiercely at her. "We've gotta fight for it. We understand."

Their hearts were strong now, but when the bullets fly and you're up to your elbows in the blood of your friends, it has the tendency to weaken resolve and make high ideals seem very small. The only solace that Lee took from them was the fact that they were here, living and breathing before him. They had survived the collapse, which was a trial by fire. And if you were able to survive that, if you were still functioning on the other side of something so horrible, then there must be some steel inside you after all.

These were not some random civilians who toted assault rifles around with them for no reason. They were the survivors. The only reason they were alive right now was because they were smarter and stronger, or at least luckier, than every other civilian who had died or succumbed to the pandemic and the incredible violence that followed.

"Okay." Lee's smile was thin. "If you all understand what you're getting into and wish to volunteer anyway, then I'm honored to have you."

A ripple of excited murmurs went through the group.

Lee stepped forward to the thirty-something man and extended his hand. "I recognize you from camp, but I don't think we've ever met."

The man took his hand and shook it vigorously. "Nate Malone."

"Good to meet you, Nate." Lee looked over Nate's shoulder at the others. "For now, I'm going to leave you unofficially in charge of these folks."

Nate nodded. "What do you want us to do?"

"Nothing for now." Lee clapped him on the shoulder. "For now, rest up. I'll have you guys training tomorrow, but today we're on hold. So enjoy it. You won't see it again for a while."

"What about Sanford?" Nate worried. "Don't you guys need us for Sanford?"

Lee shook his head. "No, we need you guys to train as a team so we can rely on you. I'm sure you're all good shots, and I'm sure you're all outstanding people, but working as a team takes practice, and we only have about a week. I need you and your group spending all that time getting ready."

Nate considered this for a few moments, then finally nodded.

To the entire group, Lee raised his voice. "Thank

you, folks. This is gonna be a tough road, but I couldn't have asked for better volunteers."

Lee left them and immediately went to find Harper. He rounded the building and could see the little fire pit where he and Angela had sat and talked, but she was no longer there. He headed for the door, and once inside found LaRouche and Jim just walking out from eating breakfast. He stopped them in passing.

"Either of you guys seen Harper?"

LaRouche pointed up to the foreman's office. "Yeah, he's up there with Bus and the dude from last night."

"Eddie?"

"Yeah, the mechanic."

"Thanks." Lee turned for the stairs.

"Hey, we're gonna see if we can't scrounge up a little bit of extra meat and some booze." LaRouche winked secretively. "Make a little fire out back and have us a regular barbecue later tonight."

Lee made a face. "Good luck with that. You might have to barter the clothes you're wearing."

"The ladies might like that."

The two men departed with a wave, and Lee continued up the stairs. In the office, he found Bus sitting behind the desk, Harper leaning on the edge of it, regarding the map, and Eddie Ramirez standing in the middle of the room, sharing in Harper's fascination with the map.

Bus noticed Lee first and raised a hand in greeting. "Just the man we wanted to see. We've got a problem."

Lee sighed. "What's new, right?"

"You're going to the coast, aren't you?" Eddie interjected.

Lee hesitated, then nodded.

"Then I could leave my family here, where they're safe, and I'll go with you to the coast. On the way, I'll keep your engines in top shape. And when we get there, I'll figure out if I want to return there with my family or stay with your group."

Lee considered it and looked to Harper and Bus to get their take on the arrangement. They both gave him a nod of approval. "Seems fair," he concluded.

"Excellent." Eddie clapped his hands. "You want me to take a look at your trucks now?"

"Well..." Lee didn't really want Eddie fiddling with the trucks unsupervised. The guy seemed straight up, but Lee still wasn't comfortable with trusting him implicitly just yet. "Let me get up with Sergeant LaRouche and I'll have him help you out."

Eddie seemed to get the picture. "That's no problem. I'll be with my family, so you know where to find me when you need me, okay?"

"Thank you very much, Eddie."

The mechanic left the room.

Harper watched him go with one raised eyebrow. "Interesting guy."

Lee smiled. "Yeah. We'll see how useful he is."

Bus rose from his seat. "We were just talking about the plan."

"Yes." Lee put his hands in his pockets. "That's what I was trying to find Harper for."

Harper raised his chin. "You found me."

"You know Nate Malone?"

"Yeah. Decent guy."

"Good. Because I need you to train him and about twenty others who just volunteered to help."

"Oh." Harper looked confused. "That doesn't leave much time, between Sanford and heading east..."

"You're not going to Sanford."

Harper's lips tightened. "Um...what do you mean?"

"I need you training the volunteers while we're clearing Sanford."

"Why not LaRouche?" Harper gestured off to the side as though the sergeant were sitting in the room. "He's military, and he's got just as much or more experience than I do. He's way more qualified to train the volunteers than I am. Why would you want me to do it?"

Lee leaned in. "Come on, Harper. I trust you both, but...don't take this the wrong way, but I need LaRouche with me in Sanford. You're the next in line as far as trust and experience goes."

"Fuck." Harper hung his head.

"I need you to do this for me."

"But—"

"You've soaked up what I've taught you and you're one of the best people I have. Plus, you're a natural leader. People listen to you. LaRouche is just as good, tactically, but he's a little bit loose for me to trust him with training the volunteers. Father Jim is good, but not as good as you. I need Julia as our medic. Jeriah and his team are just plain green."

Harper looked up at the ceiling. "All right. Fine."

"You'll do good."

"I'd do better in Sanford."

"Agreed. But I gotta have someone to train them, and you're the best choice."

"Well…" Harper trailed off, not having anything else to say.

Lee looked to Bus. "Is there something you guys wanted to talk to me about?"

"Yes." Bus took a pen that was lying on the desk and tapped it on the wooden top. "It's about fuel."

"Right. The tanker."

"Were you planning on taking it with you?"

Lee shrugged noncommittally. "I gotta keep the Humvees running."

"Okay." Harper looked back at the map. "So are you taking both the Humvees in one direction?"

"I'm gonna have one Humvee go east and one north. Obviously there are going to be other vehicles in each group, especially the one heading east, because that group is going to need to carry a shitload of ordnance. I'm going to need to keep all the vehicles in both groups fueled."

"We also need to keep the hospital running."

Lee nodded. "I agree. Which is why I hadn't really cemented this part of the plan. Because what we have to do depends on what we find at Sanford. There was a military installation there, evacuating people. We have no idea how much of the equipment they left. If we're lucky, we might come across some fuel trucks. We'll just have to see what we come up with."

Bus put the pen to his lips thoughtfully. "Keith

Jenkins did that welding for the dozer attachment, didn't he? If we can scrounge up some more welding supplies for him and plug him into the power at the hospital, he might be able to weld us some fuel tanks."

Lee had to admit that was a good idea. "Definitely. But how big those tanks need to be depends on how many vehicles will be in each group. Which depends on how many people and how much crap we have to carry with us."

"So, essentially, planning is on hold until you guys clear Sanford."

"Correct." Lee rubbed his palms together. "Now, Harper, why don't you go talk to Nate Malone and plan for what you're putting them through this week?"

Harper looked at him blankly. "What do you want me to teach them?"

"Just drill the basics," Lee said. "Marksmanship and squad tactics."

"Right." Harper sounded despondent. "Just the basics."

After Harper left, Lee and Bus turned their attention to matters inside the camp.

"Have you heard from Jerry at all today?" Lee asked.

"No." Bus splayed his hands out across the desktop. "He's made himself a bit scarce after yesterday's performance."

"I'm worried about Jerry and Professor White," Lee stated.

"In what way?"

"They make me nervous. Professor White is just angry enough to do something stupid. And Jerry seems like he and his supporters are on the verge of leaving." Lee chewed at the inside of his lip for a moment. "You think they might do that?"

"Leave the group?" Bus's eyebrows quirked up. "I don't know. That's a big risk for them to take, wandering out there by themselves. We've built something safe here, or at least safer than it is in the rest of the world. I don't know if people will want to leave it."

"What if they don't leave it?" Lee found a small tear at the corner of the map and worried at it with his finger.

Bus rubbed his eyes. "I don't know, Lee."

"It's something we need to think about."

"What do you want me to do? Have sentries follow them around all day?" Bus snorted. "There has to be some level of trust."

"I agree." Lee stepped toward the desk. "But I want you to keep your eyes open."

"For what?"

"You have two groups of people who don't really want anything to do with how we've been running things, but I'm also sure they don't want to leave all this behind. We're no different than every other third-world country out there now. When there are dissenters, they don't picket Congress. That's the old world. If you have dissenters now, they come after you." Lee lowered his voice. "I just want you to watch your back."

Bus gave him a pointed stare. "I could say the same to you."

Lee nodded. "I already do."

Their conversation continued and eventually fell to trivialities. Jeriah Wilson and his team arrived around noon and Lee left to debrief them. They reported that everything was quiet in Lillington when they left, and that the Fuquay-Varina and Dunn survivors were still settling in but should be mounting scavenging operations inside Lillington in the next few days. They'd successfully set up a radio base station, and Outpost Lillington was currently online.

Lee made an exhaustive list of everything he would need for their operations in Sanford and began to gather those items. Most of them were readily available from the stores that he had taken from Bunker #4. Such things as ammunition and ordnance were locked away in one of the ubiquitous shipping containers around the camp.

Some of the other items like food stores and medical supplies he had to scrounge from others like Marie and Jenny, who were in charge of the food and medicine, respectively. Luckily, most of the food and medicine they had originally came from Lee, so they had no issue with giving it back to him. Several times throughout the day, Julia or LaRouche or Jim would pass by and ask if he needed help, but he would only smile and wave them off.

In truth, he just needed something to keep him busy.

And it was pleasant, in a way, to be busy with something besides keeping himself or others alive. The monotonous physical labor of hauling the heavy packages of supplies back and forth set his mind at ease and allowed him to work off some of his nervous energy. Because he had all day, he worked slowly and meticulously and checked his list often. Sometimes he would sit on the tailgate of the Humvee for a long period of time and simply enjoy the quiet and the relative solitude of being left alone.

He loaded the supplies they would need into the back of the Humvees and checked the fuel levels in both. They were each at about the halfway mark. Plenty to get them in and out of Sanford, but they would need to refuel immediately after.

As dusk threw giant splashes of amber across the sky, he finished loading the last of the supplies. A steady stream of people was now making its way toward the Camp Ryder building for dinner. Lee wanted to avoid the crowd, and he quickly cut across Main Street between two groups of survivors, all talking loudly among themselves and not noticing Lee pass by.

He found his group nestled in an open area among several shanties, close to the fence. A fire pit had been dug into the ground and ringed with cinder blocks and loose stone, identical to the dozens of other fire pits that had popped up around Camp Ryder when the weather began to chill. In the center of the fire pit, a large stack of wood was burning hotter and brighter than was usual.

Around the fire were gathered most of Lee's team members, including Jeriah Wilson and his group. They sat atop crates and overturned buckets, and others stood around holding tin cans for drinking cups. LaRouche was laughing loudly, his mouth stained by the chaw that bulged on the inside of his mouth, and he held a bottle of whiskey in one hand. The bottle was already nearly half gone.

When he saw Lee, he raised it up. "Captain! We didn't think you were gonna make it."

Lee smiled and waved a small greeting. "What happened to the barbecue? Thought you were gonna have a whole hog spitted over that fire."

LaRouche threw a disdainful glance at Julia, who was seated a few places down from him. "Well, *someone* was supposed to talk to her sister..."

"I never agreed to that," she stated blandly.

"But..." LaRouche held up the bottle of whiskey. "We did receive a charitable donation from one James Tinsley, scavenger extraordinaire. Along with his best wishes, of course."

LaRouche put the bottle to his lips and turned it up.

Julia crossed the distance in a flash and deftly snatched the bottle from him. She stared at the mouth of the bottle in horror. "You're gonna get tobacco juice in it, you nasty bastard!"

LaRouche's eyes tracked her drunkenly. "Tobacco and whiskey is an excellent flavor combination. I was only trying to share."

Lee stepped in closer, feeling the warmth of the fire on his face and hands. Julia passed the bottle to him with a sneer of disgust and he accepted. A quick label inspection revealed that this was not the cheap, bottom-shelf liquor like Bus had squirreled away in his desk. Lee was very surprised that someone had given it to them as a gift.

In the quiet glow of the dying fire, he leaned forward on his crate and cleared his throat. "You know," he murmured, "I don't think I'm gonna make it."

Lee looked at him, and then across the fire pit where Julia was watching them guardedly, as though she sensed an impending conflict and wasn't sure how Lee was going to react. Looking back to the sergeant, Lee watched him as he eyed the last dregs of amber liquid swirling at the bottom of the bottle, the flames dancing in it as though it had caught fire itself. He stared at this for a long while and then nodded once, as though confirming something within himself.

"What do you mean?" Lee asked hesitantly.

LaRouche grinned into the fire, and his teeth glistened bright and wet. "You know what I mean."

"No."

"I mean..." LaRouche looked lazily skyward and seemed suddenly enamored by the sky above him. The smile faded from his lips and he seemed in awe. When he spoke again, his voice was eerie, like he was speaking in his sleep. "I only wanted a place in the sun. Like a big, open backyard where I could sit on a lawn chair with a cold beer in my hand. And maybe a wife, maybe some kids. We'd have the neighbors over for barbecues, and they'd ask us what type of beer to bring. And we'd talk about restoring classic cars and how best to keep your lawn green."

He closed his eyes as though he were picturing it. "And I'd be able to hear the kids yelling and laughing, playing in the yard, and the lawn would just stretch on for acres of perfect green grass. And when the neighbors went home and the kids were put to bed, we'd sit on the couch, me and my wife, and we'd watch some boring TV shows before falling asleep at ten o'clock. Like real, boring, old married couples."

He opened his eyes, and the smile returned with a melancholy note. "But I'll never make it. All of that's gone now, and even if there was an end in sight to all of this, I don't think I'd make it through." He finished off the whiskey. As he lowered the bottle and sighed, his breath fogged the air before him. "You know, you live your whole life with these dreams and you know they're far-fetched but you think, 'At least they're in the realm of possibility.' But now…"

"Now you have to make new dreams," Julia stated simply.

LaRouche's smile broadened. He pointed the empty liquor bottle at her. "That's why I like you, Julia. Seriously, though…there's no guarantee that I'll even live through tomorrow. Or you, for that matter. So…will you have sex with me?"

Julia hung her head. "I think you've had enough to drink tonight."

"I know." LaRouche glanced between Lee and her. "So…yes?"

"No."

"Oh." LaRouche shrugged. "Well, I tried."

"Good effort, though."

"Well…" He stood up and swayed on his feet. Julia reached out to steady him. "I'm off to bed, then. Early to rise. Got a long day, and all of that crap." He extended his arm to her, like a gentleman offering a walk. "Would you like to walk me to my shack? I promise I will not make any more inappropriate advances."

"Or gestures," Julia said.

"Or gestures." He nodded. "And I won't cop a feel. Unless you want me to."

"Nope." Julia rose from her seat and looked at Lee. "You heading in too?"

"Yeah." Lee rubbed his knees and stood up. "I suppose I am."

He turned his back to the fire and felt the residual warmth as the two made their way between the ramshackle huts, LaRouche leaning heavily on Julia. They disappeared around the corner, and Lee left the fire. As he made his way through the camp, the cold wind quickly sapped the warmth of the fire from him. Hunched against it, Lee made it to Angela's shanty and stood there before the plywood door, staring at it for a long time.

Eventually, he went inside.

He moved quietly and closed the door behind him. In the small square of living space, Sam was curled in a ball, covered in several layers of blankets. Beside him was a smaller lump that would be Abby. She had taken to Sam as an older brother, and she slept less with her mother than with Sam now. Between the kids and the door, Angela slept on her side, facing Lee. The blankets were pulled up nearly over her nose so that all he could see were her closed eyes and her brow that always seemed to knit when she was in a deep sleep, as though something in her dreams troubled her. Beside her was an open space and more blankets. A spot she had left open for Lee.

Quietly, he set his rifle down and took off his boots and slowly lay beside her, pulling the blankets over himself. He could feel the warmth of them even through his jacket, which he still wore. She stirred as he settled beside her, and when he turned toward her, he found her eyes partially open, watching him steadily.

She reached across the small empty space between them and placed her hand on his chest. Then he reached up and took her hand in his. Her fingers were warm, and his cold. She closed her eyes, no longer scrunching her brow, and he closed his eyes along with her. Holding on to each other, they fell asleep, not knowing how tomorrow would break them down.

TEN

A NARROW WINDOW

THEY REACHED BROADWAY BEFORE DAYLIGHT.

As they approached the center of the small town, the sky was still deep and black above them, the stars peering down at them, cold and indifferent. Lee was in the lead Humvee, still seated in the passenger side, and Jim had taken Harper's place at the wheel. LaRouche remained on the gun, and Julia sat with the muzzle of her rifle protruding from the window, squinting against the cold wind that slapped at her face.

Unlike Camp Ryder, Broadway had no fence or wall. There were only two defunct vehicles pushed partially into the roadway to create a space wide enough for only one vehicle to pass through. On the other side of this vehicular barricade, two guards stood holding brand-new M4s and watching the two Humvees slow to a stop in front of them.

One of the guards looked cautiously at them, then stepped out of cover and walked to the driver's side of Lee's Humvee. Jim lowered the window and the guy looked in and relaxed a bit when he saw Lee.

"We've been expecting you."

"Anybody up yet?" Lee asked.

"Shit, we're farmers, Captain." The man grinned. "We started our day an hour ago."

"Where do you want us to go?"

The man pointed straight down the road. "Go right through. End of this road you should see Kip and a few others. They're waiting on you."

They followed the man's directions and found Kip and two other men standing at another roadblock, situated at the intersection of Harrington Avenue and Main Street. There wasn't much to the downtown area of Broadway. Just a couple of short buildings stood behind them, and then north of Harrington Avenue, there were only fields that stretched out into the darkness.

Jim stopped the Humvees there just before the intersection and Lee stepped out. Kip Greene greeted him stoically, while the other two men smiled and shook Lee's hand a little more enthusiastically.

"How are you this morning?" Lee asked, simply to be polite.

"Had another group try to pass through here last night," Kip said.

"Infected?"

A nod. "It was a little bigger than the last few. No pack mentality. Just another herd. The dumb ones. I think they're coming out of Sanford." He shrugged. "Anyway, we hosed 'em pretty good, but a couple got away."

Lee swiped at his nose, which had started to run in the cold. He wore a shemagh this morning

to keep his neck warm, and he pulled this a little tighter, used a corner of it to wipe his nose.
"Maybe they're running out of food."

"Maybe."

Lee looked back into the town. "You got a tall
place we can set up a radio repeater?"

"Yeah." Kip pointed back the way they had
come. "Couple blocks back that way, on your left,
should be a water tower. That's the highest point I
can think of."

"Perfect." Lee turned back to the Humvee.
"LaRouche!"

The man's head poked up over the fifty. "Yeah?"

Lee walked back to them as he spoke. "You
and Jim go set up that repeater. Should be a water
tower a couple blocks back on the left. Don't kill
yourself, but try to get it as high as possible."

LaRouche disappeared into the Humvee with
a mumbled acknowledgment, and a moment later,
he and Jim exited the vehicle with their rigs and
rifles in hand. The two of them were the most
familiar with setting up the digital repeaters, and
they could get the job done quickly. They opened
the rear hatch of the Humvee and LaRouche
hauled out one of the repeater sets. Then they set
off down the street and a moment later they had
disappeared into the darkness.

As soon as he lost sight of them, he knew that
they were dead.

The feeling was so sudden and so strong that he
stood there for a moment with his mouth open, as
though he were trying to shout after them but was
unable to make any sound. His conscious mind

was strangling his protests in his throat, while his midbrain, his animal brain, lit up like fireworks.

Paranoid. You're just being paranoid, his human brain told him.

His animal brain had no words, only a dreadful certainty that rammed into the bottom of his gut like a cold railroad spike. The words that did run through his mind were just a recent memory, spoken in LaRouche's voice, and they were as clear as if he were sitting at the fire next to LaRouche: *I don't think I'm gonna make it.*

"Lee..."

He turned and saw Julia looking at him, and realized his mouth was still open. He snapped it shut, and just that fast, the overwhelming feeling was gone, and in its place was a greasy trail of unease.

"You okay?" she asked.

"Yeah." He turned away and faced Jeriah Wilson's Humvee and called out to them with a deceptively steady voice. "Everyone take twenty minutes and get some food and water."

Wilson gave a thumbs-up and all the doors to the Humvee opened simultaneously as if the five men inside were all waiting for Lee to tell them they could get out. They stood up and stretched their legs and began pulling provisions out of their packs. Lee put his hand up against the Humvee and could feel a small shake moving through his limbs.

He shook his head, irritated with himself.

"They'll be fine," Julia said and stepped out, arching her back and groaning as she stretched.

"I know," he mumbled in response.

Kip appeared beside him. "So what's your plan for this thing?"

Lee swung his arms, disguising his nervous energy as getting his blood moving against the cold morning. "We'll get in close to Sanford. Then me and LaRouche will go in on foot to recon the area. See how many we're dealing with."

"Just two?"

Lee nodded. "Two is safe. More is better in a fight, but we're trying not to engage until we're ready. Two is relatively easy to sneak in and out with. More than that tends to get us noticed."

"Hmm." Kip nodded slowly. "You've really worked it to a science."

"We've done it a few times."

Kip clucked his tongue. "Well, if you're comfortable with two..."

"Oh, it's not about comfort. More like necessity." Lee stuck his hands inside his tactical vest to warm them. "If I could go in with an army, I would. But we've gotta go with what we have. Which are ten guns against hundreds of infected. The only way to even the odds is that we choose the time and place for the engagement."

"Engagement," Kip remarked with a chuff.

Lee eyed the man and wondered where he stood on the debate the other night. Did he side with Jerry and Professor White? Did he believe that it was murder to lure the infected in and wipe them out indiscriminately? Or was he simply commenting on Lee's sterile word usage for a very dirty job?

"So how long do you think it will take you?" Kip wondered.

"If all goes well, about five days, give or take."

Kip's eyes widened. "Five days?"

Lee nodded. "Smithfield took longer, and Sanford is a little bigger. But we didn't really have things down pat when we took on Smithfield. We're more experienced now, so I hope that translates to being quicker."

Kip seemed to have exhausted his list of questions, so Lee busied himself with getting a little food in his stomach and washing it down with water. It was a couple of oat biscuits that Marie had prepared, wrapped up in a piece of cloth. They got a little dry after sitting in the cloth for a while, but they were okay. The water was painfully cold in his mouth and he forced himself to drink more than he wanted to, in order to stay hydrated.

As he ate, he judged the eastern horizon with a skeptical eye. It had changed almost imperceptibly from complete black to a charcoal gray. They were entering the golden hour just before dawn when the packs that hunted the countryside at night were less active but the hordes inside the towns and cities had not yet emerged from their dens.

They needed to get going.

He rested his hands on his magazines and tapped at them impatiently. The minutes slunk by as he waited in the early morning silence. A flicker of movement from down the street caught his eye and he stood up, his hand reaching for the grip of his rifle. The figures drew closer. It was LaRouche and Jim.

Lee took a relieved breath. "Alright," he called. "Everyone mount up. We're rollin' out."

Two minutes later, they were moving.

* * *

They stopped just outside the north end of town. They had swung around the city on the 421 bypass and exited on a small two-lane road that led into Sanford. Lee wanted to start there and work his way south.

Here on the back roads, Lee took a quick scan of his surroundings. To their right was a bank of woods, the interior still shaded and dark with night while the treetops began to show the silvery glint of daylight just over the horizon. To their right, a field of corn stood brown and wilted, the ears long since shriveled away, unharvested or picked through by animals. Straight ahead, Lee could see the first few houses of suburbia, set back among stands of trees.

Lee opened his door and swung his legs out. "LaRouche, you're with me."

"Uh-huh."

Lee stood there at the door and checked through his gear. When he was satisfied, he clipped his rifle to his sling and let it rest against his extra magazines. He motioned for Wilson to join him and the young cadet jumped out of his Humvee and jogged over. Youth often went hand-in-hand with inexperience and a general lack of wisdom, and Wilson was no exception. However, he was a clear thinker under pressure and decisive. Lee trusted him for one reason only: He felt confident that Wilson could handle everyone on the team if it came down to any sort of engagement.

Lee glanced between Jim, Julia, and Wilson. "Wilson's in charge. Me and LaRouche both have handhelds, so maintain radio silence unless we're calling you. Keep an ear perked up, though—if shit hits the fan, we're gonna need you to come in and extract us."

They all nodded.

He continued. "Hold tight right here, and Wilson, make sure we're maintaining a solid three-sixty defense. You guys are out in the open here, so keep your eyes peeled and no fuckin' around."

"I got it, Captain," Wilson said.

Lee eyed him. *Of course you do.*

Lee trusted him to get the job done, but that didn't mean he was without misgivings.

He kept his thoughts to himself and looked over Wilson's shoulder at LaRouche, who had just finished securing his pack onto his shoulders. "You ready?"

"Ready."

Lee took the radio from its pouch on his chest and switched it on. He waited for it to light up, then keyed it and spoke quickly. "Radio check, radio check." He could hear the squelch and his own voice echoing back at him from inside the Humvee and from the radio on LaRouche's shoulder.

"Alright. Let's go."

The two men set out into the breathless morning, silent as a bank of fog as they moved down the road in the cadaver-gray light of dawn. Lee took point, LaRouche staying about ten yards behind him, constantly checking behind them and walking backward to watch their flanks and make sure nothing was sneaking up on them.

They walked hunched at the shoulders, tension

ratcheted through their core and legs, their progress slow and deliberate. Ceaselessly, their eyes scanned from left to right and back, checking every shadow and stopping at the slightest stir from the cornfield on their right or the woods on their left. Sometimes they would stay kneeling there in the middle of the road, silent and still for minutes on end, and they would never hear another sound or see what had made the first.

They would rise slowly and continue on, hoping that those furtive noises were not the creeping of something deadly, stalking them just out of view.

They reached the first street of the residential area and stopped there. It was an even grid of two-lane blacktop, unmarked by painted lines but littered with old trash and the strange flotsam of a town that had panicked and fled and then been overrun. Every town, every apartment complex, every housing development they had been through held some strange thing that could not be easily explained. Things that made no sense, unless you had been there to witness how it had happened.

Here on the outskirts of Sanford, in whatever community made up this grid of split-level and ranch houses, the first strange sight was the body of a woman, all the features long since decayed and blackened, lying against the base of a tree. She wore a blue terry-cloth robe, stained brown with the putrid fluids of her decomposition. In her right hand she clutched a newspaper, and in her left she held the handle to a broken coffee mug. Her cause of death was a mystery, as the rot and the animals had disguised it among the mar of flesh they'd left behind.

They didn't linger, as they never did, attempting to piece together these odd puzzle pieces left behind by the violent collapse of a society.

Graffiti seemed more prevalent here than in the other places they'd been. Various political or religious sentiments had been scrawled across doors and signs and the blank white canvases of house siding. All of them had a different scapegoat, a different person or deity to blame for the catastrophe. One simply said FUCK THE WORLD in red spray-painted letters nearly six feet high.

Red for anger.

Red for blood.

Red seemed to be the dominant color choice for graffiti everywhere.

The houses looked ransacked, which was not unusual. An intact window was hard to find. Lee thought that even the survivors broke them out of spite when they found them, some deep-seated resentment toward the civilization that had spawned and betrayed them. Maybe those glass windows were just another reminder of the things they felt they would never have again.

More mysteries to be pondered at a later time.

Loose curtains billowed from the open windows, like a dead thing's insides oozing out.

Death was the predominant medium in Lee's mind. Everything was painted in shades of it, and everything existed in some stage of it. He wanted to think in terms of rebirth, but he knew that the rebirth had not yet begun, because the decay had not yet finished.

They made their way through these abandoned

streets and occasionally caught sight of the beginnings of the urban area—businesses erected to support a populace that was no longer there. But they had not yet outlived their use.

They reached a street called McIver and made a right, heading west into the city.

Lee pointed straight ahead of them and spoke quietly. "We'll take up a position on one of those buildings and see what there is to see."

"Hopefully one of them will…" LaRouche stopped midsentence.

Lee turned and looked at him. The sergeant's eyes were scanning the houses around them. They stood about a block from an intersection with stoplights hanging dark from the power lines. They were only a few blocks now from the bigger buildings. The air was very still, no birds to sing in the cold, no insects to make a sound.

"What?" Lee asked.

"Something just moved."

Lee raised his rifle to a low-ready and scanned.

His eyes stopped on a wooden porch at the front of one of the houses. The ornamental latticework had been stripped away and the tall brown stalks of grass were matted down in front of the opening. A dead dog, recently killed and partially eaten, lay near the front steps of the house.

Lee thought back to his own house, his front deck, and the crushed grass there near his steps that should have been his first clue.

"We should keep moving," Lee whispered.

They walked forward, both focused now on the dark underbelly of the porch.

They'd gone about ten paces when some pale and sinewy thing squirmed partially out of the shadows.

"Fuck..." LaRouche whispered and sighted down his rifle.

"Don't shoot!" Lee hissed. "Just keep moving."

The tremor returned to his arms, and his pulse began to pound through his body. Shooting now would only wake every infected within a half mile of them, and there was always the chance this one would ignore them. It was rare, but it had happened before.

The thing under the deck lay on its side, its head resting on its outstretched arm. As they passed by, it regarded them with a dim intelligence that said it was sizing them up.

"Don't shoot unless you have to," Lee said quietly, trying to control the shake in his voice.

"Pick up the pace, Captain."

"Running is only going to make it want to come after us."

LaRouche swore under his breath.

The thing raised its head and hitched itself up onto its elbows, still watching them. It made a weird guttural sound and another tangle of limbs appeared from underneath the deck.

"There's two of them now," LaRouche said.

"Just keep walking." Lee tried to sound calm and reassuring, but it wasn't convincing to himself and he doubted it was to LaRouche.

The first infected lurched up to its feet in a sudden movement.

"Cap..."

It started toward them, but slowly, as though testing their reaction. Testing whether they would run. Or testing if they were wounded, if they were weak, if they were easy prey. Perhaps running was a better idea...

It barked.

The second one stood up and swung its arms loosely.

A third infected crawled out of the space.

"Lee!"

The first one began to jog toward them.

Lee broke. "Go! Run!"

ELEVEN

TROUBLE BREWING

ADRENALINE LIKE AN ELECTRIC shock went through him and Lee forced his legs to go faster, faster—*We aren't going fast enough!*

A stone clattered across the pavement at his feet and he turned to see one of the infected, now in the road less than twenty feet behind them, holding another fist-size stone in its hand. It reared back and hurled the stone at them, catching LaRouche in the leg and causing him to stumble.

Lee reached out quickly to grab LaRouche's arm and steady him. The lead infected had gained on them and was now only a few yards behind them. The others were spreading out on the lawns, cutting off their escape, while more of them kept scrambling out from underneath the house.

Lee shoved LaRouche toward a randomly selected driveway. "Into that house!"

They weren't going to outrun this pack. They were fast, and Lee and LaRouche were weighed down with gear. Their only hope was to bottleneck them at the front door and hope the house muffled their gunshots.

LaRouche made for the front door and Lee

bolted after him, turning just in time to see the pale hand reaching out for him, its gnarled fingers contorted into claws. Lee twisted and struck out with his rifle, slamming the infected across the side of the face and causing it to stumble sideways. It was still up, but it cantered to the right and gave Lee an opening to make for the front steps of the house.

Ahead of him, LaRouche hit the door without slowing down. It shattered inward with a spray of wood and plaster and LaRouche went sprawling into the foyer, landing on his hands and knees.

"Get up!" Lee shouted. "Get up!"

LaRouche turned and saw Lee topping the front porch stairs, and he rolled quickly out of the way. Lee dove for the front door and spun, landing hard on his left knee, his ankle twisting up underneath him and his right leg splaying out for balance. He brought his rifle up as a shape filled the doorway and fired rapidly. Bullets punched through the doorframe, then found flesh, bursting through the creature's torso in sprays of gristle and blood.

It wasn't enough.

The thing hit Lee full-on, knocking him back, its hungry arms wrapping around him, a grim parody of an embrace. Lee fell onto his back just in front of the door and tried to twist his rifle up, but it was squashed between the two bodies. Hot breath brushed the side of his face, yellow teeth clacked inches from his skin.

Reflexively, he pulled the trigger.

The muzzle was close to his head and the blast was like being punched in the face. His vision darkened and sparkled at the edges, but it must have had the same effect on his attacker and its death grip on his torso loosened just enough for Lee to contort his body and jerk the thing off-balance. He rolled, pinning the scrambling creature underneath him.

"Get this fucking thing off me!" Lee screamed.

Still struggling to keep the thing on the ground, Lee could feel the front door of the house batting around at his feet. His back was exposed to the other infected who would be coming through the door, and he couldn't tell where the fuck LaRouche had gone. Pulling his hips off the ground, he drove his weight down on the thing's chest and kicked out blindly with his foot, shutting the door behind him and planting his boot there.

Lee stared down at the infected he had pinned. It was arching its back and writhing about underneath him, its neck stretching up toward Lee, the cords of muscle distending through its skin, the jaws working fast like a wild animal, trying desperately to catch a piece of Lee's jugular. He registered the sound of gunfire, but it sounded muffled, like he was wearing earplugs. The door at his feet clattered and pressed in at him.

"LaRouche!"

A boot came across his vision in a tan blur, and the infected's head jerked to the right with a muted crunching sound. Blood spewed out across the floor in a brilliant flash, and the thing's jaw wobbled around, unhinged. The boot came down again and again, and this time the crunch was more distinct and the body underneath him went limp.

Lee started to rise.

"Keep that door shut!" LaRouche barked, and he began firing through it.

Lee could feel the impact of the rounds punching through the wood. He rolled slightly, trying to maintain pressure on the door, but something on the other side suddenly hit it hard and his knee buckled. The door slammed open, catching Lee's foot between the wall and the door. The infected tumbled in, and Lee could see in a flash-frozen moment that LaRouche was still firing at it, tracking it with his rifle as it fell on top of Lee. Instinctively, Lee curled into a ball, knowing, just *knowing* that LaRouche was going to accidentally shoot him.

He felt the weight hit him, but he didn't feel the bullets. He opened his eyes to the wall, inches from his face, and the splash of gore on it. He stared for a half second and the question circled in his mind, *Did that come out of me?*

Fight through it.

He heaved the body off of him.

Somewhere in the back of the house, glass shattered.

"They're comin' in the back!" LaRouche's voice was dim, like he'd gone into another room, but when Lee hauled himself to his feet, LaRouche was standing right in front of him. The sergeant put a hand to Lee's shoulder. "You okay? Did I hit you?"

Lee looked down at himself. "I don't know." If he'd been hit, he couldn't see the hole, and the blood wasn't coming out. "Post up on the front," he said, shouldering his rifle and shaking his head to clear it of the humming noise that was settling in. Two infected lay dead in the foyer, another outside on the porch.

How many more?

LaRouche put his shoulder to the front wall and scanned out the front door at the yard.

A large oak tree stood in the front yard.

No movement.

Lee faced the opposite direction. The front door opened into a spacious living room. A half wall divided it from the kitchen. A hallway to the left, leading farther into the house. Lee could see dim daylight making its way into the house from around the corner of the hallway, and just beyond, he could see that the kitchen opened into a dining area.

He could hear LaRouche's breathing, and not much else.

The house seemed quiet, tense.

"How many were there?" Lee said quietly, taking small steps toward the hall, pieing off the corner. He could see the dining area now, an ornate wooden table with chairs, tableware and napkins still set out as though prepared to receive guests. Beyond the table was a sliding door onto a patio. The glass had been shattered.

"I think..." LaRouche started.

"Shh!"

They held their breath.

Silence.

Then something in the dining room creaked.

Despite the cold, Lee could feel the sweat on his face, trickling down into his eyes. He swiped at it,

THE REMAINING: REFUGEES   173

and his fingers came away red, with a small chunk of brain matter from the infected.

The half wall extended partially down the hall, with a wide opening directly between the kitchen and dining room. A hand was gripping the top of the half wall, steadying something that was crouched down on the other side.

"Contact!" Lee grunted and fired into the wall. Plaster and drywall exploded.

The hand disappeared down and then the beast, a tall and skinny thing that seemed to be all arms and legs, came scrabbling out of the dining room with a shriek. It launched itself through the wide opening at Lee and he fired wildly as he backed up. He felt something hit the back of his legs and he fell backward over a coffee table. He pulled his finger from the trigger just as his muzzle passed over LaRouche, still standing at the front door. Lee let himself roll, feeling the floor on the top of his head, the strain as his body bore down on his neck, and then he came up on his hands and knees, having performed a complete backflip. He whipped his rifle up.

"You got it! You got it!" LaRouche waved a hand at him.

Looking down the barrel of his rifle, Lee could see the gangly form stretched out at the mouth of the hallway, only a foot or so from where he had originally been standing. Blood was shooting out of its nose onto the carpet. Its eyes blinked rapidly, then slowed, then stared, half lidded, at the growing pool before it. Lee had caught it right between the eyes.

Lee pulled himself up to his feet, feeling the shakes coming over him heavily.

"Should we call them in for extract?" LaRouche said, his voice strained.

"No." Lee shook his head. "We can still do this."

"Did we get them all?"

"Did you notice how many there were?"

"No." LaRouche scanned the yard again. "I didn't count."

"Me neither." Lee moved to the front door. "We can't just sit here, though."

"You think we woke up the hordes?"

"No way to tell until it's too late." Lee stepped out onto the porch to get a better angle at the side of the house and the rest of the yard. Through the surrounding trees, Lee could see the sky turning bright and pink, but the sun hadn't yet shown over the horizon. If they hadn't stirred them with the gunfire, any hordes in the area wouldn't emerge from their dens until the sun was out. "We're just a couple blocks away from the urban area. I say we make for the buildings now while we still have a chance."

LaRouche didn't seem to like that, but he nodded anyway. "You're the boss."

Lee took a last glance at the three bodies jumbled inside the house and the one lying at his feet. Something bothered him. Without another word, he took the stairs down into the front yard. He heard the light footsteps of LaRouche taking up the rear again.

They moved quicker now, unsure whether they'd

killed the entire pack. Four was a small pack, but then again, they'd all been crammed in underneath that deck. He couldn't see many more than four fitting under there. Maybe five. Perhaps if there were others, they'd decided that there were easier meals elsewhere.

Then it struck him what had been bothering him.

None of them were females.

Jerry rose early that morning.

Like everyone else in Camp Ryder, he lived in a shanty, and he slept on whatever he found to make his nights more comfortable. Lucky for him, he'd gone through the trouble of locating and hauling a twin-size mattress out of a nearby house. The mattress was his pride and joy, the reason he could wake up in the morning and smile at the people of Camp Ryder, rather than scowl at them like Captain Harden and his henchmen. He also felt a measure of pride in the fact that he had carted off the mattress by himself, carried it to and from the pickup truck, all the while scanning for infected.

Yes, infected.

Professor White preferred the term "plague victim," but Jerry didn't share the man's sympathy for them. He'd witnessed those creatures tear plenty of people apart, and he felt comfortable saying they weren't human. However, Professor White and Jerry agreed on one very important point: Captain Lee Harden and his sock puppet, Bus, should not be running Camp Ryder.

Jerry stood up from his mattress, oblivious to

the creaks and groans of the inner springs. Half a year ago, Jerry would have been outraged to be forced to sleep on such a mattress. Then he spent two months sleeping on dirt, and he grew to appreciate the barest of cushions between himself and the ground. Now the stained, popping mattress felt luxurious, like the finest bed, wrapped in Egyptian cotton.

He stretched and twisted, working the kinks out. Another thing that would have ruined his day in his past life, and now just a minor annoyance. Most days bore with them some sort of persistent ache or pain. You couldn't just pop some muscle relaxers for your back anymore or a couple ibuprofens for your head. You just had to tough it out, and with that came a certain sort of levelheaded patience. Because it was so constant, pain and cold and general discomfort became disconnected from the mind, like white noise just humming in the background.

It made him realize how truly weak humans had become.

If you felt the slightest twinge of pain, you took an ibuprofen. If you were sleepy, you took caffeine. Then, if you couldn't sleep later, you could take some sleeping pills. In between, if you didn't take your morning shit right on time, you took a laxative, but then if it didn't come out right, you took antidiarrheal medication. If you took too long sitting on the crapper, reading the *Wall Street Journal*, you might develop hemorrhoids, in which case you could shove a glycerin suppository up your ass. If you had a bad day, you took the white pill. But if you were *too* happy, then you took the pink pill to calm you the fuck down. Pills, pills, pills, until everyone was the same homogenous, robotic, smiling (but not *too* smiley) upper-middle-class white male with a two-thousand-square-foot house, a matching set of Volvos, 2.5 kids, a cheerleader wife, and a golden retriever named Buddy.

Hey, you achieved the American Dream!

Your prize?

A failing 401k to obsess about and a mountain of debt to make you consider killing yourself.

That was the life of pathetic stasis that Jerry had come from. He was a man defined by a checklist, as though his life culminated in whatever he could put on his résumé: $100,000-plus salary? Check. President of the HOA? Check.

Platinum American Express?

The most expensive Titleist driver?

Member of the town council?

Check, check, and check.

All of that was gone now. Now his life was difficult. It was dirty mattresses and hunger and pain and wiping your armpits and crotch with baby wipes between your weekly sponge baths. Now you had to be strong to survive, but the reward was survival itself. And there was no greater sense of purpose than to simply survive. It was, after all, one's primary instinct.

So here was Jerry, stripped of his titles, and his family, and his belongings that never really meant anything to him in the first place. He was a modern-day Job, but the destruction of his previous life was not a test of his love for God but a blessing, imparting to him a fresh sense of purpose, a new drive to succeed at the most important thing of all: *living*.

And then there was Captain Harden, some relic of the old world sent to reestablish those very things that had destroyed humanity in the first place. Society, order, government—all just a bunch of bullshit. It might work for a short time, but in the end it was destined to fail. Jerry was no anarchist—he knew there had to be some "system" in place in order for people to get along. But the larger the population, the stronger that system had to be in order to bind all of those divergent threads together. Here in the new world, it was more natural. It was tribal. And Camp Ryder was the tribe. It did not need to expand; it needed to simply survive.

The weak suburbanite that still huddled inside of him made Jerry want to cheer Captain Harden on. The protector! The savior! Come rebuild our society so we can have central air again! But the rest of him loathed the prospect of returning to that place of restriction. Here in the tribal society, every voice was heard because the tribe was small, and so the system was loose. Everyone was on a level playing field, but Jerry, already accustomed to manipulating his way around and over people, had the possibility of rising to the top.

A tribal leader.

But only if Camp Ryder remained a tribe.

When Camp Ryder became a state, then Jerry would once again simply be Jerry, and the only way to be important would be to *have things*.

As Jerry pulled his faded pair of jeans on over his thermal underwear, he once again ignored the root of the issue in all of his ponderings and rationalizations. The true problem was Jerry's own obsession with being important. Because in Jerry's mind, Jerry was number one. Jerry came before everyone else, including the wife and the two children and the golden retriever named Buddy that he'd left inside of his burning house while he ran out the side door and crawled through a hundred yards of tall grass so the hooligans that had set his house ablaze wouldn't see him escaping. And it wasn't until he had reached the woods and run another mile that he realized whom he had left behind.

When it hit him, he fell to the forest floor and he wept bitterly and clawed at the rotten leaves. He was not ashamed or grief stricken...he was angry. Angry with his wife and angry with his kids. Jesus Christ, did he have to do everything? Did he have to pick each one of them up and carry them out of the burning house? Were they fucking stupid? The house was burning! They were supposed to *RUN!*

Now their stupidity had put him in an impossible situation.

Now he was alone in the dark of the woods.

Now he had no one.

How dare they leave him alone in this world!

In spite of their selfishness, he'd survived, and he eventually found Camp Ryder.

Here, he found the true purpose, and here, once again, Jerry was number one.

Or at least tied for first with Bus.

But then G.I. Joe came along, and Jerry was number two.

This was unacceptable. Because Captain Harden wanted to fix things, he wanted to put them back together, back to the way they were. And everyone cheered and clamored, just like that sad little part of him that just wanted to be comfortable again. But all the while, the new Jerry simmered in anger. The captain was trying to take away Jerry's tribe, in which he could place himself as the leader, the elder, a person of *importance*.

So Jerry told people what they wanted to hear: that this whole thing would all be over soon, that Captain Harden was just overreacting. No need to rebuild anything, because nothing had been destroyed in the first place. Things were just a little...out of control. It would all get better. They just had to stick together, stop trying to save the world, and everything would be okay.

It was all a bunch of crock.

Jerry was good at manipulating, and he used that to his advantage. In order to maintain his tribe, he had to undermine Captain Harden. Captain Harden said that this was a permanent change, that things would not get better on their own, so naturally Jerry insisted that they only needed to wait it out. Captain Harden said that they needed to rescue survivors, so Jerry argued that it was dangerous and a waste of resources.

Then Professor White had come along and provided a new way to contradict Captain Harden.

The "infected" were victims, and they should not be killed without first determining if they were a danger. It was a proven fact that some of the "plague victims" were nonaggressive, so lying in wait atop a city building and gunning them down as soon as they came in sight was murder. History would judge Captain Harden harshly as a butcher who had committed genocide against his own people. Another Hitler. Another Mao. Another Stalin.

Pure genius.

Regardless of the fact that Jerry disagreed with Professor White, he stuck to the old adage: "The enemy of my enemy is my friend."

He pulled on his heavy wool peacoat he'd traded up a carton of cigarettes for, followed by a wool cap, then stepped into his boots. He'd disdained to accept any of Lee's "supplies" and even refused to carry one of his M4s. Instead, he carried an old coach gun he'd sawed down to a twelve-inch barrel. He left the wood stock intact, as he was a little nervous that if he made it a pistol grip it would fly out of his hands when he fired it. He carried the shortened scattergun slung at his side, inside of his coat, and one of the pockets was heavy with extra shells.

It was a good weapon for him. Simple and effective. Easy to use. Never jammed. Didn't require much cleaning.

There was a knock at the door.

"Who is it?" Jerry looked at the plywood slab of a door.

"It's me, Jerry." The voice was low.

"Come in."

The door swung out and a man stepped in quickly amid a rush of cold air, slamming the plywood closed behind him. He was short but solidly built. He'd been a little emaciated when Jerry had first met him, but with the steady stream of supplies from Captain Harden's bunker, the meat from hunting, and the food from scavenging, the man was beginning to show his build, and he reminded Jerry of one of those migrant workers who stood as high as the average man's chest but could pick up a slab of concrete with his stubby little arms and carry it on his shoulder.

"Arnie." Jerry smiled as he laced up his boots. "How cold is it out there?"

The stocky man waffled his hands. "Cold now, but I think it's gonna be warmer than yesterday."

"Good."

Jerry grabbed an empty satchel and slung it over one shoulder. It was just for show. He wouldn't really need it. He followed Arnie out of his shanty and over to the little red Geo hatchback that sat on the side of Main Street, just a short jog to the gate. Arnie got into the driver's seat and Jerry squeezed into the front passenger's.

"What do I owe you for the gas?" Jerry asked.

Arnie cranked the little four-banger to life and put it in gear. "I got it from a friend. Friend of yours too. So don't worry about it."

Jerry nodded and smiled. "Sounds good. Thank you."

"Here." Arnie pulled two red sashes out of his pocket and handed one to Jerry. "Tie it on your right arm."

Jerry accepted as they pulled up to the gate. The sentry stepped up to the window and leaned down to peer inside. He greeted Arnie amiably—he was a regular scavenger—but regarded Jerry with a look of surprise.

"Jerry?" The sentry looked confused. "You leavin' the compound this morning?"

Jerry forced a smile. "Everyone's gotta pull their weight, right?"

"Right." The sentry nodded and patted the hood of the car. "Be safe out there."

"Will do," Arnie said, and cranked the window back up.

The little Geo made its way down the worn dirt entry to Camp Ryder and exited out onto Highway 55. Jerry instructed his driver as they went, making a right onto 55 and taking it down to Highway 27. At the intersection, they could see the town of Coats beyond, which was still a regular stomping ground for scavengers. No outpost had been set up in the town, because it was so close to Camp Ryder, but it had been cleared of infected and still held some small treasures for those who wished to look.

Of course, any place that had been "cleared" wasn't necessarily safe. The packs roamed where they wished and could often be found skirting the edges of these small towns, though they seemed uncomfortable with so much concrete underneath their feet and would quickly vanish into the woods unless there was prey to run down. Anyone outside the wire kept their weapon on hand and kept checking behind their backs if they wanted to survive.

They made another right on Highway 27 and took

it west. It was a long, straight road and it changed names to Leslie Campbell Avenue as it drew closer to Campbell University. The university was a ghost town, as it had mainly been empty during the summer when the FURY pandemic hit. Jerry didn't even think Captain Harden and his crew had done any clearing operations in it, but had simply reconned the area and declared it "safe."

It was here at the entrance to Campbell University that they entered a roundabout, turned onto Howard Drive, and immediately pulled left into a small shopping center with a coffee shop on one end and a Chinese food restaurant on the other. They pulled toward the coffee shop and drove around the back of the building, where they found another small car. It was parked alongside the back of the building, facing the same direction as their Geo.

As they parked behind it, Professor Tommy White and one of his students stepped out. The older, long-haired man waved in greeting, but his face was stony, or as stony as it could be on such a flaccid little creature. White's companion was some white kid with dreadlocks—yet another one of those wannabe hippie stoners, rebelling against two yuppie parents for committing the mortal sin of purchasing shoes made in Malaysia.

The two men met in the middle, their companions standing back a bit and keeping a watch not only for infected but for any other prying eyes.

Jerry extended his hand. "Professor, I'm glad to see you."

White shook it limply and absently, as though

he had weighty things on his mind that Jerry was interrupting. "Yes, thank you for meeting me."

"Well." Jerry clasped his hands together. "I say we cut to the chase and speak in very plain terms with each other. That will make things much simpler and more efficient."

White regarded him with a quirked eyebrow but nodded.

Jerry continued. "I'm sure we have our different reasons for how we came to this position, but I think we can both agree that Bus needs to be removed from power, and Captain Harden with him."

White grimaced. "I don't know if Bus is a part of the problem here..."

"He's a part of *my* problem," Jerry stated calmly. "They have a symbiotic relationship, Professor. You must remove both if you are going to remove either. They are viewed as one and the same. The original members of Camp Ryder support the captain only because Bus supports him. All the newcomers love the captain because he saved them, but they only support Bus because Captain Harden supports him. They're two different ends of the same problem."

White shuffled his feet a bit, looking uncomfortable. "I don't want any more bloodshed."

"Nor do I." Jerry put his hands inside his coat pockets. The brass at the base of the shotgun shells was cold on his fingers. "But I also don't wish to die, and I think you and I can both agree that that is the end result for the path Bus and Captain Harden have put us on."

"We can just run. Avoid all the conflict. Band together and head for the mountains."

"Don't be foolish." Jerry shook his head. "You've got a bunch of college students who don't know anything about surviving in the wild. You haven't accepted any of Captain Harden's guns, and neither have I. We've got no supplies, no medicine, no way of surviving outside of the Camp Ryder Hub."

White's eyes widened. "But you heard the guy last night! There are millions of them coming this way. We'll never be able to survive that many."

Jerry held up a finger. "He *thinks* there are millions of them heading this way. It's an unproven threat. Don't fall victim to Captain Harden's overreaction to these things. While he uses them as an excuse to take more and more militaristic control of everyone, you're using it as an excuse to run prematurely. Both are equally dangerous."

"As opposed to what?" White's voice rose up a little bit and the young guy with the dreadlocks looked over at them. "Waiting until they attack us to start running? That's ridiculous! If we wait until they're here, we'll never make it out."

Jerry pursed his lips. "Captain Harden got one thing right. There will be a stream of refugees fleeing from the north, as these supposed millions move south—*if* they move south. That will give us all the warning we need."

"That leaves supplies." White scratched at his temple.

"The supplies are there," Jerry said. "And there will be more."

White considered this. "Harden will never just give you his supplies, and he will fight for them."

"Captain Harden won't be here." Jerry smiled. "He's recruiting more goons to go with him and start blowing up every piece of infrastructure he can get his hands on, the fucking idiot. Camp Ryder's going to be empty. But he's going to leave behind supplies, because the camp is going to need them. He said he's going to be sending all the refugees to Camp Ryder, right?"

"Right."

"That will be our window of opportunity."

"To steal the supplies."

"To take over Camp Ryder," Jerry corrected.

White fussed and growled. "This isn't a military action! We're not taking over anything!"

"We have to." Jerry looked at the older man. "Don't you get it? You're not waltzing into Camp Ryder and taking those supplies. Not without getting into a firefight. Captain Harden and his hit squads might be gone, but Bus still pulls some weight. If my people and your people are all united and they are all armed, we can take over. And once Bus is out of the way, we have control of everything in Camp Ryder."

"You said it yourself," White pointed out. "My people are just students. Besides, I don't want them shooting at each other."

"They won't." Jerry was confident. "With all of our people together, we'll completely outnumber Bus and his supporters. We go in all at once, everyone armed, and we won't even have to fire a shot. They'll give it up without a fight. As long as Captain Harden isn't there to convince them otherwise."

"And then we can head for the hills?"

Jerry dodged the question. "We'll have the supplies to do so."

"All right." Professor White looked off into the eastern sky, all the color melting out of it into a golden slag that ran across the horizon. It was already feeling warmer. "What do we need to do?"

TWELVE

RUMORS

TIMBER CREEK SEEMED MUCH smaller now. Staring out at the condominium complex from where his little truck idled at the front gates, Harper remembered how it had felt the first time he'd come there to scavenge. At that time, with nothing but a few weapons to split among everyone, a handful of cartridges, and relying heavily on Molotov cocktails, this place had seemed like an entire world of danger.

Now the burned-out buildings seemed small and familiar, like he knew every charred brick, every gutted car, and every broken piece of concrete that littered the complex. He'd been here so many times even before his first encounter with Captain Lee Harden. He remembered the man, exhausted, weaponless, blood running down his back from multiple lacerations.

Harper smiled grimly.

He remembered he'd told Lee to get lost... among other things.

Over the past three months, they'd been there many more times. It was Lee's preferred spot to take them for putting some rounds downrange and to practice their squad tactics. And now Harper was here with the twenty volunteers from Camp Ryder.

To train them, apparently.

Harper had no idea how to train people into a working unit, so he did exactly what he remembered Lee doing: swept the complex for infected, split everyone into two groups, instructed one group while the other watched their backs.

The first ten lined up, facing one of the long brick condominium buildings. Harper took a roll of duct tape and pasted ten crosses at chest height, at even intervals along the wall. One for each trainee. Then he paced them back about fifteen yards.

As he did this, he noticed the almost military rigidity of the trainees, and it pissed him off a bit.

He was no firearms expert. And he sure as hell wasn't a drill instructor. He didn't know what these people anticipated when he told them he would be training them, but it wasn't going to be any crawling under barbed-wire fences or bullshit like that. As far as Harper was concerned, that was great for what Lee referred to as "stress inoculation," when you were trying to get Johnny Doughboy out of his comfort zone. But all of these people were already inoculated to stress in the worst way, and the proof of it was that they were still alive.

He crossed his arms. "Everyone relax," he grouched. "You've all learned the basics of how to work and sight your rifle—stance, grip, trigger pull, good sight picture and sight alignment. Take your time. Put ten rounds in your target."

He stepped back and waited.

It took everyone a moment to realize there weren't any more instructions.

Then they shouldered their rifles and began sighting in at the duct-tape crosses staring back at them. The first fusillade rang out, always the loudest. It started with a single shot, then grew to a crescendo as everyone joined in. It tapered off and began to take a steadier pace as each trainee found their own rhythm.

When ten rounds had been fired, Harper walked behind them and took a glance at their targets. Not bad shooting, overall. Of course there were a few people who needed help, but there were a few people who had punched out the entire center of their target.

"Again," he called.

Ten more rounds fired out, slow and deliberate.

When they were finished, Harper re-taped the crosses and faced the trainees with a furrowed brow. They stared at him expectantly, rigidly, as though this were some intense military training. He didn't know why that bothered him, but it did, and he needed to say something about it.

"Look...let's get something out of the way here early on," he said. "Captain Harden asked me to train you folks how to work as a team and how to shoot those firearms he gave you during combat. I'm not a soldier. I'm not a professional instructor. Captain Harden asked me to do something, and I'm doing it."

He twirled the roll of duct tape in his hands. "I'm not going to yell at any of you. There's not going to be any PT or punishment. This isn't boot camp. You've already been through boot camp. It was called 'surviving the end of the world.'"

There was a brief moment of laughter and the tension eased slightly.

"I'm going to try to impart to you a little bit of what I've experienced," he said, feeling a little more comfortable as the people surrounding him began to relax. "When I put in my two cents, some of you may already know what I have to say. That's fine. Hear me out anyways. I'm not going to act like I've been through more shit than you, because we've all been through enough in our own separate ways. At the end of this, there's no promotions, no honors, no awards. You'll just hopefully be a little more prepared for what's coming. And that little bit might be the difference, right?"

The trainees rumbled in agreement.

"On that note." Harper rubbed his beard. "Does anyone have any questions?"

The small crowd looked side to side at each other, assessing how open their companions were to asking questions. It didn't seem like anybody was in an inquisitive mood, but then a younger guy stepped forward and raised his hand. He was a mousy-looking kid with red-flushed cheeks and shifty, nervous eyes.

"Yeah." Harper gestured to him. "What's up?"

The kid looked unsure of himself. "Do you think we'll have to shoot other people? Like...real people?"

"Noninfected?" Harper ventured.

"Yes." The kid glanced around at his peers. "You've done it before, right?"

Harper considered this. "What are you getting at?"

"Well, I think most of us have had to kill crazies before." He shifted his weight. "But I don't think many of us have had to shoot at real people. Do you think we'll have to do that?"

The rest of the trainees were looking at the kid uncomfortably, as though they weren't sure whether to tell him to shut up or not, but there was also the sense that most of them had the same question: Were they capable of killing a noninfected human being?

"There's no difference," Harper said steadily. As the words left his mouth, he wondered whether they were true or not. He remembered the young man at the roadblock when he'd gone with Lee to his first bunker. Back when Doc and Josh and Miller were alive. He remembered putting that rusted, pitted bayonet blade through the kid's stomach and firing the rifle. He remembered the screams, remembered the feeling of absolute revulsion. Could he tell others about that? Could he tell these volunteers, when he hadn't spoken of it since?

The kid looked confused. "Sure, there's a difference..."

"No difference," Harper said sternly. "The only difference is in your perception. Those people infected with FURY, they aren't another species. They're not animals. They're human beings. And I don't care whether a human being is in their right mind or their brain looks like Swiss cheese, if they're trying to kill me, I'm gonna rip their goddamn heart out if I have to.

"The fact is, you may come into contact with normal human beings who want to hurt you, want to kill you, and want to kill your teammates. You need to decide *right now* whether you can pull the trigger on one of those people. Because in the middle of a shoot-out is not the time to discover that you can't do it." Harper looked at them all. "And there ain't no shame in it. What's a shame is lying to yourself and then making your team pay for it.

"You want me to tell you what to expect?" He shook his head. "I can't do that. It's different for every person. Some people feel guilt, some people feel elated, some people feel nothing at all. Just depends on the person. If you decide that you can kill a person, and if that opportunity presents itself and you take someone out, my advice would be to not make a big deal about it. Don't dwell on it. People have been killing people for thousands of years, and only recently has our society decided that killing another person mentally destroys you. You hear that crap enough times, it becomes a self-fulfilling prophecy." He pointed at the kid. "You gotta kill a man, maybe you gotta kill a girl... you do it and you get it over with. Ain't no need to mourn 'em or think about them afterward. And that's all I'm gonna say about that."

That seemed to end it.

No one left.

Apparently they had all decided they were capable of killing a sane human being. Maybe they were, maybe they weren't. It wasn't for Harper to determine. He just wanted them to shut up, shoot straight, and learn how to cooperate with each other.

When he'd cycled all twenty through the warm-up, he had them take a quick sweep of the complex again to make sure nothing had been drawn in by the sound of gunfire. While they cleared the area, he re-taped the targets again. The brick siding was looking ragged and pockmarked. Holes were completely punched through in places.

When they returned, Harper was holding his own rifle.

"What we're gonna do next is some 'point-shooting' or 'snap-shooting.'" He turned so the trainees were on his right. "Having a good sight picture and sight alignment is great, but in all likelihood, when you are in a combat situation, either a shootout with noninfected or being overrun by a pack, you won't have the time or the presence of mind to look through those tiny little sights and squeeze off a perfectly aimed shot. Instead, you'll shoot instinctively."

He motioned for the mousy kid to step forward. "It's Devon, right?" Harper recalled.

A hesitant smile. "Yeah."

"You know how to point at something?"

"Of course."

"Then you know how to point-shoot." Harper smiled. "I could go into a whole lot of technical mumbo jumbo about why that is, but suffice it to say you don't have to aim your rifle to hit the target. You just point and fire. You want the long explanation, you can talk to Captain Harden about it.

"Here." Harper shouldered the rifle and faced the targets. "How I'm going to practice my point-shooting is by linking my body's muscle memory between instinctive shooting and static shooting. So I'm going to take my time, get a good sight picture, aim, and fire one round. Then I'm going to drop my muzzle to a low-ready and immediately snap it back up and fire a second round without aiming."

Harper demonstrated and impressed himself by putting both holes within an inch of each other. "When you start out, your two shots are probably going to be a little wide of each other. That's okay. As you practice, the distance between your aimed shot and your snap shot will begin to decrease until you can more or less put them in the same spot." He gestured for the line to step up. "Go ahead and do it."

They picked up quickly. It helped that most of them had probably done this type of shooting before, though they may not have known what it was called. Harper walked behind them and saw the shots striking the target in rapid succession. He had everyone empty their mags and then switch groups. The next group completed the exercise just as well.

Everyone reloaded, and he took them through some other basic move-and-shoot drills. Lee had explained to him once that he had always been taught to "aggress on the threat," which meant that when a threat presented itself, you moved toward it while you were shooting. The action of aggressing on the target was effective because it forced your targets into a fear response, where they essentially froze up, torn between the decision to stand and fight or cut and run.

The only problem was that it was completely ineffective against the infected. You could not intimidate them, could not force them to think a certain way. They were there to attack you, and moving toward them only made their job easier. Lee had quickly learned this and nixed the "aggress on the threat" portion of training. Now they trained to move laterally and to back up. Any sort of shooting while moving was difficult, but the group picked up on it as fast as they had picked up on everything else.

It was a good group.

After several hours of drills, interspersed with sporadic sweeps of the Timber Creek condominiums, they took a break for some food and water. It was late morning, nearing midday by now. Harper took an old two-liter bottle full of water and a can of sliced peaches to the tailgate of his truck and hoisted himself onto it.

The mousy kid, Devon, joined him shortly.

"What's up?" Harper asked as he struggled to get a fingernail under the pull tab of the can.

He expected the kid to have more questions about shooting and killing and frankly, Harper wasn't really in the mood to talk about it anymore. Not because it was a sensitive subject but because he had already imparted what minimal wisdom he could on the topic. He'd already said the conversation was over. What else did Devon want?

But instead, the kid furrowed his brow. "Sir, have you ever seen Jerry go outside the gate?"

Harper stared at Devon for a moment. "First, just call me Harper. Second...yes. I've seen Jerry go outside the gate. Once. To get that fucking mattress he loves so much. Why?"

"Oh." Devon shook his head. "It's probably nothing, then."

Harper was in the process of lifting the open can of peaches to his lips for a sip of the juice but stopped. "What?"

The kid waved a dismissive hand. "It's just that I saw Jerry leaving really early this morning. Thought it was weird, because I've never seen him leave the compound. But, I mean, if he's done it before, then I guess it's not a big deal." Devon shrugged and smiled. "After that big argument the other night, I just thought...Well, never mind."

Harper kept his eyes on the kid. "Yeah. I'm sure it's nothing."

It was turning into a busy day at the medical trailer, which meant it would be a busy day for Angela. She didn't know much about medicine, not like Jenny did, but she was competent and willing to help, and she'd proven that she was cool under pressure, so when Jenny was swamped, Angela stepped in to help out. With Sam off learning to hunt with Keith Jenkins and Abby with the other children her age, she either helped out with the sewing and mending of garments or she helped out in the medical trailer.

Frankly, she despised sewing. She did it without complaint when that was where she was needed, because she'd volunteered for it before she realized how much it sucked. She knew how to sew and she did it well, but having to do it for hours on end was miserable. In retrospect, she would have much preferred to learn hide tanning or even log splitting, but those were occupations largely held by men.

Sexist?

Maybe.

She hadn't put much thought into it. There were a few women who hunted and a few men who knew how to sew. Perhaps it would have offended her four or five months ago, but there wasn't the sense that she was being squeezed out by a Good Ol' Boy network. It was more that everyone was just doing what they could do well.

Those who knew how to hunt, hunted.

Those who knew how to sew, sewed.

Of course, that didn't stop her from learning. When sewing and nurse assisting were not needed, she hung around Dave, the guy who worked with all the animal skins the hunters brought in, and tried to absorb as much knowledge as possible. It was messy work, but for some reason, she enjoyed it.

But today was not a day when garments needed to be patched. And Dave didn't have any hides to work. Today was a day when the cold, or the flu, or whatever it was that was going around, seemed to be exploding inside Camp Ryder.

Angela walked into the medical trailer and found Jenny with three full cots and two worried families with red, runny noses and children who coughed unabashedly into the air, the noise wet and rattling. The nurse-turned-village-doctor wore a surgical mask over her face and sat on a stool, a boy of perhaps ten standing before her as she illuminated the back of his throat with a small flashlight.

"When did you start to feel yucky?" she asked.

"This morning," the boy answered.

"And did you notice your nose getting runny anytime before that?"

"Yes. And I had a sore throat."

The mother broke in. "Is it pneumonia?"

Jenny glanced up. "He doesn't have pneumonia."

"Can't you give him some antibiotics?"

"Antibiotics will do more harm than good right now. If he develops pneumonia, which I don't think he will, since he's a healthy young boy, then we can talk about giving him something." Jenny clicked off her flashlight. "At this point in time, he needs to eat, drink, and sleep as much as he can stand."

The father looked around, his face turning red. "How are we going to find extra food to give him?"

Jenny was now stuck. She could do nothing but shake her head. "I'm sorry. Everyone is in the same boat as you guys."

The mother took her son by the shoulders and guided him away. "Thank you anyways, Jenny."

Defeated, Jenny leaned back. "Yeah. No problem."

Angela took that moment to make herself seen with a small wave of the hand, and she offered Jenny an encouraging smile. The other woman looked exhausted. When she saw Angela, she waved sedately and stood up as though she weighed a thousand pounds.

"Thank God," Jenny said, giving Angela a quick hug. "I'm drowning in here."

"What can I do?"

Jenny glanced at the remaining family of sick people and the three patients lying on their cots, two of them asleep and the other tossing about miserably underneath a blanket, a plastic bucket within arm's reach. She ushered Angela over away from the others and produced a yellow pill and another surgical mask from her jacket pocket.

"Here. Take the pill and wear the mask."

Angela inspected the pill. "What is it?"

"Just vitamins—it'll help your immune system. But I have to treat it like contraband, because I only have a few left and if anybody sees it, they're going to want some."

Angela discreetly popped the pill into her mouth and swallowed it dry. Then she strapped the mask onto her face. "Okay," she said, the word slightly muffled through the itchy, sterile-smelling mask. "What do you need me to do?"

Jenny pointed to the three cots. "This cold-flu thing is kicking our ass right now. Some of the older folks are starting to develop pneumonia after having it for about a week. These three are today's victims."

Two days ago, the beds had been filled with different people.

"Where'd the others go?" Angela asked.

"They were still sick, but on the uptick, so I sent them back home. These folks are worse off, and I only got three beds." Jenny shook her head. "I'm running low on antibiotics too. The sooner Lee can get to that bunker of his, the better. I don't know how many more pneumonia cases I can treat with what I have here."

"He's working on it."

"I know." Jenny shook her head. "Anyway, I have to talk to this family and figure out if they have the same thing as everyone else or some wonderful new thing that's going to kick our ass. You mind dosing the three beds? And I think Mr. Clark threw up a little bit ago . . . if you could clean his bucket out."

Angela nodded. "I'm on it."

She cared for the patients as best she knew how, giving them their prescribed doses of antibiotics and talking to them, trying to cheer them up, trying to take their minds off of their miserable circumstances. She felt pity for them, though she tried not to let it show on her face. They were sick here in this strange world, forever removed from the things and the people and the places they knew. They suffered through without any of the comfort those things could bring.

As Angela finished dosing the last patient, Jenny concluded her talk with this family—which was the same talk she'd given the previous family, and the family before that, and would probably give the family that followed: Keep them fed, hydrated, and well rested. Not much else could be done.

It seemed that they might be getting a lull in business when Bus stalked into the medical trailer.

He nodded to Angela. "Glad you're here. Jenny's gonna need the help." He turned to Jenny. "There's a group of three refugees coming in from OP Benson."

"Good Lord . . ." Jenny pulled the surgical mask from her face. "It never ends."

Angela felt a measure of excitement. She'd never helped in the medical trailer when they were receiving newcomers. "What's the big deal? Is one of them hurt?"

Jenny turned to her. "Maybe. Maybe not. We're gonna give all of them a solid, full-body inspection. They either consent to it or they can find another place to stay. We're looking for bite marks, scratch marks, any wound that might look infected. We're checking them for symptoms—not just for FURY but anything else contagious. We have to figure out whether they need to be held in containment or if they're good to join the community."

"Where'd they come from?" Angela asked.

Bus shrugged. "Out east, apparently. I didn't get anything more specific."

Angela and Jenny exchanged a glance.

"Okay." Jenny stood up. "How long do we have?"

"Less than five," Bus said. "Let me know when they're cleared."

"All right." Jenny heaved a great sigh. "Let's get ready."

Angela went to retrieve water and food—most of the refugees arrived dehydrated and starving. Jenny cleared an area and dragged out some partitions made of PVC pipes and bedsheets that would serve as a privacy screen when she inspected the refugees.

They had barely finished prepping before the three refugees arrived.

Outpost Benson used an old silver Toyota Camry to conduct their patrols, and it was in this that the newcomers were driven to Camp Ryder by two of the four men currently assigned to Benson. The two men from Benson rode up front, and the three refugees were in the back. As they piled out, Angela sized them up from her vantage point at the mouth of the medical trailer.

A teenage boy and a slightly younger-looking girl who were obviously siblings stepped out and huddled together, uncomfortable, apprehensive, and clearly wary of the sentries who watched them with ported rifles. The teenagers were both dark-haired and fair-skinned.

A middle-aged man exited the Toyota last. He had a shaggy head of wavy gray hair and a beard that was playing catch-up, still dark along his jaw, though the chin was streaked with gray. He had dark eyes that immediately regarded his surroundings with suspicion. He hovered over the teenagers, his arms encircling them protectively.

Jenny didn't wait for an invitation. She marched out confidently, even showed a little bit of attitude, as though the newcomers were just another chore in the middle of her busy day. Angela was unsure how much of this was genuine and how much was a cultivated act to demonstrate her confidence to wary and untrusting patients.

Angela followed a few steps behind.

Jenny left off her surgical mask, and Angela figured there was a reason for that, so she removed hers. Perhaps wearing the surgical mask during introductions was a little too *Hi-nice-to-meet-you-can-I-have-your-kidneys*?

Jenny extended a professional hand to the man and after a moment's hesitation, he shook it warily.

"I'm Jenny. I'm the nurse here at Camp Ryder. Has anyone already explained to you what we're going to do?"

The man looked about unsurely. "I don't...I don't think so."

All three of them seemed to be in what Angela had heard Jenny and some of the others refer to as "the refugee daze." After fighting and surviving by the skin of their teeth while on the road, and then finally finding a safe place, many of the refugees would seem to mentally shut down, as though they suspected that they were only sleepwalking in a dream.

"Okay." Jenny pointed toward the medical trailer. "Come on, hon. What's your name?"

"Kyle. This is Clay and Holly."

Jenny smiled perfunctorily. "Nice to meet you guys. So, Kyle...we have food and water, which you're all welcome to. Before we agree to let you stay or to interact with any of the people here at Camp Ryder, including the traders you see over there"—she pointed to her left—"we have to do a kind of physical screening. Make sure you don't have anything catching that could hurt the rest of us. I'm sure you understand."

"Yes."

"It is a full-body screening," Jenny clarified. "So each of you will need to strip down completely. I know it's uncomfortable, but it's very necessary for our safety and yours. If you're willing to do the screening and everything is good, then you're welcome to stay, or trade, or move about as you wish. If you don't want to subject yourself, then you know where the door is and we wish you the best of luck."

They reached the medical trailer and Jenny turned to face Kyle again. "So?"

"Uh..." He looked down at the two kids. "Yes. I guess."

"Okay, then."

Angela was impressed. She would have thought that Jenny's speech would have been met with more resistance, but clearly the all-business approach worked well for Jenny. It made her seem more credible and the situation less invasive and more of just another everyday occurrence.

Jenny pointed to a couple of folding chairs against the wall. "Gentlemen, if you guys want to have a seat right there, I can get started with Holly here." She gestured toward the recently erected privacy screen. "Is that okay with you, Holly? You'll be right there on the other side of those sheets. Nobody will see you, but they'll be right there if you need them, okay?"

Holly looked at Kyle and Clay, clearly afraid of leaving them, even just to go ten feet away.

Angela stepped in, treading a little lighter than Jenny. She knelt down just slightly—the girl was tall for her age but still shorter than Angela—and gave an encouraging smile, the same smile she gave Abby when she was trying to convince her to do something she didn't want to do. "It's okay, Holly. I felt the same way when I first got here. But you know what? These are the good guys."

Holly took some time considering it, though she relaxed visibly as she looked around. Maybe it was Angela's tone, or Jenny's businesslike manner, or the people of Camp Ryder who walked by the entrance to the medical trailer and nodded and smiled and waved at them. Eventually she seemed to accept that these people were not out to get her.

"Okay," she said in a mousy voice.

Jenny took her by the hand and led her back behind the privacy screen to get started, while Kyle and Clay took their seats, their dirty hands clasped nervously in their laps like a couple of children waiting outside the principal's office.

"Would either of you like some food or water?"

They looked at each other.

"Yes," Kyle said. "He's hungry. If you have some to spare."

"Of course." Angela retrieved the jug of water and two of the three bowls of oatmeal from the table where she'd placed them. She set the water jug between Clay and Kyle and offered them both a bowl.

Kyle shook his head. "He can have mine. I'm not hungry."

Clay snapped a look at him. "You have to eat too."

"I'm fine."

"You haven't eaten…" Clay seemed to realize his protests were falling on deaf ears and turned his attention to Angela. "He hasn't eaten in two days."

"I'm fine."

Angela forced herself to smile, even as her throat thickened. She gave Clay his bowl and pushed the other into Kyle's hands. "Kyle, there's enough for both of you to eat, okay? Please, just eat. I can get more."

As if eating were an unbearable shame, Kyle stared down into the bowl.

The argument apparently settled, Clay attacked his bowl. Kyle followed, pacing himself as though to prove the point that he was, in fact, not that hungry.

"So." Angela rubbed her hands together for warmth. "Where are you guys from?"

"Out east," Kyle said, still intently focused on his oatmeal. "Little town called Snow Hill."

"How long have you been on the road?"

"Couple weeks."

"Oh." Angela was surprised. "So you stayed in Snow Hill for a while?"

He took a big bite of oatmeal and looked at her quizzically. "Yeah. We had a farm. Did okay for ourselves. Why do you ask?"

Angela shrugged. "Just curious why you left."

Kyle tapped his spoon against the side of the bowl and considered this for a moment. "The Followers. You ever hear of them?"

"Yes. Mostly just rumors."

"Yeah, well." Kyle turned back to his food. "Same here. But it was enough to scare their father, and he made me promise to get them out of there."

Angela's eyebrows went up. "So you're not the children's father?"

"He's our uncle," Clay said quietly.

Kyle eyed the teenager. "Yes. I'm their uncle."

Angela leaned forward. "So what about the Followers scared you guys so much?"

"Pretty much everything, really." Kyle glanced up at the privacy screen. "But I think...what they say about the women and girls...I think that's what scared him the most."

Angela shifted in her seat. "Kyle, this might sound a little silly...but what have *you* heard about the Followers?"

The man sucked at his teeth and regarded Angela with that same piercing stare, as though there were many questions rolling around inside his brain, but in the end it seemed that he shrugged them away and left them unspoken. "Marty Wiscoe. I heard he was some hellfire-and-brimstone televangelist before all this happened. Then when people started going crazy, he said it was God's judgment on the world for being so wicked. Bunch of people joined his congregation right before things fell apart. Called themselves the Followers of the Rapture. Kind of a cult, I guess."

Kyle took a heavy breath. "The rumors about them are pretty far-fetched. Some people say that Marty Wiscoe's the Antichrist. Some people say he's going around preaching the gospel. Most of the rumors are that when he comes to town, his 'congregation' is more well-armed than you'd expect church folk to be. He makes all the men in town repent of their sins and promise to follow God, the Bible, and him. If they agree, they become part of his 'Lord's Army.' If they refuse, he hangs them on crosses." Kyle shook his head. "But they also say that he forces people to eat their own children, that he's growing horns, and that he can make people burst into flames with the power of his mind."

Angela shook her head. "And what is it they say about the women and girls?"

"They say he kidnaps all the girls of childbearing age. Gives them the great honor of bearing the next generation of his Lord's Army. Keeps them as wives and"—he lowered his voice slightly—"sex slaves for his men."

Angela swallowed. "Sounds like a lot of rumors."

"Yeah." He set his bowl aside, empty. "There's probably not much truth to it."

Kyle and Clay exchanged an uncertain glance.

Neither looked convinced.

THIRTEEN

SANFORD

COLD DAWN HAD GIVEN way to a relatively warm day. Lee's estimate was that it was around fifty degrees. Tendrils of white clouds streaked the sky like contrails, running east to west. The sun was between them now, and Lee enjoyed its momentary glow on his face.

They made it into Sanford, to the tallest building they could find. Some four-story structure on the corner of Steele Street and Carthage Street that bore a sign of faded white paint across red brick that declared it the Sanford Business College. The doors and windows were already busted in, so Lee and LaRouche made their way to the stairs and went up to the roof.

Clearing the entire building would have taken too much time, but as they ascended the stairwell, they opened the door to each level and listened carefully. Their concern was with any human occupation, rather than infected. Except in the pursuit of prey, infected tended to stay on the ground. They heard nothing at each floor, and if the building was occupied, those inside were staying very quiet.

As they went, Lee thought about the lack of females, and the more he thought about it the more he began to insist to himself that they would see some today. Sanford had the biggest population of any city they'd cleared since Smithfield, so it stood to reason the horde would be larger or there would be several hordes inside the city. It was just a numbers game.

Surely there would be females here.

And when they saw the females, that knot in the cradle of his stomach would go away. Things would go back to their relative normalcy. The infected would be the same enemy, and he would continue to deal with them in the same ways. The lack of females in the last few cities would be a curiosity but nothing more. There would be nothing new to worry about.

They reached the roof, dropped their packs, and settled in.

They waited.

Hours passed.

The hard roof and brick abutment became uncomfortable, and the two men shifted positions often. They sipped water to stay hydrated and occasionally ate a strip of deer jerky to stave off hunger. Frequently one of them would poke his head over the ledge to see if a horde had emerged from their den, but they both knew before looking that there wasn't—they would have been able to hear it or smell it.

The knot in Lee's stomach cinched itself a little tighter.

Around midday, LaRouche rose to his knees,

exposing his entire torso, and let out an exasperated sigh. "What the fuck, man? This place is a goddamned ghost town."

Lee wanted to tell him to settle down, that they would show up, but the truth was that LaRouche had taken the words right out of his mouth. He hitched one arm onto the abutment and pulled himself to his knees beside the sergeant. Together, they looked out over the city.

Across from them stood a bank, more shops, a diner. There were no cars parked alongside the road, which was odd. Plenty of trash, though. More than a few shell casings glittered on the concrete below them. Here and there, an empty magazine ejected from an M4. Trails of pockmarks ran across brick walls like ellipses on an unfinished sentence.

Something violent had happened.

Nothing unusual.

There were a few bodies, decayed and beginning to skeletonize. Other than their quiet presence, the place was deserted.

"I dunno," Lee said tightly.

"I feel like we usually have eyes on them by now."

"Maybe they're in another section of the city."

"Could be."

"Maybe we should move." Lee raised one knee and rested his elbow there.

LaRouche made a face and looked out at the city again. "Well, we've already wasted half the day."

Lee nodded. "I say we move south toward the other end of town, see if we can catch sight of the horde."

"If there is one."

"Why wouldn't there be?"

"I don't know." LaRouche shrugged and said no more.

Lee stood and shouldered his pack. "There'll be a horde."

Almost as though he hoped for it.

On his feet, he could see farther over the abutment to the south end of town. Steele Street stretched out and continued on through several intersections. He wished they could cut across the tops of the buildings. Roofs had become a sort of safety zone for them. The ground was where the danger was.

Lee moved toward the door to the stairwell. "Let's get going."

"Hold up..."

Lee glanced behind him, expecting to see LaRouche dawdling with his pack, but instead the man was standing, his neck extended out, focused intently on something to the south, tense like a bird dog with its eyes on a quail. Lee instinctively tried to follow LaRouche's gaze, but there was so much to see from this vantage point that he had no idea what the sergeant was looking at.

"What is it?"

LaRouche waved a hand and knelt. "Get down... Come here."

Lee watched him duckwalk quickly to the southern-facing abutment and peer over. Lee followed closely behind, settling to his knees but looking at LaRouche rather than over the abutment. "What is it? What do you see?"

"I can't tell," LaRouche whispered. "Way down there at the intersection."

Lee rose slowly so he could just see over the abutment to the intersection south of them. "What am I looking for?"

"Across the intersection, you see that two-toned building? Red on top, white on bottom?"

"Yeah."

"You see the entry to that building? Right there next to the square pillar. I think it's a person."

Lee stared at the building, squinting against the low-slung sun. "I don't see..."

The words rolled to a stop on his tongue as a head poked out from behind the pillar. He couldn't see its features from this distance, but he could see it looking around as though scanning for threats. After a moment of this looking back and forth, it disappeared and then emerged again, dragging something behind it—what looked like the lower half of a dog.

"Shit," LaRouche whispered.

"That ain't a person," Lee murmured.

It dragged its prize quickly across the street, then paused on the other side to look around again.

"Why can't it be a person? You've never eaten dead dog?" LaRouche was trying to make a joke, but when Lee snapped a look at him, there was a thin sheen of sweat across his brow that belied his lackadaisical attitude.

The person, the creature, the infected—whatever the hell it was—must have determined that the coast was clear again. It reached down and grabbed one of the dog's legs and pulled it around the corner toward an open building door, and then disappeared inside.

"Where's he going?" LaRouche asked shakily.

"Den, maybe."

"What, are they hoarding food?"

"I don't know. I'm watching the same damn thing you are."

A minute passed.

The infected came out from the darkness of the building, this time without the dog's hindquarters. Still in the shade of the building's portico, it looked back and forth, and then scampered across the street where it had come from.

"I've never seen them that cautious before," Lee said quietly, as though the infected might hear him from so far away.

"You think it's a pack or a horde?"

"There's only one."

"What do you think he's a part of?"

Lee shook his head. "I've never seen a pack this far into an urban area."

"So you think it's a horde?"

Lee didn't answer.

"What do we do?" LaRouche asked after a moment.

"I wanna know what the fuck is in that building."

LaRouche suddenly ducked and pointed. "There he is again!" he hissed.

The same movements. Stopping at the building across the street, poking the head out, looking back and forth a few times, running across, looking back and forth...but this one was different.

"Not the same one," Lee said. "The other one was wearing a shirt and jeans. This one's just got some khaki shorts, it looks like."

"What's it holding?"

They both squinted. The infected at the corner was holding something cradled in its two spindly arms but they couldn't tell what it was. It disappeared into the building and came back out a moment later with nothing in its arms. Before crossing the street again, it looked both ways, as though it were a pedestrian concerned about vehicular traffic. For a moment, its gaze lingered in their direction and Lee felt his heart jump into his throat. But then the creature jogged across the street and disappeared, following the same trail as the other infected.

"They're like ants," Lee stated with sudden certainty. "They're out there scavenging something and bringing it back to their den. They've got a fucking den inside that building."

LaRouche kept chewing at his lip. "We could take 'em out in their den while they're sleeping."

Lee looked at him like he was insane. "Not a fucking chance. I'm not wandering into that building in the dark to fight some infected. That's nuts."

"Okay." LaRouche didn't put up an argument. Apparently he didn't like the sound of his own idea.

"No." Lee looked back toward the south. "We'll do a trap in the morning. Catch 'em right outside of the den. Once we've wiped 'em out, we'll check out the den."

"We should do some more recon."

Lee nodded. "We need to get a head count on them, and I want to see what they're scavenging."

"All right." LaRouche took a deep breath, like he was preparing to take a dive. "Let's do it."

They made for the stairs and headed for the ground floor. They were quicker going down than they'd been coming up, and in a minute or two Lee peeked out of the building and took a glance at the city around him. It was devoid of life, just as before. They faced north, onto Carthage Street.

Moving with cautious urgency, they slipped out and hugged the wall of the building, jogging west for a short distance and then quickly cutting down an alley that ran behind the storefronts. The intersection where they had seen the infected crossing was only one block down from them. On that corner, another tall building stood, some sort of apartments or condos.

When they reached it, they found a steel door standing closed and locked between them and the inside. If they checked the street side for doors, they would expose themselves, so it was this door or nothing.

"I got it," Lee whispered, and he pointed to the corner of the building where a narrow alley led out to the street. "Watch that alley."

LaRouche moved to the corner, keeping back away from it a few feet and leaning out just far enough to see down the alley. He scanned back and forth quickly, then leaned back into cover. He looked to Lee and gave him a thumbs-up. "Alley's gated off at the street."

Lee nodded. "Watch my back."

He dropped his pack near the steel door and unzipped the main compartment. After his first few scavenging trips, Lee had learned the value of two items: a crowbar and a bolt cutter. Without the proper tools, it was incredibly difficult to make his way through an urban area after everything had been boarded up, chained up, and locked up by business owners hoping to eventually come back and reopen their doors. It was times like these that the crowbar and the bolt cutter justified the extra twenty pounds they added to his pack.

He pulled out the crowbar and shifted his sling so his rifle hung on his left side, out of the way. He glanced over his shoulder as he stepped to the door. LaRouche was still at the corner, peeking out, and then scanning behind them.

All appeared quiet.

Lee set the flat, curved head of the crowbar into the narrow crack between the steel door and the jamb, right above the latch. The head of the crowbar was just a sliver too thick, so Lee put his weight onto it and struck it three times with the palm of his hand until it was embedded nicely into the crack. Then he took the end of the crowbar and began leveraging up and down, bending the frame away from the steel door.

"Psst!"

Lee looked up.

LaRouche made eye contact with him and held up a single finger, then pointed down the alley.

Lee bit his bottom lip and went back to work, that old familiar shudder working its way through his limbs. He focused on his task, kept prying up and down, up and down. Not worrying about what LaRouche's hand signals meant. He was close now, but these industrial doors were tough.

"Come on, you bitch," he mumbled to himself, straining hard to bend the metal.

Light but rapid footsteps behind him.

Lee turned and found LaRouche beside him, eyes wide. "Gate's not latched!" he hissed. "One's coming down!"

From the alley, the faint sound of rusted hinges.

The clatter of a metal gate on a brick wall.

"Open it!" LaRouche urged under his breath.

Lee set himself into the door, fingers aching from their grip on the crowbar, his forearms beginning to burn from the strain. "I'm fucking trying!"

LaRouche made an angry growling noise low in his throat and turned his attention to the alley, raising his rifle. "This is about to be bad."

"I'm almost there..."

From the alley came that distinctive chuffing sound.

Something sniffing the air.

"Captain..."

Lee gritted his teeth, trying to work fast, but trying to work quietly at the same time. If he rushed, he would make noise, and noise would only draw the infected to them faster. And the others would follow.

"I got it...I got it..."

He pushed in the crowbar one more time, and this time instead of leveraging up and down, he pried with steady, firm pressure.

The door popped with a little scrape. Lee ducked in, leaving his pack outside on the ground. LaRouche slipped in just in time for Lee to close the door as quietly as he could, plunging them into darkness. In the brief flash of sunlight when he'd opened the door, Lee had seen a long hallway, white walls, and red carpeting. It smelled like death.

Something farther down the hall.

A hunched figure.

Alive or dead?

He felt his stomach tighten involuntarily as the stench of the rot, held in so long in this dark, enclosed space, permeated his mouth and nose and seeped into his throat and sinuses. He could feel the churn in his gut, and his mouth began to water, preparing for vomit. He tried to bury his nose in the fold of his shemagh that lay wrapped around his neck but couldn't quite reach.

He wanted to ask LaRouche if he had seen anything down the hall, but he was afraid to speak. He wanted to click on the flashlight of his rifle and illuminate this petrifying dark, but he was afraid to move. He remained glued to the outward-opening door, both hands clamped on the handle and pulling it shut as tightly as he could. If he made a move, if he allowed himself to vomit or even breathe too loudly, the infected would hear him.

It would cry out to the others, knowing there was something to feed on inside.

Lee and LaRouche's chances of survival went downhill from there.

He strained, sweat on his palms making his grip

on the handle slippery. His ears searched for any sound but heard only the overwhelming silence of the building. Whatever he had seen down the hall, real or imagined, it was not making any noise.

Movement from the other side of the door.

Shuffling feet, noisy breathing.

It was sniffing the air.

It was just a human. It was not another species. Nothing had changed, anatomically or physiologically, in the infected. Its nose was no more sensitive now than it had been when it was a whole and healthy person. However, there was a part of Lee that thought perhaps that mammalian, instinctive part of the brain—the only part left over after FURY—might be capable of interpreting scent data more clearly than the conscious and logical mind was able to. The infected may not be bloodhounds, but that was not to say their instinctive brains were not able to cipher from the air whether a person had been standing there recently.

His arms began to fatigue, tiring from holding the door shut so tightly.

The sniffing, scenting noise became more pronounced, as though the infected were pressing its nose against the doorframe, trying to inhale their scents from the other side. Abstractly, Lee wondered whether bathing made their scent more or less obvious. Was it the strange smell of soap that tickled its brain, or was it the smell of a living thing's body odor?

On the other side of the door, the creature began to make a guttural sound: "Guh…Guh…Guh…" It wasn't loud, and Lee didn't think it was any sort of call to other infected. Perversely, it reminded him of a toddler trying to sound out new syllables.

"Guh... Guh..."

From the outside, the door handle jiggled and the door moved slightly under Lee's grip. He gritted his teeth and held tighter. In his mind he pictured losing his grip, the door being yanked open, and the infected bursting through, biting and grasping at them. He would move back quickly, as soon as he felt he was going to lose his grip...

"Cap."

Lee jumped at the hot breath in his ear. He turned and thought he could see the faintest outline of LaRouche's face in some dim, ambient light. He was standing very close to Lee now.

His voice was the barest thread of a whisper. "I think it's gone."

Lee listened and heard only silence. No more sniffing, no more shuffling feet. No more grunted syllables. But Lee didn't release the door or open it to retrieve his pack. Not just yet. He waited in the disorienting darkness, steeped in the smell of rotted flesh, for what could have been a minute or possibly ten. It was difficult to tell.

The smell of the air became a physical image in his head, like a series of close-up photos of every dead and corrupted thing he'd ever seen: bloodless skin, stretched to bursting with noxious gases; brown fluids leaking; maggots squirming busily.

He tasted vomit.

Unable to wait any longer, he used every bit of control he had to open the door only an inch or so and look out. The small vertical shaft of light bisected his face, and compared to the deep black-ness of the inside, the outside seemed completely white. It took a few seconds for his eyes to adjust to the light.

His stomach heaved.

He pushed the door open a little farther.

No infected.

"Clear?" LaRouche croaked.

"Yeah..."

LaRouche fumbled past Lee—to his credit, still moving quietly. He went down to his hands and knees and stooped until his face was only inches from the pavement, and then he vomited. He'd had the presence of mind to spill his guts close to the ground so that it wouldn't make a splashing sound.

Seeing LaRouche blow didn't help, and Lee fol-lowed suit.

Between bouts of quietly purging mostly stom-ach acids, water, and bits of deer jerky, they both looked up and around but saw no threats. The ordeal lasted less than a minute before the two of them wiped strings of sputum from their noses and mouths and dragged themselves back into the building, along with Lee's pack.

Feeling marginally better but still queasy from the inescapable smell, Lee slung into the backpack and closed the steel door behind him. He clicked on his rifle's light and shone it down the hall, his face squeezed tight.

There, down at the end of the hallway, Lee could see that hunched thing he'd seen before, and also the likely source of the smell. It was so badly decomposed, the only reason Lee could tell it was human were the soiled clothes it wore.

"Stairs." Lee burped and spat.

Directly to their right rose a stairwell. They moved to it and began to climb. The air in the stairwell may have still smelled like the corpse, but to their overwrought noses, it seemed cleaner and fresher as they rose. They took deep breaths and blew hard out of their noses, trying to clear their sinuses.

"Never get used to that smell," LaRouche remarked.

They worked their way up the stairs and found the rooftop access. It was nearly identical to the roof of the business college, but here they found something interesting: a couple sandbags, some empty 5.56mm ammunition cans, and some discarded aluminum box magazines were scattered in a corner. Brass shell casings made a glittering carpet in the corner. A few feet away were the remains of a case of MREs and a case of bottled water.

"Looks like some of our boys picked a nice overwatch," LaRouche commented and poked at the empty box of MREs with the toe of his boot.

Lee eyed the discarded brass. "They hosed *somebody* down."

"Bet I know who."

They moved to the edge of the roof, crouching low, and peered over at the intersection where they'd seen the infected crossing earlier. They could see the building where the infected had entered—the likely location of their den. The streets were pockmarked with bullet strikes. There were a few old corpses off to the side but not enough to justify the expenditure of ammunition sitting at their feet.

"Where are all the bodies?" Lee wondered.

"Maybe they ate them." LaRouche glanced at Lee. "The infected, that is."

Lee scanned up the street a little farther in the direction they had seen the infected coming from. He tapped LaRouche on the shoulder and pointed, hunching low and trying to keep his body flush with the roof's abutment. "There. You see 'em?"

About two blocks west of the intersection, there was a large box truck, halfway embedded into a storefront. Lee could not read the words on the side, but he could clearly see the enlarged picture of a cornucopia of grains, vegetables, fruits, and meats.

A grocery truck.

The back end of the truck hung halfway open, and all around it and inside of it was a crowd of tattered, filthy souls, all clambering to get inside. Lee could hear them occasionally barking at each other, but they were quieter than normal, he thought. There were perhaps fifty of them. They would climb into the back of the truck, disappearing inside. Then they would emerge a moment later, their arms full.

"They are rat-fucking the shit out of that truck," LaRouche whispered in amazement.

Lee watched, quiet and still.

He was overtaken by the pure oddity of what he was seeing. Lee's first instinct was to try to explain it away, but he couldn't deny it. They were gathering food from the truck and taking it back to their den, or what Lee *assumed* was their den. It was not a free-for-all. They were not eating whatever they got their hands on.

And Lee didn't know how he felt about this.

Fear.

Uncertainty.

Loathing.

Fascination.

"Those are cans they're carrying," LaRouche mumbled suddenly, as one of the infected passed by on the street below them.

"Jacob said he'd seen them get into cans," Lee breathed out. "They understand that it's food."

LaRouche turned and looked at the captain. "What else do they understand?"

Lee didn't answer.

"Where's the rest of them?" he asked.

"I dunno."

"You know what else?"

"What's that?"

"No females," Lee said.

LaRouche took a long moment to look but could find none for himself. "Not a goddamned one," he confirmed.

FOURTEEN

EVOLUTION

ANOTHER MOMENT OF OBSERVATION PASSED.

Lee sidled a little closer to LaRouche and pointed in the direction of the truck. "You see the one across the street? Standing on the car? He's got a red hoodie on."

"Yeah."

"He's keeping watch."

"How do you know that?"

"He hasn't moved. Everyone else is gathering food, and he's been standing on that car, looking back and forth the whole time."

"Keeping watch," LaRouche repeated, as though testing to see if the words made any sense. "What the hell are they keeping watch for?"

"Prey, maybe?"

"Maybe."

Their answer came only a moment later when it suddenly let out an eerie, ululating cry unlike any Lee had heard come from the infected. At first Lee thought they had been spotted up on their high overlook, but somehow he knew that was not right. The noise from this infected was not a screech or a bark. It was a scream.

"The hell…?" LaRouche jumped back at the noise but didn't take his eyes off the scene unfolding.

All at once, the fifty infected gathered around the box truck began to stampede for the den. The ones carrying food dropped it to the concrete. Boxes and packages spilled out and were trampled underfoot; canned goods went rolling and scattering across the road. As each of the infected horde began to run, they echoed the cry from the watcher.

"What are they doing?" LaRouche looked like he wanted to run too. "Should we get the fuck out of here?"

"No!" Lee put a hand on his arm. "Stay put!"

"What are they running from?"

"I don't…"

Any further words were cut off.

From a side street just behind the box truck burst three figures. None of them wore but the barest tatters of clothing, and even from this distance Lee could see the lean, almost athletic musculature. Were they regular people? No…there was no mistaking that animal run, the sprinting form of a hunter. But it had been months since Lee had seen an infected that appeared so…

Well fed?

The truth hit him like a slap in the face.

"Holy shit," he said out loud.

As the running horde of infected came abreast of Lee, he watched as two more of the larger infected loped around the corner directly across from them, cutting off a portion of the fleeing horde. The horde slowed partially as they began to try to squeeze by.

One of the first three who had attacked from behind, a powerful-looking dark-skinned man with wild tangles of black hair down to his shoulders, leaped straight forward and tackled a member of the horde from behind. The two of them tumbled across the asphalt, the victim lashing out like a cornered dog, biting and kicking and slashing viciously. But the dark-skinned infected was too large and too strong for it. It pinned its flailing prey to the ground and placed one of its massive hands on its prey's head and the other on his chest, and the muscles in its back rippled as it flexed, forcing the smaller infected to expose his jugular.

The hunter opened its mouth inhumanly wide and lunged.

In one quick twisting motion, it ripped out its prey's throat.

The sun was a red ball hovering just above the horizon, a retreating source of heat, taking the relative warmth of the day with it. Cold dark approached from the east, doggedly borne in on gusting winds that cut right through the fabric of Harper's jacket and made him pull the collar up over his face and swear that he would find himself a fucking pair of gloves or convince someone to make a pair for him.

The group of twenty volunteers stood, cold and tired from a day's worth of exercises. Beside them, just inside the Camp Ryder gate, their vehicles ticked and cooled from the drive back. The smell of cook fires surrounded them, emanating from Marie's kitchen and from a few others strewn about the camp.

"All right, folks." Harper jerked a thumb toward the Camp Ryder building. "Dinner should be ready in a little bit. We're done for the day, but we're doing it all again tomorrow. Make sure you get some sleep."

The group began to disperse with quiet mumbles of "Catch you later" and "See you in a bit." Harper watched them disappear into the streams of people walking about, packing everything in for the day and setting up for another cold night. He adjusted the strap of his rifle, felt the cold metal on his fingertips, and turned toward the Camp Ryder building.

Devon's words from earlier rolled through his head.

What was Jerry up to?

Sure, Jerry didn't make a habit of leaving the gates—he was a bit of a pussy in Harper's opinion—but that didn't mean that he didn't occasionally go out if he needed something. After all, everyone had to have something to trade nowadays. Perhaps Jerry just wanted to find himself a little creature comfort or something he could trade up for it. Case in point, he'd gone through a lot of trouble just to get his mattress.

Harper hadn't made a big deal about it when he spoke to the kid, because honestly, he didn't know what to make of it. But he thought he had better talk it over with Bus anyway. Bus would know what to do. The big guy didn't give himself much credit for being a leader, but there was a reason that everyone in the Camp Ryder Hub deferred to his judgment.

Harper made his way into the building. It was warm inside, to the point of stuffiness, and crowded, which didn't help. Whatever Marie was cooking had a strong, robust smell to it. For some reason, it turned his stomach. Harper smiled and nodded at the people he recognized and quickly made his way upstairs.

As he walked, he realized why the smell cloyed at the back of his throat and soured in his gut.

It smelled like chili.

He stopped halfway up the stairs and looked down at all the people milling about, getting in line for food. It was noisy, and busy, and underneath the scent of the food, a million other smells wafted. He breathed shallowly, as though he might escape the smell of the chili and thought to himself that this was a strange reaction, even as his tongue became suddenly dry and his knees felt weak.

Screaming.

Skin parting under a blade.

Panic.

The sensation of concrete, scraping the very tip of the bayonet as he ran the kid all the way through. The feeling in his hands of the rifle jumping as the young savage tried desperately to push the blade out of his belly. Wide, animallike eyes, staring down at the mortal wound.

Screaming and blood.

"Hey!"

Harper jerked and grunted like he was being pulled back through some invisible membrane that separated the real world from the world of his memories. It had felt so real in that moment that he'd had the fleeting, maddening thought that everything he had experienced after and up to the present had in fact been a jumble of daydreams, and that in reality he was still there, spiking a kid to the ground with the rusted blade at the end of an SKS.

"Huh?" Harper looked up the last few stairs and found Bus standing at the top, his bushy eyebrows narrowed as though he were suspicious of Harper. "Yeah?"

"You okay?" Bus asked.

Harper nodded and felt sweat, cool and greasy, across his receding hairline. "Fine."

Bus flicked his eyes out to the floor of the building. Then he jerked his head toward the office. "Come in and talk to me. I've got news."

Bus retreated into the office without another word and Harper stamped up the last few risers, trying to shake that hollow, stretching feeling in his stomach, that sensation that had no name. Like a backlog of emotions that you just can't process so you leave it in a dark corner, forgotten and spoiling as time passes, and you maintain your unwillingness to dissect it. The more wretched it becomes, the more you try to ignore it.

In the office, Bus collapsed into the chair behind the desk with a great huff.

Harper stepped up to the desk, trying to discreetly wipe the sweat from his head, but Bus took notice anyway. He gave Harper that same strange look he'd given him on the staircase.

"Everything okay with you?" he asked.

Harper nodded. "Yeah. Fine. What's been going on with you?"

Bus shook his head. "Just the usual—every problem under the sun. Jenny's running low on antibiotics and this flu thing going around camp is ending with half the older folks getting pneumonia. Keith Jenkins misplaced that little .22 revolver he had and now he claims someone stole it, but who knows…"

Harper raised an eyebrow. "You call me up here to talk about antibiotics and missing revolvers?"

"Just venting." Bus sighed and jabbed a finger at the radio. "Captain Harden just reported in."

Harper wiped his moist fingers off on his pants. "Is everybody okay?"

Bus stroked his beard for a moment. "As far as our people go, yes. Everything is fine."

Harper waited for him to continue.

"In fact," Bus continued, folding his hands on the desk, "from Captain Harden's recon on Sanford, it sounds like they'll be able to clear the place sooner than expected."

"That sounds like a good thing."

"It does, doesn't it?" Bus didn't look happy. "He said there were approximately fifty infected in the horde and no evidence of a larger group, at least on the northern side of the city. They located what they believe to be a den, but they haven't been able to get inside."

"Only fifty?" Harper was taken aback.

Bus pointed. "Close the door."

Harper stepped back and pushed the door closed. The rumble and scrabble of people moving and talking and laughing below them was suddenly diminished to a quiet background hum. Harper stood there, facing the door for a moment, feeling certain that he would not like what came next.

He turned back to the desk. "Where'd the others go?"

Bus looked at the map. "Eaten, it sounds like."

"Eaten." Harper took a breath, still too confused to truly have a strong reaction to the news. "They're eating each other?"

"Yes and no." Bus met his gaze. "According to the captain, he watched the horde of fifty that had managed to break into a box truck, and they were taking foodstuffs. Things like canned goods. And they were taking them to the den. Then in the middle of all of this, the horde was attacked by a small group of what the captain referred to as 'hunters.' He described them as slightly larger and much more aggressive than the infected in the horde. He told me they showed no signs of malnutrition." Bus's nose curled in disgust. "That they appeared well fed."

Harper stood very still and looked straight ahead.

Bus leaned forward. "We have multiple problems here, Harper. We've got these infected, not only scavenging our food, but they're showing the intelligence to do so."

"Frankly..." Harper swallowed against a dry throat. "I'm more concerned about the hunters."

"Why? Let the infected eat each other. Save us all the problem of how to kill them."

Harper finally took a seat in one of the folding chairs. "We don't have the time to let them wipe each other out. It could take months, even years for that to happen. Besides, if they run out of other infected to hunt, who do you think they're going to turn to? The infected are easier prey for them now because they're undefended and they can't think like we can. But once that food source is gone, they'll come after us. In the meantime, the hunters are getting stronger, and that creates a problem for me."

Bus seemed confused. "Which is..."

Harper could feel himself getting flustered, and he couldn't quite pinpoint where it was coming from. His neck felt hot and his shoulders felt tense and his face and scalp prickled. He was getting pissed, but why?

He stood up out of his seat and put both palms against his eyes and groaned. "Because they were dying, Bus! All the infected we've seen over the last few months have been getting skinnier, and weaker, and sicklier. It was the light at the end of the tunnel that one day after a good, long, cold winter we'd wake up and they'd all be gone." His voice hitched. He realized he was feeling the shock of crushing disappointment. Something so close to his grasp had just been ripped away. "This doesn't mean they're going to wipe each other out! All it means is that they're adapting!"

"But they've always hunted." Bus stood up. "These packs aren't anything new..."

"It's not about the packs." Harper turned to face him. "You heard what Jacob said about them. They might be fucking crazy, but their bodies haven't changed. Their bodies can't process all the crap they eat, he said." Harper hung his hands on the back of his neck and shook his head. "That's why he said they were skinny and always hungry. But if you've got these ones, these hunters, the ones who look 'well fed,' that means they *are* changing. They *are* processing what they eat, and they *are* getting stronger."

Bus seemed to realize that his friend was taking this news harder than he was, albeit for different reasons. His face softened and his head hung.

"There's something else he mentioned. Something that bothers me."

It just keeps getting better, Harper thought.

With a measure of exhaustion, he sighed. "What's that, Bus?"

"He said that when the hunters attacked the horde, they ran back to the den but stopped short of running inside. He said they just stood outside and turned back toward the hunters like they were ready to fight, but the hunters took their kills and disappeared."

Harper forced himself to think about it at length.

He gave up after a few moments. "Okay. Beats me what the hell they're doing."

"I think we should talk to Jacob."

Harper nodded. "I think that's a good idea."

Jerry stood in the dinner line with the rest of the people. In his own mind this was a chance to rub elbows with the common man, a demonstration that he was just like everyone else. For him, being among everyone else was an act of goodwill on his part, despite the fact that he wouldn't be fed if he weren't there.

While he smiled and laughed—or looked gravely concerned, depending on the conversation topic— he saw Harper and Bus slip out of the upstairs office and tread swiftly down the stairs. They glanced out at the people in line for dinner, but if they noticed Jerry there, they gave no indication.

Jerry had spent a lot of his lifetime being under- handed, and he was able to recognize it when he saw it. Old Bus and his lapdog Harper were up to something, sure as shit. Those were the expres- sions of men who were trying to keep a very wily cat inside its bag. And if they wanted it in, it stood to reason that it could benefit Jerry to let it out.

"What do you think?"

Jerry refocused on the tall lady in front of him and her rather short and stubby spouse. Interest- ing combination. Had they been married before the collapse or was this an arrangement of circum- stance? More importantly, what the hell had they been talking about?

He took his cue from the couple's intensely serious faces and affixed a somber look of contemplation to his features. "Hmm," he said, as though interested. "I think it's something that bears consideration."

They nodded knowingly.

The man spoke quietly, leaning in so Jerry could smell his breath, sharp and sour. "We appreciate that you actually take the time to think and don't just shout out whatever answers you think people want to hear. You know we're behind you, Jerry. Anything you need."

Jerry smiled. "Thank you. I'll keep that in mind."

He reached the folding table where Marie was dishing out some thick reddish stew or chili, made with some unknown meat, a bit of corn, a bit of beans.

"This looks delightful, Marie." Jerry smiled as the woman dished him a bowl of the stuff.

In truth, he resented how Marie couldn't make shit except stews, soups, or chili. He understood that there were nearly a hundred mouths to feed, but it certainly wasn't the five thousand, and even that had come with a fish option. He looked down into the pot of ruddy mush and tried hard not to sneer.

Marie pushed the bowl into his hands and smiled, syrupy sweet to the point of being a little sarcastic. "Anything for you, Jerry. I'm just glad I could please you."

His smile became wooden. "Yes. That's very nice of you. Thanks again."

He stuck his spoon into the chili/stew/mush and turned toward the open area inside the building, all the tents and huts thrown up on top of the grease-stained floor where trucks used to park and mechanics would tune them up. Still, underneath all the smells of the food and the stink of the people and the little bit of smoke from the cook fires and candles, he could still smell that little tinge of *eau de grease monkey.* His father had been a mechanic, and the smell still gave Jerry a hollow feeling in his gut.

On the other side of the little indoor shanty-town, there were a number of folding tables and chairs, as well as crates and buckets and anything else you could sit your ass on. This was where the community came together and shared their evening meals in the company of their peers, and a quiet conversation off to the side could go unnoticed among the rabble.

Jerry took a bite of the food as he made his way over. The same mystery-meat-and-beans taste as every other dish Marie made. Would it kill her to make a fucking steak every now and then? Couldn't she make steaks with deer meat? He had to admit, prior to surviving the collapse, he'd never eaten venison, but it was just a meat like every other four-legged animal. He was sure steaks could be made out of it. Or, Christ, at the very least some hamburgers.

A man with a dirty old Yankees hat was waiting for him in the corner.

"Jerry." He nodded and spooned up a mouthful of chili.

"Greg. How's the kid?"

"He's doin' all right." Greg glanced under the bill of his cap at the people closest to them, but they were all lost in loud conversations. "You talk to White today?"

"This morning." Jerry pushed his food around. "He's in."

"He's worthless."

"He gives us a majority."

Greg smirked. "Who's gonna train them how to use those weapons?"

Jerry shook his head. "Won't be necessary. We have enough of his students to stand around holding them and it should be enough to discourage a firefight."

"If you say so."

"I do."

Greg regarded him for a brief moment, and in that time Jerry felt that the other man was scanning him up and down to determine whether he should throat-punch him or not. In the end he took another monstrous bite of food. He chewed, swallowed, and sucked at something in his teeth before speaking again. "How many will there be?"

"Five." Jerry set his bowl on the ground, no longer interested. "You'll take four. You're gonna need to rough one of 'em up before you let him go. Make it believable—it's gotta convince Old Man Hughes that something happened. He's my weak link in this whole thing. If he thinks something is suspicious or doesn't add up, he'll say so to Captain Harden."

"How believable do you want it?"

"Don't break any bones or anything. Little black eye, cut lip. That should be enough."

"I can do that. Where you want me to take the other four?"

"Hole 'em up in the university somewhere."

"Okay." Greg scraped up the last of his meal. At least he seemed to be enjoying the stuff. "When?"

"The morning after tomorrow. They'll meet you across the Cape Fear bridge, right outside of town."

"All right." Greg smiled unpleasantly. "We'll be there."

FIFTEEN

DIVERSION

JACOB STOOD, LOOKING OUT over a fire at the thickening darkness in the woods beyond their protective fence. He posed a peculiar figure: skeletal, long-limbed, pale-skinned. He wore boots and a pair of the olive drab pants he'd received from Lee, a tan pullover, and a matching watch cap. They'd given him back Captain Mitchell's M4, and he wore it in a single-point sling, hanging across his shallow chest.

If he didn't look so damn weird, Harper thought he might look like a soldier.

"That is very strange," Jacob said quietly and looked down into the fire.

No, he isn't a soldier, Harper decided. His eyes showed no hardness in them. Not like he'd seen in Lee. But there was something there, something Harper couldn't put a finger on, but he felt it was the reason why Jacob had been able to survive the trip from Virginia to North Carolina by himself.

Probingly, Bus said, "Thoughts?"

Jacob flexed his spidery fingers and began cracking each knuckle. "My thoughts are that it creates yet another disadvantage for us. Well..." He eyed the two men. "Primarily for Captain Harden. Besides the obvious issue of them appearing to be faster and stronger, there's the added issue of their sleep cycle. Up until this point, I've seen packs work at night in the rural areas and the hordes during the day in the urban areas. This seems to be a pack, preying on the hordes, and working in an urban area during the day."

He grabbed a long stick and jabbed at the fire, his free hand cradling his rifle against his chest to keep it from swinging into the fire as he bent over. His train of thought seemed to jump tracks and drifted off into the night with the fog of his breath in the air.

Harper shuffled a little closer to the fire and held his hands out to warm them. "What about the adaptation? I mean, this is the first time we've seen this..."

Jacob held up a finger. "Not the first time."

They waited for him to elaborate.

He held the stick in the fire until the edge became blackened. "And I wouldn't call it 'adaptation' necessarily. Not in the sense that I think you mean it, as though they are evolving." He held up the tip of the stick and stared at the smoking point. "No. Evolution can't happen that fast. Not in the period of three months. Not even in three years. It takes generations for changes to occur. So to see what makes them different from the other infected, we have to look at normal, everyday differences.

"Chemicals in the body can play a part. For instance, some races produce more testosterone than others. Certain people are more capable of accessing instinctive memories. Some people are genetically predisposed toward violence. Physiologically, some people can eat certain things, including raw meat, and others cannot." He smiled faintly. "We're not all as homogenous as our previous popular culture would have us think."

"So..." Harper closed his eyes and tried to think. "Some people are naturally better at being an infected. Is that what you're saying?"

Jacob watched smoke rise from the stick. "Essentially...yes. Genetic predispositions. While they are not evolving in the sense of growing tails and cat's eyes to see at night, it is an evolutionary principle that we are seeing take place here: survival of the fittest." He rammed the stick into the dirt and looked at the two men, his eyes glistening in the firelight. "You have to understand that civilization has been breeding the survival instinct out of humanity for generations upon generations. Survival is based upon aggression, but aggression is rooted out in modern society. If a modern human being is then infected with FURY and the bacterium eats through his frontal lobe, all he has left to rely upon are his animal instincts. The more intact those instincts are, the more successful that human will be at surviving. The instinctively weak will become food for the instinctively strong."

That hollow feeling was back in Harper's stomach. "How do you figure out which ones are instinctively strong?"

Jacob scratched at the crook of his neck with a single long finger. "Obviously a person who was athletic when he got infected will be more able to catch prey. Some people see better than others, some people hear better than others, and some people smell better than others. Then there will be people who exhibit several of these...survival attributes. If I'm correct, then what Captain Harden saw in the hunters was just the cream rising to the top, so to speak."

"I don't believe this," Bus mumbled.

Harper tilted his head back a bit. "What area of science did you say you were in?"

Jacob smiled patronizingly. "Microbiology on all my paperwork. But genetics is something of an interest. I've probably done enough research on my own time to constitute a doctorate."

Harper clenched his jaw. "You can tell us all about the genetics, but you can't tell us where the bacteria came from?"

Jacob's expression soured a bit. "A large part of genetics is simply observing and understanding key characteristics, whereas microbiology requires a lab. It is, by definition, the study of things that can't be seen with the naked eye." He sniffed. "Hence the 'micro' in microbiology."

Harper loaded a retort but was stayed by Bus's voice.

"So this isn't going away," Bus said. "They're not just gonna...die out."

Jacob looked at the big man with something akin to pity. "I wouldn't hold my breath."

Thirty miles away in Broadway, the discussion was much less detailed. Lee and his team asked the same questions but mostly had no answers. A few people had some theories, but none was worth seriously considering. In the end, the discussion of what Lee and LaRouche had witnessed petered out in about five minutes.

They ate cold MREs for dinner and bedded down for the night. There was no joking and no quiet laughter in the darkness, as there usually was. They were all serious and stone-faced, lost in thoughts of what had been and what was still to come.

Jim had the last watch and he woke them two hours before dawn.

They ate a hasty breakfast and Lee took a stick and began to draw in a patch of dirt, using the light from a single gas lantern. What he produced was a reasonable facsimile of the intersection of Wicker Street and Steele Street. Lee used small stones to illustrate buildings and shallow lines in the dirt to show roads. As he finished, his team gathered around him, some of them still eating or drinking, but all of them geared up and ready to go.

Lee knelt down on his haunches and pointed to each item and named it. "This is the intersection of Steele Street and Wicker Street in Sanford. The southeast corner is where the suspected den is located. It's a tan-ish, sandstone-colored building. Two stories." He moved his pointer. "On the northwestern corner is the building we'll be taking. It's an apartment building, and it's about..." He looked to LaRouche. "What would you say? Five or six stories?"

"I counted six."

"Six stories, then." Lee swept the pointer down along what was Steele Street. "We're gonna come in from the north, since we didn't see any activity in that section during recon. We'll park the Humvees back a few blocks and hoof it into the apartment building. Once we're on the roof, we'll overlook the southern-facing wall and set the traps right here." He circled the street in front of the building.

"Uh…" One of the guys from Jeriah Wilson's group popped his hand up. A short, redheaded man-boy whom everyone had originally taken to calling Lucky Charms and now just referred to as Lucky. "Isn't that a little close to the den, Captain?"

"Yes." Lee pointed to it. "I want it close, because as soon as we take out the infected, we're going to go in and see what's inside that den."

The group grumbled, but no one spoke up.

Lee nodded with a small smile. "I know it sounds unnecessary, but from what we saw yesterday, it seems the infected are storing up food there and are very protective of it. I would like to see what's inside."

"Won't the food be tainted?" Wilson looked disgusted at the prospect of eating food from an infected den.

Lee shrugged. "Maybe. Maybe not. Things like canned goods should be fine. Besides, who knows what else they're squirreling away up in there. It's worth a look."

LaRouche nodded. "It might also give us some insight into how the infected work."

Lucky sneered with sarcasm. "What is it, a fuck-ing safari?"

"It's called intelligence," Lee said evenly. "And you're welcome to stand guard outside if you don't want to go in." He tapped the stick across his knee. "Does anyone else have any questions or concerns before we get going?"

Ten people shook their heads and remained silent.

Lee stood up and flexed his stiff ankle. "Then let's get going."

They moved silently along Horner Boulevard, a road that paralleled Steele Street. Their boots, even the ten pairs of them moving in tandem, made only the barest of whispers across the concrete, and their presence inside this small burg created no more stir than a moon-cast shadow sliding between the dark places between buildings.

Lee had never taught them how to move stealthily, whether in the cities or in the woods. By the time they'd joined his team, they had all learned everything there was to know about avoiding detection. The infected had taught them, as had the thieves and the murderers who stalked the roads. Mistakes were paid for in blood and the lives of the ones you loved, so you learned quickly or you paid dearly.

No do-overs.

No second chances.

Though they lacked the overall discipline and knowledge of a military unit, when Lee considered the world around him and the social collapse

they had all survived, and thought of it as a prov-
ing ground with an attrition rate of 90 percent,
it made these select few more qualified to survive
and operate in this world than even the best the
military had to offer.

In these moments of clarity, crouching silently at
the corner of a redbrick building, with an old blue
mailbox to his left and a leathery, skeletal corpse to
his right, when his eyes scanned down these dim
streets and saw the shapeless shadows of his team
moving in a tactical column, Lee felt an immense
pride. Not the pride of the teacher looking at his students, but the privilege of a man who is astonished
at the capabilities of the people he fights alongside.

Lee watched them for a half second longer before turning his gaze south again. These
moments were always fleeting in the midst of his
work, like shapes in a cloud quickly swept away by
the wind. The brief thought was swallowed by the
night once more and he was refocused.

He stood at the corner of Horner Boulevard
and Carthage Street. Ahead, LaRouche was on
point this time and he was on the southern side of
Carthage Street, near the alley that led to the rear
of their target building. He moved to the mouth
of the entrance and put his shoulder to the corner,
leaning out partially to get a view of the dark area
behind the buildings.

Lee watched, his rifle resting on his knees. He
waited for the signal for the rest of them to move
up, but LaRouche seemed to be fixated on something. Impatiently, he wanted to call out to him, but
he knew it would be unwise. You had to trust your

point man. His whole purpose was to feel out the danger, so if he needed an extra minute, he got it.

Lee scanned east and west on Carthage Street, then north and south along Horner Boulevard. Behind him, the others crouched quietly, spaced out along the sidewalk with Wilson taking up the rear and dutifully facing the way they came.

No threats.

Lee turned back to LaRouche and found the sergeant looking at him.

LaRouche held up a hand and signaled them with a wave.

Lee reached behind him and tapped Jim, who was next in line. "Moving," he whispered.

The tap and word was repeated all the way back as Lee stood and quietly made his way across the street to join LaRouche. Once at the corner, LaRouche gave him a palm to signal to slow up a little, then held a finger to his lips. Lee turned and held up a finger to everyone else. They moved to positions along the storefronts, glancing uncomfortably through the shattered windows at the dark interiors of the businesses.

Lee leaned in closer to LaRouche, who had refocused his attention down into the alley. They spoke in soft whispers.

"You got something?"

LaRouche nodded. He switched positions with Lee so that the captain was at the corner and leaning out slightly. He pointed to the end of the alley, where the small parking area terminated in the back of their target building and the steel door they had jimmied the day before.

"You see it?" LaRouche asked. "Leaning up against the door?"

Lee squinted into the darkness.

Something was there, slumped in the shadows. His first impression was of a person, sitting with his back up against the door.

"Fuck," Lee breathed out. "You gotta be kidding me."

"What's it doing outside of the den?"

"Have you seen it move?"

"I think it's asleep."

"Too cold out here for it to be sleeping by itself, exposed."

"You think it's dead?"

He leaned out a little farther from the corner and whispered to LaRouche, "Just get ready to take it out if it starts coming."

"Okay." LaRouche blinked. "What are you...?"

Lee waved one arm around the corner, and then braced for the reaction from the infected.

"Oh, Jesus." LaRouche hunched a bit and tightened the grip on his rifle.

Down inside the alley, the slumped form did not stir.

Lee repeated the wave twice. He garnered no response.

They both watched in silence, holding their breath. Eventually they turned and looked at each other. LaRouche raised his brow in question.

Lee looked back at the still figure. "What I wouldn't do for a bow."

Finding a compound bow or a crossbow had been a frequent topic of conversation, as they had encountered several situations where the ability to make a silent kill would have been nice. Lee had a suppressor, but contrary to popular belief, it did not "silence" the weapon, and would still be loud enough to wake the infected in the nearby den.

The other option was trying to sneak up and smash the skull with Lee's crowbar. Historically, it had been unsuccessful, simply because the damn things were impossible to sneak up on. Like cats, they would perk up and look around at the smallest sound.

"Alright." Lee ducked back in. "Stack up on me. Hold fire unless it starts coming at us."

LaRouche blew out a breath. "You got it, Cap."

The ten stacked up tightly on each other and moved around the corner, hugging the wall to their right. The alley jogged down for about twenty yards, where the wall to their right ended and opened into a paved parking lot with the barest traces of paint still clinging to the concrete, framing the parking stalls that now sat vacant and purposeless.

Lee forced himself to remain hard on the target as he approached.

Whatever or whoever was slouched against that steel door to the apartment building still had yet to move.

He was now within ten yards of it.

In the crisp moonlight, Lee could see it was an older man with wisps of gray hair still holding stubbornly to his liver-spotted scalp. He wore only a set of stained white underwear and one black sock on his left foot. His limbs were sallow, his chest sunken in, with a tuft of white hair poking up from the hollow of it. From its nose to the top of its chest, it was covered in dried blood.

What's it doing out here? What's it doing away from the den?

It definitely wasn't one of the hunters. It was too old and too frail. Lee had seen these old and sick ones in the hordes. Occasionally, he'd seen one of them lying in the street, either dead or dying, or too sick and weak to move. It was disturbing to leave them lying on the ground, for in their last moments, they seemed less insane and aggressive and more like the people they had once been.

Lee motioned for everyone to fan out. The single-file stack split up and LaRouche began moving to the right, while Lee remained stationary, covering the infected at the door. When they had the thing effectively surrounded, Lee glanced to his right and found the man next to him was Jake. Gone was his joker's expression and twinkling eyes. Now his lips were pursed in concentration, his brow wrinkled up into a fierce glare of intensity.

"Relax," Lee said very quietly.

Jake nodded once.

"Move up with me." Lee let his rifle sink down to his chest and quietly withdrew his KA-BAR from its sheath on his vest. "Stay hard on him, but don't fire unless I tell you to. Okay?"

"Okay."

Lee stepped forward, and Jake moved with him, close enough for their shoulders to brush. Lee held his knife overhanded and flexed his fingers on the grip, squeezing in as tightly as he could go. If the old infected made a move for them, Lee would lunge forward, seize him by the throat, jerk him back, and plant the knife wherever he could get it into the brain—either through the temple, the palate, or the base of the skull.

It can't make a sound, Lee told himself. *Not a sound.*

SIXTEEN

GOING UP

STANDING BEFORE THE INFECTED, Lee tensed and drew back his hand, ready to strike out. Jake stood directly beside him, and to either side the others trained their rifles on the form and held their breath.

"He's not breathing," Jake mumbled.

Lee stared at the man, at the bib of crusted blood around his neck and chest. Dark, almost black-stained skin. The blood was not smeared, as though the old man had been feeding, but instead was caked as though it had poured from his own nose and mouth. Now standing closer to him, Lee could see the malformation of his head, caused by the explosive compression and decompression of a high-powered bullet.

Lee bent down to look closer. "He's been shot in the head..."

A thunderclap obliterated the silence.

The sound was so sudden and overwhelming that Lee felt every muscle in his body jerk simultaneously like he'd stuck his finger in a light socket. Strangely, nonsensically, he thought that the body of the old man had been booby-trapped and it had exploded. But it still sat before him, crumpled and motionless against the door.

He looked up at Jake to see what the noise had been.

The younger man leaned over, one hand on his knee and the other steadying himself against the wall. He looked right at Lee, dumbfounded, confused, terrified.

Then he coughed, and blood spewed out.

Lee watched a thick gobbet of red as it flew through the air. It seemed slow and lazy as it arced its way down to the ground. He could hear the sharp intake of his teammates' breath, the shuffling of feet, the movement of fabric. He could feel his gut tightening, forcing the words out of his mouth.

"Get inside!" Lee shouted.

The sensation of time warp dissipated.

He reached up and snatched a handful of Jake's sleeve as the kid's knees buckled and his body sank against the wall.

LaRouche began to fire his weapon rapidly. The sound of his rifle was like an explosion that set off an avalanche. Lee was suddenly surrounded by a ring of fire and noise as everyone opened up, the muzzle flashes like tongues of flame licking out into the darkness, everyone aiming for the rooftops.

Lee pulled roughly at Jake's arm, forcing him to flop onto his back. His eyes were wide and pale, the blood like tar around his mouth. His chest rose and fell, and Lee could see the gaping wound in the glitter of the muzzle flashes, like dozens of cameras going off. He jammed both of his hands under the kid, the concrete rasping away the skin of his knuckles, and hooked his fingers into Jake's armpits. He jerked the kid partially upright.

"Open the door!" Lee screamed behind him. "Open the fucking door!"

Someone—Lee couldn't tell who it was—stepped around and kicked the dead body out of the way of the door, and then yanked it open. Lee didn't wait for an invitation. He immediately began backpedaling, trying to maintain his grip on Jake, but the guy had begun to squirm around and claw at his chest. In the back of his mind, Lee registered the sound of Jake's breathing—ragged, gurgling, wheezing.

The sound of air passing by a wet valve.

Lee hauled himself into the doorway, pulling with everything he had. The stench of the rotting corpse enveloped him again like a soggy, putrid blanket. He pulled Jake just inside the door and then collapsed with one giant last effort that landed them both on the ground.

Lee twisted up and onto his knees and leaned over the wounded form beside him. The sheer surprise of the moment was giving way to the pain, and Jake's body was beginning to shake, his throat finding the ragged threads of a voice and issuing those horrible noises of the wounded.

Lee ripped open Jake's parka, exposing the hooded sweatshirt beneath. All of it was drenched in blood. Quickly, he traced his fingers over the glistening red fabric and found the hole and the torn flesh under it. The wound was on the right side of Jake's chest, maybe three inches from his sternum. If the bullet hadn't clipped the heart, it had come damn close. It was welling up, deep and fast. Too fast to just be capillaries. Lee pressed his palm to the open wound and bore down on it with all of his weight.

Jake cried out and his eyes went wide.

Lee looked up. "Julia! I need some help here!"

Outside the door, the rifle fire slowed. LaRouche held the door open with his foot and screamed at the others to get inside as he took evenly spaced shots, putting suppressive fire down on something, though Lee wasn't sure what it was.

"Get in! Get in!" LaRouche shouted.

The members of the team tumbled through the door, tripping over themselves to get inside. Were they still taking fire? Lee couldn't hear over the sound of LaRouche's shots, but he didn't think so. There had only been one shot.

Lee kept watching the faces come through the door, looking for Julia but not finding her. His stomach suddenly dropped inside of his body cavity, and for a brief moment he forgot that his hands were pressed tightly against the warm, wet flesh of Jake's chest wound.

"Where the fuck is Julia?" he barked, trading fear for anger.

LaRouche lowered his weapon and looked at someone who was still outside the door. "Julia! Get the fuck inside!" He reached out and grabbed her, pulling her into the doorframe and then shoving her inside. He followed quickly, letting the door close behind them.

It had seemed dark in the predawn light, but

with the door closed to the outside world, the blackness inside the apartment building was absolute. It was only the sound of footsteps, heavy breathing, and Jake's tortured groans.

In the palm of his hand, Lee could feel the pulse, rapid and still strong, but he could also feel the blood seeping through his fingers, warm and steady. It pushed through his fingers with the insistent rhythm of Jake's heart.

Arterial bleeding...

Lee pulled his right hand away and began searching his tactical vest for the flashlight he kept clipped there. Underneath his other hand, he could feel Jake writhing and his groans were beginning to become screams. He found the flashlight and clicked it on. The tiny spear of light suddenly illuminated Jake's face and his eyes were shut tight, his teeth clenched and red.

"Hey, buddy." Lee tried to sound calm. "I need you to hang on. This is gonna hurt like a motherfucker." He pulled his other hand off the wound and probed it with two fingers. "You ready?"

"No!" Jake gasped. "Don't hurt me!"

"Just hang on..." Lee gritted his teeth and pushed his fingers into the wound.

The breath caught in Jake's throat. He jerked away from the touch, and Lee could feel the muscles in Jake's chest contract around his two fingers. The breath came out of him in a shriek.

"Hold on!" Lee shouted over the cries and tried to concentrate. He could feel the blood squishing past his fingers. He just had to find where it was coming from. He had to find it and clamp it off.

Three other flashlights came on, bathing everyone in harsh white light that blanched their features into pale, haggard masks.

Julia appeared, kneeling down at Jake's other side and ripping open her medical pack. She pulled out a pair of shears and went to work on the hooded sweatshirt. "Gimme some light!" she ordered. "On the wound!"

The flashlights all shifted to focus on Jake's chest, the different angles casting the shadows of Lee's hands off in separate directions. "He's got a clipped artery, I think." Lee looked at Julia. "Maybe a collapsed lung."

She nodded quickly, hair flying in her face as she delved into her pack.

"Hey, Cap!" LaRouche hollered. "We gotta move it upstairs! There's no way the infected didn't hear that shit!"

Lee looked at Julia again to see what she thought. She had one hand touching Jake's femoral artery and the other on his carotid. After a brief moment of concentration, she made eye contact with Lee and shook her head quickly.

"BP's already too low." As she spoke, she began riffling through the contents of her pack, withdrawing sterile dressings, hemostats, scalpels, and some sterile-packaged items that Lee didn't know the name of. "He's bleeding out too fast. We gotta stabilize it right now, or we're gonna lose him."

"OH JESUS!" Jake suddenly screamed. *"FUCK!"* He tried to say something else but dissolved into a coughing fit. He thrashed around as he coughed and swatted at Lee's fingers, still inside the wound.

"Jim!" Lee called out. "Hold him down!" He could feel the pressure of the bloodstream on the tip of his finger. "I almost got it...Almost got it..."

Julia held out a pair of hemostats. "When you find it, clamp it."

Jake's breathing became rapid and shallow.

"He's hyperventilating," Julia said with a note of detachment. "Try to breathe deep, hon. Slow, deep breaths."

Jim knelt down at Jake's head and took both of the kid's hands in his. "That's it, Jake. You're doing great. Slow down your breathing for me, okay? Slow it down. All the way in, all the way out."

Jake gaped up at Jim, tears streaming down his face. "It hurts...It really hurts."

"I know, buddy," Jim said soothingly. "You gotta hang on for just a little longer, okay?"

"Okay."

"I think I got it," Lee said. He closed his eyes. In the slick moving parts of Jake's chest cavity, the blood spewing from that artery was pressing at his fingers, but the pulse was growing weaker by the second. Lee realized that he was kneeling in a puddle of Jake's blood. He pushed deeper.

A faint cry and a groan. Jake was close to passing out.

"Cap!" LaRouche's voice sounded out. "I've got contact!"

Lee's eyes snapped open and he looked up. LaRouche was leaning partially out of the door, the barrel of his rifle nosed out of the crack. "You gotta give me some time!"

"Fuck!" LaRouche's stance tightened up. "I got five infected comin' around the corner..."

There. The firm, fleshy tube of a large artery.

"I got it!" He grabbed the hemostat from Julia's fingers. "Everyone get ready to grab Jake and haul ass up these stairs!" Lee put his flashlight in his mouth and tasted the sharp coppery tang of Jake's blood.

"We gotta move!" LaRouche bellowed and started pulling the trigger.

The confined space shook as the rounds blasted out.

Lee hooked his finger around the throbbing artery and fed the tip of the hemostat down along his index finger until he could feel its tiny jaws around the blood vessel, and then he clamped it down. If he'd been in a hospital or any other setting, he would have checked to see if he'd stopped the bleeding, but they just didn't have the time.

He pulled his fingers out of the wound, leaving the hemostat dangling out, trembling with each of Jake's hitching breaths. "It's clamped! Go!"

Hands shot forward in a flash, seizing Jake's arms and legs, and they bore him up so quickly that it seemed to Lee that Jake simply disappeared from beneath him. By the time Lee grabbed his rifle from where it lay in the coagulating red pool, they'd already hauled him up the first section of stairs, Julia following beside with a rifle in one hand and her medical pack in the other, shouting at them not to knock the hemostat loose.

The clatter of a magazine across the floor.

"Reloading!" LaRouche called.

Lee surged toward the door as LaRouche slammed a fresh magazine into his rifle. He shouldered past him and pulled the door shut. Immediately the door lurched under his grasp, a live thing trying to get away from him. Angry fists pounded the other side, nails scratching in panicked desperation at the door. The infected on the other side made short, sharp barking calls, excited, signaling to the others that they had found live prey.

"Get the crowbar out of my pack!"

LaRouche looked around blindly for a moment. With the rest of the team retreating up the stairs, they were taking their flashlights with them and the room was falling into darkness again. Then, at the base of the stairs, another light appeared and it was Jim holding it.

"What are you doing?" Jim yelled at them.

"We're gonna block the door," LaRouche shouted back with a little anger. "Gimme some light here!"

Something hard hit the door and it jerked outward so hard that it almost pulled Lee off his feet. The door cleared the jamb for a second and through that tiny crack, Lee saw a flash of what waited on the other side. Dozens of faces with wide eyes and bloody maws leered in at him and pressed themselves forward. Behind them, he could see the corner of the building that led to the alleyway, and more of them were coming around the corner.

He heaved and managed to close the door again. "Hurry the fuck up!"

"Got it..." LaRouche yanked the crowbar out of the pack and rushed to Lee's side with it. He worked it around Lee's white-knuckled hands and into the door handle, then jammed it all the way through. "Move!"

Lee didn't wait to see if the barricade would hold. He spun on the balls of his feet and sprinted for the stairs, scooping up his pack as he ran. Ahead of him, Jim stood at the base of the stairs waving them on, his rifle held at a low-ready. Lee shoved him as he ran by, encouraging him to follow them as he and LaRouche pounded up the stairs two at a time.

Behind them, the door rattled violently. Lee's legs felt frail and wobbly, his muscles soft, and his blood diluted and watery. He couldn't take the stairs fast enough, had only cleared the first landing…

The sound of metal clanking on the ground.

The door burst open.

Screeches and roars and the tumble of bare feet.

It was over. They wouldn't be able to outrun them, so now they had to fight. He dipped his head into the loop of his rifle's sling, letting it hang on his neck like a gigantic pendant, and then slung into his pack—it contained everything, including his GPS, and he could not leave it behind. Then he turned and looked down the stairs as the first of the mad creatures came scurrying around the corner, one filthy set of claws clutching the banister and the other reaching for him, its mouth agape.

A well-placed double tap sent the thing sprawling backward into its den mates, where it fell to the stairs and was trampled under their feet.

As Lee swung his muzzle toward the next and nearest target, he began backpedaling up the stairs.

He moved his feet blindly, feeling the edge of the step with his toes and then launching himself backward until he pulled his foot behind him and it caught.

He felt his balance leave him.

Only a few steps down from him, an infected loped toward him on all fours, its mouth spread grotesquely wide, its tongue hanging out.

Lee fell backward, clinging to his rifle.

This was it.

But then he felt a hand grab the drag strap of his tactical vest and he felt himself get a little lighter. Someone had ahold of him and they were dragging him backward up the stairwell. In his right peripheral he could see the muzzle of an M4 resting against his shoulder. It blossomed a white-hot rose of fire, and Lee felt the heat on his face, but he didn't hear the noise, didn't seem to hear anything outside of his own huffing breath and rushing blood.

The face of the infected on all fours seemed to suddenly flatten in on itself, as though it had run headlong into an invisible wall. It fell instantly, spread-eagle upon the steps.

Lee shouldered his rifle again.

Targets popped up.

Flashing thunder knocked them down.

Just like the reactive steel targets in basic.

Reload.

Keep shooting.

Keep backpedaling.

Reality seemed warped. In the strange darkness of the stairwell, lit by the strobing of his muzzle flashes, each section of stairs looked the same as the last, with dark, hollow eyes and snarling teeth below him. His legs burned as he thrust himself up each riser, and he could not remember how many flights of stairs he had ascended.

It seemed without end.

He reloaded his rifle for a third time, and when he brought the muzzle up and slapped the slide release, feeling the bolt clunk forward, chambering that next round, there was nothing below him to target. The stairs were a hollow well beneath his feet that hung heavily with swirling clouds of cordite.

"Did we get 'em all?" Jim's voice wavered breathlessly.

"I dunno." Lee turned. "Keep going."

From the dimness below them, crawling up the bloody flight of stairs, a wounded infected appeared, gibbering as it clawed past the bodies of its den mates, the concept of its impending death lost behind the urging of its own bloodlust. Its dark eyes fixed them with a blank stare, devoid of emotion, and it reached for them, eyes dark and alien.

"I shot that thing in the head!" Jim said shakily. "How's it...?"

Lee put two in its chest and it collapsed backward.

"Why didn't it die?" Jim demanded, his voice on the edge of panic.

"Just go!" Lee shouted and hauled himself up the last flight.

As they reached the top of the stairs and stumbled into the muted light of dawn, Lee could no longer hear the thing clinging to life. On the rooftop, they found the other members of the team huddled in the center of the roof. Julia was bent over Jake, working feverishly at starting an IV. The others crowded around her, and among their bodies, Lee caught glimpses of Jake. His mouth was open and his eyes stared vacantly at Julia. The only evidence that he was still alive was the rapid rise and fall of his chest.

No one watched the stairwell door that he and LaRouche and Jim had just emerged from. They were all watching Jake and mumbling encouragement to him, leaving their backs exposed.

"Hey!" Lee barked. "Someone gonna watch the fucking stairs?"

Wilson popped up at the sound of Lee's voice and shouldered his rifle. "I got it, Cap."

Lee strode quickly to Julia's side and knelt down beside her. Jake's eyes tracked him, still glassy and out of it. "How's he looking?"

Julia's lips were set in a thin line, her jaw clenched, red smears across her face and neck. "He needs blood. I don't have the equipment to do a transfusion, and I don't have time to test everyone's blood types." She swabbed the inside of Jake's elbow and then looked up at Lee. "We need to get him to Smithfield, and fast."

"Okay." Lee nodded, but he had no idea how possible that would be. "Gimme a minute."

Lee stood up, caught LaRouche's eye, and motioned him over. They kept low, below the line of sight from any rooftops around them.

"Cap?"

"What do you think?"

"That was a high-caliber rifle, and close." LaRouche glanced out beyond the edges of the roof. "I didn't see a muzzle flash, but I'd think he was on top of one of these adjacent buildings." He looked at Lee. "Who do you think it was?"

"I have no fucking idea," Lee growled. "Some asshole, trigger-happy scavenger."

"Let's check it out." LaRouche nodded toward the edge of the roof.

They moved toward the edge, hunching lower as they went toward the abutment until they were duckwalking. Without prearranging it, they separated so they were about ten yards apart.

Lee put his shoulder to the abutment and looked at LaRouche. "On three."

"Okay."

He counted with his fingers, *one, two, three,* and they both popped up and looked out over the nearby rooftops. In the brief moment they were exposed, they searched for movement, for anything that seemed unnatural, for the glint of gunmetal or the flash of a scope lens. When they ducked back into cover, they looked at each other and shook their heads.

"Nothing," LaRouche said.

"I got nothing," Lee confirmed. "One more time, a little slower."

Again they counted down, and on three they both stood up partially and looked out over the small-town rooftops laid out around them, but they could find no evidence of the sniper. Lee had to agree with LaRouche's assessment. That had been a high-powered rifle round, and it had come from someplace very close to them. And yet there was no one on the roofs. None of the nearby buildings had facing windows from which a sniper could have made the shot.

LaRouche swore. "He must've bugged out already."

Hit-and-run tactics? Lee thought.

"What about the infected?"

Lee leaned farther over the edge. There was no movement in the alley below him, and when he switched to overlook the street, there was none there either.

"Should be about fifty, right?" Lee asked.

"Yeah."

He turned and looked at the kid in the center of the roof, lying on his back and barely there anymore. "Jake needs to get to Smithfield ASAP. We'll clear the stairwell and do a headcount on the way, see how many we took down. That'll give us an idea of how many are left."

"Okay." LaRouche looked pained. "We're not pulling out, are we?"

Lee stared at the den. "No. We need to get in there." He jogged over to Wilson and tapped him on the shoulder. "Wilson, I need you and your team to come with me."

Wilson nodded firmly. "Will do, Cap."

Lee moved back into the stairwell and Jim followed, LaRouche remaining behind with Julia and Jake.

SEVENTEEN

THE DEN

LEE CLICKED ON HIS gun light, illuminating the darkness. His knees felt rubbery and fatigued as he made his way down. On level five he found the last infected Jim had claimed to have shot in the head. He and Jim leaned over the body and inspected it. The lifeless eyes stared at them, wide and lemur-like. A jagged groove ran from the top of the infected's forehead, all the way back to its crown.

"Is that where I shot him?" Jim asked.

Lee nodded. "Sometimes the round skips off the skull. I've seen it happen before."

They continued on down the stairwell and Lee started counting heads. As he went down, the bodies got thicker and he hesitantly stepped among them, certain that at any moment one of them would explode up and latch its filthy jaws into his jugular. On level two, the stairwell was so choked with bodies that Lee had to walk over them, their soft flesh and blood squirming under his boots as he put his weight on them. Here, the walls were spackled with red dots and white chunks of brain and bone. Bullet holes marred the wall like a hidden picture could be revealed if all those dots were connected.

At the bottom, he stopped and looked around.

"Forty-two," he said aloud.

They moved to the door, which had closed on its own. Lee pushed it open partially and took a quick sweep outside, finding only three more infected bodies and no snipers on the rooftops sighting in on him. He stepped out and held the door, motioning Wilson and his three teammates to pass through.

He grabbed Wilson and looked him in the eye. "Be quick, but don't be stupid."

Wilson nodded curtly. "We'll be back in a second."

Lee and Jim made their way back up the stairs, having to stop on level three to give Jim's legs a rest. Lee didn't push it. To be honest, his legs felt fatigued as well.

At the rooftop again, he found LaRouche kneeling near Julia and Jake. The sky above them was gray and purple like a contused body. Lee called him over, away from Julia and her patient. The three men huddled together, but their eyes lingered on their wounded comrade. They knelt about fifteen feet away and eventually they dragged their attention back.

"Is he gonna make it?" Jim asked.

LaRouche looked away. "Julia says it's pretty bad. The artery can be closed to keep him from losing blood pressure, but there are complications that go along with sealing a major blood vessel. It sounds like the bullet might have collapsed his lung too. She won't know until they open him up."

They all knew what that meant.

They'd found a medical professional to replace Doc, but Dr. Hamilton was a general practitioner, not a surgeon. The equipment was there at Johnston Memorial Hospital in Smithfield, but the experience and the knowledge were not. He did the best he could, but often it was not enough.

"Damn." LaRouche shook his head.

Lee couldn't disagree. "Let's try to stay focused here." He pointed back toward the stairwell. "I got forty-five dead bodies, and we estimated fifty yesterday."

"We didn't count to the man," LaRouche pointed out.

"I know." Lee sniffed at his nose, which was beginning to run in the cold. "So, worst-case scenario, there are some still inside the den, but I don't think that's likely. I've never seen the hordes separate into groups. They're all or nothing."

LaRouche cleared his throat. "We keep putting these rules on them, Cap. Like they've got Rules of Engagement, but they don't. They're just wild fucking animals. They're unpredictable. The truth is, we don't know what those bastards are gonna do next."

Lee rubbed his forehead. "I'm just judging from past behaviors. Look, I know going in there doesn't sound very pleasant. But if there's something we can find out by doing it, I don't want to pass it by because we were afraid to get our hands dirty."

LaRouche sighed. "Yeah, I know. I'm with you."

The sound of a diesel engine rumbling below them drew their attention.

Lee stepped to the edge of the roof, first taking a glance at the rooftops around them, and then looking over at the big green vehicle below. Wilson leaned out of the front passenger's seat and looked up. Lee gave the younger man a thumbs-up and then turned to the others on the roof with him.

"They're ready. Let's get Jake down there."

LaRouche and Jim each took an arm and Lee took the legs. Julia followed behind, holding the IV above the wounded man. Jake was in and out of consciousness as they moved him and he made thin, high-pitched mewling sounds at random intervals as he became more wakeful. Then shock would take him over again and his body would sag heavily in his comrades' arms.

Lee made eye contact with Julia.

He could see the detachment in her gaze. Jake was no longer a friend; he was a patient, and a patient was nothing more than a broken machine that needed to be fixed.

Lee had seen her like this before. There'd been another member of their team, Rob Kiker, a middle-aged guy from Jim's congregation. A firefighter with some basic recreational-weapons knowledge. They'd gotten in a scuffle with a pair of unknown scavengers just outside of Camp Ryder, and he'd been stabbed twice in the chest with a pocketknife.

He'd been one of those guys that was everyone's friend. No one had a bad thing to say about him. And when he was lying on the concrete among some overgrown weeds pushing up through the cracks, bleeding out into a growing pool, Julia had been there with this same blank, emotionless expression on her face. She never said his name

once when she was working on him. She kept
referring to him as "patient."

"Patient's BP is dropping pretty low" and "I
think the patient's aorta got nicked."

And in that moment, Lee resented her. He
resented that she refused to call him Rob and that
she'd never cried a tear for him and probably would
never cry a tear for Jake, and yet she grew sick and
pale and she trembled at the thought of the system-
atic killing of these creatures, the same ones who
hunted them, who killed them, who fed on them.

They deserved her emotion, but not Rob? Not
Jake?

Lee looked away from her, feeling his expression
beginning to reveal his thoughts.

They loaded Jake into the back of the Humvee
as quickly and as gently as they could, and Julia
climbed in the back with him, the IV pack nearly
empty already. Lee shut the back hatch of the
vehicle and slapped it twice. Without any further
acknowledgement, the Humvee took off, bearing
Jake toward Smithfield.

In the settling dust, the three men moved out.

They emerged from the blue shadows between
the buildings and discovered that the sun had cau-
terized the bruised sky and now sat on the horizon, that kind of white-hot that was too bright to
look at but gave off no heat. At the mouth of the
alley, Lee stood as point and he looked right and
then left, studying the street in both directions.
When he felt it was safe, he moved on.

They crossed Wicker Street and stood at the
south side of the intersection, looking across Steele

Street at the entrance to the den. It was strange to stand there with the wind blowing at their backs and bearing with it that silent and empty sound, like a missed note from a woodwind instrument that is held indefinitely. It was the call of vast and lonely places, and it settled into these ghost towns like a thin layer of dust, coating everything. It was not the complete absence of sound, but instead the presence of sounds you are unaccustomed to hearing because they are normally drowned out by the busy noise of human existence.

Here in this abandoned city, it was the creaking of the stoplights hanging from their hinges, the skitter of dried leaves and trash along the concrete, the steady trickling noise of water moving beneath them in the sewers. It is these noises that make you so acutely aware that there are no other people around.

"You smell that?" Jim said quietly.

Lee sniffed. It was faint, but it was there.

"Might be some more in there," Jim observed.

"It's where they sleep. It's bound to smell like them." Lee curled his nose. "Come on, let's get this over with."

He crossed Steele Street and found himself facing the tan brick wall. Only a few inches of masonry were between him and whatever was inside. He found himself pulling away from the wall, as though the building that contained these creatures' den was itself alive and predatory, its entrance just another hungry mouth waiting to consume them.

A bank of three windows above them, the glass that used to be in their frames now littering the sidewalk under their feet. He listened but did not hear anything coming from inside.

A blue mailbox on the corner.

A NO PARKING sign, bent almost in half.

Two trees, one on each side of the corner.

Lee pushed up to the turn and glanced around. The stench there in the alcove of the building's entrance was enough to make him curl his nose and take short breaths. "All right...slow and deliberate. Take your time. Make sure you check everything."

The front door was open.

Lee faced it straight-on and clicked on his gun light. It gave him a direct view down a hallway with white walls. He approached, angling first to the right, and then to the left of the door to see what was on either side.

Trash.

Empty cans of food.

Dark piles of excrement.

He moved through the door. The hallway extended down about forty feet and terminated at a pair of double doors. Lee could see that the doors were open but the inside was dark, and the angle of the doors only allowed tiny slivers of his light to punch through. On either side of the hall, there were doors. Two to the right and two to the left.

"I'll hold the hall," Lee whispered. "You two clear the rooms."

"Moving," LaRouche acknowledged.

The two men slipped behind Lee and into the first room, moving at a steady pace, smoothly taking the corners of the room and clearing it quickly of threats. It was empty. Just more of the same refuse as in the hallway. While they cleared, Lee remained in the hall, his rifle snug in his shoulder, and he scanned, taking each door and trying to see farther into that big room past the double doors, but failing.

"Clear."

"Clear."

"Behind you." LaRouche touched Lee's shoulder as he crossed the hall to the next room.

Their flashlights played across the walls in glowing phantasms.

Lee found himself fixated on the room at the end.

With each breath he took in, smelling dank and ripe with all the odors of these filthy animals, his grip squeezed tighter on his rifle, his cheek pressed harder against the buttstock, the little red dot of his scope burned hotter in the abysmal darkness at the end of the hall.

"Clear."

"Clear."

"Moving."

Lee stepped closer to the door. It was a deep black square in the center of his gun light's bright halo. Movement inside? Something pale and slick flitted across that tiny shaft of light that the double doors allowed in. A trick of the light, perhaps.

"Clear."

"Clear."

"Moving."

Another few paces forward.

Now Lee faced the door, only about ten feet

from it. His angle was still poor to see inside and he considered adjusting, but then again, if he could see them, they could see him.

If there were anything there at all.

"Clear."

"Clear."

"All clear, Cap."

"There's something in that room straight ahead. I think I saw it move." He didn't take his eyes off the door as he spoke. "You still got your frags in your vest, LaRouche?"

"Yeah."

"We're gonna frag and clear. Two frags—one from me, one from you. Jim, you're gonna pull hard cover on that door until we slip those frags in, then hug the wall so you don't get hit with shrapnel."

"Okay." Jim's voice was tight.

"Go ahead and cover us." Lee waited until he could see the ring of light created by Jim's gun light, squared up on the door. Then he lowered his rifle and plucked a fragmentation grenade from a pouch on his vest and moved closer to the door, hunching down as he went. LaRouche moved alongside him. Lee took the right-hand side of the door, and LaRouche took the left.

The base of the doorway was cluttered not only with trash but with rotting, discarded carcasses that appeared mostly consumed. Cats, dogs, rats, a rib cage from something larger that Lee couldn't identify.

From inside, something muttered and drew a harsh breath.

Lee looked up at LaRouche. In the illumination of Jim's gun light, half of LaRouche's face was plunged into deep shadow and he looked otherworldly. They both held up the green spheres in their hands and pulled the soft metal pins. Lee held up one finger, then two, then three, and then the two men leaned forward and chucked the fragmentation grenades into the room.

There was a hiss of alarm.

The sound of both heavy objects striking the floor, the spoons flying off and clattering across the floor.

Lee turned away from the doorway and pushed himself up against the wall, one ear shoved tightly against his shoulder, the other plugged with the fingers of his left hand, while his right took the grip of his rifle and prepared to start firing.

It seemed to take forever for the grenades to go off.

In Lee's mind, he was sure that before they could go off, the infected would exit the room and tear them to pieces.

He knelt there, huddled against the wall, and looked down between his legs. A feline corpse smiled up at him with one cloudy eye, its skin drawn back and displaying its full set of teeth. Such a small thing, with so many sharp teeth. What was mankind's obsession with domesticating predatory creatures?

He felt the shock waves punch him through the wall, one after the other, hammering his chest and jarring him to the bone. A billow of smoke loomed in the entrance, both doors blown open wide. He could hear a sound like hail on a tin roof, but it was debris and dust and chunks of plaster skittering across the tile floors of the hallway.

Lee hauled himself up and stabbed the button of his gun light.

When the light came on, the cloud of dust and smoke rolled over them, and it was like high beams in a thick fog, blinding them. He turned in the general direction of where he thought the door was and began moving forward. Through the smoke, he could see the glowing cone of LaRouche's gun light moving swiftly through the open doors.

LaRouche was yelling. "Get on the ground! Get on the ground!"

Old habits...

Lee cleared the doorframe and the room began to materialize in the smoke, as though it were being born of the smoke itself, and the particles floating through the air were converging in the room to form the long conference table that had been shoved to one side, the office chairs piled atop it.

And bodies.

There were bodies in the room.

Not carcasses that had been fed upon, but the bodies of infected they had just killed. Lee wanted to look down at them but he passed them by, chasing that cone of light from LaRouche that was beginning to fade into a crisp silhouette. Still, as he stepped over the bodies, his subconscious registered something important, even if his conscious mind was ignoring it.

"Did we get 'em all?" LaRouche shouted.

"Keep checking," Lee called back.

He found the corner of the room he'd been seeking, and it was unoccupied by anything alive. He turned and looked out into the room, his light now able to push clear through the smoke and darkness and see the far wall. He registered the mounds of flesh in the center of the room—perhaps five or six of them. Their limbs were tangled together, and some of those limbs were detached from the bodies they belonged to, blown off in the blast.

Look at them . . . Look at them . . .

But he looked past them, and he could see LaRouche, still moving deeper into the long room. The shadow of his body and his cone of light kept retreating, getting smaller, and it gave Lee the false sensation that this room was not a conference room at all but some massive underground cave that just kept on going.

Look at the bodies!

Lee forced his eyes down into the bloody mess before him.

Pale, thin limbs. They seemed small and childlike. The flesh on these seemed softer somehow than the other infected he'd noticed, like there was more fat on them, as though they had not been starved as extensively as the others. Long tangles of hair, matted and dreadlocked in places. All of the infected had somewhat overgrown hair, but the hair on these was longer than normal. Some of their faces were contorted, as though they were enraged by what had happened to them. Others stared serenely at the ceiling.

"Oh my God . . ."

Lee took a step forward and blazed his light down onto the one closest to him. Splayed out in a twisted position, legs spread in different directions, one arm trapped beneath the body, the other reaching out as though clawing its way across the floor. Fair skin and blond hair, sullied by clumps of dried gore and filth. Fresh, bright-red blood flowed from the nose and ears, over its blank face and down in bright red ribbons across the mounds of breasts.

"LaRouche!" Lee said, but his voice was quiet, either truly without volume or lost under the roaring sound in his ears, like shouting into a hurricane.

"Captain?"

Lee moved his gun light to illuminate another body.

"Captain?"

He looked up to find LaRouche standing there on the other side of the bodies, shining his light onto them. It seemed that they had died, clinging to each other in terror.

Lee's voice was a croak. "It's the females. They're all here. Why were they keeping them here? I don't...I don't get it."

"Look at them," LaRouche said with an empty voice.

But Lee had not taken his eyes off of them. There were more than he'd thought at first—probably about ten, though it was difficult to tell in such a pile of arms and legs. They were so tightly packed together...

"Look at them," LaRouche repeated.

"I'm looking at them..."

"No." LaRouche leaned over and pointed, very deliberately, very slowly. "You see that?"

In the wreck of flesh before him, among the obliterated remains jumbled together like the rest of the garbage strewn across the floors, under all that red-painted skin, he hadn't noticed it. He saw the first one and felt immediately sickened. The roaring in his ears was the rush of a million pointless thoughts. And when he looked to the next female, lying dead and dismembered on the floor, he saw that it was the same with her, and with all of the others.

He could barely find his voice. "They're all pregnant."

EIGHTEEN

A SIMPLE EQUATION

LEE'S STOMACH DID SOMERSAULTS around his other organs. His brain went to work, interpreting and extrapolating what he was learning with what he already knew and trying to shove the images that his eyes were generating into place along with all the other things he knew, like unwieldy pieces of a jigsaw puzzle with a picture that made no sense.

Some of them were close to giving birth, the skin of their bellies stretched tight.

Some of the other females were not far along at all, and just beginning to show.

Could they have mated even after they were infected?

Why wouldn't *they reproduce?*

How stupid had he been to believe that those instincts for survival were relegated only to the hunt for food? Their instincts clearly went further than that. The males in these hordes, they still looked emaciated, despite all the food they were scavenging, because they were gathering it for the pregnant females and eating only what their bodies needed to survive. Ancient instincts of the hunter-gatherer, buried under millennia of civilization, and now resurrected before their eyes.

Each conclusion only carried with it another question, and each question required greater understanding than he had. They spun around in his head like debris caught in a tornado.

Lee suddenly wanted to take a seat. He wanted to be in his Humvee, surrounded by the familiar things, the smell of diesel fumes and grease and metal, the smell of gun oil and cordite, of the musty bedroll he slept on every night. Instead, he took in a deep breath of the rank air and tried to ignore his churning stomach.

Compartmentalize. Make the problem small.
First, let's get the fuck out of this room.

Lee turned toward the door and took one step before the room flashed and jumped.

He spun, his mouth and eyes wide open, swinging his rifle up, and found LaRouche standing over the dead females with a cold, blank look in his eyes. His rifle was pointed down at one of the females, and a tiny hole had appeared in the center of her bulging stomach. No blood came out of it— her heart was no longer pumping.

"Are you okay? Was she still alive?" Lee took a step forward. "Did she try to bite you?"

LaRouche didn't respond, didn't look at him. He stepped over the body he had just put a bullet into and pointed his rifle at another, aiming for the belly. He pulled the trigger and shot her too.

"Jesus!" Lee shouted. "What the hell are you doing?"

LaRouche stepped over to another one. "I'm

killing those fucking things before they can crawl out." He pulled the trigger again.

"Stop!" Lee took a step toward the man, though he wasn't quite sure what he was going to do if LaRouche didn't obey. Was he going to fight LaRouche over it? Over dead infected? Over the very same thing he argued with Professor White about?

LaRouche turned and sighted down the barrel at another target.

Lee grabbed the foregrip of the rifle and jerked it up. He didn't know why. His heart was slamming in his chest. For the first time in a very long time, Lee didn't know where his head was. But he pulled that rifle in close so that the two men were face-to-face, and LaRouche gave no more reaction to being stopped than he'd had to shooting the dead bodies.

Lee shook his head, looking into the sergeant's vacant eyes.

"Stop." His voice trembled. "Just...stop."

"Okay." LaRouche blinked, but the look of emptiness did not leave him.

"You guys..." Jim's voice cut through the room like a rope to drowning men. Something tangible to hold on to. They turned and watched the ex-priest as he stood in the doorway, his rifle hanging from its sling, both his hands clutching his temples. "Oh my God."

Lee took LaRouche firmly by the shoulders and pulled him away from the corpses on the floor. They stepped over the arms and legs of these lost females, sequestered away, protected in this god-forsaken hovel from the dangers outside.

Lee pointed the other two men toward the exit. "Let's go."

Outside, the cold breeze scoured the stench from their clothes and the three men stood in the street for a moment, just breathing fresh air. Lee was the first to snap out of his daze, and he chastised himself for letting the shock of the moment set him off balance. All of the survivors had their perceptions about how the great and highly trained Captain Harden should act, and to be truthful, he held some of these perceptions himself.

But sometimes the moment just got the better of you.

"We need to get out of the open," he said over his shoulder.

They crossed the street at a jog, and Lee decided to just keep going. They needed to get to the Humvee anyway and get in contact with Wilson's group and Camp Ryder. Jim and LaRouche didn't ask any questions, and Lee didn't give them any explanations. He just kept heading north, away from the den, and they followed him.

The Humvee with the dozer attachment was still sitting where they'd left it. Jim climbed in the driver's seat, LaRouche in the back, and Lee in the front passenger's seat. They shut the doors and the heat from their bodies and breath began to fog the windows.

Lee picked up the handset to the radio, but then set it back down again. His fingers lingered on it as he spoke. "We can't tell anyone about what happened in the den."

Silence.

Then Jim said, "Uh, Captain...I think..."

Lee turned to face him. "People have a hard enough time accepting the traps. You think they're gonna go along with blowing up a dozen pregnant women?"

"Infected," LaRouche spat.

"Do you not see the fucking difference? Jerry and Professor White are gonna use this to sway everyone's opinion. It's gonna fuel the fires and burn us, I guarantee it. I know we feel like we should report everything back, but this seriously jeopardizes my mission." Lee stabbed at the dashboard with a finger. "We've come too goddamned far to have it fucked up by some bullshit like this. It even took *us* by surprise, and we're out here doing this shit every day. How do you think the average person is going to take it?"

Jim looked wary, like he was making his way across an unsteady footbridge. "Captain, I understand this is not going to be popular, but I think we have a moral obligation to tell people. I mean, not only could this give Jacob useful information, but it's also a safety issue. If there's a den here with females in it, there might be one of the same in Lillington."

Lee thought about it and knew that Jim was right. "Let me handle that."

Harper bounded up the steps to the Camp Ryder office. Concrete walls blurred by, metal stair risers clanging under his feet. He found Bus standing and facing the radio. He turned when he heard Harper come through the door.

"What's wrong?" Harper said, breathing hard. "Did someone get hurt?"

Bus nodded. "Lee's on the line. He's telling me to go to 'private channel,' whatever that means."

Harper had to think about it for a moment. "Private channel" was a particular frequency that they could switch to and not be overheard by the other base stations around the Camp Ryder Hub that might be monitoring the main channel. Lee had only told the people on his team about the private channel.

Harper stepped to the radio and switched the frequency, hoping he'd remembered correctly. He took the handset and keyed it up. "Lee, you there?"

"Yeah, I'm here."

"What happened? I heard something bad happened."

"Jake's been shot. Julia is with him, and Wilson and his team are taking them to the hospital."

"Sonofabitch…" Harper thought Lee sounded a little dazed, and that, above everything else, made him worry. "Who shot him? And who the hell is with you if everyone left for the hospital?"

"Jim and LaRouche are with me; don't worry. We're fine. As for the shooter…" Lee paused for a long time, and Harper could hear him breathe into the microphone twice, thinking. "We don't know who it was. We didn't see who shot him. We think it was from the rooftops, but we haven't had a chance to check it out yet."

"No one else got hurt?"

"No, it was just Jake. The guy only fired once."

"Is Jake gonna make it?"

A pause before the transmission came through. "I don't think so, Harper."

Harper looked at Bus and could see that his face was gray and worn.

"Look, we'll talk about that later," Lee said over the radio. "It's not what I called you for."

"Okay." Harper was still processing the news of Jake's imminent death. "What do you need?"

Lee's voice was distant. "I need you to get Jacob and a couple of the people you trust from your group of volunteers, and I want you to go to Lillington. You don't need a lot of guys, just three or four of them. You're going to comb the downtown area of that city. You're looking for a den."

"A den? Like an infected den?"

"Yes. It's gonna be pretty nearby where we set up the Lillington outpost. I would say within a few blocks, but go out at least five blocks in each direction. You'll smell it when you reach it. It should be a low place with open doors, easy to access. Probably dark, not a lot of windows."

"Okay. I got it." Harper touched his forehead. "What are we doing?"

Lee's words became very deliberate. "Before you do any of that, I need you to work with Jacob and come up with a way to safely capture a live infected, to safely transport it, and to safely keep it contained."

"Whoa, Lee..." Harper stared at the radio as if it had bitten him. "You wanna tell me what's going on here?"

"Is anyone in the room with you, and is the door closed?" Lee asked.

Harper glanced over at Bus, who nodded. "Yeah, Bus is in here. Door's shut."

"Okay." An audible intake of breath. "What I'm about to tell you does not leave that room."

Harper placed the handset back on its cradle. He felt shaky. Weak. Unsure of himself. The concept, the dream of one day making it through this alive, felt like land receding quickly from his view as a riptide carried him out to sea.

He turned around and found Bus, still contemplative, sitting at his desk.

"What do you think?" Harper asked him.

Bus looked up as though he'd forgotten Harper was in the room. He shrugged. "I choose to trust the captain because—let's be honest—I don't have much of a choice. I'm sure some people call it blind faith, but that's not really accurate, because I do take the time to think about everything he asks me to do. And you know what?" Bus smiled. "Sometimes I don't agree with him. But I weigh that in the balance of his track record and the consequences of *not* going along with him."

"How do you mean?" Harper slid his hands into his pockets. "You think he would pull support if you refused to do something?"

Bus shook his head. "No. I don't think Captain Harden would do something like that, especially after everything we've been through. The consequences I speak of are more...intangible. Such as, if me and him are divided, what kind of precedent does that set for everyone else? And what if he's right and I'm wrong? What if I refuse to do something, and it turns out that I should have? How many people are going to be hurt? At the end of the day, you have to realize that the captain is very utilitarian. In other words, he might risk the lives of five people, but it's only to save the lives of a hundred."

Bus leaned forward and regarded his rough hands, folded on the desktop. "You know, I think he sees things as a very simple equation: how many people risked versus how many people saved. If the number of people saved is greater than the risk, he'll do it. And sometimes I resent his thinking." Bus looked at Harper with a pointed stare. "But I wouldn't want to make the decisions he makes."

Harper found himself on the cusp of jumping in to defend Lee—he knew the captain, and he knew he didn't make his decisions lightly. But when the survival of a nation was in jeopardy, the needs of the many outweighed the needs of the few. Lee had the survival of more than just himself to think about, and when you began to get into numbers that spanned an entire region, an entire state, then the computations became very complex indeed.

And realizing this, Harper knew where his heart was.

He nodded to Bus and turned for the door. "I need to find Jacob."

Lee and his two companions worked their way through Sanford. They drove cautiously up and down the side streets, their pace slow and deliberate. Not so fast that they would miss something important, but not so slow as to make an easy target. They scanned for signs of further infected but found none. They looked for evidence of raiders, but the roads were deserted. As they continued their sweep, they made mental notes of places that could provide good scavenging.

Lee scanned left, found a pair of boots on the radio console.

"LaRouche. Your feet. On my radio. Again."

The boots retracted. "Sorry."

In the southern section of town, they eventually found what they were looking for.

The school sat in a slight hollow, the surrounding streets overlooking it. From their vantage point on Bragg Street, they could see that barriers had been erected around the school. It was a combination of chain-link fencing, concrete blocks, and concertina wire. This metal and concrete wall extended around the entire perimeter of the school. The perimeter had been breached in several sections. Not just man-size holes but gaping swaths of chain link and barbed wire that had been trampled and pushed out of the way.

Inside the complex, the tattered remnants of tents occupied the sports fields, giant decontamination domes that sat crumpled and collapsed in the center of the football field. The parking lots where students used to congregate and engage in their secret teenage rebellions were now cleared as landing pads for helicopters, but only one remained: an AH-64 Apache, parked slightly askew in the right corner of the parking lot, as though its pilot had set it down hard and quick. Lee could see the cockpit was open and empty. The rotors hung limp and motionless.

"Why the fuck they need attack helicopters for an evacuation?" LaRouche asked from the back.

Lee shook his head. "Someone thought they were needed."

There were boxes and crates strewn everywhere, but they looked looted and torn apart, either by scavengers or by the infected searching for food. Among these, bodies lay where they'd fallen. It was difficult to tell due to the level of decay, but some of them were whole, and Lee presumed these were the infected, shot down by defending troops. Others were in pieces—the civilians who hadn't made it to safety before the infected caught up with them.

In another, lower parking lot, Lee could see a collection of school buses. They would have been used to ferry survivors back and forth to the airport. He saw himself for a moment, sitting in one of those buses, the air hot, the vinyl seats sticking to his skin, sweat and panic thick in the air. Driving down these deserted back roads with an armed escort of Humvees, a pair of Apache attack helicopters making flybys overhead.

Discomfort.

Terror.

Lack of control.

These were someone's last memories.

Behind the school buses, parked closer to the buildings, were the hulks of OD green and desert tan. He leaned forward in his seat and pointed. "See 'em? Coupla LMTVs and a tanker."

The LMTVs were two-and-a-half-ton trucks that had replaced most of the old M35 "Deuce and a Half" trucks. Lee supposed they could share the same name, but for some reason most people just called them LMTVs. Two of these were parked alongside a HEMTT truck, with the M978 fuel tanker modification.

LaRouche whistled. "That's a couple thousand gallons for you."

"If they left anything for us." Lee waved his hand toward the high school complex. "Bring us in there, Jim."

The Humvee rolled forward through a gap in the Jersey barriers that had been left open for vehicles to pass in and out of the complex. A rollaway section of barbwire-topped fencing lay bent and toppled to the ground, what was left of a body clad in ACUs lying on top.

Jim took it slowly and tried to avoid the dark mounds of decaying flesh that littered the parking lot, but there were far too many, and occasionally Jim would cringe and the tires would thump across some old corpse. The sound of brittle bones snapping would be muffled through the rotting meat.

"You're doin' good, Jim."

The ex-priest nodded hastily. "You want to go all the way back to those trucks and the tanker?"

"Yeah." Lee looked out his window and scanned the rooftops with a suspicious eye. "All the way back."

The smell was not as bad as Lee had thought it would be. The sun and wind and rain had soaked and leached most of the putrid odor from these remains. In tiny updrafts of air, carried on the heat of the engine block, Lee could smell the faintness of their death like disturbing memories that cannot quite be grasped.

"Movement!" LaRouche called.

"Shit." Lee hunched lower over his rifle.

"You want me to keep rolling?" Jim asked.

"Where's the movement coming from?" Lee called out.

"Down near the vehicles...I can't tell what it is..."

Lee slapped the dash. "Stop here."

The Humvee jerked to a halt.

"I saw it behind the HEMTT." LaRouche pronounced it *heh-mit*. "It's like an animal or something."

Lee peered at the cluster of vehicles. They all faced outward, the bulk of the building casting a pallorous shadow over half their bodies, while bright sunlight lit their hoods and reflected off their windshields. Beyond the glare, Lee could see nothing in the shadows.

"Jim, honk the horn and be ready to haul ass," Lee instructed. "LaRouche, if it's infected that come popping out of there, light 'em up."

"Yeah, I gotcha."

"Ready?" Jim asked, his hand on the horn.

Lee nodded.

The vehicles were perhaps fifty yards out, maybe a little more.

Jim punched the horn.

The Humvee gave its uncharacteristic squawk.

They waited.

From underneath the wheelbase of one of the

LMTVs, Lee thought he saw a shadow move. A pair of dark-colored winter birds flitted across the sky, swooping and jabbering at each other. A steady breeze gusted through his open window, dried his eyes, and chilled the sweat on the back of his neck. The Humvee hit a rough patch of idling and rumbled underneath them before smoothing out and returning to normal.

The smell of diesel fumes and decay.

His pulse was steady.

"All right." Lee's door creaked slightly as he pushed it open. "Jim, you're with me. LaRouche, maintain overwatch and cover our retreat if we start running back to the Humvee."

NINETEEN

TALKS

JIM STEPPED OUT WITH LEE, leaving the vehicle running. The two met at the front of the Humvee. The warmth of the engine washed across Lee's back as he pulled his rifle in tight and squeezed the foregrip. They maneuvered toward the vehicles, splitting up and flanking, trying to get an angle on what might be hiding behind the bulks of metal and mechanics.

They were within about twenty yards of the vehicles when Lee saw a flash of brown fur from underneath the chassis of the HEMTT. As he brought up his rifle, a long black snout poked out from behind a tire and evaluated Lee with suspicious eyes, tan ears erect and oriented toward him.

Irrationally, Lee's first thought was, *Tango?*

He stepped forward, let the muzzle of his weapon drop.

The dog took two hesitant steps out from behind the tire, still watching Lee, its head level with its haunches and sniffing the air, catching his scent. The resemblance did not go further than the first, immediate impression. It clearly had some German shepherd or maybe some Malinois in its bloodline, but it also just as clearly was a mutt, though Lee wasn't sure what else it was mixed with. The fur was lighter, almost gray across its flanks where it was clumped with dirt and grime, charcoal around its snout and eyes.

As it cleared its hide, it caught sight of Jim moving in from the other side, and it stiffened. It looked back and forth a few times and backed away one step, its tail slung low but making nervous wagging gestures, as though it hoped they were regular humans but just couldn't be sure.

"Lee," Jim called, addressing his rifle toward the dog.

Lee held a hand out. "Hold your fire."

Most domesticated dogs had either been infected or turned feral. In either case, when they were encountered, they were shot and chalked up to target practice. As cold as that sounded, it was better than having them rip one of their scavenging crews apart, as they'd been known to do. They might look like old house pets, but their instincts quickly reasserted themselves and they were just as dangerous as wild animals.

But this one was alone.

"You gonna shoot it?" Jim asked.

It was a valid question. In addition to being a danger to people, as long as a dog didn't display any signs of infection from FURY or rabies, it was a decent meal. The taste was similar to beef, but a little gamier. They'd found the smaller the dog, the more gamy the taste, so if you bagged yourself a large-breed dog, like a Labrador or a Rottweiler, you could almost pretend you were eating steak.

This one was smaller, maybe fifty pounds, if that. But Lee wasn't interested in killing and eating it. This one seemed less inclined to attack and more inclined to give them a good long inspection, which made Lee believe that perhaps the dog had not gone feral. He stood there and forced his body to relax, to be loose and controlled, like he was the owner of this dog and expected it to heel.

"Lee?"

"Shh." Lee held a finger to his lips.

The dog quirked his head at the sound from Lee.

It kept its eyes mainly on him, as he was the closest, but chanced a look at Jim every few seconds to make sure the other man hadn't gotten any closer. It kept sniffing the air, as though it wasn't sure who these people were, but whatever scent particles it was pulling from the breeze weren't alarming it either.

Lee patted his leg and spoke calmly. "Come 'ere, boy."

Jim took an audible breath, something akin to exasperation, and Lee flicked a glance in his direction. His rifle was still addressed toward the dog, but it was held at a low-ready, and Jim's eyes were on Lee. "What're you doing?"

Lee didn't give him an answer. Whatever the reason, Lee felt confident that there was a good reason for this dog. He patted his leg again and called out to the dog, but it just wagged its tail hesitantly and moved its paws as though it truly wanted to come closer but couldn't bring itself to do so.

"What if it's feral?" Jim called out.

"If it's feral, it won't come when I call."

"It doesn't look like it's coming."

"It will." Lee reached his hand slowly into his left cargo pocket and brought out his little bag of jerky. Luckily, he hadn't finished it off earlier and still had a few pieces left. Keeping a steady eye on the dog, he opened it up and pulled out a single, small piece. The dog was skinny, and Lee could see its ribs showing. It would be hungry. He held the piece of jerky into the air and he could see the dog focusing on it, lifting its snout to test the air as the breeze carried the smell of the jerky over to it.

The dog sniffed and licked its chops once, then let out a little whine and worriedly moved its feet a few times, closing the gap between them by only a foot or so.

"It's okay." Lee spoke calmly. "Come on."

The dog wouldn't come any closer after that, so Lee gently tossed the jerky toward the dog and it landed about halfway between them. The throwing motion spooked the dog and he backed up. When the piece of meat hit the ground, the dog watched it with incredible intensity and crept forward a few feet. Then it bolted and snatched up the morsel before drawing back again.

Lee smiled. "Yeah, I got you now."

The piece of jerky was gone in a flash and the dog was standing there, now attuned to Lee's every move.

Lee looked over to Jim. "Let's walk back."

Jim began sidestepping in the direction of their Humvee, not quite willing to turn his back on the dog. Lee, however, turned completely and strode casually on. As he did, he took a strip of jerky and pulled smaller pieces off, then dropped them on the ground as he walked.

As they neared the Humvee again, LaRouche grinned and shook his head. "I'm guessing we can't eat your new friend."

Lee turned and found the dog, still standing about fifteen feet away from Lee, scarfing up the little pieces of meat from the ground. He walked up to his passenger's side door and dropped another piece there. He opened the back door and stood there expectantly.

The dog regarded the piece of jerky at his feet, and then him.

"Come on, boy." Lee motioned toward the backseat. "You wanna go for a ride?"

The dog wagged its tail.

"Yeah, you know what a ride is." Lee set the rest of his jerky on the backseat and then climbed into the front passenger's seat. "Let's go for a ride."

To his left, Jim settled into the driver's seat. "I'm not giving you any of my jerky to replace what you fed to that mutt."

Lee ignored him and kept his eyes on the dog outside. A little closer now, it gave the Humvee a wide berth but was intent on the backseat. Lee could see the wheels in its head turning, trying to figure out whether the vehicle was a good thing. Lee could see its tail still wagging, and he could almost picture the dog's faint memories of riding in cars with its face out the window and its tongue hanging out, a pure rush of smells with each breath.

Then, abruptly, the tail stopped wagging.

The lean muscles all along its body rippled and tensed. The head snapped out toward the sports fields and rose up, the nose working furiously. Lee followed its gaze but couldn't see anything. Its lips curled in a low growl, and then, without warning, it shot into the backseat of the Humvee.

"Whoa!" LaRouche jerked his legs back.

The dog thrust its dark muzzle between Lee and Jim, facing forward, and then began to bark savagely. Lee and Jim both drew back away from it, but then realized it was barking at something out beyond the front of the vehicle, out in the sports fields.

Frothy spittle speckled the windshield as the dog continued to bark.

"You think it smells something?" Jim asked over the sound of the dog's panicked barking.

Lee opened his mouth to speak but LaRouche interrupted him.

"Contact! Infected!"

Lee leaned out and slammed the rear door, and then his own. "Let's go, Jim!"

Jim stomped on the gas, lurching them forward and whipping the vehicle to the right. Lee tumbled into the radio console and the dog, feeling the hot breath and the grungy fur against his face. Jim snapped the vehicle in a complete 180, LaRouche shouting obscenities from the turret as he held on for his life. He straightened out and headed for the gap in the barriers that they had come through.

Righting himself and leaning forward, Lee was able to look back and see out his window to the football fields, where the dark shapes of three infected were visible, sprinting toward them in a wide skirmish line. The one in the center was bulky and brown-skinned with wild black hair...

"Jesus! They're fast!" Lee exclaimed.

The Humvee shuddered and the dog in the back-seat yelped in surprise as LaRouche opened up with the fifty. Just before they shot through the barriers and turned back onto Bragg Street, Lee could see the white streaks of the tracers lancing out at the pursuing infected, kicking up chunks of concrete.

Then they were on Bragg Street, and Lee could no longer see them.

Harper knocked twice on the plywood wall and then pushed open the blue tarpaulin curtain that served as a front door. Inside, Jacob knelt on the dirt floor and appeared to be stuffing his backpack with the personal items he'd arrived with, and a few things Julia and Jenny, who most often served as the welcome party, had provided him. Beside the pack, the plate carrier that had once belonged to Captain Mitchell from Virginia sat on the floor, three aluminum box magazines lying across the chest.

Jacob looked up at Harper and regarded him enigmatically.

The guy's a real puzzle, Harper thought. Obviously, he was sharp as a tack. Not just book smart but street smart. There was a bit of a fighting dog lurking under all that education.

His eyes, expressionless, returned to his work. "Can I help you, Mr. Harper?"

"Mind if I come in?"

"Come on."

"Thanks." Harper slipped through the door and pulled the tarpaulin back into place. "You goin' somewhere?"

"Yes." Jacob zipped up the main compartment of his pack. "I think I can do some good at the hospital in Smithfield. I found a pair of scavengers who are making a run out past that direction. They're going to drop me off on their way."

Harper chewed at his lip. "Yeah, uh…"

Jacob pointed to the three magazines. "Would I be able to get some extra magazines from you? Those three are the last I have left, and one of them is only half loaded. Is there any way I can get three more mags and, say, two hundred rounds of ammunition from you?"

Harper rubbed his nose. "Jacob, we need your help with something."

The scientist tilted his head back. "Oh?"

"Captain Harden and his team made a very interesting discovery today. He wants me to take you and a team to Lillington to…check something out."

Jacob smiled. "Mr. Harper, you're going to have to be more specific."

"Captain asked me to keep it quiet, so what I tell you stays here."

"Of course."

Harper stepped closer and knelt down so that they were on eye-level, and then told him what there was to tell. As he spoke, Jacob continued to work at packing his things, but as the truth of the matter came out, his movements began to slow until he appeared frozen in place.

"Pregnant?" Jacob's mouth worked silently for a moment. He seemed both terrified and dazzled by this news, and the edges of his mouth ticked up as though he wanted to smile but couldn't bring himself to. "I don't believe it."

Harper looked at the floor. "I didn't either, but—"

"Do you know what this means?" Jacob suddenly demanded.

"Uh…"

"It's reproduction. It's continuity in the line." That scared smile again. "There will be mutations—there *have* to be mutations. It would take years and years…unless the gestation period is decreased. It could be. I just don't know." He snapped his head up and looked at Harper gravely. "Please tell me…"

Harper shook his head. "They were killed before the captain realized what they were."

Jacob threw his hands up with a loud groan.

"Listen." Harper looked around as though someone might be in the shadows of the room, eavesdropping. "The captain doesn't think this is the only den with females in it. That's why he wants us to check Lillington."

Jacob had been in the process of smearing his hands down his face, but he stopped when he heard this last part. His forehead and cheeks looked flushed from the pressure he'd exerted on his skin. "Because you wiped out the Lillington horde, but you didn't check for the den."

"And there might be females there."

"Are you going to kill them?"

"We're gonna try to get a test subject."

Jacob turned, his hands at his sides and the fingers working back and forth with a manic energy. "And if she's pregnant...that'll answer so many questions. I'll be able to watch the gestation period. And see how the baby grows." He turned to Harper. "What effects does the plague have on the fetus? We don't know. We can assume a lot, but until we watch it with our eyes, observe and record it, it's just bunkum."

Harper gave him a questioning look. "You seem excited."

Jacob shook his head. "Not excited. Fascinated, though. Truly, truly fascinated. But very scared. This isn't a laboratory anymore. This isn't studying something that's safely contained. This is studying something that is right here, right now, wiping us out." He took a deep breath. "It's a lot of pressure."

Harper put a hand on the scientist's shoulder. "Don't get bogged down just yet. We still have to catch one of them."

Jacob stalked over to a corner of the small cube that he called his home and snatched up a metal pole with a thin cable coming out of the top, a makeshift dogcatcher's pole. "Same as you catch any other animal that wants to bite you. I'd suggest the use of a heavy tranquilizer, but I don't want to take any chances with the fetus."

Harper eyed the pole. "Where'd you come up with this thing?"

"I made it." Jacob set it beside his pack. "I took to heart what Captain Harden said to me the other day, when I was about to throw myself out of the gates for a chance to snare one of them. Admittedly, that was not smart. He was right; I was wrong. So I made the catch pole, and if I'm not mistaken, there are many unused rooms at Johnston Memorial Hospital that might serve perfectly for housing a test subject."

"I believe there are."

Jacob nodded, very serious. "Then I believe I'm in."

They met at Broadway just before sundown. Lee, Jim, and LaRouche had already made it back and downloaded their gear, and by the time Wilson's Humvee pulled past the roadblock at the eastern end of Broadway, Jim had already started a fire and pulled out food.

At the telltale rumble of the Humvee, Lee and his two companions looked up and watched the vehicle roll down the strip toward them. The last they'd heard from Wilson was that they were firing up the generators and blowing the dust off the equipment they needed to operate on Jake. No prognosis outside of Dr. Hamilton's general assessment that things didn't look good.

They waited tensely as the vehicle stopped and the doors opened. Wilson stepped out, but his expression remained blank. The other members of his team followed, and they looked mostly exhausted. They hoisted their packs onto their shoulders and began meandering their way toward the glow of the fire like moths drawn to the light.

Lee and Jim offered quiet encouragement as

they dropped their packs and took their places around the fire. Lee looked back to the vehicle and watched as Julia slid out last. Her clothes were soaked in blood and the pale skin of her arms was smeared with it. Like a fierce blush, it reddened her neck and face. Strands of her hair were stained from the base of her scalp all the way back, clumped together from constantly brushing her hair away with bloody hands.

It appeared that she made a conscious effort to avoid eye contact with Lee, looking everywhere else as she slowly approached. Wilson stepped to her side, put a gentle hand on her shoulder, and said something that Lee couldn't make out. Whatever he said, Julia offered a faltering smile and a nod.

Lee looked down into the flames. "What's the news?"

Julia answered, her voice stone-cold. "Doc Hamilton is operating now. He said he'd hit us on the radio as soon as he had news."

Lee glanced up and saw her eyelids flutter.

"He's gotta go in," she said in a flat monotone. "Repair the artery. Close up the chest wound. Hope the blood pressure doesn't drop too low."

"Julia did phenomenally," Wilson said to Lee. "She was on point the whole way there. If Jake makes it, he owes it to her."

Julia shot Wilson a withering look. "Let's not play pretend, okay?" She looked at Lee for the first time, angry, though he wasn't sure if it were directed at him or some nebulous power responsible for what had happened. "Jake's not gonna make it. He was shot through the chest with a high-powered rifle round, and it took almost forty-five minutes for him to get anything but the most basic battlefield care. He already lost too much blood by the time we got him into surgery, and Doc Hamilton poking around in there is only going to make him bleed more. They can pump him full of IV fluid to keep his BP up, but at some point in time it's going to dilute the blood too much, and they don't have anything to replace it with. And then Jake's going to die."

The group looked at her, awkward and silent. They waited for her to continue, but she had apparently spoken her mind. After a stretch, Lee stepped around Wilson and put a hand on her arm, firm but gentle. "Come on, let's get cleaned up."

"I'm fine," she said.

"You still need to clean up." Lee pulled slightly, and she allowed herself to be removed from the circle. "Jim, why don't you get some food going?"

Jim nodded. "You got it."

Lee grabbed his pack as he walked with Julia toward an area where Kip Greene had told them there was a rain basin. The last little bit of crimson light coming from the sunset lit up Julia's face and blended all of the gore together so that Lee could not tell where it stopped and her skin began. She stared straight ahead, her face immovable.

"What's the problem, Captain?" There was a bite in her voice.

Lee chose not to take the bait. She was looking for a conflict, looking for some way to exorcise those emotions she kept under lock and key, but fighting with him wasn't going to solve anything. "No problem, Julia. You said your piece, and now it's time to get cleaned up. You know...wash your hands for supper and all that?"

"And I need an escort to do that?" She jerked her arm away from him.

Lee looked behind him, feeling his blood rise, and wondering who might be watching them. "Cool it," he said in a warning tone.

"Why you gotta walk with me, huh?" Julia shook her head and turned the corner of a single-story brick building where a rain catch sat, filled almost to overflowing. "Make sure that crazy Julia doesn't go off the fucking deep end? Screw you. I can handle myself just fine."

Lee clenched his hands at his sides. "Clearly."

"Yeah." She looked up at him, fire in her eyes. "Clearly. Now why don't you go play army man with your buddies out there and leave me the fuck alone."

Lee took two quick steps and his fist shot out, almost involuntarily, but he got control of himself well before it touched her. He extended his finger so it pointed right into her face. "Is that the best you can fucking do?" he spat. "Is that the best you can come up with?"

Julia swatted his hand out of her face. "Leave me the hell alone!"

Lee faced her, putting his hands down but not leaving. "No. You give me a fucking answer. Is that the best you can do?"

"What the fuck are you talking about?"

"I'm talking about Rob, and I'm talking about

Jake." He leaned forward so their faces were separated by only a few inches. He could smell the blood on her and the sweaty scent of her. His words came out of him, strained and hot and barely controlled. "You never even reacted to Rob being killed. You can cry a goddamned river for the infected we shoot, but when it comes to your own people, your own friends, you shut down and strike out at the people who *are* here for you."

She looked like she was about to hit him.

Lee didn't care. "So is that the best you can come up with? One of our own is about to die, and the most emotion you can wring out of yourself is to be a fucking bitch to your friends? To the people who care about you? Is that the best we can expect?"

Her voice trembled. "You don't know what the fuck you're talking about."

"Then tell me, Julia! Tell me that I'm wrong!"

She hit him in the chest with both palms, rocking him back on his heels. "This coming from you? What about you, Lee? I've never seen you shed a fucking tear!"

"If I thought twice about all the people who have died because of me, I'd never be able to make a decision again." He threw out his arms. "What's your excuse?"

"Don't you tell me what I feel." Her whole body shook with rage. "I think about Rob every damn day. And now I'm gonna think about Jake. And the two of them are going to be stuck in my head forever and I'm never going to be able to get them out, along with all the other people I've lost." She took a step forward. "What is it you want to see?

You want to see me cry? Is it not good enough for you until I come and dry my tears on your shoulder like a good little girl? Fuck you!"

She spoke with such force that Lee found himself searching for a response but coming up empty-handed.

Julia raised her head. "You wanna see tears? You're gonna wait a while, because all I am is pissed." Her voice dropped in volume. "I'm bitter, and I'm angry, and I can feel it just sucking the life out of me. Because every day I wake up and I'm confused." The stiff aggression of her body suddenly slacked, like high-tension wires snapping. He shoulders sagged, her head lolled, and her arms flopped to her sides. "I look around and I wonder where my house went, where my family went, and I have to remind myself *every day* that all of that is over. I just keep thinking that I'm not supposed to be here. That maybe tonight is the night that I go to sleep and I wake up and things are back to normal." She shook her head. "But it's never going back. I'm stuck here. I'm trapped."

Lee stared at her for a long moment. The resentment, the frustration, and the fear all came out of him in a breath, and he leaned forward onto the rain catch, hanging his head just above the water, smelling that clean smell of rain, seeing the shimmering image of his silhouette against the darkening sky.

She waited for a long time before speaking again. "You think about them too."

He felt the side of the rain catch shift as she put her weight on it.

She continued. "Because if you weren't think-ing about them, you wouldn't be so worried about whether I was thinking about them."

A grim smile touched Lee's lips.

"You're just as fucked-up as the rest of us," she said. "You just do a better job of hiding it."

Lee looked at her. She had her back turned to the rain catch, leaning on it with one elbow and looking down at the ground, her face set in an expression that had no name. Not quite resigna-tion. Not quite determination. More like the res-ignation to be determined. It was something that spoke of the drive to gut it out when crushing defeat was all one had to look forward to.

It was the look of a human being who no lon-ger saw, nor cared to see, anything of beauty, but instead focused solely on the concept of survival. Same as a wild animal will not appreciate the splendor of the jungle it lives in, but instead sees only the danger that lurks inside.

This was not a moment of absolution or enlight-enment. It was a hard realization that while the infected seemed to be moving forward, the rest of mankind seemed headed in the opposite direction. The two were still worlds apart, but they seemed bound and determined to meet in some wretched middle where fighting for food and water and pro-creating the next generation was an all-consuming task. Simple propagation of the species and noth-ing more.

"Friend of yours?"

Lee saw her looking out toward the street. He followed her gaze and found the stray dog they had rescued—or who had rescued them, depending on how you looked at it—standing at the corner of the building and regarding the two of them cautiously.

Lee stood up. "Yeah. We found him in Sanford today. Still pretty skittish, but he's even more afraid of infected than he is of us. And he can sniff 'em out way before we can."

Julia raised an eyebrow. "An infected-sniffing dog."

Lee bent down and held out his hand. The dog approached, still timid, but it gave a demure wag of its tail and stretched itself out to tentatively lick Lee's fingers. "Good boy." Lee turned his wrist in an attempt to scratch the dog behind the ears, but it backed away quickly. Lee stood straight again. "He's still a little shy."

"What's his name?"

Lee wiped the dog slobber off on his pants. "I'm gonna call him Deuce."

Julia held out a hand. "Hey, Deuce."

The dog regarded her with a tilt of his head, but didn't come any closer.

"He's still warming up to us," Lee said quietly. He looked back at Julia. "Listen, I didn't mean . . ."

Julia shook her head. "You're right, though. I can't take it out on you and the others."

Lee nodded once but didn't respond. He put his hands in his pockets and decided to leave the whole conversation where it was: a mutual understanding that they were both dealing with these things in their own ways, and they both needed their space to mourn in the way they saw fit. He turned back to the street and put one foot in front of the other. Behind him, he could hear Julia gathering a bucket of water to clean herself off with.

Deuce backed away from Lee as he crossed the street but paralleled him, keeping about ten feet of distance between them at all times. He was interested in whatever food Lee might drop but still not willing to roll over and show his belly just yet.

LaRouche met him before he reached the fire. "You guys okay?"

"Fine." Lee waved it off. When they reached the fire, Lee hitched his foot up onto an overturned bucket and leaned on his knee, looking at his group gathered around the fire. "Listen…" He cleared his throat. "You all did great today. Every one of you. It's just…sometimes it doesn't matter."

They all nodded and looked down into the fire.

At the edge of the amber light, Deuce grumbled and trotted around them.

Wilson raised his head. "Cap…I don't know if you thought about it already, but we were talking about what happened earlier. The shooter…"

Lee spoke without emotion. "He was aiming for me."

TWENTY

HARD TRUTHS

WILSON LOOKED SURPRISED. "What are you talking about?"

"The only reason I didn't get shot was because I bent down when the shooter fired. Otherwise, the round would have gone through both of us."

"How do you know the shooter wasn't just aiming for Jake?"

"I don't." Lee shrugged. "But that infected was put there to slow us down, to get us to bunch up around the door. And yet the shooter only fires one shot. Whoever it was, he wasn't just trying to ambush us, or he would have hosed us all down. He was trying to take out a specific target. And I have a hard time believing that someone was gunning for Jake."

LaRouche scrunched his brow. "Well, why would anyone try to kill you?"

Lee shook his head. "I really don't know." But then he thought, *Yeah, you know.*

LaRouche shifted his weight, appearing uncomfortable. "Well...should you continue going on operations with us?"

Lee scratched the back of his head. "I'm not

going to run and hide, if that's what you mean. Honestly, I don't really give a shit about this guy's motivations at this point in time. I'm not sending you all out to do my dirty work for me and staying back behind the lines."

The electronic sound of a voice being transmitted over the radio trickled from the Humvee a few yards from their fire, and it cut off any further debate. Lee looked over at the Humvee, along with everyone else. The words were inaudible, but they all knew what they were. And yet they hoped.

Jim was the first to stand up. "I'll get it."

The group watched silently as Jim stepped over to the Humvee and sat inside, retrieving the handset and speaking in a hushed tone. Julia appeared, staring with her cold blue eyes at Jim as he talked inside the vehicle. She was wiping her hands off with a small red cloth, and then she dabbed her face with it as she approached the fire. Her eyes retreated from Jim and grew hypnotized with the writhing flames.

The embers crackled and popped in the absence of their voices.

The handset clacked as it was set back into its cradle.

The Humvee's door groaned, its hinges needing lubrication.

Jim stood with his hands folded in front of him.

They all knew without him speaking a word, so he said nothing at all. Instead, he walked back to his spot, where he had arranged a large pot next to the fire. It trembled and stood ready to boil over. Inside was rice and split peas, and he stirred them

with a metal spoon that clanked on the sides of the
pot. They all watched in the quiet of the deepening night as he took a small spoonful and tested
whether the food was done. His eyes glistened and
shone red, but he did not make a sound.

Seeming satisfied with the texture of the food,
he removed the pot from the fire and set to opening some canned meat. As he worked, his tears
traced down his nose, and he swiped at them with
his sleeve.

They ate in silence, unable or unwilling to put
into words yet another loss.

In the morning, Harper woke to what promised to
be a dismal day. The clouds that stretched unending across the sky were a uniform, primer gray, and
they spit out rain slowly and steadily, an excruci-
ating pace common only to November and the
beginning of December in North Carolina. Summer rainstorms were a panicked rush, as though
the clouds were trying to empty themselves as
fast as possible in order to cool the parched earth
beneath them. But in these late months, the sky
leaked like a loose-fitted pipe, as though the clouds
were sullen and depressed and could not be bothered to work harder.

Harper stared out from behind the door of his
shanty and cursed the sky. He could feel the ache
in his joints. The hard times and the grief were like
bitterness in his bones. He felt old. Out of shape.

Used up.

Tired.

He sighed and closed his door.

"Too much work to be done for a pity party," he mumbled to himself as he lit his camp stove—not the one he used to burn deer guts. He'd scrounged up a little treat that he hoped would brighten his morning. It was a pack of instant oatmeal, brown-sugar-and-cinnamon flavored. He'd traded up three packs of AA batteries for a box with five packs left in it, and he saved them for when he needed a pick-me-up.

Diet food was what he would have called it four months ago.

Now it was an indulgence.

He boiled the water and poured the packet in, and for a long time he stood there over his little tin mess pot with his eyes closed, just breathing in the aromas and imagining a different place. The rich, spicy pungency of the cinnamon. The warm, robust sweetness of the brown sugar. There were so many things associated with those two smells, it was like running a dragnet across the riverbed of his mind, dredging up those memories of family and holidays that had been drowned and buried so long in the silt of his subconsciousness.

Holidays.

When the cold was cozy and it didn't seep into his chest and make him worry about pneumonia. When the big concern of the day was what wine to bring to Thanksgiving and whether his brother-in-law Frank would get tanked at Christmas dinner. When he spent hours on the couch with Annette, listening to Bing Crosby with only the glow of the tree lighting their living room. Colored lights only on odd years, because Annette thought they were tacky, but he loved them and she conceded once every other year. Her stupid ornamental nutcrackers displayed on the mantel, their jaws dropped in perpetual shock.

She loved those silly things.

The ridiculous cornucopia she put in the center of the dining room table every year for Thanksgiving, with the fake mini pumpkins and the plastic gourds and the velvet leaves in fall colors. The little things that were *absolutely necessary* in order for her to enjoy the holiday properly.

Annette.

He opened his eyes and stared down at the thickening oatmeal. All around him were dirt floors, plywood walls, blue tarp to seal him from the rain, and a cold emptiness with nothing to fill the void. The memory of her was like a dying tree that he tried time and time again to pull up from the soil of his mind, but her roots were dug in too deep, inextricably intertwined with every thought, every recollection of his old life. There was not a place, not a feeling, not a scent or a taste or a sound that did not carry with it some tiny bit of Annette. She haunted him ceaselessly.

He missed her so hard that it became a very real, very physical pain in his chest. It was a tightness and a melancholy, but there was also a note of frustration that he felt each time he thought of her, some distant realization that no matter what he did, no matter how hard he tried or how long he waited, he could not have her back.

In life, you are often set apart from the things that you desire only by your willingness to work tirelessly to gain them. So many things are unlikely to be achieved but still within the realm of possibility. But death is not conquerable. It cannot be overcome or outmatched. You cannot outthink it. You cannot outmuscle it or even wait for it to be over, because it is truly, perfectly infinite. And this realization caused in him each time a new uproar from a small, petulant child in the back of his mind who threw a tantrum because he could not get what he wanted.

Because what he wanted was impossible.

Not impossible, the way the word was used to describe a daunting task that the lazy person simply did not want to take on. But *impossible* in the coldest, most pragmatic sense of the word. There was no way to fix it. It was simply unattainable. And goals that were unattainable were best left alone, for they destroyed men's minds and weakened their resolve to live.

He ate his oatmeal slowly, wishing to relish it but failing miserably.

These memories were not worth their weight in grief.

He looked at the box of oatmeal, swallowing against a lump in his throat. "Fucking waste of good batteries."

He finished his breakfast and strapped on his gear, checking to make sure his magazines were all topped off, and then slinging into his M4. Looking down at himself in his BDUs and army-green parka, with all of his gear and his rifle hanging off of him, he almost laughed. *If you could see me now, Annette…you'd get a kick out of it.*

He left his shanty and threw the Gore-Tex hood of the parka up over his head to keep the rain off of him. It was misting steadily and he watched clouds of it billow down out of the sky, falling not at the speed of rain but more like the steady drifting of snow on a windless day.

He met Jacob, Nate, and his three volunteers at the front of his pickup truck near the gate. Nate had chosen Devon and a middle-aged man and woman whom Harper knew to be a couple, though he couldn't remember their names for the life of him. He nodded to them all as he walked up.

"Morning, everyone." He extended his hand to the middle-aged man. "I'm sorry; I don't remember your name."

"Mike Reagan," the guy said, taking Harper's hand. "This is my wife, Torri."

"Glad to have you guys." Harper motioned for the pickup truck. "I think we can fit everyone in. We need to hit the road, and I'll tell you guys what's going on while we're on the way."

They all managed to squeeze into the bench seats. Harper drove with Nate and Jacob up front with him. Devon, Mike, and Torri sat in the back. As they left the gate, Harper kicked it into four-wheel drive, as the dirt road had turned into a boggy mess overnight. The old Nissan crawled steadily through the muck and found its way eventually out to Highway 55. Dirt and gravel clinging to the tires pelted the wheel wells noisily as he brought the truck up to speed.

When the worst of the noise had subsided, he told them what the situation was. He warned them to not talk about this with anyone else, that they should consider it confidential until further notice. Then he explained Captain Harden's belief that there would be a den in Lillington, and in that den there would be some live infected hiding out. He paused here for a long time, considering the ramifications of telling them the part about the infected being females and being pregnant. But he figured it was best to get the arguments out of the way now, rather than when they had the damn things cornered in whatever hovel they were hiding in.

The reaction to the news was not quite shock but more just a general disbelief. Without having Captain Harden there to explain to them why he thought this, most everyone, with the exception of Jacob—who already knew—screwed up their faces and asked why the hell the captain thought there would be pregnant females in the den. That was ridiculous.

"These people are crazy violent." Devon was shaking his head. "No way they're out there... making babies. Secondly, I just don't see them having protective instincts."

Mike's eyes were incredulous in Harper's rearview mirror. "You know, I'm usually on board with whatever the captain has for us, but this seems a little far-fetched. Jacob, is there any realistic basis for thinking there are dens of females out there, and that they might be pregnant?"

Jacob gave Harper a sidelong glance and looked uncomfortable. "Well, uh, yes. In fact, there is."

"So..."

Jacob studied his dirty fingernails. "The FURY

bacterium did its business already, eating through
the brain. We already know that it didn't leave
behind much—just enough for basic primal functions. We've grown accustomed to considering
these...people...to be hyperaggressive. But much
of the hyperaggression was simply a by-product of
the plague's effect on the brain during the primary
stages of infection, and I believe most of what we
see now isn't mindless aggression but simply the
drive to hunt for food.

"Another primary instinct for survival is the act
of procreation. Primal instincts are primal instincts,
and sex is one of them. We think of it as separate,
because we like to romanticize it, but it really is just
a basic biological function in order to ensure the
survival of the species." Jacob looked back at three
faces that all seemed extremely uncomfortable.
"Other basic functions are maternal instinct—a
very powerful instinct, mind you—and a male's
instinct to protect. So no, I don't think it's far-
fetched to believe that they are mating, procreating,
and protecting the pregnant females. It actually
makes perfect sense from a biological perspective."

The interior of the truck was silent for a long
moment, everyone digesting this latest bit of bitter
truth.

Torri looked distraught. "So what are we going
to do if we find them?"

Harper pointed toward Jacob with his thumb.
"That's why I brought Jacob along with us. It's his
deal to catch one of 'em, so that's what we're going
to do. Captain Harden has reason to believe that
the pregnant females might not be aggressive..."

"Yes, about that." Jacob smiled hesitantly. "W
shouldn't expect that. If they hold as true to bio
logical nature as they've done in the past, the
what we'll see is the same thing we see in othe
pregnant females of the animal species. Namely
up until the point of giving birth, they will avoi
a fight at all costs, but if you corner them or ge
too close, they'll definitely attack. This is true o
almost every animal. What we don't want to do i
enter a den where perhaps they have already giver
birth, because I believe we will find the female
to be even more aggressive than the males in tha
situation."

"You don't think..." Harper took his eyes of
the road for a moment. "But it's only been fou
months since the outbreak!"

"Some of them could have been very preg
nant when they were infected," Jacob observed
"Whether or not they could maintain a viable preg
nancy after that is a point of speculation. Anothe
thing to think about is the gestation period. W
already know the plague causes massive increase
to the metabolism, and that affects a whole slev
of other biological functions, including aging. It
possible that the gestation period grows shorter."

They drove the rest of the way in relative silence

It was just after seven in the morning whe
they pulled up to the back lot of Outpost Lilling
ton. Harper had radioed ahead the previous nigh
to let them know they would be arriving in the
morning, but still the sentry regarded them with
suspicion. One of Old Man Hughes's people, h
believed. Harper rolled down the window and fel

the cold wetness on his arm as he hung it out the window to display his yellow armband.

Still, the sentry approached with caution, trying to peer through the rain-mottled windshield at who was inside. When he finally looked in the open window, he immediately recognized who he was dealing with. His face became sharp and urgent. "Mr. Harper! I'm glad you're here. Something bad happened. I think some of our people got hurt. You'll have to talk to Professor White."

Well, isn't that just fucking dandy. Harper pursed his lips. Always a goddamned emergency.

The sentry ran back, and he and his partner pushed the car they used to barricade the entrance out of the way—Harper supposed they kept it in neutral so they could roll it back and forth with relative ease. When the car was clear of the little alley, Harper goosed the gas and trundled noisily into the parking lot, where he parked in the center—angry, a little concerned, and not really worried about where he parked his truck.

He had barely put his boots to the muddy gravel ground by the time he heard someone shouting his name. He looked up and found Professor White running toward him, his face twisted in panic, and Old Man Hughes trailing closely behind. Unconsciously, Harper slid his hand onto the grip of his rifle.

"Harper! Harper!" Professor White wailed. "Thank God you're here!"

Harper couldn't help himself; the guy brought out the worst in him. He extended his hand swiftly and stopped the professor's forward progress with a palm to his chest that nearly knocked him over. "Calm the fuck down, Professor." Harper nodded politely to Old Man Hughes as he plodded up in his dirty overalls. "Now, what's the problem? Why are you running up on me like that?"

The panic in Professor White's face disappeared for the briefest of moments, and Harper saw a flash of irritation—and what was that, a bit of hatred?— before the needy fear reasserted itself. He stammered to get the words out: "F-four of our people were just kidnapped!"

"What?" Harper looked at Old Man Hughes like White had just spoken a foreign language and the old man was going to translate it.

Hughes nodded. "Five of his kids went out to do some scavenging. One of them just came back beaten to a pulp. Said the other four got jumped and kidnapped."

Harper took a second to absorb this information, his eyes bouncing back and forth between Hughes and White. It appeared they were deadly serious. He turned to his pickup truck and handed the keys to Nate. "You guys continue on without me. I'm gonna figure out what the hell is going on here."

They were back at the high school by what Lee supposed was daybreak, although there was no definitive point in time when the sun shone through the dreary sheen of clouds. Deuce was willing enough to climb in the Humvee, but when everyone else began to pile in, he retreated to the rear of the vehicle and hunkered down there for the ride.

They rolled slowly through the break in the barriers that surrounded the high school complex and came to a stop amid the dead bodies and ravaged crates of supplies. Lee stepped out, keeping his eyes on potential hiding places while he walked to the back of the Humvee and opened the rear hatch. Deuce was huddled there against the tailgate and tumbled out as soon as the fastback was open. He jogged a short distance away, taking occasional glances back toward Lee while his nose worked the air.

Lee watched him for a moment, but the dog didn't seem to react to anything. "I think it's all clear for now." He patted the side of the Humvee and the others stepped out.

The drivers stayed inside their Humvees.

They made their slow and cautious progress across the high school's parking lot. The rain turned from a cloying mist to a drizzle, and then tapered off again. The Humvees followed behind and stopped short of the jumbled collection of abandoned military equipment. Lee and LaRouche jogged forward slightly, doing a quick sweep of the undercarriages and all around and behind the trucks before waving in the two Humvees.

The two LMTVs were desert tan in color, both equipped with cargo beds. Along either side of each bed were fold-down benches so the two-and-a-half-ton truck could serve as a troop transport or carry cargo and equipment in its hold. The cab was a two-seater with a little more room in the interior than the Humvees.

The HEMTT was of a similar construct but wider and longer, and painted olive drab. In place of the cargo bed, there was a long oval tank that extended the length of the machine from the cab on back. It was less than a commercial eighteen-wheeler would carry but still plenty of fuel.

They flipped the switch in the diesel vehicles and crossed their fingers as they waited for the ignition light to go off. Maybe they waited longer than normal, or maybe it was just that the wait seemed interminable, but they rejoiced in a stroke of good luck when the little orange lights went off and a press of a button brought the big machines to life. Further inspection of the gauges revealed that all three had more than half a tank of fuel, and that the HEMTT's tanker still contained three quarters of its payload.

They fueled their two Humvees, which were both down to less than a quarter tank. Lee kept an eye on Deuce as the dog explored the area with a relaxed familiarity. Deuce trotted around the perimeter like a guard dog, constantly sniffing, his nose up high, testing the wind, then down low, searching the ground.

They split up their nine people into two-man teams—a driver and a gunner—with the odd man out being Jim, who volunteered to drive the HEMTT, stating he had some experience driving bigger vehicles. In the Humvees, the extra passenger would man the gun, and in the LMTVs he would simply ride shotgun with his rifle out the window. Lee would drive, and LaRouche would be on the gun. They would take point. Julia volunteered to drive the other Humvee, with

Wilson in the turret. They would bring up the rear of the column. Jim in the HEMTT would be in the center of the convoy, with an LMTV and a Humvee behind him and in front of him.

It wasn't ideal, but limited manpower demanded some sacrifices.

They loaded everyone up and managed to convince Deuce to get in Lee's Humvee again. Then they formed into their column and made for the exit. They left the high school behind them without spotting a single infected or any other suspicious person who might have been gunning for Lee the previous day. The roads stretched before them, empty and abandoned, and apparently safe for passage.

In the rural area outside of Sanford, the scenery looked like every other country road in central North Carolina—two-lane blacktop that had been neglected even before the collapse, with potholes deepening and the painted lines fading and cracking. Now, with no traffic to keep them down, weeds had grown in the cracks, and the narrow grassy strip to either side had begun to encroach on the cement. Beyond that, the forest rose up in gray streaks of timber.

Eventually they came to a rural road, off of which a nondescript dirt road would lead them to the bunker. Here Lee found the familiar bucolic setting to be slightly different. The road stretched narrowly, the trees crowded in on either side, with no open fields to let them breathe. The shoulder was sharp and the culvert deep and marshy with overgrowth, leaving no room to turn around.

They turned right onto this road.

At the corner, a weathered street sign rose from coils of brown creeping vines, stalwart in its losing battle against the relentless advance of kudzu. The name of the narrow road, according to this sad signage, was DEVIL'S TRAMPING GROUND ROAD.

Lee grimaced at the road name and pressed down on the accelerator pedal, at which point several things happened at once.

The engine wound up, as though to accelerate as normal.

Then the hood of the Humvee very suddenly warped, changing shape in front of his eyes.

The entire vehicle jolted violently and Lee felt it all the way through him like the crack of a baseball bat in his hands, felt the shock wave in his chest like getting the wind knocked out of him.

And then the engine lost power.

TWENTY-ONE

IN THE WOODS

FROM THE CAB OF the LMTV directly behind Captain Harden's Humvee, Wilson not only heard but *felt* what sounded like a hammer striking an anvil, except louder, more overpowering. Wilson wasn't sure whether he had imagined it or whether somehow his eyes had zeroed in on just the right focal plane at just the right moment, but he would later swear that he saw the bullet that took out Captain Harden's engine block, or at least the path of spatial distortion left in its wake.

To his right, his passenger, Zack, stared slack-jawed, his face more confused than scared.

Odd, intrusive thoughts collided in his brain in that half second as Captain Harden's Humvee swerved wildly on the road and began to slow as it lost power to its drive. The thoughts were calm and meticulous, calculated and rational, and he thought this was very odd.

.50-BMG is one of the only bullets capable of reliably taking down an engine block.

7.62 and 5.56 just don't cut it—not enough mass, not enough velocity.

But the average .50-BMG FMJ projectile is

approximately 650 grains, delivered with over 13,000 foot-pounds of muzzle energy.

A single shot? Could be from a Barrett or a McMillan.

But you can also shoot a single shot from an M2.

Snipers in the Korean War would put telescopic sights on their M2s.

"What the fuck!" Zack wailed.

Zack's scream snapped Wilson back into real time and he slammed on the brakes. The LMTV's tires groaned and chirped across the asphalt and they came to a halt there in the middle of the road.

"Get out! Get out!" Wilson reached across and shoved Zack toward the passenger side, trying to get him to open his door and run.

A sudden, incredibly loud whine, almost simultaneous with a *snap-clap-crunch* sound.

Wilson felt a pressure in his hand and when he looked, the first thing he saw was that Zack's head and neck were lolling, almost detached from his torso, exposed muscle fibers twitching about madly amid jutting bone. In the slopping mess of Zack's avulsed upper torso, his own hand was shaking about, his ring finger and his little finger missing at the first knuckle.

Small-arms fire from ahead.

Wilson looked up, his mangled right hand still lying on Zack's body. The Humvee was turned almost sideways in the left shoulder and Captain Harden and LaRouche were crouched at the front end, using the engine block for cover. LaRouche fired blindly over the hood of the Humvee while

Captain Harden yelled at the rest of the convoy to get the fuck in the woods.

Wilson turned and grabbed Zack's arm with his injured hand, and he took ahold of his rifle with the other. "I got you, buddy. Hang on."

He kicked his door open and heaved himself backward. He felt the seat disappear underneath him and he fell to the ground, losing his grip on Zack's arm. His head bounced off the concrete, bringing stars to his vision, but he clambered quickly to his feet, still holding his rifle.

Jim was suddenly there beside him, hauling him up. Wilson reached back into the cab, looking for some part of Zack to grab so he could haul him out of the truck.

Jim's hands grabbed his shoulder, staying him. "Get into the woods!"

"I gotta get Zack!" Wilson shook Jim off and reached over the driver's seat to where Zack's body was collapsed in a strange contortion across the seats. "Where's Julia? Maybe if we just stop the bleeding…"

Wilson felt himself being yanked out of the cab. Jim was in his face. "Get into the woods!"

Wilson bellowed back, "I've gotta get Zack!"

"You let me get Zack!" And then Jim turned him roughly and shoved him hard in the back.

Wilson stumbled but recovered, and he continued into the woods. When he looked back, Jim was right behind him. He hadn't rescued Zack at all. He'd lied to him!

Wilson stopped ten feet into the wood line and turned. "What the fuck are you doing?" he

screamed at Jim and launched himself back toward
the truck. Jim was having none of it, and he tackled Wilson straight to the forest floor.

"He's dead! He's dead!" Jim barked at him.
"Now keep your head down!"

Wilson laid his head back into the leaves, and
that was when the pain finally surfaced. It welled
up so suddenly, he just started breathing rapidly
and then finally pulled his hand in front of his face,
could see the little white shards of bones sticking
out of the meat, could see the tendons flicking back
and forth as his hand trembled, and he screamed,
"My fingers! My fingers are gone!"

Lee hit the woods with LaRouche close behind
him. Deuce had made it out of the Humvee with
them, but then he'd sprinted off into the woods
and Lee couldn't see him anymore. Another *zip-
snap-BOOM* and a small sapling suddenly splintered into pieces to his right. The time between
the impact and the report was negligible—the
shooter was within a few hundred yards of them.

He didn't stop until he could just barely see the
road, and he hoped to God it meant that whoever
was shooting at them wouldn't be able to see him.
Then he slid to the dirt and came up on his knees,
his chest heaving and sweat beginning to break
out over his face.

LaRouche leaned against a tree, gasping. "Fuck
me! Was that a fifty?"

Lee nodded. To their right, he could see the
others huddled maybe a few dozen yards from
them but still far enough into the woods to be

relatively safe. "Jim!" he shouted in that direction. "Jim!"

The tall man suddenly appeared from off the ground, seeming to emerge from an invisible hole. He scanned around and when he saw them, he ran over, hunched low, with his rifle in hand. He pulled to a stop in front of Lee.

"What the heck was that?"

"Fuckin' ambush." Lee gritted his teeth. "They must have realized we were gonna try to run through it—*FUCK!*" Lee put a hand on Jim's shoulder. "You and LaRouche need to get back up to the vehicles. *Do not let them take out any more vehicles.* I can't stress that enough. Wherever they're shooting from, they're close, so if they can see us, we can see them. Keep them busy, try to see where the shots are coming from, and start laying into that position on the Ma Deuce." Lee looked them both in the eyes. "Do not fucking get yourself killed. Do you understand me?"

They both nodded.

"Where you going?" LaRouche asked.

"You guys hold their attention; I'm gonna shoot them in the back."

Lee didn't wait for further discussion, because there was no time for it. He turned, facing perpendicular to the road, and sprinted deeper into the woods.

He slipped through the trees, just pumping blood and gulping air.

The sameness of the forest became soothing in its monotony, almost hypnotic like the lines on a highway. The ground dipped down now—that was

good. It would cut off the line of sight even better. At the bottom, there was a stream. He headed
for it, angling to his right a bit. He didn't want to
be in the stream, because it would be freezing and
also because it was noisy. But the low point of the
banks would keep him out of sight.

The earth was squishy beneath his boots as he
ran along the banks. The extra power it took to
keep up his pace made his thighs burn and his
lungs stretch out for more oxygen. He had to balance speed and stealth. He wanted to come in
from behind these guys, and his best guess was
that they were in the woods, maybe two or three
hundred yards out from where they had stopped
their vehicles.

How many were there?

Only one person shooting at them with a
.50-cal, it sounded like.

But he might have a buddy to watch his back.

Regardless, it was one of those shitty situations
where it didn't really matter. You had to do what
you had to do, and if it turned out that you made
the wrong choice, you were going to have to adapt
and overcome. Even a wrong action is better than no
action. Stasis is the enemy on a dynamic battlefield.

As he ran, he shucked a 40mm grenade from a
pouch on his vest and slipped it into the launcher
under his M4. In his mind, he pictured two men,
lying side by side in a sniper's hide, facing away
from him as he crept silently up behind them and
put a 40mm grenade right between them, ripping their bodies apart. He held onto the image,
clutched it like a talisman.

He slowed to a jog, glancing up the steady incline in the direction of the road.

BOOM.

It almost halted him in his tracks for a moment. The attackers had fired out another round, and he hoped and prayed silently that it had not hit one of his people. Who the fuck were these guys? Were they just your average raiders who had stumbled across a .50-caliber rifle?

No . . .

They seemed to have discipline in their fire. The superb round placement when they took out his engine block. That was precision, to hit a moving vehicle right where you wanted it. Precision and discipline.

Lee waited for the sound of LaRouche and Jim returning fire on one of the M2s, but it didn't come. Just the sporadic, random crack of the 5.56mm rifles, striking out ineffectively into the woods.

They had not yet pinpointed the sniper.

He kept going.

It seemed like he had been running a while, but he knew how adrenaline could distort your sense of time. The last rifle shot he'd heard seemed omnidirectional, with no real way to triangulate where it had been coming from. He had to make sure he was past the sniper before he cut back in toward the road. If he didn't run far enough, he ran the risk of walking right up on them and giving away his advantage.

Go for thirty more seconds.

Lee kept count as evenly as he could, and when

the thirty seconds were up, he knelt down next to the creek bed and shouldered his rifle. To his left, the creek was petering out into a muddy, rock-filled hole. A faded can of Budweiser was half submerged in the silt. To his right, the slope was shallower.

He'd already passed the highest point of the hill.

That was where the sniper would be.

BOOM.

Lee's head snapped to his right. This time the rifle report had a definite direction.

More muffled chatter of return fire echoed through the woods, suddenly bolstered by the much louder sound of one of Lee's M2s spitting out rounds. Lee heard the rounds snapping branches way over his head and saw one of the tracers burn through the woods.

"Yes," he whispered, hunching low. "Light 'em up…"

Low to the ground now, Lee moved quietly up the side of the slope toward the sound of the last rifle report. As he gained ground, he sank lower, to the point where he was on his hands and knees, scooting forward a few yards at a time. Tension stretched his eyes wide and caused his bladder to tighten. He kept moving.

Close to the top now, he heard voices, but he couldn't make out what they were saying.

Another rake of fire from the M2, and this time one of the rounds hit a tree so close to Lee that he could feel the splinters of wood tickle the back of his neck.

The voices ahead of him cried out in alarm.

Then there was the sound of running feet.

Shit! Lee's heart squirmed into his gullet. He rose up on one knee, pulling his rifle in tight and sighting down at the crest of the hillock. The red dot of his Aimpoint hovered there just above the carpet of leaves.

Two shapes suddenly appeared, sprinting to get over the hill. One of them carried an M4 at the ready, with what looked like a scoped bolt-action rifle strapped to his back, and the other carried a Barrett M82 by its carrying handle, the bipod still extended out like he'd simply grabbed it and run.

They both wore ACUs.

There was a moment when the man with the M4 saw Lee kneeling there on the ground, and they made eye contact. There was hesitation. Just looking at him, the way he wore the uniform, the way he carried his rifle, he was a copy of every soldier Lee had ever known.

He didn't want to pull that trigger.

The man shouted, "It's him!" and raised his rifle.

Lee squeezed off two shots, striking the man once in the head and once in the chest, and spinning him backward to the ground. As the man fell back, Lee swung on the other and began aggressing on him, shouting, "Drop that weapon! Drop it!"

The giant Barrett rifle clattered to the ground, but this man had no intention of sticking around. He turned and threw himself down the hill with all the speed and desperation of a rabbit running from a coyote. Lee tracked him with his rifle, the red dot leading him just slightly as he plunged down the hill.

Lee intentionally aimed low and fired a quick burst of rounds. He wasn't sure how many of them connected or where they hit, but the running man jerked and tripped and then tumbled all the way down the hill until he rolled into a tree. The man groaned and grabbed his ass, his legs grinding out grooves in the wet forest floor that showed black underneath the ochre leaves.

Lee turned quickly to address the first man he'd shot. He lay flat on his back with his head tilted up and his mouth open. Red bubbles were still gurgling out of his nose, and everything above his nostrils was coated in it so that Lee could not see his eyes, nor where the bullet had entered his skull. He was positive the man was dead, even if his heart would still be pumping blood for the next few seconds. He'd seen that type of bleeding before, and it only occurred when there wasn't much left but pulp between the ears.

The rifle strapped to the man's back was a Remington 700.

Probably the rifle that had killed Jake.

Lee lowered his M4 and turned back to the man who still writhed at the bottom of the hill. The rain began to fall harder, its patter across the leaves of the forest floor drowning out the murmurs and curses. It would also cover the sound of approaching infected. With all the gunfire, it was just a matter of time before they showed up to investigate.

Maybe they were already there.

Lee made his way down the slope. The man on the ground caught sight of Lee approaching and twisted himself so that his back was against the tree, baring his teeth in a grimace. Lee stopped short just a few feet and pointed at the man with the muzzle of his rifle.

"Who the fuck are you?"

The man groaned and clutched at his wound but did not respond. The crotch of the man's pants was dark with blood, and it soaked the entire pant leg. It looked like the round had caught the man high on the inside of his thigh and exited near his buttocks. The amount of blood suggested damage to the femoral artery.

Lee got the sensation that he was being watched and he turned to glance behind him. The woods stretched on in a glistening, rainy pallor. There was no wind to cause anything to move, and the forest sat preternaturally still in the steady downpour. Over the sound of the rain, he thought he heard a distant growl, but when he listened, it was not repeated.

He turned back to the man and knelt down. "Let me lay this out for you, hotshot. I give it three minutes before you pass out from blood loss." Lee rubbed his beard thoughtfully. "I don't know how long it will take the infected to find you, but I can't imagine it will be long. So...you think you'll still be awake to be eaten alive, or do you think the blood loss will get you first?"

The man blinked rapidly and began looking around.

"All that shooting?" Lee said. "There's gotta be a pack of them somewhere around here, coming to investigate. So you tell me...you wanna sit here and see how it ends for you...or do you want some help?"

The man shook his head. "I don't wanna die."

Lee's face became flint-rock hard. "Who are you?"

A moment's hesitation, and then: "Sergeant Prestone."

"You Army?"

A shaky nod. "Eighty-second Airborne."

"Why are you trying to kill me?"

The man's eyes glinted and a red smile touched his lips. "Because you're a fucking traitor, Captain Harden...a fucking traitor."

Lee reacted without conscious thought. He leaned forward and struck out with the buttstock of his rifle, hitting the wounded man in his upper thigh, right where the bullet had entered him. The man's eyes went wide, he made a tortured sound, and curled in on himself like a little gray pill bug.

Lee sidled closer and grabbed the man by the face, forcing eye contact. "Do not fuck with me."

"It's the truth," the man moaned. He was beginning to shake and his skin was becoming pale. "It's the truth..."

Lee shook him. "Who sent you?"

"No. Get me out of here...The infected..."

"The infected are going to rip you to shreds unless you tell me who sent you."

"Save me and I'll tell you." The sergeant's voice was faint.

"It doesn't work like that." Lee shook his head. "You tell me who sent you."

The man's bloodless lips moved, forming words

before he found a voice to put to them. "...you know who sent me...you know." His eyes swam around in the deeper end of unconsciousness and then came back to the surface for a moment. "Your time is coming, Captain."

"You're not answering my question."

"We weren't the only ones."

"What are you talking about?"

"They sent others."

"To kill me?"

"Yes."

"Why?"

"I'm tired."

Lee leaned away from the man as though the sight of him was repugnant. Deeper in the woods, but this time much clearer, he heard the howl, echoed back and forth. He stood and wiped rainwater from his eyes and from where it had gathered around the mouth of his beard.

Sergeant Prestone watched him as he stood. "You gonna help me?"

Lee shook his head. "Won't do you any good."

The man tried to haul himself upright but was too weak. "But you said..."

"I said you had about three minutes left to your life. But you've gone and wasted time trying to bullshit me, and the infected are getting too close." Lee rubbed his chin. "Guess you should have talked faster."

"Then kill me."

"No."

"Please...just shoot me." Sergeant Prestone sounded panicked. "Don't let them get me."

Lee pulled the hood of his parka up over his head and turned away from the dying man. "You won't distract them if you're dead."

Lee turned himself back the way he had come and began walking quickly away.

"You sonofabitch!" the man cried out weakly from the ground. "You sonofabitch! Don't leave me here!"

But Lee had already left him. His parting hope was that the man would pass into shock before he felt much. He could not imagine the pain of being eaten alive.

As he worked his way back to the group, he thought he heard the sounds of growling and barking, and perhaps a scream of terror, muted by the woods and the rain.

TWENTY-TWO

Odd Cargo

HOLD HIM DOWN!" Julia ordered.

Wilson squirmed beneath the bulk of two of his teammates, one holding onto each arm while Julia took hold of his right wrist and held it tight, then took the first stump of a finger, what used to be his little finger, and forced it out straight.

"Waitwaitwait!" Wilson cried out. "Don't do that, Julia! Please!"

She showed no pity when she looked at him, only honesty. "Wilson, this is gonna hurt, but we gotta do it. I gotta close up your fingers somehow, and there's not enough skin to stitch them shut."

"Can't you sew my fingers back on?" His voice shook.

"No, I can't sew them back on." She turned to Jim. "Bring it over here while it's still hot."

Jim knelt down, holding his M4, barrel up. The barrel burned hot enough to sizzle the raindrops off into steam as they hit it. The look on Jim's face was pained, as though he felt the agony of what Wilson was about to experience.

Julia pulled Wilson's wrist toward the hot barrel. "Put that cloth in his mouth. Wilson, you bite down on that thing hard, but *do not* jerk your hand around. You gotta be strong."

His response was a shake of the head. "Fuck! Jesus! Oh no..."

Lucky knelt over his head, holding a towel from one of their packs, rolled up tight. He placed it apologetically in Wilson's open mouth, at which point the young Air Force cadet closed his eyes and bit down hard.

Julia pushed the stump of Wilson's little finger into the barrel.

It took a moment for the sensation of his own burning flesh to hit him. Then his eyes shot open and he issued a sound that would have been a scream if not for the towel in his mouth. His teammates urged encouragement to him, but their voices were overcome by the desperate noises coming from him.

"One more," Julia said. "One more."

Wilson shook his head fiercely, but it did not save him. With one grown man forcing his arm out straight, Julia held on to the remains of his ring finger and pulled it inexorably toward the scalding metal, touching it amid muffled shouts and jerking, and holding it there while the skin and meat and blood vessels seared into one raw, red mass.

"Done," Julia said and immediately released Wilson and stepped back. Two of his teammates jumped back with her, but the one holding onto Wilson's right arm was too slow. As soon as Wilson got his left arm free, he swung out wildly and clobbered his teammate, causing him to stumble backward.

Wilson backpedaled away from them, the pain blinding him to the fact that they were only helping him. He clutched his three-fingered hand to his chest and ripped the towel out of his mouth, and like it was a plug in a spigot, he spewed out swears and curses as he huddled on the ground, his eyes squeezed shut again.

Julia breathed heavily with a shake of her head, wiping her bloody hands off on the hem of her parka and then swiping the rain out of her eyes. Beside her, LaRouche grimaced, looking down at Wilson's form.

"Damn," he muttered.

The sound of boots in the wet leaves behind them.

Lee trotted up to the group, soaked and breathing heavily, rainwater steadily dripping from his beard. He pointed to the road. "We gotta go..." His words trailed off as he caught sight of Wilson, still lying on the ground. He took a deep, rapid breath to catch his wind again, then he looked at Julia questioningly.

She zipped up her pack with a jerk and hauled it off the ground. When she spoke, she avoided Lee's gaze. "We lost Zack."

Lee seemed taken aback. "What happened?"

"They got him in the chest," she said tightly. "Nothing we could do for him."

Lee put a hand to his face, pulling it slowly down over his eyes, as though the anger and the frustration and the pain could be wiped from him like the rainwater. He stared warily back in the direction he'd come from, but when he saw and heard nothing, he looked once again at Wilson, who was just now sitting up, still cradling his hand. "What's wrong with him?"

Julia pulled one backpack strap onto her shoulder. "Lost two fingers on his right hand."

Lee nodded slowly, not responding.

"We just seared them closed with a hot rifle barrel."

"Oh." Lee took a step so he was standing over Wilson, and then extended his hand. "Come on, man. We gotta get mobile again."

Still grimacing, Wilson took the offered hand.

Lee hauled the man to his feet, then turned to the rest of the group and pointed for the vehicles. "We need to get the fuck out of here."

LaRouche pulled up beside Lee as they headed for the vehicles. "What about the Humvee?"

"We'll come back for it later," Lee said. "For now, just grab our supplies and the radios and put them in the other Humvee and let's get going."

"Hey." LaRouche touched the captain's shoulder. "Who the fuck was that shooting at us?"

Lee looked at him, and something strange passed over his eyes.

"Just some guys," he said, and left it at that.

Moving quickly, they dismantled the M2 on the now-defunct Humvee and pulled the SINCGARS radio off its bracket, stowing both of them in the other Humvee. Then they pulled Zack's body out of the cab of the LMTV and put it in the back cargo area. They would take it back to Camp Ryder and bury it with Jake.

Bury it with the others.

The windshield in that LMTV was still usable, despite the gaping hole on the passenger's side.

Lee hurriedly took a cloth from Zack's pack and wiped down the seats. His face remained stolid, and he gave no more reaction to this grisly task than if he were simply cleaning a dirty window, even when he found a long tendril of flesh hanging on to the rough hole in the seat back. He eyed the thing and then picked it up with his thumb and forefinger, and flicked it out the door behind him.

All the while his eyes kept tracking back to the woods.

With only a few seconds to spare, Deuce reappeared. He was quiet, but clearly concerned with something in the woods, as his golden eyes remained locked and his ears perked in that direction. Lee was not the only one who took note of the dog's attentions—the rest of the group quickly piled into their vehicles.

LaRouche took the driver's seat and from there watched the captain warily. As they drove it became obvious that Lee's eyes were unfocused, staring straight ahead through the rain-dappled windshield, blinking in time with the windshield wipers. His eyes only became sharp again when he glanced down at his GPS to monitor their progress.

An error message popped up on the screen of the GPS unit and Lee's eyes narrowed. He held up the device, then off to the left, then off to the right, up against the window. Finally, the error message went away. Lee held the device in the air and muttered something under his breath.

"Something wrong with it?" LaRouche asked.

Lee turned to face him like he had forgotten the sergeant was sitting there next to him. There was that same weird look again, but it quickly disappeared. "Maybe the satellite orbits are starting to decay." He looked back to the screen. "That's the second time it's happened this week."

They were silent for a while.

After a time, Lee pointed out the windshield. "There, to the right. That's our road."

LaRouche cranked the wheel to the right and they pulled onto the unpaved road. It was just plain dirt turned to mud, and mostly overgrown. Lee consulted his GPS again, but the screen was frozen with the error message again.

"Sonofa*bitch*..." Lee shook the device as though maybe a wire was loose. Finally he gave up. "Just go straight down. We'll find the damn thing."

It took five minutes to find the bunker—a big cement lump protruding from the forest floor with an iron door that looked as formidable and secure as a bank vault. A large tree branch, still adorned with wilted and crinkled brown leaves, had fallen over the door, partially obscuring it from view.

After they found the bunker, it took more than two hours to load everything into the trucks. The first LMTV—the one with the .50-caliber bullet hole in the windshield—was crammed full of a thousand pounds of C4, fuses, blasting caps, and det cord. There were another thousand pounds from Bunker #4 back at Camp Ryder. It sounded like a lot, but cutting bridges took a lot of explosives.

P is for Plenty, Lee thought absently.

The other LMTV held crates of claymores, grenades, and ammunition that only took up about half of the cargo bed, so they filled in the cracks with M4s, boxes of magazines, and a jumble of the six-magazine shoulder bags, haphazardly thrown on top of everything else. There was room in the Humvee and in the cab of the HEMTT, so Julia hauled up as many medical supplies as she could fit in those spaces.

By then it was early afternoon and it had stopped raining.

Lee closed and secured the bunker and convened with his team. Strapping back into his rifle and gear, which he'd doffed to carry supplies back and forth, his eyes traveled from person to person. Tired faces, but hard as well. Hard with violence and loss.

"I know it's been a rough couple of days," he said. "Sanford didn't take as much time as we thought, but we paid the price for it. I know you guys want to get back to Camp Ryder, and I don't blame you, so I'll leave it up to you guys." He situated his sling around his neck. "Eventually, we're going to need to scavenge whatever vehicles the National Guard left for us at the airport outside of Sanford. We can do it now, on the way back to Camp Ryder, or we can go straight home and make another trip tomorrow." He shrugged. "I'll leave it up to you."

They looked between each other and murmured.

A consensus was quickly reached.

LaRouche nodded. "Let's do it now. Get it out of the way."

"Alright." Lee gestured for the trucks. "Then let's not burn any more daylight."

The unpaved road dead-ended in a slight clearing with a few sapling trees trying to push up out of the shadows of their brethren, their growth frozen for the time being as they stood dormant for the winter. It was tight, but with some maneuvering and some spinning of the tires through the muck and mud, they were able to get the trucks turned around and on the move.

They drove on, kept turning through bends in the road, and Lee expected to see a roadblock with rifles pointed at him, but there were none. They had not seen any sign of roadblocks in more than a month. Lee had heard them referred to as *bandits*. Such an old word for such a seemingly new problem.

But it wasn't really new, was it?

It was the same old humanity, suffering from the same old problems.

These problems didn't stem from a fallen government. They lay within humanity's base instincts, and the collapse of society only made it easier for them to manifest themselves. Perhaps Julia was right. Perhaps there truly was no difference between the infected and the uninfected. They all had the same problem lurking inside of them. One simply had the ability to cover it up, and the other did not.

Because society is just a mask that we wear, constructed to look like something else, something better, something we *wish* we could be. If you live in that society long enough, if you wear the mask long enough, then you eventually forget that you're only a few generations removed from savagery, and you let yourself believe that it's no longer a part of who you are.

You're better than that now.

You're "evolved."

But it's an inescapable part of you, just as it's a part of a dog, and the infected hordes, and the packs of hunters. It's the rabid selfishness of an animal that knows no morals or laws. It's a common bond between humans and everything else that lives and breathes. The only thing that sets humans apart is their often-errant desire to distance themselves from it. To be greater than that small creature inside of them.

Sometimes it works, and sometimes it doesn't.

But if humanity was anything, it was stubborn.

And resilient.

And self-deceiving to the extreme.

So we rebuild, Lee thought to himself. *For better or worse, we're gonna try again.*

He sighed and rubbed his face. *I'm just tired. Just fucking tired.*

The twists and turns of the empty roads led them on for nearly an hour before they finally reached the narrow two-lane road that led into the regional airport.

Lee could see what it had been before and also what it had become. To either side of the road stood old farmhouses. These had been walled off with hastily erected chain-link fencing, staked into the shoulder of the road with metal poles. Lee could remember the monumental amount of trash his unit had left behind them everywhere they went during the invasion of Iraq, and here was no different. Even simply transporting the refugees from the high school in Sanford to the airport for evacuation had resulted in such a trash clog that the edges of the fence were cluttered with it up to about knee height. Water bottles, MRE wrappers, diapers, cigarette butts, and even bits of clothing, sneakers, and electronic accessories like iPods and cell phones littered the sides of the road. It was like everyone had simply started shedding dead weight at this point, throwing whatever they didn't need over the side and into the street.

The houses and the chain-link fencing stopped as they crossed over a bridge with a single set of railroad tracks underneath. On the rails, a freight train sat stalled, its lengthy bulk trundling motionless off into the distance in either direction, its cargo of coal and cedar chips and whatever else it carried stuck in limbo forever.

After the bridge, the trees to either side of the road disappeared and the land opened up into a sprawl of white hangars and a squat brick building right in the center of it all. The municipal airport had no security measures to speak of. No gates to block their progress either into the airport or onto the tarmac. The road led to a parking lot in front of the brick building, and there was a cluster of military vehicles there, spread out onto the tarmac. Immediately, Lee could see a couple of "gun truck" Humvees, as well as a few more LMTVs and a HEMTT with a wrecker attachment.

Jim pulled the truck up over the curb, the other two vehicles following in a slow parade as they circled the compound at a steady twenty miles per hour. As they did, Lee counted the vehicles, including several that he had not seen, parked hurriedly beside and behind some hangar buildings as though the operators had abandoned them in a rush and caught the last flight out of town.

There were no aircraft left on the field save for a few civilian propeller planes, now just abandoned chunks of fiberglass and metal. All the helicopters were gone, and if anything like a C-130 had been here, Lee saw no evidence of it now.

The vehicles that remained were three Humvees, two of them with guns, and the other just an old two-seater cargo truck; two more LMTVs identical to the two they had; and two more HEMTTs, one with a wrecker attachment and the other with a tanker on the back.

After taking a long, cautious loop around the perimeter of the airport, they saw nothing to make them believe there were any infected in the area. Lee directed LaRouche onto the tarmac, and they parked there, about fifty yards from the cluster of abandoned military vehicles.

Lee pushed open his door. "Sit tight for a second."

He jumped down, scanning around him carefully as he jogged back to the other Humvee. Lucky was driving, and Wilson sat in the passenger seat, his jaw clenched and sweating profusely. Tough kid to lose two fingers and have them seared shut with no pain medication.

"How you holdin' up?" Lee asked.

Wilson just grunted and nodded.

Lee patted him on the shoulder, then directed his attention to Lucky. "Hand me that radio."

Lucky reached forward for Wilson and plucked the handset from the console and leaned across

Wilson's body to give it to the captain. Lee nodded in thanks and keyed the radio. He called for Harper twice before garnering a response.

"Yeah, go ahead, Captain. This is Harper."

Lee turned and faced away from the Humvee as he talked, scanning the area behind him. He could still hear Deuce complaining from the back of the LMTV, but he had quieted some. "Harper, you still in Lillington, or have you headed out?"

"We're still here, but we were about to hit the road." A pause. "Jacob has his... thing."

"Copy. Switch over to private channel," Lee said quickly.

After a moment and a few adjustments, Harper was the first to transmit. "Are you sure about this?"

Lee rubbed his eyebrows. "No. How's it look? Is it secured?"

"Yeah, it's secure." There was a level of resignation in his voice. "It makes a lot of noise, but it doesn't seem to want to attack us. It just kind of lashes out if you get too close."

Natural instinct, Lee thought. *Lot of posturing, but a pregnant female won't go for a fight unless she absolutely has to. Too much risk to the fetus.*

Aloud, he said, "What about the others?"

"There were no others." Harper's voice was flat. "This was the only one left. The others were dead and this one was eating them to stay alive."

Lee made a face. "Has anyone from Lillington seen you guys?"

"No, we're a couple blocks from the outpost, and we're outta sight."

"Good. How many do you have with you?"

"I've got five, besides myself."

"Count Jacob out," Lee said. "He needs to stay with his...subject. Send one other person with him to help if the thing gets out of hand, then let him take your pickup straight to Smithfield, and don't let anyone see them. You and the other three beg, borrow, or steal a vehicle from Lillington—I'm sure Old Man Hughes will loan you one—and get up to this airport."

"Okay. What do you have up there?"

"I've got some vehicles that need to be appropriated."

"We'll be on the way in ten."

They signed off and Lee had those present with him get out and begin sweeping the compound on foot. The ride through had not revealed anything, but they still proceeded with caution. They left their convoy in the center of the small airstrip and gradually made their way between the hangars toward the other vehicles.

As they passed by a particularly large hangar, Lee noticed Deuce giving the building a wide berth, his head hung low and his tail tucked in. He growled almost a constant stream of uncomfortable noises and kept his eyes fixed on that hangar.

Lee sniffed the air, and it may have only been his imagination, but he thought there was a tinge of that rank, unwashed odor, tainting the smell of fresh rainfall. At one point, while the others continued on, Lee hung back and inclined his ear toward the hangar, standing perhaps twenty feet from it. He could not be certain, but he thought he heard something scrape and slide against the corrugated walls of the hangar.

He did a visual check of the doors and found them padlocked.

He thought perhaps there was good reason for that and decided not to go near it again.

The small white pickup truck pulled into the parking deck of the Johnston Memorial Hospital in Smithfield and began working its way up to the top level. It drove quickly and bore with it two occupants and an interesting piece of cargo.

Jacob drove, while in the passenger seat Devon sat askew, clutching a rifle and staring uncomfortably out the back glass at the blanket-wrapped and rope-tied bundle lying secure in the bed of the pickup truck. Every time it moved, whether under its own power or because of the movement of the truck taking the turns, Devon tensed.

They'd restrained it with Jacob's homemade dogcatcher's pole and then fallen upon it with the thick blanket, terrified and hoping that its teeth would not be able to bite through. Then they'd tied it around the waist and ankles with rope, pinning its arms to its torso and rendering it the squirming form in the back that now set Devon's pulse racing.

When they reached the top level of the parking deck, Doc Hamilton was already exiting the stairwell doors that accessed the main wing of the hospital. He was a small-framed man in his late forties, with a ring of black hair growing wild around a spotlessly blank dome of scalp. He had a sort of permanently paternal expression engraved on his face, and even now it only showed concern and perhaps a bit of confusion.

Jacob put the pickup truck in park and stepped out, immediately making his way to the truck bed. Devon followed after a moment's hesitation and a pained look that spoke of his desire to be anywhere else. Doc Hamilton watched the two men go to the rear of the pickup bed and lower the tailgate, craning his neck to see what was inside.

"What can I help you with, gentlemen?"

Inside the truck bed, the brown-bundled form suddenly thrashed and growled.

Doc Hamilton took an involuntary step back. "What the hell is that?"

Jacob looked quickly around to make sure there was no one else watching. He took three large steps and seized Doc Hamilton in a firm handshake. "I'm Doctor Jacob Weber, microbiologist with the CDC."

Recognition showed through in Doc Hamilton's features. "Oh, you're the guy from Virginia."

"Yes." Jacob nodded curtly. "And I'm going to need a bed and as many soft restraints as you can find."

"Uh...okay..."

Jacob laid his hand on Doc Hamilton's shoulder. "And Doctor..."

"Yes?"

"Do you know anything about sedation or anesthetics?"

"Not really."

Jacob flashed a nervous smile. "I'm going to need you to learn...quickly."

TWENTY-THREE

THE PRISONER

ONLY TWO OF THE vehicles on the airstrip were out of commission: one of the LMTVs would not start for some unknown reason, and one of the Humvees looked like it had been cannibalized for parts. After finding the vehicles that were in good working order, they moved them over onto the tarmac and arranged them in a single-file line, so that the convoy was ready to go as soon as Harper arrived.

On the northern end of the tarmac, they located the vestiges of what looked like an ammunition drop. The National Guard troops, assigned initially just to evacuate people, were ill equipped to handle the combat they were forced into. It was likely they had depleted their small armories in a very short amount of time. The ammunition drop had probably come out of the back of a Chinook from Fort Bragg.

They found it splayed out like the carcass of an animal attacked by wolves. The parachute was cut away partially, still attached by two lengths of cord, and the cargo netting that held the pallet together was flayed open like a skin. The tops of the wooden boxes were scattered about, some of them in pieces, and most of the boxes were empty. About half of the pallet bore boxes designated as 5.56mm, but the other half was .50-cal. There was not a single box of 5.56mm left, but they were able to find three untouched boxes of .50-cal.

They took what they could get and made sure each Humvee had at least one hundred rounds in its gun.

Thirty minutes after their conversation on the radio ended, Harper and his three people showed up, crammed into an old Toyota Camry that puttered onto the airfield. Lee waved to them as they pulled up and extricated themselves from the car.

"You guys made good time," Lee remarked, shaking Harper's hand.

"I was eager to get away from Frankenstein and his creature."

Lee half smiled. "He'll get good information. Maybe even something that can help us."

Harper shrugged. "Maybe. But I don't wanna be around the damn thing."

Lee changed the subject by pointing to the vehicles. "Right now, let's get these things rolling toward Camp Ryder."

"Okay." Harper regarded the convoy stretched down the tarmac, hands on his hips. "What's the plan?"

"Me and LaRouche will take the lead Humvee, Wilson and Lucky in the rear Humvee. Everyone else just grab a vehicle and follow the leader." Lee shifted his feet. "Soon as we get out of this airport, I'm gonna pick up speed, and I'm not letting up until we get to Camp Ryder, so stay with me. I don't want to get bogged down."

Harper nodded but looked concerned. "When we get back, we gotta talk."

Lee met his gaze. "Yeah. Same here."

The group split up to their separate vehicles and the convoy got rolling. Lee kept his Humvee at a steady forty-five-mile-per-hour clip as they moved away from the airport and back onto the surface streets. The fencing and trash flowed by them in streaks without detail or texture. A small break in the clouds showed a glimpse of white, sun-brightened clouds, cresting above their dark, damp underbellies. The hole in the sky drifted with the wind, opened wider, and then eventually collapsed on itself after revealing a sliver of blue sky.

The wind was picking up, blowing the dreary rain clouds out, and bringing colder weather in behind it. Flurries of brown leaves skipped across the roadway, caught in the gusts. Lee eyed the occasional house as they passed by. There was a quality to everything now, even in the houses that were not clearly ransacked, a grainy, worn-out feeling about them. This indistinct quality to everything was as pervasive here as it was in the cities, and Lee believed probably across the entire country. Without the people who had once inhabited these areas, a wasteland was all that was left, and you could feel it like a chill in your bones.

Scavenging from these houses, Lee felt like an archaeologist, staring in wonder at the things humanity had once held dear to them. Ornate clocks and sets of fine china. Placards and degrees and trophies. The things people were most proud of, the things displayed on mantels and walls, were now the things that were the first to be left behind.

They continued down unused streets, driving through long stretches of country and short clusters of neighborhoods and intersections with old abandoned gas stations long since tapped of any fuel. At intersections they slowed just enough to make the turn, but never stopped. And if they were passing straight through the intersection, Lee didn't even tap on the brakes.

Just before it happened, Lee had sunk deep into a memory, triggered by some unique and fleeting sensations, a combination of numbers on a mental lock that opened up the dusty safe where things long forgotten and pushed aside were stored. The things locked inside were impressions, images and bits of time, like clips of film. Sometimes just a feeling or an emotion.

The trigger was a gust of wind through the open windows that bore with it that musty, oaky scent so reminiscent of fall. The cold air seeped down past his collar, and the smell was the smell of leaf piles on an autumn day, and the sensation of lying there, the chill on his neck and on his cheeks and nose.

He was young in this memory, and his soul was still light, and the world maintained its wonder.

His memory was the sensation of the leaves, dry on top and wet on the bottom.

The feeling, almost slick against his fingers, of cold dew clinging to old wood in the early-morning shade—a ladder of boards nailed to the side of the tree that led up to the top and felt so incredibly high that his pulse raced.

It was the image of his childhood hiking boots with their red laces, and how they felt, heavy with mud as he tramped through the woods after his father.

It was the feeling of his blue jacket, the inside flannel so warm, but the metal zipper cold every time it touched his neck.

The earthy smell of pecans and the ripe, gritty feeling of their hulls as he gathered them in his pockets.

And it was into these memories that a ghost suddenly appeared, a being from another time, another place, transposed there strangely into his childhood among fall leaves and tree forts and hiking trails. All those images disappeared like a sudden gale of wind dissipating a cloud of smoke that hung in the air, and his memories became his perceptions of the present.

Blacktop stretching out before him.

Empty trees to either side.

A sign that stated the speed limit was fifty miles per hour.

And the ghost—a man—standing there in the center of the road, his legs straddling the double yellow line and his arms spread out wide, his hands open, palms revealed and empty. He wore a MultiCam uniform, and a matching boonie hat shrouded his bowed head.

Lee stamped on the brakes and the Humvee skidded to a stop just a few yards short of the man. Lee must have grabbed his rifle and exited the

Humvee, because the next thing that registered was how much colder the wind had gotten in the last half hour of driving. He stared down the barrel of his M4 as he approached the man in the road, and he realized he was yelling.

"Get on the ground! Get the fuck on the ground!"

The man complied, moving slowly and deliberately as he lowered himself so that he was facedown on the roadway, his legs and arms spread-eagle.

"Do not look up!" Lee shouted as he continued to approach.

He could hear boots behind him. LaRouche was there beside him, also pointing his rifle at the man on the ground, but his eyes were fixed on Lee. "Captain! What are you doing?"

"Make sure this motherfucker doesn't have any weapons, and get him in the back of a truck," Lee ordered. "I'll keep him covered, but we need to move quickly."

"Uh, Captain, I think he's military..."

"I know he's fucking military!" Lee snapped. "You're gonna hafta trust me on this one, LaRouche. Pat him down and detain him!"

LaRouche gave a slight shake of his head but turned his eyes toward the man in the road. "Sir! Keep looking down at the ground. Put your hands on your head and interlock your fingers. Don't move from that position, or you will be shot."

Again, the man on the ground complied.

Lee stood with his feet spread wide, his rifle addressed toward the man's torso, and his finger hovering outside the trigger guard. LaRouche crossed the short distance between them and took hold of the man's arms, pulling them behind his back and then securing them with a single large zip tie from his vest. As the hands were secured, Lee shifted his attention from the man in the road to the woods around them. He felt naked and exposed.

"This is not a trap," the man on the ground said loudly. "I'm not here to hurt anyone."

At the sound of his voice, Lee jerked, tingled uncomfortably, like a star bursting from his core out to his extremities.

When he looked back around, LaRouche was pulling the man to his feet. Lee took two steps and stood directly in front of them. The boonie hat was unsettled and fell from the man's head. Short, sandy hair with a long, crescent-shaped scar running from the top of his head down to his ear—a scar Lee knew came from a boating accident many years ago.

The man raised his head. "How are you, Lee?"

Lee bared his teeth. "Brian Tomlin..."

The man smiled hesitantly.

Then Lee delivered a right hook to the man's jaw and knocked him unconscious.

On the ground in front of Lee, the man called Brian lay on his back, his eyelids fluttering, while that strange knockout groan came from his throat. Lee ripped the shemagh from around his neck and used it to quickly blindfold the man on the ground. As he worked, his eyes scanned the woods again.

Harper appeared, wide-eyed. "Uh...what the hell was that?"

"Come on." Lee bent down and hooked his arms through one of the man's elbows. "We need to move."

Harper's voice bore a little more edge to it. "What the fuck is going on?"

Lee straightened his legs, dragging the man's torso off the ground. "Could I get some fucking help here? I'll explain things later. This is not the time or the place."

Harper's jaw protruded angrily, but he snatched up the man's other elbow and they began hauling him toward the nearest LMTV. "Why not, right?" His voice was rank with sarcasm. "We trust you on everything else, so what's one more time? You know, one of these days you're gonna have to actually tell us what the fuck you're doing!"

The man dragging between them mumbled something, forming words with the noises coming out of his mouth. Lee shook him hard. "Don't talk." His eyes came up to Harper as they shuffled around the corner of the LMTV, regarding the older man from under his eyebrows. "We've lost two men to ambushes. You wanna stand around with your ass in the wind, be my guest. But we need to get mobile ASAP."

They hauled the man into the back of the LMTV. Lee grabbed the handle on the lifted tailgate and hauled himself up. He looked over the side and saw LaRouche standing around, looking a little confused. "LaRouche, you're driving. I'm gonna watch our man back here."

LaRouche nodded and jogged back to their Humvee.

At the tailgate, Harper clenched his jaw. "You want help back there?"

Lee shook his head and looked down at the blindfolded man. "No. I got it."

Harper disappeared with a huff.

Lee knelt down over his prisoner. The man's mouth worked, probably feeling out the damage to his jaw. As the sound of engines shifting reached him and the LMTV lurched forward, Lee searched himself to see how the presence of this man affected him. Was he off balance? Was he shocked? Perhaps confused?

No.

He was cold inside. Like the surface of his mind was a frozen lake, and he knew there were things moving beneath that hard numbness. Powerful emotions that could hurt him, cloud his judgment, and drive him crazy. Fatalistic thoughts. Feelings of hopelessness. But he couldn't see or hear or feel them. He only had the knowledge that they were there.

Now there was nothing but the cold, flat hardness.

He took a deep breath and it felt rotten in his chest.

He would have preferred anger.

Lee sat back on his heels as the truck rumbled along. Over the sides, the tops of trees clawed at the darkening sky. He lifted his head and felt the wind on his face and neck, colder where his shemagh had kept his skin warm.

The man at his feet shifted and touched Lee's boot.

He directed his face upward, searching like a blind man. "That you, Lee?"

Lee didn't respond for a long time, just sat there, staring down at the captive and considering what to do next. Finally, he spoke. "What are you doing here, Brian?"

Brian triangulated on Lee's voice. "Listen to me. I know you're confused, but you have to trust me. I'm here for you."

"What about my men? What about them?"

"I can't help what happened—"

"Just shut the fuck up." Lee shook his head. "Who's taking care of South Carolina?"

"You've been out of the loop, my friend. What the hell happened to you, anyway?"

"How about you answer my questions first."

"There is no South Carolina, Lee. Not anymore."

Lee's eyes narrowed. "What do you mean?"

Brian shook his head. "No. Not here. You get me someplace safe and you keep me under lock and key and you have someone you *really* trust guard me. I'll talk to you in private. But not here."

Lee's jaw jutted out. "Suit yourself."

Five minutes later, they pulled up to the Camp Ryder gate. Lee peered over the top of the cab as the guard opened the entrance and the convoy rolled in, barely fitting all the vehicles inside. As the diesel engines trundled in, people began to notice and their eyes went wide at the line of military vehicles. Many of the people began to clap, smiling up at Lee as the LMTV came to a halt. Perhaps the presence of the military vehicles gave them an increased sense of security.

But Lee's mind was in another place, and he gave them a curt nod and hopped down off the tailgate. Harper was immediately there with him, and curious onlookers who wanted to see the vehicles pressed in on them. As they edged around the back of the truck, they saw the huddled form in the back, bound and blindfolded, and a slight hush fell over their excited talking.

"Help me get him out of here," Lee mumbled to Harper.

"Where we gonna put him?" Harper asked.

As he said it, Bus edged through the crowd, followed closely by a group of three that Lee recognized as some of the volunteers. Lee nodded to Bus and they pulled Brian over.

Bus's eyes widened a bit. "Who's this?"

Lee looked between Bus and Harper. "Please, just give me a minute so I only have to explain things once to the both of you."

Bus nodded. "Okay."

Lee pushed Brian into the hands of the three volunteers. "Find a shipping container for him and lock it up tight."

"Wait!" Brian protested, twisting his still-blindfolded face around. "Don't pass me off to these people, Lee! You have no idea what you're doing!"

"Get him out of here."

Two of the volunteers, both younger men, took hold of Brian and dragged him off.

Lee reached out and put a hand on the shoulders of Bus and Harper, simultaneously pulling them slightly closer as though to confide a secret to them and pushing them toward the Camp Ryder building as he started to walk. "Let's talk."

The three men stood in a tight circle inside the office. Bus leaned back against the desk and folded his arms across his chest. Harper stood in a similar repose but with one hand worrying ceaselessly at where his beard extended down onto his neck. Lee stood as the third point in the triangle, his rifle leaning against the chair behind him and his unbuckled tactical vest providing a support for his hands.

He told them what had happened over the course of the past few days and left nothing out. From the sniper who'd killed Jake, to the ambush as they neared the bunker, to the conversation he'd had with the dying man as he bled out on the forest floor, Lee recounted everything in detail, his voice rote and emotionless. He ended with his discovery of Brian Tomlin and his suspicions about the man.

Lee pursed his lips. "The two men sent to kill me knew which building we were going to use in Sanford, and they set a trap for us there. And then they clearly knew what route we were going to take to get to the bunker—which *no one* should know." He took a long, deep breath. "I personally believe that whoever is controlling them is someone with intimate knowledge of the operation. And that's where Brian Tomlin comes in."

Harper looked confused. "The guy we captured?"

Lee nodded.

"Why would he…" Harper trailed off, and Lee could see the dots connecting in his head and revealing an unpleasant picture. The older man's gaze fell down to the floor and his face tensed. "Sonofabitch. That's how you know him."

Bus stuck his head out and opened his arms. "Am I missing something here?"

"Brian Tomlin," Lee said quietly, "is *Captain* Brian Tomlin. The Coordinator for South Carolina."

Bus stood frozen in place for a moment, his eyelids blinking rapidly as though he were struggling to process the information he was receiving. Gradually, his arms retreated back to his sides and his blinking slowed again.

"Well, shit," he muttered.

Lee shifted, turning around and slowly stripping his vest from his shoulders and draping it over the back of the chair where his rifle leaned. Then he turned back to the other two men, his eyes on Harper. "That's why I treated him like I did."

"Yeah." Harper touched his forehead. "I see."

"He claims to be on my side, but right now, he's suspect number one." Lee sat down. "And that's my bit of news."

"Jesus." Bus looked briefly overwhelmed. "I'm afraid to ask, Harper...but do you have something for me as well?"

Harper suddenly looked troubled as he was forced to switch gears from one worry to the next. "Uh...yes. It's about Professor White and Lillington." He paused. "It sounds like a group of his students went missing—well, actually, they were kidnapped."

"Kidnapped?" Bus looked startled.

"Yeah," Harper continued. "Five of them were out scavenging along the edges of the town and apparently a group of guys in an old panel van pulled up and ordered them all on the ground. Kidnapped four of them, but one of them fought and got away. They beat the fuck out of him, though."

Bus's expression turned from surprise to suspicion. "Why didn't they call this in to us?"

Harper shook his head. "White said some bullshit about not wanting to make it public. He was afraid it would start a rash of vigilantism."

Bus rolled his eyes. "That guy is unbelievable."

"Yeah, well...all of that to say, White's requesting guns now."

It was Lee's turn to look surprised. "Guns?"

"Yeah." Harper shoved his hands in his jacket pocket. "I thought it was weird, but then again, I guess he's just worried about safety. And apparently, he doesn't want you or any of our people to get involved with trying to track down the bad guys and get the kids back. He says he'll handle it on his own, if we give him the tools."

Lee knew this would have been much more ironic in the old world, but he supposed now it was just a sad circumstance. If White and his students hadn't been idiots and rejected the firearms he'd initially tried to give them to protect themselves, they would not be in this situation, and those four others would be safe inside the walls with an unpleasant war story to tell around the fire.

Lee leaned his elbows onto his knees. "Alright. I guess we can give him some guns."

Harper crossed his arms. "I guess that brings us to the topic of the mission."

"Yes," Bus said. "When are you planning on leaving?"

"Tomorrow if possible. The day after at the latest." Lee looked at Harper as he said this. "I plan to meet with my entire team—the volunteers as well—and make sure everyone has everything in order before we go. If we can leave before noon tomorrow, we'll do it. If not, we'll wait until the following morning. But we need to get a move on. Who knows how close those things are to crossing into North Carolina, or if they're already here."

Bus nodded. "Just let me know, Captain. If you need the extra day to relax…"

Lee grimaced. "That would be great, but I don't think we have the time to relax. Every day we need to wait drives me nuts. I keep wondering how many of them are migrating south into the state, crossing that river, every day."

"It might not be any," Bus pointed out. "Jacob said he didn't expect them to cross into the state until late this month."

"Even if that's the earliest they'll make their way down here, we're still behind the eight ball." Lee looked up at the map on the wall. "It's going to take time to blow those bridges and set up in Eden. And that's all assuming that Jacob's estimation is correct. They could be knocking on our doorstep next week, or they might all die before they even reach the river. We just don't know."

"I agree." Harper looked stern. "We can't play the odds on this one. We need to assume the worst."

Lee stood, favoring his ankle slightly. "I need you to gather everyone up after dinner. We'll meet here." He looked around the room. "It'll be tight, but it's better than standing outside in the cold."

"All right. Where are you going to be?"

Lee took up his rifle. "I'm going to have a talk with Captain Tomlin."

TWENTY-FOUR

OLD FRIENDS...

IT HAD BEEN A decent day of scavenging for Greg and Arnie. They'd left in the morning when the sun was positively over the horizon and they knew the packs would be bedded down. Now as the afternoon waned into evening, they hit the road, aiming to be back at Camp Ryder before dusk.

For the last week, they had been working the Cedar Cove subdivision off of Highway 210. It was a few streets of approximately eighty middle-income houses sitting on half-acre plots of land. It didn't look like anything special, but the houses were still curiously full. The only things obviously missing were some clothes, cash, and a few family photos, absent from conspicuously blank spots on the walls.

Several of the houses at the front of the neighborhood had suffered from looters, back in the days when people were still grabbing big-screen TVs and video game consoles. One of them was fire-gutted, with a collapsed roof. But the houses nestled back into the neighborhood's cul-de-sacs were surprisingly untouched.

Today they'd been able to clear ten of those houses, Arnie pulling guard in the front while

Greg worked each house over meticulously, dragging along an old military-surplus duffel that grew heavier with each house until it weighed so much that Greg could hardly lift it into the hatchback of Arnie's Geo.

When he'd first started scavenging, he would take nearly everything from a house. But experience came with a little more discretion, and now he chose to take only the items that were in high demand and simply make mental notes of where everything else was, in case someone specifically requested those items later.

The Big Three, as he called them, were food, water, and clothing.

A close fourth was what he considered "drugstore items," which included everything from medicines to toiletries. As a rule, to prevent him from taking up real estate in his duffel with items that were low on the totem pole, he only took with him whatever drugstore items he could fit in the pockets of his coat. Usually a couple bars of soap and some medications.

The medications were a growing priority for Greg, but not the kind that Jenny and Doc Hamilton could use. More and more people were trading up pretty valuable items to get their hands on antidepressants, pain medications, and any other mood-altering drug to make their lives in this savage landscape feel less horrible.

Greg allocated his deepest coat pocket to those little orange bottles.

So Greg had a methodology for scavenging these houses.

First, you had to sweep it for threats—make sure nothing was hiding in the dark closets or under beds, ready to take a chunk out of you when you had your back turned. Then it was straight to the kitchen and pantry. Take everything that hasn't been expired for more than a year. Off to the closets and dressers. Take all the socks, and all the underwear. Hooded sweatshirts and micro fleece pullovers, if they were size large or above. Any pants of sufficiently sturdy construction— never touch the designer brands. Check if there are any solidly made boots. Finish up with a trip to the bathroom for medications, first-aid supplies, and bars of soap. Before leaving, check under the bed, between the mattresses, in the nightstand, and in the closets for guns or ammunition. If there's a garage, take note of what's inside so you can maybe come back through for it later. If there are cars, siphon the tanks.

So with the back of the Geo laden with a good haul of food, clothing, and even a few gallons of gasoline, they piled in with maybe an hour and a half to go before dusk and one more errand to run before returning to Camp Ryder.

Arnie drove while Greg stood up in the back-seat with his Remington 870.

"I don't get why Jerry gives a shit about these fuckers," Arnie griped.

Greg could just barely hear him over the sound of the wind rushing by his ears, but he shrugged and hollered back, "You know how he is. Fostering goodwill and shit like that."

"Whatever."

That concluded the conversation.

Greg kept an eye on the time and the distance from the sun to the western horizon.

They arrived at Campbell University with about forty-five minutes to spare.

Greg hopped down out of the Geo and opened up the duffel, retrieving from it several food items, along with a couple of thick blankets. He used the blankets to wrap up the canned goods and a sleeve of sandwich cookies—a little care package for the kids in the dormitory.

Greg resented having to give away what he'd scavenged, especially to the brats from Fuquay-Varina, but he had already told Jerry he would do it. Besides, he supposed the kids had earned a little food and some warm blankets, going through all of this bullshit at Jerry's request. Who knew how long they would have to stay holed up in the dormitory?

They had their own motivations, of course.

Namely, complete hatred of Captain Harden.

He supposed that got them through some of the cold nights.

"You want me to come with you?" Arnie asked, still sitting in the driver's seat.

Greg shook his head and hauled the satchel of goods up over his shoulder. "Nah. Sit here and guard our shit."

One arm holding the satchel, the other his shotgun, Greg made for the four-story dorms to his right. The four kids from White's group who had pretended to be kidnapped would be up on the top floor, where the infected wouldn't wander and other scavengers or raiders generally wouldn't venture—there just wasn't a lot of usable loot in a college dorm.

The sidewalk cut through a gently sloping lawn, a few stately oak trees framing it like a gateway. The once-manicured lawn was now an uneven and patchy mess of overgrown clumps of brown fescue and dead weeds as tall as sapling trees. Through the oak trees and up to the redbrick building, the bushes surrounding the base of it were wildly untrimmed, their carefully shaped branches just barely visible beyond a screen of new-growth off-shoots, slightly lighter in color.

Greg rounded one of these bushes and then stopped.

A cold wind pressed at his back.

The dormitory door stood open.

Not so unusual, but for the bloody smear across it.

Greg dropped the satchel. It made a muted metallic *clank* as it hit the concrete. He shouldered his shotgun and stepped back, away from the door, and then to his right, so that he was back behind the overgrown bushes.

The sound of a car door opening.

Greg glanced back and saw Arnie running across the waist-high lawn, his old hunting rifle in hand. They knew better than to call out to each other, but when Arnie had jogged up within a few feet of Greg, he took a gulp of air and whispered, "What's wrong?"

"Blood on the door."

Arnie raised his rifle.

The two men edged toward the door.

Taking a longer moment to look at it this time, Greg noticed blood on the floor of the entryway as well. A few drops and then a long, coagulated smear that zigzagged across the tile floors and disappeared into the dark hall. Far down that hallway at the opposite end, a single window let in pale gray light and illuminated a small area in its glow, but everything between them and that window remained invisible in its shadow.

"Should we go in?" Arnie asked.

"I think we're gonna have to."

"Got your flashlight?"

Greg fished the little yellow light out of the back pocket of his jeans and flicked it on. The light was a mottled circle that probed dully at the heavy shadows, barely lighting their way. Slowly, the two men entered the dormitory, the candle-like orb of light guiding them along the trail of blood on the floor like wheels on a track.

It terminated in a door left ajar.

The placard to the right of the door read STAIRS.

Greg pushed the door open with the barrel of his shotgun, holding the pump action with the little flashlight pinched between his fingers. The door swung open and a draft of rank air hit them both, causing throats to clamp shut and eyes to water.

"Jesus Christ…" Arnie stepped back, fanning a hand in front of his face.

Greg handled it more stoically and pushed into the stairwell.

It was not the smell of rot, but the smell of bowels spilled.

In the corner of the bottom landing lay the top half of a body. The head was largely untouched, dark brown hair, a young man's face, grotesquely serene atop its masticated corpse, reminding Greg of an obviously Photoshopped picture. Sharp ribs standing out from a spine stripped of meat. The organs scattered across the floor as though they'd been dug out and indiscriminately flung in random directions.

"Is that...?" Arnie choked.

"Yeah." Greg turned away. "It's one of the kids."

"Where are his legs?"

"I'm guessing that's where the blood trail came from." Greg started up the stairs. "Whatever took him down dragged the other half of him off somewhere."

At the fourth floor, they found a single dorm room with a splintered door. A crowd of bloody footprints stampeded back and forth down the hallway, but they centered there at the door that barely hung onto its hinges. Inside, the walls were red, like some hellish brothel, and textured with flesh. It stank of copper coins and sewers. It was too difficult to determine what parts belonged to whom, so they counted heads and came up with three.

Arnie shook visibly. "I thought the infected didn't like to leave the ground floor."

Greg shook his head. "I don't know."

"What are we gonna tell Professor White?"

Greg looked at his partner. "We're not gonna tell him shit."

* * *

The shipping container was located back behind the Camp Ryder building and had become something of a storage shed for unused mechanical parts and other pieces of junk that people didn't want to throw away, fearing it would be needed in the future. Cracked radiators, empty oxygen tanks, old hubcaps—they wasted nothing, but what they couldn't find a use for eventually found its place inside this out-of-the-way container.

Two of the volunteers who had carted Captain Tomlin away still stood at the closed doors of the shipping container, a lock and chain around the bottom. These were new additions to the box.

Lee carried with him an unlit LED lantern, though the sky was not yet completely dark. He set this at his feet and eyed the padlock. "You got the keys to that thing?"

One of the volunteers responded by stretching out his hand, a single key held delicately between his thumb and forefinger.

"Is he still restrained?"

The man with the key nodded. "We put him in there exactly how you gave him to us."

Captain Tomlin had all the same training that Lee did. And off the top of his head, Lee figured there were a dozen ways he could have gotten free from zip-tie bindings if he were left alone like Tomlin. There were a lot of sharp metallic edges in that shipping container. All it would take was some patience and the willingness to get cut a few times.

Lee bladed his stance toward the door, his rifle

ported against his chest. "You mind pulling those doors open for me? Just in case."

The man looked at the key in his fingers. "Oh. Yeah. Sure."

The man with the key bent down at the lock and undid the chain. It clanked noisily across the metal as he pulled it away and yanked at the two doors. Lee raised his rifle fractionally, half expecting to see Tomlin crouching in the shadows with a piece of rebar, or some other such weapon of opportunity, clutched in his hand. He pictured this in his mind, because it was exactly what he would have done if their situations were reversed. He would have hidden with something sharp or something heavy, and he would snag the first idiot to walk into that box and he would either open him up or bash in his skull. Then he would grab that man's weapon and take out whoever else was standing around before heading for the nearest exit.

Yes, that's what I would do, Lee thought. *But I would not have stood in the middle of the road waiting to hitch a ride. Clearly, we are not thinking on the same page here.*

The doors opened wide, and it took a moment for Lee's eyes to adjust fully to the dark interior of the shipping container, but he was able to immediately see the form of someone lying on the ground; he could see the pale palms of his hands still secured behind his back and the slumped, almost fetal position in which he lay.

At the sound of the doors opening, the figure stirred, craning his neck up and around. He was lying on his side, with his back to the entrance, probably in the very same position in which they'd thrown him in the container. He'd managed to pull the shemagh-turned-blindfold off his eyes and it sat limply on the ground next to his head.

Tomlin craned his neck far enough that he was able to see Lee approaching out of the corner of his eye. As Lee stooped to place his lantern on the ground and turn it on, the man's face immediately went from hesitant curiosity to anger.

"What the fuck is this shit, Lee?" He twisted wildly until he was in a sitting position, partially facing Lee where he stood, just a few feet away. "Are you fucking off the reservation, man? I told you I'm here to help you and you throw me in this fucking shithole with two random guys?" Tomlin's eyes flashed. "If you had any idea why I was here, you wouldn't be draggin' ass comin' to talk with me."

While Tomlin spoke, Lee circled around him slightly and visually inspected the bindings to make sure they were still secure. He didn't want to step too close to Tomlin until he had a few questions answered. He waited until it seemed that Tomlin had said his fill, and then he looked him in the eyes.

"What are you doing here?"

"Close the door and we can talk."

"Brian, answer the question."

Tomlin's eyes jerked to the two men standing at the door. His jaw stuck out defiantly, but when he looked toward them, his eyebrows twitched upward, almost imperceptibly, but Lee knew the look. It was a look of concern. Whatever he had to say, he really didn't want those two to hear him.

When he spoke, his voice was very quiet so that Lee had to lean forward to hear. His eyes remained fixed on the guards as he whispered, "Please. Please just close the door and tell them to go away." His eyes turned to Lee and they seemed earnest. "Give me five minutes, Lee. Five minutes and you can do what you want with me."

Lee searched the man's eyes. He knew his face well, knew his facial expressions. It was strange to look at a face that he knew so well in his memory and try to see if it was the person he knew, as though what he saw before him now was only Brian Tomlin's body, and some sinister force was controlling it. The face was so familiar to him, it almost broke him down to see it like this.

He knew this face in so many different ways, as he knew all of the Coordinators like family. He'd known this face when it was gaunt and tired after sixty days of Ranger school. He'd known it covered in face paint and lit by night vision, and he'd known it when it was heavy with a twelve-pack of beer and lit by the glow of the football game on TV.

He knew the man sitting before him.

He knew him like a brother.

But as Harper would surely agree, even brothers betray each other sometimes.

Nevertheless, Lee found himself standing up and turning his head partially, his eyes still locked on Tomlin while he spoke to the two men outside the shipping container. "Close the doors, please. You guys are relieved. Go get some chow."

A brief pause.

"Uh...okay. Thank you."

The doors swung closed. The flimsy glow of twilight went out completely, and everything in the shipping container that existed beyond the five-foot bubble created by the lantern seemed to disappear, as though Lee and Tomlin had suddenly been launched into deep space and were floating there in an abyss of dark matter.

Lee backed up a single step. Now the light was evenly between the two of them. Lee shifted slightly so that he was not pointing his weapon at Tomlin, but the threat was very clear. "You have five minutes, Brian. Please tell me what the hell is going on."

Tomlin's eyes closed, and Lee could see them twitching back and forth underneath the lids as he gathered his thoughts. He took a deep breath, his eyes still shut. "The long and short of it is that your life is in danger."

Lee almost laughed. *"Really?"*

Tomlin's eyes snapped open. "I'm fucking serious, Lee!"

What trace of black humor Lee had taken from that statement suddenly disappeared like a match puffing out in the wind. It struck him that Tomlin's concern was not only for the secrecy of what he was about to reveal, but he appeared to be genuinely concerned for Lee.

"I know you already know about the other two guys," Tomlin said. "They weren't hard-core killers or anything, but they were no slouches either, so count yourself lucky they didn't get you. Both designated marksmen out of the 82nd. But they aren't the only ones out for you."

Lee stared, felt something stir in the pit of his stomach.

Tomlin took his silence as an invitation to continue. "There's someone else, at least one other. And I think he's on the inside, Lee. I don't know whether he's close or just close enough to feed intelligence, but that's how those two boys knew where to set up and wait for you."

"You saying I have a mole?" Lee's nose wrinkled a bit, like he'd smelled something foul.

"Mole. Informant. Spy. Whatever you want to call it, Lee. Why do you think they knew you were heading to Sanford that day? How do you think they knew where and when to set up to catch you before you got to your bunker? Because someone was feeding them intel from the inside."

Lee canted his head. "Interesting. The way I saw it, whoever was controlling this little operation to kill me had to have knowledge of *where* my bunker was, not just when I planned to go there. And that's information that only I have. But maybe another Coordinator would know."

Tomlin smiled savagely. "Like me, right?"

"Yes. Like you."

"Fuck you, Lee." He lurched up onto his knees. "You and I both know that's not true!"

Lee had to suddenly restrain an urge for violence. "Yeah, well, apparently I'm kinda out of the loop these days. So why don't you tell me what the fucking truth is?"

"You *are* out of the loop!" Tomlin nearly yelled it. "That's where all this shit started from!"

Lee held up a hand, his lips curling in a snarl.

"Before I listen to any more of your bullshit, just answer one question for me. Did you come here to kill me?"

That one froze him.

Tomlin lowered his chin slightly, then sank back onto his heels.

A moment stretched by, and Lee arched his eyebrows, looking for an answer.

"Yes." Tomlin shook his head. "That was the original plan."

Lee crossed quickly, knocking over the lamp and causing the light to slant up at them and cast their faces in strange shadows. He grabbed Tomlin by the collar. "The original plan was to work together! The original plan was to save what we could and reestablish some sort of government! Why aren't we sticking to *that* plan, Brian? What happened to *that* plan?"

"Things change," Tomlin said bitterly.

Lee shoved him to the ground and shook his head in disgust. "I'm done."

Tomlin squirmed into his side. "Lee, wait! You have to let me finish!"

But Lee had already turned his back on him. He pushed open the two doors and stepped out into the gravel lot of Camp Ryder. He turned back around, one hand on each of the double doors, his face just a shadow in the darkness. "I don't have to let you do shit, Brian. I'll deal with you later."

Lee slammed the doors on Tomlin's protests, but not before he could hear the other captain screaming at him—not in anger but in what appeared to be a sincere warning. "Watch your back, Lee! Watch your back!"

TWENTY-FIVE

...AND NEW ENEMIES

IT FELT LIKE TUNNEL VISION, walking through Camp Ryder, the closed and locked shipping container behind him. The only thing visible was what lay directly ahead of him. Each question was a dropping anvil, smashing into that ice-cold, frozen surface over his mind and causing hairline cracks, weaknesses to be exploited when he least expected it, fissures to make him lose control.

His breathing came in rhythm with his rapid stride. He wasn't quite sure where he was going. Simply escaping that shipping container, escaping whatever else Tomlin had up his sleeve, whatever other lies he had to spew out of his mouth. He rounded the corner of the Camp Ryder building—it was as good a destination as any.

But as he came around to the front of the building, he could hear the voices filtering out, cheerful in each other's company.

He did not want to be with these people.

He did not want to put on a face for them, to make them believe everything was okay.

He did not want to endure their concern for him if that face faltered.

He wanted to be left alone.

Standing there at the front of the building, still swimming silently in the shadows, he stared at the entrance to the Camp Ryder building and the banner that Harper had hung there three months ago. A symbol of what had been and what could be again. Weather had turned the midnight blue to gray twilight, the red had become blanched, and the white was dingy at the tattered edges where hundreds of hands reached up to touch it every day, to honor it in their own way, to try to remember what the fight was all about.

The flag stirred only slightly in the breeze.

Where is the line between determination and stupidity?

He slumped against the cold concrete wall, felt it leach the warmth from him, pulling it through the fibers of his parka. Every bit of him felt heavy like cast iron, his feet like they were encased in concrete. His rifle dangled loosely from his hands, an anchor weighing him down, and he got the very real sensation that, like any heavy, immobile object, if he were to stand there long enough, he would sink into the ground and the earth would swallow him up.

Still staring at the flag, he thought, *I've given you everything. When is it going to be enough? When have I given enough that I can just be left the fuck alone?*

He'd fought the fight. He'd run the race.

But the enemies never stopped coming, and the race had no finish line.

He'd spent much of his adult life considering

himself a sheepdog of sorts—a creature that lived to confront the wolf, that protected the sheep because doing so was instinctive for him. But maybe he wasn't a sheepdog anymore. Maybe that was a younger man's game.

Perhaps now he was just a tired mutt with a scarred muzzle and a limp, who had battled his fair share of beasts and rescued as many sheep as he could manage. Perhaps he didn't fight nowadays for the same reasons he had a decade ago. Maybe now he only hobbled out to confront that threat because it was the only way he could buy himself some peace and quiet. Maybe all he wanted was a place in the sun to lie down and rest and to be left alone, like any old dog that wishes to while away his days, lying on the front porch with his eyes half lidded in the sunlight.

He closed his eyes and imagined himself at peace.

And he thought, *Maybe that's worth one more fight.*

He opened his eyes again and there in the fore-front of his vision was the flag. He tried to dig deep and feel that pride he had once felt, and perhaps it was there, buried beneath the exhaustion and the resignation.

The only easy day was yesterday, he thought. *Because yesterday, at least I knew whose side I was on.*

Devon returned from Smithfield in Harper's pickup truck, bearing Jake's body. He rode by himself and no one asked him why he had made the drive alone, and he did not offer an explanation. They carried Jake's and Zack's bodies to a corner of the compound where crudely made crosses marked the graves of fourteen others, and the two men were interred by firelight. When they were finished, no words were spoken, because all the words of loss and death had already been said, and to say them now only smarted like a reopened wound.

A somber procession made its way into the Camp Ryder building, and upstairs to gather in the office and discuss the coming days. Nearly thirty of them crammed into the tight space—standing room only. The desk and the chairs had been pushed back against the walls and the door to the office remained open because one or two people stood in the frame of it, peering in over the heads of the others. Their attention was focused on Lee, Harper, and Bus, who stood with their backs to the map of North Carolina and faced the crowded room of volunteers.

Lee waited until the murmur of conversation lulled. His eyes scanned the faces before him as he spoke. "I wanted to take a moment to thank all of you. You knew what I was asking of you, you knew the risks involved, and you volunteered anyway. There is nothing in this world that has any meaning or value without people such as yourselves who are willing to put themselves in harm's way to try to ensure that other people have a future. Without that future, without that probability of survival, everything loses its meaning."

He cleared his throat softly. "People lose hope when that happens. They lose their sense of purpose. But people like you are the reason the rest of them can plan for tomorrow. You're the reason they can hope." He paused, then nodded, as though he felt he had communicated what he'd wanted to say.

Then he quickly held up a piece of paper and focused on it. "First group, I'm going to call your names. If I call your name, please step to this side of the room." Lee motioned to the left of the doorway. Then he began to call the names.

He called out twelve in all. Among them were Julia, Nate Malone, Mike and Torri Reagan, and Devon Mills. As he called their names, they began to filter to the left side of the room.

When everyone was situated, Lee went on. "You folks who I just called out will be with Harper. Your group will be going north. I'll talk more about it in a minute." He looked to the others who had naturally drifted to the opposite side of the room. "I'm going to call the rest of you, and you will make sure you're on the right side of the room, if you aren't already."

Among the next thirteen names that he called were Jim, LaRouche, and Wilson. When he was done calling the names, he asked for LaRouche to step forward. The sergeant looked around hesitantly but stepped to Lee's side.

Lee gestured to everyone on the right. "If I just called your name and you are standing to the right, you will be under the control of LaRouche. And you'll be heading east."

There was a stir in the room.

Lee had expected it.

He knew the question before it was asked,

but it was LaRouche who voiced it. "Uh, Cap...
shouldn't it be you?"

Lee drew a lengthy breath, still staring at the
sheet in front of him. "I won't be leaving with you."

The noise was one of confusion. Heads were
turning back and forth, questioning each other,
wondering if they'd heard right.

Lee raised his hand. "Quiet, please." He waited
two breaths until he could speak without yelling.
"I know the rumor mill works fast around here,
but for those of you who haven't heard or who
have heard an incorrect version, I will explain to
you the reality of the situation." He folded the
paper crisply. "The individual we captured and
brought in earlier today is Captain Brian Tomlin.
He is a Coordinator for Project Hometown, just
like myself. His assigned area was South Carolina.
Without getting into too many details, I will tell
you that he has brought some issues to light that
require my attention right now. I don't know how
long it will take to get to the bottom of it, but as
soon as I figure it out, I'll be heading out to join
the rest of you in the east."

Nate Malone stepped forward. "How do you
know he's telling the truth?"

"I don't. That's why I need to get to the bottom
of it."

Lee could tell that the others had many questions about this odd decision, but none of them
voiced their concerns, so Lee moved the briefing
on. "Harper's group. You'll be given one of the
HEMTT tankers, the wrecker, two of the LMTVs,
and one of the Humvees. Your primary objective

will be to establish a defensive stronghold in Eden, North Carolina. Your secondary objective will be to use the wrecker while you are working your way north, to clear a supply-and-escape route from Eden to Camp Ryder. Your tertiary objective will be to assist any refugees who are fleeing south." He nodded to Harper. "You're my right-hand man. I trust you to get it done."

Lee turned to the right. "LaRouche's group. You have one objective and one objective only: limit the amount of infected crossing the Roanoke River. You'll be given the other tanker, the rest of the Humvees, and the last LMTV, which we are going to load with more than two thousand pounds of ordnance, ammunition, and rifles." He looked at them very pointedly. "That payload is our life, guys. You're going to use it to buy cooperation where you can, blow up the bridges that can't be defended, and mine the shit out of the ones we can't blow. We're on a time crunch, and you guys are my hammer—I need you to hit hard and fast." He put his hand on LaRouche's shoulder. "Sergeant LaRouche has extensive experience with demolitions, so you'll all be in good hands. Just do what he tells you and you'll come back with all of your limbs."

Nervous laughter ran through the group.

"Last issue to address," Lee said, folding his arms across his chest. "I know it's short notice, but is anyone here unable to leave Camp Ryder by tomorrow?"

Silence fell over the room. Glances were exchanged, shoulders were shrugged. Some people just bowed their heads slightly.

Lee nodded. "If no one objects, then plan to leave late tomorrow morning."

The group seemed to be in consensus. All heads nodded the affirmative.

"Does anyone have any questions?"

For a moment, Lee thought he might escape without questions, but Lucky poked his carrot top out of the crowd and raised his hand. "Yeah, I got a question."

Lee pointed to him. "Go ahead."

Lucky looked around briefly. He was part of Wilson's team, and therefore in LaRouche's group. "Since we're headed east, I figured we should probably know what to do if we come across the Followers."

There was an audible groan from several members of the group. From the other side of the room, Nate rolled his eyes and lifted his hands. "It's just an urban legend, man. Just people spreading scary stories. I doubt there's a group of people out there simultaneously cannibalizing and Bible-thumping."

"You don't know that," Lucky said defensively. "Have you been east? Has anyone in this room been out that way in the last few months?"

"I'm with Lucky," Wilson said quietly, inspecting the bandaged stumps of his now three-fingered right hand. "It's possible that the Followers are a complete fabrication. It's also possible that everything we've heard is true. I think a more likely scenario is that the truth lies somewhere in between, as with most other things like this." He looked up at Lee. "I think we should have a plan to deal with them if we come across them...even if it is a big 'if.'"

Whether out of pity for the man who had just lost his fingers or in deference to the fact that he was probably right, no one continued the argument. Instead, all eyes shifted to Lee, looking for his answer to the problem of the Followers.

"Because we don't know truth from fiction at this point in time, we can't really make a plan to deal with them," Lee said thoughtfully. "However, I would simply say to use common sense. If you encounter a group—any group—that is hostile, you blow them the fuck up. But if you think you can get them to cooperate, then go that route. If the Followers do exist, and they are expanding out from the east coast, they might end up being a valuable ally." He smirked. "And if they don't want to be an ally, then they'll make a great barrier between us and the infected."

LaRouche nodded. "I think we can handle that."

A few more people asked a few more questions. Some of them Lee deferred to Harper and LaRouche. When the general questions became more specific, Lee dismissed the group so they could each meet with and speak to their respective leaders and get some answers.

As the group trickled out of the room, only Lee and Bus remained.

The big man leaned on his desk and took a long look at Lee. "What happened in there?"

"With Captain Tomlin?"

A nod.

Lee fiddled with the piece of paper still in his hands and considered the question. "No disrespect to you, Bus, but I think it would be best if I kept this between him and me."

Bus made a *fair enough* face.

"I need more time to speak with him. When I get everything sorted out, you'll be the first to know."

"What about Professor White and the rifles?"

"Once we see Harper and LaRouche off tomorrow, we'll worry about getting those rifles to him."

A knock at the door interrupted them.

Lee turned to find Eddie Ramirez standing, half inside the room. He looked rapidly back and forth between Lee and Bus.

"Help you?" Bus asked.

"Yes." Eddie's tone was clipped. "You told me I would be heading east with the others. Is that still true?"

"Actually"—Lee faced the door—"I didn't get you in on the briefing because I need you here for a little while longer. I've got some business to take care of, but I'm going to catch up to LaRouche's group afterward and head east. I wanted you to stick around because there's a few vehicles out by the Sanford airport that I want you to have a look at and see if we can't get running again."

Eddie's face became neutral. "Oh."

Lee peered at him. "Is that okay? I'm hoping it will only take a couple of days."

Eddie seemed to be considering it. "Yes," he said finally. "That should be fine. What's a few more days?"

Lee nodded. "I appreciate it. I'll get up with you."

Eddie left and Lee and Bus exchanged a look.

Bus's white teeth shone underneath his beard. "Antsy little guy, isn't he?"

"Well…" Lee tossed the paper on the desk. "He's got a family to worry about."

Bus headed to the door. "You sleeping in here tonight?"

Lee looked around as though he were feeling out the emptiness of the room. "Yeah. Probably."

He lay on a wooden front porch, one of the long-planked kind that takes up the entire front of a ranch house, like the kind in old Western movies. He lay there with his eyes closed, but he could feel the warm sunshine on his cheeks, across his forehead, on his lips. The light came through his shuttered eyelids deep and red. The sound of a steady, warm breeze blowing gently through trees crowned fully with green. This was his place in the sun. His place…

"Get up."

Shadows flashed across his eyelids.

He opened his eyes.

His father stood over him, his hand outstretched as though to help him to his feet.

"Get up, Lee," he said. "Get up and look."

"Look at what?" His own voice was small and childlike.

"They're coming."

He shook his head. "I'm tired. Just let me sleep."

"Get up and look, Lee. They're coming."

"Who's coming?"

"You know who's coming."

Lee accepted his father's hand and stood up. Before him, perfectly manicured grass stretched out. A large oak tree stood to the right, its expansive limbs moving slowly, undulating and seeming to glimmer in the light, sighing quietly. A dirt path led away from the porch and edged straight away from them through the front lawn. It then rose, bisecting a hill that sloped up from the yard.

"There." His father pointed to the hill.

Lee squinted and could see figures atop the crest of the hill, just black silhouettes against a sun-bleached sky. They stood shoulder to shoulder and chest to back, and had he not looked carefully he would have thought they were the top of the hill themselves, as completely as they covered it. "I see them."

"They're coming."

"I know."

"Take this."

Lee looked down and saw what his father offered. It was an M4. Lee accepted the weapon. He ejected the magazine, looking down into it and judging its weight. It was less than half full. "There's only a few rounds in this thing."

Harper appeared to his left, so that Lee was standing between him and his father. "It's all we have left."

"What happened to all the ammunition?" Lee asked.

"We used it up."

"How did we use all of the ammunition?"

Harper shook his head and repeated himself. "We used it all up."

Lee slammed the magazine back into the rifle. "Okay."

His father put a hand on his shoulder and looked him in the eyes. "You're gonna have to make it count."

Lee opened his eyes and felt immediately that he was not alone in the room.

He rolled to his right and reached for his rifle.

"Don't."

Lee blinked and looked up to the darkness above, where his hand reached out across the floor. He did not have to take time to realize who was seated in the folding chair, one boot placed securely on Lee's rifle. He knew Tomlin from his voice.

"Before you try to kill me," Tomlin said quickly, scooting the rifle farther away from his fingers, "keep in mind that if I wanted you dead, you would be."

Lee's voice was ragged with sleep. "What happened to the man who was guarding you?"

Tomlin's teeth flashed like blue pearls in the darkness. "He'll be fine. Probably just embarrassed about falling asleep on the job. Don't worry, I didn't touch him."

Lee curled his fingers into a ball and considered attacking. He would need to extricate himself from his sleeping bag in order to be able to use his legs to balance himself—any hand-to-hand would be pointless without his legs, especially against someone as good as Tomlin.

"I know you're thinking about taking me, Lee." Tomlin's voice maintained its calm. "I don't have a weapon, so I won't be able to stop you. I didn't come here to kill you. I came here to help you. Just give me a chance."

Lee took that moment to push the sleeping bag off his legs. He moved slowly, not wanting to broadcast an attack, but wanting—needing—to get himself ready. As he moved, he kept his eyes on Tomlin, and he could see the faintest of smiles on the other man's lips, his eyes twinkling slightly in the darkness. When the bag was clear of his feet, he shifted his weight so he appeared relaxed, but Lee could feel the muscles in his torso and legs, ready to explode if necessary.

Lee kept his voice low. "Convince me quickly. Or I'm going to break your neck."

"I believe you." Tomlin's face grew serious. "I'm going to tell you why they want to kill you. And I'm going to tell you who 'they' are." He leaned forward slightly. "You're not going to like what you hear. But I'm going to tell you anyway."

Lee waited, stock-still.

Tomlin traced the lines of his mouth with his thumb and forefinger. "You remember the term *nonviable asset*?"

Images came to Lee's mind of endless stacks of Standard Operating Procedures clumped together by sections with a stapled corner. Do's and don'ts associated with Project Hometown. What was approved. What was unapproved. The acceptable and the unacceptable. Rules on things and situations Lee thought would never happen to him, and so they were relegated to a dusty storeroom in the back of his mind, dredged up now as though some servo in his mind had been cued to pull all documents associated with the term *nonviable asset*.

"Yes," Lee said thickly.

Tomlin ventured on. "It's when someone violates mission protocols to the extent—"

Lee cut him off. "I know what it is."

The back of his neck began to tingle hotly.

He thought about the map hanging on the wall behind him. The cities and towns, some of them highlighted in red. The viable and the nonviable. What could be useful and what was a waste of resources.

A waste of resources...

Tomlin's brow shifted and Lee could see the question in his eyes, like an old sadness. When the other captain spoke, his voice was heavy with disappointment. "Why'd you do it, Lee? What the fuck were you thinking?"

Lee turned his head slightly, finding it difficult to look Tomlin in the eyes now. His gaze went to the office door and rested there. Even in the dim light he could see the paint peeling and the metal rusting underneath. Growing old. Wearing down. Breaking. Entropy. The gradual, eventual, and inevitable destruction of everything in the universe.

Nothing was built to last.

He heard his voice, calm and monotone. "It was an accident."

"An accident?" Tomlin said incredulously. "You left your fucking bunker! More than a week early!"

Lee pulled himself to his knees. "Leaving the bunker was a mistake," he growled. "But not coming back to it was an *accident*. You think I wanted to be lost out here by myself? You think I wanted to lose communication with the rest of you guys?" He shook his head, the snarl in his voice causing his nose to curl. "It wasn't a fucking option. Shit happened, and I had to adapt to and overcome the new situation. And the new situation was that I was cut off. I didn't go AWOL. I didn't abandon the mission."

Tomlin nodded. "I know, Lee. I know what happened. I saw where your house used to be."

Lee shook his head as though he were about to say something else about it, but then stiffened as something else had struck him as odd. His brow furrowed and his eyes zigzagged across the ground, and then rose to meet Tomlin's. "How'd you know I left my bunker?"

"They were watching us the whole time, Lee. Sensors in the hatches and in the bunkers. So they could tell when you came and when you left, and which bunkers you'd gone to." Tomlin snorted. "None of us realized it, but we should have."

Lee rubbed his face. "I don't understand. We lost communication with Frank. Everyone was gone. Who the hell was watching us?"

Tomlin didn't seem to want to answer the question directly. "He sent me and the others to kill you because you were a nonviable asset. He didn't want you using the equipment in your bunkers. He didn't want you using up the resources."

Lee's mind reeled with possibilities. "Was it Frank?"

Slowly, Tomlin shook his head. "Frank's dead, Lee. This was one of us."

Lee found himself stiff as a board. "Then who was it?"

Tomlin exhaled shakily. "It was Abe. Abe Darabie."

TWENTY-SIX

NEW REALITIES

THE BLUE GLOW OF the computer screen.

Electricity, cool air, running water.

The sensation of being trapped.

The Hole.

He remembered it, felt it, familiar to him like an old childhood house, even the distinctly cold, cement-like smell of it that no amount of carpet and furnishings and living in could remove from the place. It was a bunker, not a home.

A place of restriction.

Seclusion.

Madness.

He watched himself from four months ago sitting before his computer and wrestling with himself whether to send an e-mail, whether to violate those precious policies. It was like he was there in the room, standing behind himself. He could even see the message, though he knew it was just a memory.

You hear anything from Frank?

A message addressed to Captain Abe Darabie.

His closest friend.

He clicked send, and the response did not take long.

Neg on coms with Frank. I'm at 48 hours...did you open your box?

Lee's response: Yeah, I opened mine. Is this for real?

I hope not...prolly shouldn't be talking...just keep your head down and wait for them to cancel us...I'm sure they will.

Abe Darabie.

His closest friend.

The image of himself sitting at his computer inside The Hole disappeared and instead he was staring at cement walls and sniffing the smell of people and smoke and under all of that the rusty smell of old grease and oil. Before him was a man who wore a uniform so intimately familiar to him. A man who had been his friend, and then his enemy, and now was supposed to be his friend again.

"I don't believe it," Lee said hollowly.

Tomlin didn't react, as though he had expected this response.

His voice calm and even, he went on. "When forty-eight hours ran out, you and I both got the same mission packet. Same as the other Coordinators." A pause to swallow and moisten his lips. "Except Abe. He got a different packet. When he opened his, he was promoted to *Major* Darabie, and his job was expressly outlined as monitoring and controlling the rest of us. None of us knew about it until five days before leaving our bunkers. We were able to conference our computers and he spoke to all of us and explained his mission packet, what we were to do. But by then, you'd already left your bunker."

Lee didn't speak, but he shook his head, breathing through flared nostrils.

Tomlin looked pained. "I know it's a tough pill to swallow, Lee, but I'm trying to tell you the truth. Abe didn't like it, but he declared you a nonviable asset, because you'd violated the procedures and you were out of contact. He was just gonna drop the whole thing if you came back online before the rest of us left our bunkers. He was just gonna act like it had never happened and move on. He didn't want to blacklist you, Lee."

"Then what the fuck happened?"

Tomlin's face tightened and his voice grew cold. "Things got complicated."

Lee clenched his fist. "Complicated how?"

A long pause. "When Abe briefed us a week out, he put you on the back burner. He didn't order anyone to find you or kill you—we all had enough to worry about. He told Mitchell and me privately that if we came across you, he wanted us to detain you so he could figure out what happened." Tomlin pushed himself back in the seat. "He gave you the benefit of the doubt. We all did."

"And have I not been doing what I'm supposed to be doing?" Lee asked quietly but forcefully. "Am I not completing my mission?"

"Better than most, actually."

"Then why is he trying to kill me?"

"Things were a little easier for Abe in Colorado. He maintained steady contact with us throughout August and September. Then about a month ago he found a large group of US Army, just a hodgepodge of various units. They were under the command of a colonel. The secretary of state was with them, along with a few other cabinet members."

Lee stared on, a question scribbled across his features. "Okay..."

"The secretary of state is number four in succession to the president," Tomlin said, verbally tiptoeing. "Which is currently the highest-ranking cabinet member they've found. According to the secretary of state himself, the others are dead."

It wasn't that Lee didn't understand what Tomlin was saying. He understood the concept of presidential succession, understood the purveyance of the presidency over the military—namely *commander in chief*—and he understood that whoever fell into that office by virtue of their rank took that job and everything it entailed.

He understood all of these things, but suddenly the concept seemed repugnant to him.

He'd lived his entire military career with the attitude of, "I may not like it, but if the CIC says go to Bumfuck, Iraq, I go to Bumfuck, Iraq, and there's really no use overthinking it." The politics and the reasons were immaterial to him, and generally too convoluted to truly understand anyway.

Now, several months and a world-altering societal collapse later, after putting himself on the line and ordering others to do the same, and losing so many of them, losing such a large part of himself, and fighting for every goddamned inch, for every meal, for every day of life, the idea of simply handing the reins over to someone else seemed ridiculous.

Lee worked moisture into his mouth. "So Abe's no longer calling the shots."

"No." Tomlin's voice reflected disgust. "For the last month, he's been handing down orders from the secretary of state, who has completely hijacked Project Hometown. He's forcing the Coordinators to ship the resources in their bunkers out to the interior states. After Mitchell was killed, they decided that everything east of the Appalachians and north of the gulf region was a total loss. And they're close to making the same call with the west coast."

Lee felt his heart rate rising. "So why send people in to kill me?"

Tomlin spoke with exasperation. "Because you're just a waste of resources to them, Lee! Abe's been keeping tabs on you. He knows you emptied out one of your bunkers, and you just started on another. But you're out of contact for them, and you're serving a state that they've decided they don't want saved." Tomlin shook his head as though he couldn't comprehend why Lee wasn't following. "Don't you get it? They want you gone so you're not wasting what's in the bunkers. If the infected ever die out along the east coast, they want to be able to come back in, and they want to be able to use your bunkers to resupply."

"They can't open the bunkers if I'm dead!"

Tomlin shook his head slowly. "Not true, Lee. Abe was issued a master code. He can hand it out to whomever he wants, and if they put it in their GPS instead of the individual code, they can access whatever bunker they want." He paused for a long time, as though waiting for Lee to ask a question, but Lee only stood there, shell-shocked into silence.

"Mitchell was one of the last northeastern states. The only ones who survived were Pennsylvania and New York, only because they were able to get onto the other side of the Appalachians. They took heavy losses when they did."

"Chris and Lucas..." Lee said, picturing their faces.

"Yes. They had to abandon portions of their states. And the others—Mark from Delaware, James from Maryland, Ian from New Jersey— we lost contact with all of them within the first month. So when Acting President Briggs began running things, and then Mitchell disappeared, Abe contacted me and ordered me to discontinue my operations in South Carolina, find you, kill you, and retreat across the Appalachians."

In the strange midnight light of the room, Lee could see the tears in Tomlin's eyes. "I had people, Lee. Women and children. Entire fucking families." His face suddenly contorted. "And I left them behind. I left them with supplies running low and the weather getting cold. And I came up here, and I watched you. I watched you putting everything you had into this; I watched you taking the people and keeping them safe...doing what you were supposed to do." He blinked to clear his eyes. "I couldn't do it. I couldn't kill you."

Overwhelmed, Lee slumped against the wall and buried his face in his hands, as though the barrier of them would block out any other unpleasant things trying to force their way into his mind. His dream just prior to waking still clung to him like strands of spider silk. The distinctness of the threat, the inevitability of demise. But also the nearness of his father and the determination and the strength he drew from it.

Tomlin's voice hijacked his train of thought. "It's bigger than my personal convictions."

Muffled by his palms, Lee said, "How's that?"

"I told you about the master code, but there was something else. Apparently, our GPS devices can link to each other and be controlled remotely. With the proper codes, one can be slaved to another. When Abe briefed us before we left our bunkers, he had us all link our devices." Tomlin looked down at his hands. "When they made the decision to abandon the east coast, he remotely accessed my device and changed the security restrictions so I couldn't even access my bunkers if I wanted to."

Lee removed his hands from his face.

Tomlin was staring at him with bald intensity.

"They couldn't slave my device," Lee said, the voice of someone coming to a severe and unwelcome realization. "Because I wasn't there to link mine with everyone else's. I'm the only one who can still freely access the bunkers."

Tomlin nodded. "I need your help, Lee."

"Why should I help you?"

Tomlin's voice rose. "Because it's not right. They can't just decide who lives and dies, who gets rescued and who gets left behind! We were given a fucking job, and I'm not done doing mine, and you're not done doing yours." Tomlin pointed to the ground with his index finger. "We're still here! North Carolina and South Carolina and Georgia are still here. We haven't been overrun yet. Why give up when we've got a plan to stop it?"

Lee looked at him sharply. "You mean *I* have a plan to stop it."

"We can help each other here, Lee."

Lee looked at the other man for a long time. He drew up his knees and leaned his elbows on them. The question was whether he could trust Captain Tomlin or not. To that question, he had to ask himself, *Has he done anything to hurt you?* And of course the answer would be *no.* Tomlin may have come there with the intention to harm him, under misinformation and a misguided sense of duty, but he hadn't carried it out.

Then, of course, the next question was, *Has he done anything to earn your trust?*

Well, he didn't kill me when he had the chance.

Lee cleared his throat. "What do you know about my plan?"

They spoke for a long time. Lee explained his plan in detail, because, in his mind, he didn't have much of a choice. Sometimes when the stakes were high, you had to make a bet that you wouldn't normally make. In this situation, Lee just had to bet that Tomlin was on his side. He also told Tomlin what Jacob had briefed them on when he'd first come to Camp Ryder, and the threat they faced in the coming months.

As they talked, Lee found that they were slipping easily back into sync with each other, the familiar rhythms of an old friendship that fit you like a well-worn pair of boots. The Coordinators were a family, and they all knew each other well. Lee had been closest to Abe Darabie, but he'd naturally founded friendships with Tomlin and Mitchell, simply because they were both within a couple hours of him.

Then, with everything that had happened the previous day, with the uniformed soldiers trying to kill him and Tomlin suddenly surfacing, Lee had struggled to reconcile what he was witnessing with what he knew about these men. Particularly Tomlin. Now, in the dim glow of a lantern, standing shoulder-to-shoulder and addressing the map that hung on the wall of the office, Lee felt an immense relief, like hot water relaxing his muscles and releasing the tension in him.

Tomlin was still a friend.

Which left the question of Abe Darabie, who was clearly having his hand forced by the acting president...

Tomlin turned and looked at Lee, very serious. "Lee, you need to decide right now whether or not you recognize the authority of Secretary of State Briggs as acting president of the United States. It's a tough question to resolve, but don't wait until you're backed into a corner to figure it out."

Lee cocked his head slightly to one side. "What have *you* decided?"

"I decided I don't recognize the authority of the secretary of state, because I have no proof that the presidential successors preceding him are indeed dead. All we have is his word, which is worth zilch to me right now. Until it's proven otherwise, in my mind, the president is still commander in chief, and I will abide by the last orders that I know came from him—rescue and rebuild. Not leave the eastern seaboard for the infected."

Lee smiled. "I second that."

From inside the Camp Ryder building, Lee heard a door slam—what sounded like the front double doors. Then came the pounding of footsteps on metal risers.

"What time is it?" Lee asked, glancing over to the small window in the office. The window was clouded with condensation, but Lee could see it was still dark outside.

Tomlin cringed. "This is probably going to be about me."

The door to the office burst open and a man was there, one of the sentries, standing with his rifle at the ready. He took a moment to process what he was seeing, and his body went rigid. He swung his rifle in the general direction of Tomlin but didn't aim.

"Uh, Captain?"

"Lower that rifle for me." Lee gestured with his hand.

The man lowered his rifle but pointed with his free hand. "He escaped! He got away!"

Lee felt a smile on his lips. "Clearly."

The sentry seemed to realize that Lee and Tomlin were in no life-and-death struggle, and that there was a little bit of amusement in their eyes as they looked at him. His face flushed and his eyes searched the ground. "I'm sorry, Captain…I fell asleep."

Lee shrugged. "Well, luckily, this time no one got hurt. In the future, if you feel like you're too exhausted to perform your duties, try and find someone to replace you. It's almost freezing temperatures out there. If you're dozing off when it's that cold, you probably need to get more sleep."

The sentry relaxed a bit. "I'm sorry."

Lee waved him off, and the man disappeared through the door, his shoulders slumped slightly. Looking to Tomlin, Lee raised an eyebrow. "How *did* you get out of a locked shipping container?"

Tomlin smiled sheepishly. "One of the back corners is almost completely rusted through. A little prying with a metal pipe and I was able to squeeze out." His eyes narrowed thoughtfully. "He must really have been asleep not to hear that shit."

"Guess we won't be using that container for a holding cell anymore." Lee turned his attention back to the map. "Listen, Brian . . . I'm sorry for all of that."

Tomlin considered that for a long while. "We're in desperate times, Lee. I'd have done the same damn thing if I were in your position. There's no need to apologize for taking precautions."

Lee's lips tightened. "It's good to have you."

Tomlin looked at the floor. "Yeah."

"Do you think you'll be able to go back?"

"To South Carolina?"

"Yeah."

"I dunno. Probably not to the same people. I left them without explanation. There one day and gone the next." Tomlin smiled grimly. "No, all I can do for them now is help you stem the tide.

Maybe once all this is over and I can explain why I left..." He trailed off.

"Once all of this is over?" Lee said with a chuckle.

"Yeah. Why? You don't think it's going to be over?"

"I'm sure it will one day. But it's going to be a long damn time."

LaRouche woke up slowly from a poor night's sleep. He'd slept for periods of perhaps an hour, only to wake up with strange dreams that flew away from the grasp of his recollection and left him feeling on edge. The last time he'd awoken it was past three AM and he figured there was no purpose in continuing to try to sleep. He felt more exhausted each time he woke. The nervousness of the coming day would not allow him to rest tonight, so he would wait, and perhaps tomorrow, when they were on the road and the mission was in progress, he would sleep better.

He lay in his bed—a few thick blankets laid atop cardboard—for a long time, staring at the ceiling of his shanty and watching the tiny space between the two sections of plywood that comprised his roof shift from black into deep hues of blue. Cold air surrounded him, and the air from his lungs turned to fog and drifted up to the crack in the ceiling. He waited for the sounds of other people, but it was still too early and time was sluggish in the cold predawn hours.

He was only growing more impatient.

"Fuck it," he mumbled and threw the covers off.

He was still mostly dressed. It was just too damn cold at night to strip down, so the only thing missing was his boots. He slipped them on and shuffled his feet around in them, trying to impart his body heat to the cold leather interior by creating some friction. He left them unlaced and grabbed his rifle. It was too early in the morning for his tactical vest.

Too early for rifles, for that matter.

He pushed away the multiple layers of blankets and one tarp that served as his door. He probably had more blankets in his shanty than most, and he rarely left a blanket behind when he found it. They were cushion, warmth, and insulation. LaRouche had never realized how essential and how useful a blanket could be.

Outside his shanty, he looked up at the sky and found stars staring down at him, clear and crystalline. Dawn was still an hour away, and to the untrained eye, the sky was still dark. But a person who lies awake in the cold nights can see even the slightest change in the color of the sky.

Gonna be a clear day. Maybe even a little warm.

He meandered among shanties full of sleeping families and couples. People who had someone else to cling to in the night. Someone to give them warmth and comfort. It struck him that modern society had robbed something from people when their lives and beds were so comfortable that they preferred to sleep alone. Man wasn't meant to spend these nights by himself. The pleasure of human company in these hard times overcame any number of personality quirks that would have become "deal breakers" in the old world.

We got so picky, he thought to himself. *My steak's not cooked right, and my bed doesn't align my spine properly, and my wife just put on some weight.*

Who gives a fuck?

LaRouche could recall any number of women he'd dated, only to delete them from his phone and avoid them at all costs because her laugh was weird, or she left her wet towel on the bathroom floor, or she had too many cats.

Now he'd give anything to have one of those women in his bed at night, warm and soft, and maybe, just maybe, he'd sleep the whole night through.

Like the rest of these fuckers. LaRouche made a face as he passed a shanty that was rumbling with someone's loud snoring. How did you sleep that deeply when it was only thirty degrees out? Unbelievable.

He reached the large circle of ash ringed with stones. He knelt down over the rocks and held his hand close above the ashes. There was still some heat there. He stepped over to a large and mysterious mound that sat a few yards from the fire pit, covered by a tarp. He lifted the tarp and tossed it back halfway, revealing a stack of wood and kindling.

God bless all the people who did the chores around here. The hunting and the gathering and the splitting wood for fires. Of course, LaRouche had his own job to do and it came with its own unique set of challenges, but not once had he gone to this stack of wood and found it depleted.

He grabbed up an armload of kindling and two split logs and carried them to the side of the fire.

He brushed the ashes away and revealed the glowing embers underneath. He placed the kindling over this patch of coals and blew on it steadily until the embers began to blaze hotly and the kindling caught. Slowly but surely, he nursed the fire back to life.

He stared into the flames for a long time, feeling the heat on his face as the fire began to envelop the split logs, the splinters burning and curling back on themselves, the bark beginning to steam and bubble as what little moisture was left inside of it boiled. In those long, hypnotic moments, his mind left him and traveled to a kitchen with white cabinets and gray granite countertops and the smell of strong coffee. His parents' house in Tennessee. The bright, early-morning light seeping through the bay windows of the breakfast nook. The way the sun felt warm coming through the windows, but he could look outside and see the frost shimmering on everything. The way the house felt almost too hot when he came in from the outside, the vents kicking out air that smelled of home, a box of a dozen fresh doughnuts in his hand. That was breakfast, and it would be the only thing they ate until Thanksgiving dinner in the early afternoon. A dozen doughnuts to fuel a day of turkey frying, cigar smoking, and backyard football playing.

He thought of their faces. His mother, his father, his younger brother. Faces that would gather around the island and look at each other with that tired affection of waking up to a full house of long-lost family, in town for the holidays. Tired, but comfortable in their belonging.

He missed them, but he tried not to think about them, because he knew they were probably dead. It felt cold of him to think it, but he wouldn't fool himself into a false hope. The LaRouche family was nothing if not pragmatic, and they would not want him to labor under the assumption that they had survived against all odds. They'd lived just outside of Nashville, and so likely hadn't made it. His dad would run a hand over his thick salt-and-pepper goatee and adjust his glasses and say, "Son, you worry about yourself. We can manage just fine."

"I see you couldn't sleep either?"

LaRouche jerked at the interruption to his thoughts and looked up from the fire to find Father Jim standing there beside him, his arms tight around his chest and the hoods up over his head of both the parka and the sweatshirt he wore underneath.

LaRouche smiled marginally and looked back into the fire. "I gave up on it about an hour ago."

"Yeah. I've been lying awake for a while."

"What's bothering you?"

Father Jim chuckled. "Death? Dismemberment? The unknown?"

LaRouche laughed quietly. "Yeah, that'll keep you up at night."

"Let me guess: big responsibilities and fear of failure?"

"Swing and miss, Father." LaRouche rose up and stretched his legs.

"Well, I'm not a mind reader." Jim held his hands out to the fire.

LaRouche let the silence stretch for a minute. "You have family, Jim?"

"Yes."

"Wife? Kids?"

"No. Never married. I've got a mother and father, but they live in upstate New York, so..."

"Oh."

"I guess I should say 'lived.'"

"Do you know that they're dead?"

"They were pretty old."

"Still..."

"Yeah. Maybe."

LaRouche eyed the ex-priest. "Any thoughts? Devotionals? Words of wisdom?"

Jim smiled. "How about a verse of the day?"

"Okay. I'm listening."

Jim squeezed LaRouche's shoulder and spoke with the quiet confidence of a clergyman. "'But we are not of those who shrink back and are destroyed, but of those who believe and are saved. Faith is being sure of what we hope for and certain of what we do not see.'"

"Hmm." LaRouche considered the words for a time. "How do you keep all of those scriptures in your head?"

Jim laughed. "Oh, I don't have an encyclopedic knowledge of the Bible, unfortunately. I know... that doesn't make me a very good priest, but then again, I never pretended to be a very good priest." He sighed. "No. The scriptures that I'm able to quote directly are only because I've quoted them to myself every day since this all began, trying to remind myself that I'm gonna get through this."

"You have doubts?"

"I always have doubts. It's human nature to doubt. But faith isn't the absence of doubt; it's the decision to believe in something contrary to what you observe."

"So you believe that we'll come out of this okay?"

A faint smile. "I've made the *decision* to believe that there is a purpose to all of this, that everything works together for the glory of God, and that whether or not my own personal survival is in the cards, what we're doing here needs to be done and will be done."

"What if the purpose is to wipe out the human race?"

Jim looked at him askew. "What if there's no God?"

LaRouche seemed taken aback by the suggestion.

"You can gloom and doom it all day long, and I guarantee you won't beat me at it—my family's Irish Catholic."

LaRouche chuffed and rolled his eyes.

"Positive thinking to us is expecting the worst and hoping it's over quickly."

"Okay." LaRouche laughed. "You've got me beat."

"Hopefully you've learned your lesson." Jim adjusted his glasses and spoke sternly. "Don't ever try to one-up me on depressing thoughts."

"So, you're ready for this?"

Jim thought about it. "I suppose so. You?"

"Yeah. I suppose so, as well."

TWENTY-SEVEN

TRAITORS

MARIE MADE A SPECIAL breakfast that morning. She began cooking when it was still dark and continued on until everyone had eaten. She viewed it as her job to keep everyone fed, and with the two groups due to depart later that day, she felt it was her duty to cook an extravagant breakfast, or at least what passed for extravagant at Camp Ryder. It became apparent as she cooked that she'd been hiding away stashes of goods a little bit at a time. Things that she normally didn't use in the regular cooking. Things like sugar and cinnamon—things that were hard to come by.

So Camp Ryder and its members, who had volunteered to go out to the east and to the north to blow bridges and rescue refugees, felt like kings at breakfast and full of good food and lifted by the lighthearted conversation that went with it, when they left to gather their things and say their good-byes.

Lee, Harper, and LaRouche began to arrange the vehicles into two columns and to load the LMTVs with their respective payloads of ordnance and munitions, as well as stocking the Humvees with extra ammunition, food, and water. After a while, Wilson and Lucky joined them, and helped load in the last couple hundred pounds of C4 and several crates of claymore mines.

As they worked, the day began to warm slightly, and they even started to sweat, though it was quickly chilled from their foreheads once they stood still for a moment. The jackets came off, and they worked in just their hoodies and sweaters.

Gradually, the vehicles were filled to capacity and the volunteers began to trickle into the Square, stowing their packs in the rears of the vehicles they would ride in or drive. As the work became lighter and more and more of them stood around in quiet conversation, the jackets were donned again.

When they were finished, Lee met Harper and LaRouche between the two columns of vehicles. He'd left Tomlin upstairs in the office to avoid having to explain things repeatedly. Bus was aware of the situation, and Lee was sure that everyone in Camp Ryder would hear it from the good old-fashioned grapevine soon enough.

He put a hand on both of their shoulders. "You guys feeling okay about this?"

"Sure." LaRouche nodded.

"I guess," Harper said, a little less confident.

"I have to work with Tomlin to resolve a couple issues," Lee continued quietly. "As soon as I can make sure everything is secure back here, I'll be joining you, LaRouche, out east. You both have a half dozen repeaters in your supplies, so make 'em count and stay in contact so we can coordinate, okay?"

"Roger that." LaRouche sighed. "How long do you think you'll be?"

"No idea." Lee shrugged. "I'll ballpark it at a week."

Harper looked at him gravely. "Just be careful, Lee."

Lee smiled. "I'm always careful."

"Okay."

Lee took his hands from their shoulders. "Take it to 'em, guys."

Without another word, they mounted up and a chorus of diesel engines rumbled to life up and down the columns of vehicles. Lee stood in the middle of them and crossed his arms over his chest, feeling sick to his stomach. If there was anything more nerve-racking than being in danger, it was sending others out to be in danger without you.

The sentries pulled the front gates clear of the road.

In the side-view mirror of the lead Humvee, Lee could see Harper looking at him. His face was pure concern, but when Lee made eye contact with him, he smiled bravely and flicked a salute off his forehead. Lee returned the gesture, and the Humvee rolled away.

Harper's convoy left first, followed immediately by LaRouche's. The long train of vehicles kicked up dust as it trundled out of Camp Ryder, slowly and deliberately into a hostile world, and in less than an hour they would be in unknown territory, among unknown threats and unknown people. They would adapt and overcome—they would have to. Everything depended on it.

Out of sight from Camp Ryder, down the wind-
ing dirt road that led away from safety and security,
Harper's lead Humvee reached the end of the dirt
road and the beginning of the blacktop of Highway 27. The column slowed to a stop as though
waiting for a break in traffic before continuing.
Then the Humvee's tires scratched over the gravel,
turning right toward Highway 421, which would
take them north toward their destination.

The column of vehicles split in the middle, half
going right and half going left.

Jerry leaned against a shanty, quietly regarding
the gates as the convoy of military vehicles disappeared from sight. His lips were pursed in concentration and his mind was working quickly now, his
heart beating quickly in his chest as he thought
about his plan. Camp Ryder was empty of Captain
Harden's thugs—all the volunteers who had any
training had just left in a cloud of dust.

His fingers and toes tingled with excitement.

The gates were closed and locked again and Bus
and Captain Harden, walking side by side, disappeared back into the Camp Ryder building. Something was going on between them and whoever
the guy was that they'd captured yesterday. Eyes
and ears around the camp were telling Jerry that
the captive was no longer so captive, and possibly he was up in the office with Bus and Captain
Harden.

Interesting.

Jerry turned quickly and strode through the
rows of shacks toward the fence line. When he

reached it, he hung a left and followed the chain-link fence all the way to the quiet northwestern corner of the compound, where a jumble of shipping containers had yet to be put to good use and no shanties had been built. He sidled between two shipping containers and found Greg waiting.

"What's the news?"

Greg looked around conspiratorially. "Just got word from Doc Hamilton in Smithfield. Apparently that guy from Virginia—"

"Jacob?"

"Yeah...apparently he shows up last night with a 'package.'" Greg's voice dropped even lower and he leaned forward. "It was an infected. They captured an infected!"

Jerry's face screwed up. "What? Why the hell would they do that?"

Greg shook his head. "That's not all, man. Doc Hamilton says that Jacob had him help with the infected. They have it secured in a room so that Jacob can study it, but here's what really freaked me out..." Greg swallowed. "The infected is a female...and she's pregnant."

The two men stared at each other.

"You're sure about this?"

Greg shrugged. "I haven't seen it. I'm just relaying what Doc Hamilton told me. And Doc Hamilton was freaked out by this shit. If you're asking my opinion, then yes...I believe it's true."

Jerry rubbed his stubbled chin. "This changes things."

"They're procreating. They're not dying off."

Jerry looked at his compatriot. "No, they're

not. I don't think it would be wise to wait until the refugees from up north get here to make our move. This is something we need to get ahead of immediately."

"We need to move now."

Jerry nodded. "Send the message to Professor White to be ready to move. The minute he gets his weapons, I want him staging right outside Camp Ryder. Out of sight. You know the plan."

Greg nodded. "I'll take care of it."

Jerry turned to leave, but then stopped himself. "Greg..."

Greg raised an eyebrow.

Jerry wagged a finger. "Don't tell him about the pregnant infected. Lie to him if you have to, but he *cannot* know about that."

Greg looked like he didn't quite understand, but he nodded anyway.

Jerry slipped quietly out from between the shipping containers.

There was work to be done.

"Let's talk about this informant," Lee said, taking a seat in the office.

Tomlin was center stage between Lee and Bus, his hands clutched in his lap, the subject of Bus's intense scrutiny. The bigger man sat leaning forward and glaring unsurely at the newcomer from underneath bushy brows. Lee had explained the situation in short form, and to his credit, Bus simply absorbed the information without reaction.

Tomlin nodded to the question. "Okay. But I should be clear: I don't know the guy."

"You knew the two marksmen," Lee pointed out. "Didn't you? Would you know of anyone else he might send?"

"First, I didn't know the two marksmen." Tomlin met their eyes. "I found out about them after they'd already been sent, but I couldn't have picked them out of a crowd. And I have no idea who they would have sent to do this job." He shrugged. "I can make some educated assumptions, though."

"Such as?"

He directed his attention to Bus. "How many people does Camp Ryder take in, let's say, on a weekly basis?"

Bus, still showing some hesitation, glanced at Lee, who nodded. Bus didn't seem to want to give Tomlin extra information, but if Lee trusted him…

"Maybe three or four a week? Usually families or groups."

"I don't think it's going to be hard to find this person." Tomlin unfolded his arms and looked a bit more confident. "They would have come within the last month, so you're talking about a maximum of maybe a dozen potential suspects. I think we can narrow it down from there."

"I imagine he would have come alone," Lee suggested.

Bus grimaced. "I don't know if we've had any single folks come in lately… except maybe Jacob."

"Jacob, the guy from Virginia?" Tomlin asked.

"Yes."

Tomlin shook his head but didn't look very sure of himself. "I don't know. He came straight from Mitchell. I mean… I guess it's *possible*…"

Bus made a grim noise. "If it's possible, we should pursue it."

Lee rubbed his neck. "No one else has shown up by themselves?"

Bus thought about it for a moment, mentally flipping the pages of an imaginary ledger. Finally, he shook his head. "No. And I personally oversee everyone who comes into Camp Ryder."

"What about groups?" Lee said. "He might have inserted himself into another group that was traveling."

"That would help hide him," Tomlin agreed.

"Most of the groups we get are families." Bus tapped a finger. "But we've gotten two groups of three in the past month that have not been related to each other. One was two men and a woman, and the other was three guys—a little younger, like maybe fresh out of college."

Now Tomlin leaned forward, interested. "The younger guys...anyone in the group stand out? Anyone strike you as military, or maybe the other two didn't seem as comfortable with him?"

Bus shook his head. "No, there was nothing really noteworthy about them. But they did get here at the beginning of last month...maybe the first week of October? Is that too early?"

Tomlin waved a hand. "It's a bit early, but not out of the question."

"Let me ask you a question, Brian." Lee steepled his fingers. "You told me earlier that you were basically concerned for my safety. Whoever this guy is...is he going to try to take me out?"

"Lee..." Tomlin seemed uncomfortable. "I don't

know. I don't know how he's communicating with Abe or any of that other shit. But I can tell you that eventually the powers that be will realize I'm no longer working for them, if they have not realized that already. And when they realize that I'm out of the equation and the two marksmen have been killed, the only person they have left to take you out is whoever snuck into Camp Ryder." Tomlin rubbed his legs. "And they want you dead, Lee."

Lee sat still for a moment. He took a heavy breath and puffed it out. "Okay. Then here's what I propose: I've got to run a batch of rifles out to Professor White's group at Lillington ASAP. While I'm doing that, you two work together to make a list of potential suspects. Then we'll question our potentials and hopefully root out the one we're looking for."

Bus shifted uncomfortably in his seat.

Tomlin nodded slowly.

Lee eyed them. "Problem with the plan?"

"Those are heavy charges to bring on someone," Bus said quietly.

"Brian's a good interrogator." Lee gestured toward his fellow captain. "He knows how to read people, and he'll know when someone's lying to him. We won't need to make any accusations—we'll keep things as friendly as possible. But we can't just sit around and wait for him to reveal himself, Bus. We're going to have to go in and pull him out."

Bus changed the subject. "You're not making the trip out to Lillington by yourself, are you?"

"Well, I figured I'd grab Eddie Ramirez and see

if we couldn't swing by and take a look at some of those vehicles we left behind. Figure out what he needs to fix 'em."

"You sure you don't want me to come with you?" Tomlin asked.

"Yes." Lee nodded. "I want you here with Bus, figuring out who we need to talk to."

"I've gotta ask..." Bus turned to Lee. "What are we gonna do when we find this person?"

Lee rubbed his hands together and inspected the ground at his feet. "I dunno. We'll just hafta cross that bridge when we come to it, Bus."

When he looked up, he found Tomlin staring at him with peculiar intensity. The look conveyed everything that Lee did not want to say, did not want to put into words, because it was nasty and divisive and would ruin relationships with the people of Camp Ryder.

Lee gave Tomlin an almost imperceptible nod.

Yeah, I know, he thought. *It's gonna be ugly.*

When Lee left the office, there was a long moment of awkward silence between Tomlin and Bus, the two men sitting across from each other, each sizing the other up. Apparently out of deference to the man who ran Camp Ryder, Tomlin kept his mouth shut and waited for Bus to say something. However, after an unsettling sixty seconds, Bus made it clear that he had no intention of being the first to break the silence.

Tomlin smacked his lips. "All right. I'll go first."

Bus cleared his throat and tilted his head back slightly.

"I think it's pretty clear that you don't like me."

"I would say that I'm . . ." Bus looked like he was trying a few different words in his mind before settling on one. "Ambivalent."

Tomlin gave him a long-suffering smile. "Ambivalent."

"Yes."

"Fair enough. Let's start out this relationship with some honesty."

"Honesty sounds great."

"There's someone in your camp who is going to try to kill Captain Harden. We're not going to let that happen, because if it were to happen there would be dire consequences for both of us. Aside from the fact that neither of us wants to see him hurt because he's our friend, we're gonna have a helluva time fighting this battle without him."

Bus nodded once.

"If you agree with that, then I'll make you a deal: I help you find this guy. I won't poke my nose in any other place it doesn't need to be, as long as I get the information I need. I come up with a list of suspects, question them, and figure out who the bad guy is. And in return for that, you trust me."

"Captain Tomlin." Bus sighed. "Trust, much like respect, is something you have to earn. It is not freely given."

"And what would earn your trust?"

Bus took a moment and realized where Tomlin was going with this. It was a good move—come up with the terms, and then make it sound like they were Bus's idea. But in reality, what other terms were there? What else could he ask Tomlin to do that would earn his trust? In the end, it all came back to the same answer.

"Help me find this guy." Bus smiled without humor. "And we'll see where you stand after that."

Tomlin grinned, causing the scars on his scalp to shift. He extended his hand. "Sounds like a deal."

Begrudgingly, Bus reached out and shook the man's hand.

There was something uniquely disquieting about knowing someone wanted to kill you, Lee discovered. Feeling both heavy and jumpy at the same time, Lee exited the Camp Ryder building into what was turning into a bright, cloudless fall day. A day that would have made him want to throw a pack together and take a trip up to the mountains in better times. Now he stood on the steps, feeling slightly sickened, and looked out at the people of Camp Ryder, bustling about their chores, gathering water, splitting wood, preparing for scavenging trips outside the wire.

Everyone seemed suspicious. They all moved too purposefully for Lee, as though they were trying too hard to be nonchalant. He felt eyes on him and when he looked, they smiled fake smiles with hidden meanings, and he could not force himself to smile back.

A grumble next to his side drew his attention back. He looked down and found Deuce standing close—but not too close—to his side and gazing up at Lee with hopeful eyes and a tail that wagged hesitantly. He'd tried to get the mutt to come inside with him, but Deuce wasn't keen on the Camp Ryder building and chose instead to lurk around the corner from the front door and mumble at passersby, as suspicious of everyone as Lee had just become.

"Hey, boy," Lee murmured. "You hungry?"

The dog bobbed his head as though he were nodding in response.

"Course you are." Lee had already brought the dog a hefty plateful of scraps after breakfast, but dogs were always hungry, it seemed. "How about a ride? You wanna go for a ride?"

The dog tilted his head.

Lee smiled and started down the steps. "Come on."

The dog followed. Lee was under no illusions that Deuce was obedient, but more so that Lee was the only one who brought him food, so naturally he tagged along, hoping for more. But that was where obedience began with dogs. Good old Pavlovian training.

He found Eddie Ramirez walking across The Square, away from the front gates. Lee called out after him and he turned and waved with a half smile. "Hey, Captain. What's up?"

"Got plans for the day?" Lee asked, shaking the man's hand.

Eddie looked back toward the gate. "Actually, I was just about to go out with a scavenging crew. See if I couldn't rustle up some car parts. Try to earn my keep a little."

Lee nodded. "I'd like to borrow you, if you can rain-check them."

Eddie looked down at Deuce, who took up a position to Lee's right. "Uh...yeah, I guess. What do you need?"

"I've got to run some rifles and ammo down to Lillington. I need a second to ride with me, and I figured we could drive over and take a look at some of those vehicles we had to leave at the airport. Maybe you can figure out what you need to fix them."

Eddie nodded. "Yeah. Absolutely."

"You know where we keep all the rifles and ammunition?"

Eddie pointed to a shipping container between the front gate and the Camp Ryder building. "I'm assuming that one you got everything out of earlier today."

"Yup. I'm gonna pull the Humvee around so we can load up."

All the gun truck Humvees had been taken by Harper's and LaRouche's groups, which left them only with the cargo variant they'd retrieved from the airport the day before. It was equipped with a radio but no turret. That was fine. If they got into any trouble, they'd ditch whatever they were doing and hightail it, rather than fight it out. It was not infected that Lee was truly concerned with—they could be outrun in a vehicle. It was hostile people with guns that worried him. But the patrols out of Outpost Lillington were now including the roads to Broadway and a few miles past, and they had not reported anything.

Lee backed the cargo Humvee up to the shipping container. It was close to the front gate so that the sentries could keep an eye on it during their normal duties. As Lee opened it up, Deuce lingered around the Humvee and took a piss on one of the tires.

The shipping container was mostly empty, save for a dozen rifles and a few thousand rounds. Everything else had gone with the two groups to help them bargain with and recruit other groups of survivors to join the fight. What was left would go to Lillington and Professor White's group. Lee didn't like having an empty gun locker, but there were more rifles and ammunition at Bunker #8. Perhaps he would make another trip out there before he left to catch up with LaRouche's group.

"Anyone give you a rifle yet?" Lee asked.

Eddie shook his head, looking a bit dubious of the little black M4. "No...didn't realize that was the welcoming gift."

Lee smiled. "Yeah, no fruit baskets here. Just an M4 and a couple hundred rounds." He took one of the rifles and one of the shoulder-sling magazine pouches and handed them to Eddie. "You ever use one before?"

"Can't say that I have."

Lee gave him a two-minute crash course on the operation of the weapon. Eddie nodded along, his eyes intense and never leaving the rifle, as though it might jump and bite him if he handled it incorrectly. Lee wasn't sure how good Eddie would be with the thing, but he still wanted his passenger to be armed.

When Lee felt that Eddie had a good enough grasp of how to use the rifle, they loaded the rest into the cargo bed of the Humvee and piled in, Deuce taking a watchful position in the back with the goods. They got their armbands from the sentries at the front gate—blue today—and then they left Camp Ryder. As they drove down the dirt road, Eddie nervously clutched his new weapon and stared at the front gate as it retreated in the side-view mirror.

TWENTY-EIGHT

TIPPING POINT

THEY REACHED LILLINGTON AT NOON.

Over the course of the last week, Professor White's group from Fuquay-Varina and Old Man Hughes's group from Dunn had built the outpost into a defensible location. The wide entrance to the south was blocked with a clutter of Dumpsters and concertina wire. A sentry manned the western entrance at all times, and there was another who roamed the rooftops, looking out for signs of trouble from infected or human threats.

As they neared the compound, the sentry atop the roof waved to them and they slowed. Lee dropped his window and hung his left arm out, displaying the blue armband they'd affixed when they left Camp Ryder. The sentry took a good look at them and Lee recognized him as one of the guys from Old Man Hughes's group. When the sentry was satisfied, he waved them on and they pulled around the corner into the eastern entrance where the second sentry, a middle-aged woman with auburn hair, was in the process of removing the white car from where it blocked the narrow alley. Lee nodded to her and she smiled and motioned them through.

"Hey, Captain," she said as they pulled abreast of her. "We've been expecting you." She leaned on Lee's door and her face became grave. "After what happened with Professor White's group, he's been pretty panicked to get his hands on some rifles."

Lee nodded impassively. "I guess he should have taken them when I first offered them."

She shrugged. "Maybe he won't give you so much grief now."

"Maybe, but I wouldn't count on it."

She cracked a smile again and allowed them to pass through.

A younger man with blond dreadlocks sticking out of a black watch cap met them in the parking lot. He regarded them coolly as they stepped out of the Humvee. He offered no greeting to Lee and kept his arms crossed defensively over his chest. "Did you bring the rifles?"

Lee gave him a look that he hoped communicated how stupid the question was. Then he pointed to the cargo bed in the back of the Humvee where all the black rifles and green cans of ammunition were stacked, plainly visible. Deuce maintained his spot in the bed and looked curiously between the two men as though he found their quiet animosity fascinating.

Dreadlocks kept up his haughty stare for a moment more before following where Lee pointed and seeing the weapons in the back of the truck. He nodded. "For the record, I don't agree with this."

Lee closed his door behind him. "Where's White?"

"Busy."

Figures, Lee thought. *He wouldn't have the balls to face me.*

"Okay," Lee said. "You wanna call your people out here so I can hand out the rifles?"

"You can just drop them here." Dreadlocks put one hand on his hip and pointed to the ground at his feet with the other, like he was some factory foreman commanding a workforce. "I'll distribute them."

Lee's expression remained impassive. "Or you can call your people out here so I can hand out the rifles...and explain how they work." He touched his chin. "Unless you have some extensive firearms experience I don't know about."

Dreadlocks rolled his eyes. "Fine."

He retreated quickly and disappeared into one of the buildings.

Eddie had crossed over to Lee's side of the vehicle and was leaning against the cargo bed, shaking his head. "Damn...they really like you."

Lee smiled. "That's my fan club."

It took a few minutes for Dreadlocks to corral his people into a loose bunch at the side of Lee's Humvee. When he had their attention, Lee spoke slowly and clearly, going over the basics of the weapon system he was about to hand out. He explained how to load the weapon, how to aim and fire, how to change magazines, and how to *tap-rack-ready* if they experienced a jam. Lastly, he went over how to disassemble, clean, and reassemble the rifle.

To their credit, though a few appeared to have the same attitude as Dreadlocks, most of them listened attentively and seemed to be absorbing the information.

It took nearly half an hour to explain and issue everyone a weapon and six magazines in a shoulder sling. They had no questions for him, and they all took their rifles and filed silently away. Lee watched them go, feeling less than enthused about handing out weapons to this group. If he were going to hand them out, he preferred it be to people who would actually help when shit hit the fan. With these people, God only knew what they would do when the bad times came. Just toting a rifle didn't make you a badass. It took a certain mental edge for a person to put a rifle to good use, and looking at their eyes, their faces, the entire way they carried themselves, Lee just didn't see it.

But who knows, right?

I've been wrong about people before.

He turned and opened the door to the Humvee. "Come on. Let's get the fuck out of here."

The waiting was unbearable.

Jerry sat in his shanty, going over everything in his mind, picturing all the outcomes like a chess player anticipating the movements of the board several steps ahead. His whole body was jittery at the thought of it, alive with tension. He found his hands becoming increasingly clammy. They were ice-cold, but somehow the palms would not stop sweating. He'd urinated three times within the last hour. Noon came and went and he couldn't find the appetite to eat anything for lunch.

He lay down on his mattress and stared at the

ceiling, but the recumbent position was too much for him to hold. He had to be up, he had to move, but he feared stepping out of his shanty. He felt his plan like a bright neon billboard strapped around his chest, and anyone he came into contact with would know.

They would know, and then they would blow the whole damn thing!

He jumped off of his mattress and paced the tiny confines of his room.

Fuck! What time is it?

He checked his watch and discovered only three minutes had passed since he'd last checked.

Jerry darted to his door and opened it a crack. If he craned his neck out just right, he could see The Square and the front gate. The sentry stood, idle at his post, his rifle slung on his back, his face relaxed.

Still no sign of Greg.

"Jesus Christ!" Jerry whispered to himself. Where was that bastard?

He closed his door and set to pacing the room again.

He could feel his bladder spasming.

He tried to ignore it, shuffling around his room like a child on the verge of wetting his pants during a game of hide-and-go-seek. The sensation persisted and finally won out. Jerry snatched up a gallon jug that sloshed at the bottom with a murky, yellow-tinted fluid. He pulled himself out of his pants and stuck the head of his penis in the top of the jug. A weak stream dribbled forth for all of five seconds.

He swore and put himself away.

It would all be worth it. It would all be worth it to see the look on Bus's face.

And Lee, Jerry thought, baring his teeth. *Fucking G.I. Joe himself...*

He straightened suddenly, tilting his head. Was that the sound of the gate opening?

Jerry rushed to his door again, pushing it open a little farther this time and sticking his head out. His heart leaped as he saw that the gate was indeed drawing open. On the other side, waiting patiently for the path to clear, was Arnie's old red Geo. What would Greg say? Was it time? Was everything in place? Or was it bad news? Did something go wrong? There were so many things that could go wrong...

He closed his door and put his back to it, only to realize that he needed to exit his shanty. He pushed through the door, forcing the unbearable nervousness to shed off of him as though he were shucking off a clingy robe. He took a deep breath as he left the safety of his little shack and walked with as much confidence as he could muster, raising his chin and relaxing his face into the barely visible smirk that he usually wore. The look of someone who is always supremely pleased with himself.

Ahead of him, the tiny gray SUV pulled through the gate and the sentry closed it back. The Geo whirled around, kicking up a tiny amount of dust, and parked in the same spot that Greg always parked in to open the tailgate and barter with whatever items he'd scavenged. There would be no bartering today, which was no loss—the little trade market was slower than usual today and only a few people were hanging out with anything to offer, and only one person had come in from Broadway to scout around for some mechanical parts.

Greg stepped out of his vehicle and his eyes went immediately to Jerry, who was just now emerging from the rows of shanties. His eyes were clouded and serious, and he gave the slightest of nods. An affirmation that made Jerry's pulse quickstep. Jerry motioned to the right with a subtle gesture of his head and the two parties converged in the center of The Square and began walking toward the northeastern corner.

"They're on their way," Greg said.

"What's their ETA?"

"They were a few minutes behind me. Might already be in place."

"And you explained everything? The signal and what I want them to do?"

"Yes."

"Good." Jerry felt almost light-headed.

They passed the last row of shanties and looked around cautiously to see if anyone was observing them. When it appeared that they were not, they walked quickly to the collection of unused shipping containers. This time, rather than squeezing into the hollow space between them, they approached the doors to one and Greg quickly knocked twice, then twice again. Then he pulled one of the doors open and he and Jerry slipped quickly inside.

The interior was dimly lit by a kerosene lantern, dangling from a hook in the roof of the container.

Lined up along each wall were ten men from Camp Ryder. They all held the M4 rifles and the shoulder-sling magazine pouches that Lee had given them. There was something vicious and ironic about that, but Jerry supposed it was not the first time someone from the US government had handed out weapons like candy and it had backfired on him.

The US had always been far too trusting.

Captain Harden had always been far too trusting.

Hubris or stupidity, Jerry wasn't sure.

All of that changed today. The world was a harsh, cold, cruel place, and people outside these walls were not their friends. They were only drains on their resources that would cut and run as soon as being a community became inconvenient for them. Jerry recognized that this was how the world worked, this was how the world had always worked, and anyone who put their best foot forward was only looking to get it lopped off.

You had to close yourself off, wall yourself in, cut out the rest of the world. That was how it had always been, and nothing had changed with the collapse of society except for the apparent nature of it. Any society that opened its doors would sooner or later be destroyed. A closed society might not be a rich society, but it was a *safe* society.

But it took strength, and purpose, and perseverance to maintain that safe society. Bus was unwilling to turn anyone away because he was an incapable leader, and as a result they had become weak. They had re-created the very same weaknesses that had doomed the United States to begin with. This time around, things would be different. Because Jerry was going to lead this community, and he was going to correct their course. He was going to set a path for them that was sustainable and promised that they would survive, and not simply starve to death a year down the road, happy that they had a clear conscience because they'd allowed any person with a sob story to come into their gates and suck down their resources.

Jerry smiled at the men before him. "Gentlemen...our future begins today."

Solemnly, they nodded. Their lips were bloodless lines on their faces, their jaws struck hard from stone, their eyes cold and ready.

"Arnie will take the post at the front gate any minute, and then Greg and I will move in." Jerry pointed back behind him. "The rest of you wait until you hear the signal before you move. You know what to do from there." Jerry smiled confidently. "This is our time. We've got one golden opportunity to take back Camp Ryder. Let's do it right."

One of the men stepped forward slightly. "We're ready, Jerry."

Jerry turned to Greg. "Do you have the flare gun?"

Greg patted his cargo pocket. "Ready to go."

"Good." Jerry took a deep breath. "Any minute now..."

Arnie Brewer hitched his baggy pants up over the loose skin of his gut, which used to hold the substantial potbelly that he could have rested a beer can on while he watched TV. Now his mid-section was floppy and weird, all the fat sucked out of it, but the skin was still there, hanging off of him like a deflated balloon. He had to position the waistband of his pants in the right spot—slightly low on his hips—so that it pinned the folds of loose skin to his crotch. Otherwise, if he ran, it would constantly flail around and smack him repeatedly in his groin.

Very uncomfortable.

With his gut-sack securely pinned to his nut-sack, he hitched the rifle up on his shoulder and approached the front gate where a young, bright-eyed kid, Jamie Bechtold, stood watch. Arnie smiled and waved as he approached.

"What's up, Jamie?"

The younger man waved back. "Fuckin' starvin'."

"Sorry, man." Arnie took a spot to the side of the gate. "Had some shit to take care of. Go get yourself somethin' to eat. I got this."

Jamie stretched tiredly. "Awright, bro. 'Preciate it."

Arnie watched the kid work some life back into his legs as he sauntered away, taking entirely too long to disappear. He looked around. The Square was almost empty. Only one or two people, standing around, shooting the shit with each other. There wasn't much trading going on today, and most people were either out scavenging or taking a break for lunch.

Arnie's gaze broke off from The Square, and he looked through the wide dirt space that cut through the shantytown. At the end of it, in the northeastern corner, he could see the shipping containers that had stood there in the same position since he'd arrived at Camp Ryder. The doors of a single container faced him, and one of them hung slightly open, the darkness inside creating a black frame around the door. A tiny half-moon face peered out at him, pale and stark in the space.

His mouth dry and gritty, Arnie shifted his feet and sidled his belt around his midsection again. Then he stared right at the face and nodded, just once.

A hundred yards away, in the quiet darkness of the shipping container, Jerry saw the signal.

He turned to Greg. "That's us. We're on."

He reached inside his jacket and felt the sawed-off shotgun slung at his side, felt the rough wooden grip of it, and took confidence from it. Moving with as much restraint as they could muster, trying desperately to look casual, Greg and Jerry slipped out of the shipping container and began making their way toward the Camp Ryder building.

Angela made her way across The Square toward the last row of shanties. She moved with purpose and carried a satchel slung onto her arm and two blankets over her shoulder. As she made her way toward the last row, Jerry and one of his friends passed by. They both looked very serious and intently busy, but when they saw her, they smiled.

Snakes in the grass, she thought to herself, but nodded and smiled politely to them. She did not like Jerry, and it wasn't at all because he had opposed Lee on so many occasions. There were some people who disagreed regularly with how Lee did things and she'd found them to be great people. She prided herself on being a pretty good judge of character, and Jerry had always struck her as...conniving.

She didn't trust him one bit.

She hung a left at the last row of shanties and walked down to the end to the brand-new shanty that had been erected for the Ramirez family. Vicky Ramirez was standing outside, banging dust and dirt out of a large quilt. She smiled widely when she saw Angela approaching.

"Hey, Vicky."

"Angela, how are you?" She gestured to the blanket. "Just doing a little cleaning."

"Where're Elise and Anton?"

"They're on the other side of the complex, playing with the other kids." Vicky balled the quilt up in her arms and stepped through the doorway to her shanty. "Come on in."

The two women ducked through the low entrance. The roof was just a tarp draped over a simple A-frame to allow rain to slide off, rather than gathering in the middle and eventually collapsing on the family while they slept. Vicky had pulled the tarp back so that the daylight illuminated their little living area.

Angela laid the blankets and satchel down on the floor. "How are you guys acclimating?"

"Oh, you know." Vicky's smile had a sadness to it. "Doin' the best we can."

Angela touched her arm comfortingly. "I understand. I felt the same way when I first got here. I know it's tough starting out, but these are all great people."

Vicky nodded. "Yes, we appreciate everything."

Angela clapped her hands. "Hey, I brought you the extra blankets you asked for." She bent down and picked up the two blankets, passing them over to Vicky.

Vicky took the blankets, looking truly grateful. "Thank you so much for that."

"Well, it's been cold." Angela smiled. "And I know how it is to take care of little ones." She opened up the satchel on the floor, revealing a collection of canned goods and a bag of beans. "A few of the others and I put together a little care package. I know it's not much, but it'll hopefully help you guys out, at least until you can get on your feet."

Vicky gazed down at the goods before her, clutching the two blankets tightly to her chest. Her face tightened and her lower lip trembled just slightly. She looked as though she was on the verge of an outbreak of emotions, but she took a breath and nodded. "Thank you. You didn't have to be so generous."

Angela smiled and waved her off. "It's the least we could do. I mean, your husband is out helping Captain Harden right now. We should at least take care of his family."

When she said this, Vicky's face did something different. Her eyes averted down and to the right, blinking rapidly as her hand came up and touched her lips. Then it seemed as though she'd realized that her strange reaction was apparent, and she turned herself away from Angela, as if to hide. She busied herself with straightening the folds of the blanket and placing them on the bed.

Angela studied the other woman for a moment, then clasped her hands in front of her. "Listen, Vicky...is everything okay?"

"Yes." Vicky faced her quickly and Angela could see shame etched on her features and the beginnings of tears glistening in her eyes. "Yes, everything's fine."

Angela took a step forward and raised her eyebrows, an expression that clearly communicated that she was not buying it. "Vicky..."

The other woman's shoulders slumped and she turned, looking at the ground. When she spoke, her voice shook and cracked. "It's just that you and the others have been so kind...and I...we've all..." Her eyes rose to Angela's and she seemed to draw herself up. "I have to tell you something... before something bad happens."

TWENTY-NINE

BAD THINGS

LaRouche stood at the hood of the Humvee, feeling the engine hot underneath the paper map laid out across the hood, the steady rumbling of it vibrating the pen in his hand. He turned and, keeping one hand on the map to pin it to the hood, shielded his eyes from the sun with his other hand and looked up at the water tower perhaps a hundred yards off to his left.

The convoy sat idling along a straight and barren stretch of road known as Memorial Church Road. Ahead of them, the intersection of Highway 581 cut across their path, surrounded by wilted and brown remnants of crops: corn on the right, and what appeared to be beets on the left.

At the base of the water tower, Jim and Wilson stood with their rifles to their shoulders, carefully scanning the surrounding fields and woods for any sign of danger. Halfway up the ladder that rose along one of the tower's legs, Lucky climbed, trailing a pack that contained another repeater set. They were slightly less than thirty miles east of Smithfield.

As he watched, Lucky reached the top and scrambled onto the catwalk to post the digital repeater. LaRouche looked back to his map and used his pen to mark the intersection with a big black dot. If they ever needed to do repairs, they would know where the repeaters were posted. After making the dot, he traced his fingers along the line of the road they were on, heading east. They were a short distance from the town of Fremont, and LaRouche immediately began to look for the best route to skirt around it.

A whistle drew his attention to the water tower.

Lucky was clattering down the ladder at an unusually fast pace. On the ground, Jim and Wilson had their rifles at the ready and were scanning out to the east.

"Shit." LaRouche banged on the hood and hurriedly folded the map. "Heads up, everyone," he yelled out to the other vehicles. "Cover the road to the east. I think we've got company."

LaRouche shoved the crumpled map into his jacket and shuffled around the Humvee to the passenger's side. Jim, Wilson, and Lucky were sprinting across the gravel lot between the road and the water tower. Lucky was waving his hands wildly while his rifle jittered about on his chest.

"Two pickup trucks comin' down the road!" he yelled as he drew close.

"How far out?"

"Less than a mile…"

"Eyes on!" Jim yelled, turning his body east and bringing up his rifle.

Down the road about half a mile, the lead pickup truck came into view, a late model, small-size pickup, burgundy in color. Following close behind it was another pickup, this one larger and newer. LaRouche could immediately see that there were people in the beds of the pickup trucks, but he couldn't tell if they were armed or not.

"Wilson, get on the fifty." LaRouche turned and faced the rest of the convoy, stepping out from the column so that everyone could see and hear him. He held up his hand. "Everyone hold your fire!"

"They saw us," Lucky called out.

When LaRouche turned, the vehicles were halted in the road like two deer caught in a spotlight. They sat abreast of each other as though their drivers were conferring about whether or not to proceed. LaRouche made himself small up against the side of the Humvee, rifle addressed toward the two unknown vehicles.

"Should we signal that it's okay?" Jim asked.

"No, fuck 'em," LaRouche snapped. "We're not here to make friends. That's the captain's job. The sooner they move on, the better."

Jim shrugged. "Your call."

"My call is 'fuck 'em,'" LaRouche repeated.

The better part of a very long minute passed in silence. For some inexplicable reason, the two pickup trucks then began to roll slowly toward them, creeping on as though their speed had something to do with their visibility. Perhaps it was a lack of common sense that told them to keep rolling toward the convoy of vehicles with guns pointed at them.

Or perhaps it was the exact opposite. Maybe the fact that they had not immediately fired upon them when they clearly had more than enough firepower to do so had convinced this mysterious third party that it was safe to proceed.

"Here they come," Wilson called out from the turret.

"Keep your gun on them." LaRouche bit his lip. "I'm gonna step out there. They do anything fishy whatsoever, please—*please*—light them the fuck up for me."

"Roger 'at." Wilson tracked the two pickups with the M2.

LaRouche swore and stood up, still holding his rifle in tight, but taking his left hand off the fore-grip and raising it high over his head, palm out. The vehicles were a hundred yards out and closing steadily, probably going less than ten miles an hour. He could see that the windows were rolled down and he called out to them. "Hold up! Yeah, stop right there!"

The lead pickup obediently lurched to a stop in the roadway.

LaRouche lowered his rifle, but only slightly. As quickly as his eyes could work, he traced them over everything he could see, in the windows, in the beds of the trucks, but the only thing he could see was weary faces, all of them fearful, grimy, and smudged with what appeared to be soot. Many of them were young, kids maybe ten or twelve years of age. Even the adults were young, with the exception of the driver of the lead vehicle, who looked to be in his mid-forties, and an elderly woman in the bed of one of the pickups, who stared blankly on at LaRouche.

Seeing this pathetic bunch of refugees, he lowered his rifle just a bit farther.

LaRouche made eye contact with the driver of the lead vehicle. "Step out of the truck. We're not going to hurt anyone, and we don't want to take anything from you. We just need one of you to hop out and come talk to me."

There was a long moment of hesitation, but the middle-aged man in the lead pickup truck finally gave a shrug, resolutely opening his door and stepping out onto the road. His hands were raised, and in his eyes was a look of defeat. "What do you want from us?"

LaRouche shook his head. "We don't want anything from you. We wanna pass on our way without any trouble, and without you causin' us trouble down the road."

The man turned, and for a moment LaRouche thought he was looking back at his people sitting in the pickup trucks. Then LaRouche realized he was looking back down the road, as though picturing whatever he had come from. When he turned back to face LaRouche, he shook his head. "Ain't nothin' for us back there."

Suspicion squinted LaRouche's eyes. "Where you comin' from?"

The man looked grim. "Ain't much left of it now." He pointed back east. "Had a little settlement outside Fremont. Me and a few of the others were in the city, pickin' through the scraps when we saw the smoke. By the time we got back to camp they'd burned everythin' to the ground. We picked up the rest of these folks about a mile down the road—they'd managed to run before the camp got taken over."

LaRouche tasted something sour. "Who are you talking about? Who's 'they'?"

The man wiped his brow and seemed to just move the soot and dirt around. "I'm guessin' it was the Followers."

LaRouche wanted to roll his eyes, but in the face of this man's tragedy, he thought it would simply be rude. So he restrained his response to a slightly sarcastic, "And what makes you think it was the Followers?"

"Well..." The man put his hands on his hips and spat on the road. "Prolly because they hung ten of our men from crosses." His face twisted just slightly and his eyes blinked quickly. He met LaRouche's gaze, and there was grief but also anger. "See, what they do is use the telephone poles. First they nail 'em to a two-by-four, then they lash that to the telephone pole." The man began to visibly shake, and his words became more strangled.

He appeared to be trying to say something else but couldn't quite do it. He brought a white-knuckled fist to his mouth and breathed ragged, furious breaths for a moment before regaining his composure enough to speak. "I can't tell you the other thing they do. I can't get it out of my mouth. You'll see... if you're headed that way."

LaRouche found himself staring at the man with his rifle hanging loosely at his side. Cautiously, he pressed forward. "The Followers are real?"

"Hell, I dunno." The man swiped at his eyes. "Whatever the fuck you wanna call 'em. Don't matter to me. But we've been hearing the rumors of them from folks traveling out of the coastal region. Thought they was fake..." He grew quiet for a moment, then shook his head again. "Didn't think they'd come this far west."

"When did this happen?"

He raked his dirty hair and rubbed the back of his neck. "We saw the smoke about an hour ago. I'm guessin' it took some time to...do what they did."

LaRouche stepped closer to the man and spoke softer. "We don't have much to spare for you folks, and I'm sorry for that. But we come from a large community, and it's less than an hour's drive from here. They'll be able to help."

The man looked up, dumbfounded. "You guys from Camp Ryder?"

LaRouche drew his head back slightly. "Uh... yeah, actually."

"Are you...are you Captain Harden?"

LaRouche was so stunned by the question that he wasn't able to muster an answer for a moment. He almost told the man that he was Captain Harden, not because he wanted to take credit, but simply because the man's eyes looked so completely hopeful. The look of defeat and desperation had fled from the man's face for that brief moment, and LaRouche didn't want him to be disappointed.

But in the end, he shook his head. "No, I'm not Captain Harden."

"Oh." The man almost looked like he didn't believe him. "Do you know him? Is he real?"

LaRouche smiled. "Yeah. He's real. We're actually out here on his orders."

The man looked confused. "What are you doing?"

LaRouche shook his head. "It's complicated. Look, you're less than thirty miles from Smithfield. They're part of the Camp Ryder Hub, so they'll help you out. Go there and tell them Sergeant LaRouche sent you, okay?"

"Okay."

"Listen…" LaRouche took another step forward. "Anything you know would be helpful. Up to this point, I've pretty much dismissed the Followers as bullshit. If you know what we're heading into…"

"Yeah." The man shoved his hands in his pockets and his shoulders drew up. "Everything we've heard has turned out to be true…except that, as far as I can tell, they didn't eat nobody. But they did kill most of the men, and several are missing, along with most of the women." The man's chin quivered. "They say they take all the girls who are old enough to bear children. They give the males a choice to join them. The ones who don't join willingly are…put on the crosses."

"You know where they went? How many there are?"

The man shook his head. "Went back east. Don't know how many there were. They was gone by the time we got back. Had to be at least fifty of them to take over our settlement that quickly." He swallowed hard. "We had a lot of people in that camp." His hands searched for something to do as he spoke and eventually just flopped down to his sides like dead meat. "This is what they do. They send out raiding parties and they kidnap people. Force them to work in the Lord's Army."

LaRouche absorbed the information. "Anything else you can tell me?"

The man thought for a moment. "No. I'm sorry, but there's nothing else I can think of."

LaRouche nodded. "Thank you. Please, go to Smithfield. They can help you."

The man eyed him. "You're really from Camp Ryder?"

"Yes, I am."

"Tell me something about Captain Harden… so I know you're tellin' the truth."

LaRouche almost laughed at the man, but he could see how fragile the courage was in his clouded eyes, and he didn't want it to break. He could have given the man some random factoid about Lee Harden that might have sufficed for the moment, but he knew the power of rumors and the power of legends, and he knew how they imparted hope and inspiration to the people who heard them, even if sometimes the truth was stretched to its limit.

"Once, when we were fighting the infected," LaRouche said, "I saw him fall down a three-story elevator shaft. Shoulda broken every bone in his body after that fall. But you know what the bastard did when I went over to try to wake him up?" LaRouche balled his fist. "He got up and punched me right in the nose because he thought I was an infected trying to attack him."

The man smiled widely. "Is that a fact?"

"That's a fact." LaRouche nodded. "When you get to Camp Ryder, you watch him walk. He's got a limp in his right leg. That's from his fall down the elevator shaft."

"Alright." The man extended his hand to LaRouche, and they shook firmly. "I believe you."

"Go see for yourself."

The man stepped back a few paces, then faced eastward, where it seemed that he paused for half a beat, perhaps struck by the forlorn appearance of his friends and family in their filthy rags and downtrodden faces. Or perhaps staring down that stretch of road and picturing the things that lay beyond that cold horizon.

Then he continued to his truck.

Just as the man reached his truck and opened the driver's door to get in, he stopped and looked back at LaRouche, his face once again grave. "You boys be careful if you're headed east. Ain't nothin' out there anymore but madmen. All of 'em... madmen."

LaRouche swallowed. "We'll keep that in mind."

"Best you do," the man said. "Best you do."

As they left Lillington and drove toward the Sanford airport, Eddie grew quieter and quieter. For a while, he held onto his rifle as though it were a blanket, but gradually he released his death grip on it and now it rested between his legs, leaned forward on the dash.

Lee chalked it up to nerves—it was the first time the guy had been out since he got to Camp Ryder, and his last experience hadn't exactly been pleasant. Now Eddie had his left hand planted firmly on his knee and the other hand was inside his jacket pocket, and he looked out the side window at the countryside as it moved by them at a steady clip. He didn't speak, but when Lee took occasional glances at his passenger, he saw the man's jaw bunching quickly.

"Listen," Lee said. "I'm not saying it's going to be clear when we get there, but when we were here yesterday, there were no infected in the area. And if there are any today, we won't stick around." Lee wrangled the steering wheel as he made a right-hand turn. "Trust me. I'm not trying to get in a fight today."

"How far are we away from Lillington?" Eddie asked.

"I dunno. Maybe fifteen miles?"

"And how far from Camp Ryder?"

"Twenty or so."

Eddie finally looked away from the window, looking at Lee for a brief moment, and then at the rifle in front of him. "Do the patrols come up this way?"

"Yeah, but not often." Lee stretched his neck. "They run between settlements mostly, so they'll cover the roads between Lillington and Broadway more than out here."

It was an odd question, but he was obviously worried about the dangers of the road.

Lee did his best to set his passenger at ease. "We

haven't seen any raiders in a few weeks—we've done a pretty good job of pushing them out of the region. And as for infected...well, they can't out-run a Humvee."

Eddie listened with his eyes closed, nodding. His lips were pressed down and pale.

Lee looked at him with a measure of concern. "Hey...you all right, man?"

Eddie's eyes opened. "Yes. Can we stop?"

"Right here?"

"Yes. Stop right here."

Is he carsick? Lee thought. *Having a panic attack, maybe?*

Eddie looked at him. "Please."

Lee let his foot off the accelerator and looked around, checking through the windows and the mirrors and scanning the woods and the fields to the side of the road. Everything was empty and barren. Just more anonymous American wasteland.

He pressed on the brakes and brought them to a slow stop, straddling the faded double-yellow line.

Lee looked to his right, saw Eddie was staring straight ahead, and followed his gaze out the front windshield. He saw nothing of note. The road led straight forward, the painted lines seeming to draw in on themselves to a single point far down the road. To their right, a barbed-wire fence with cedar posts, only a few yards from the shoulder, and beyond that just a rolling set of hills once used to pasture cows. To their left were stands of commercially planted loblolly pines, standing perfectly straight in their distinct rows like soldiers in rank and file.

Nothing else.

Lee's eyes went back to his passenger. "What's up, buddy? You gonna puke or something?"

Eddie shook his head. "I have to tell you something."

Lee had been through so much and heard so much, been shocked so many times, that he became surprised at his own surprise sometimes. He swore to himself that he should be immune to the unexpected, but somehow it still had the power to knock him back a few steps. And whenever these revelations came around, they were usually preceded by something along the lines of "I have to tell you something" or "I have bad news."

So Lee mentally hunkered down, determined that he would not let this shock him, not like the news of Abe Darabie's betrayal had shocked him, not like the news of the acting president deciding to leave the east coast to die had shocked him. He was ready for this one.

He lowered his chin, as though he were about to take a hard blow. "What is it?"

Eddie looked right at him and held his gaze this time. There was regret there, and fear. "I think you're a good man, Captain Harden. I think you're doing the right thing...and you didn't deserve this."

Lee's brow wrinkled in confusion.

"I'm sorry," Eddie said, and then he pulled a small silver revolver from his jacket pocket and shot Lee Harden in the head.

THIRTY

THE COUP

TOMLIN AND BUS WERE huddled over the desk, poring over a very short list of names and trying to figure out whom they were going to speak to first and how the hell they were going to broach the subject, when Angela burst through the door of the office, holding the hand of Vicky Ramirez.

Bus jerked upright when the door came open and stared, wide-eyed, at the two women as they stood in the center of the room. The look on Angela's face was one that bordered on panic and her companion seemed to be resisting slightly as she was pulled forward, her eyes red-rimmed as though she had been crying.

"I'm sorry!" Vicky protested. "I didn't know, I swear to God!"

Bus spread his arms out, surprised. "Um... someone mind explaining what's going on?"

Angela released her grip on Vicky's hand and stepped forward a bit. "Bus, you need to hear this. And this isn't Vicky's fault. She said she didn't know, and I believe her. Promise me she won't be punished."

Bus shook his head rapidly. "I don't even know what you're talking about yet."

Angela stomped her foot on the ground. "Promise me!"

"Jesus!" Bus threw his hands up. "Okay! I promise!"

Tomlin stepped in and spoke in a level voice. "Why don't we calm down, folks?" He turned to Angela. "No one's gonna be punished, but it sounds like pretty sensitive information. Why don't you tell us what we're talking about so we can be on the same page."

Instead of responding to Tomlin, Angela turned her gaze to Vicky and prompted her with a nod of the head. "Tell them what you told me."

Vicky's whole body tensed. "I didn't know."

Tomlin nodded. "It's okay. We just wanna know what's going on."

Angela reached out to touch her shoulder, offering gentle encouragement.

"It's Eddie," Vicky continued. "He's...uh... he's not really my husband."

Tomlin shot Bus a look. The big, bearded man still seemed somewhat bewildered by the suddenness of it all, but he lowered his chin and looked at the dark-haired woman standing across from him. The look on Bus's face was one of intense focus.

"What do you mean he's not your husband?"

Tears were appearing in Vicky's eyes again. "He's not my husband! I barely even know the guy. He met me and my kids on the road, maybe three weeks ago." She let out a tiny sob, then covered her mouth with her hand and closed her eyes for a moment. Twin streaks glistened on both of her cheeks. When she opened her eyes again, she seemed slightly more in control. "He said he knew of a place, but we couldn't get in unless we said we were a family. I know it was weird, but we were desperate...we hadn't eaten in days, and we couldn't find any clean water. I don't know anything about surviving! I was a hairdresser before all of this! But he seemed to know what he was doing, and he promised us...he promised us everything would be okay."

Tomlin leaned into Bus. "Three weeks is just about the right time frame."

Bus stood as still as a stone statue, the only motion the throbbing of the arteries in his neck. When he spoke it was like rocks grinding together. "What else?"

Vicky and Angela exchanged a worried look.

"He's got a phone...it's like a big cell phone or maybe a radio," Vicky said. "He sneaks off in the middle of the night and uses it. I don't know who he's talking to. I know I should have said something...but I just thought it was weird. I didn't think anyone was going to get hurt by it."

Tomlin tapped his finger rapidly on the desktop. "Fucking satellite phone. That's how he's been staying in contact with Abe. It's gotta be him."

Bus nodded.

Vicky raised a single finger. "There's something else."

Bus looked at her. "What?"

"I heard one of the old men lost a gun." Vicky couldn't hold Bus's gaze and looked instead at the floor. "I don't know much about guns, but I think

I saw it in his pack this morning. In Eddie's pack, I mean. It was small and silver, and I don't know if it's the same gun or not, but Eddie never said anything about having a gun before we got here." She shook her head as though she felt foolish. "I should have known..."

Angela stepped to the desk. "I think Lee's in danger."

Bus immediately whirled to the radio and snatched up the handset. "It's him. Eddie's the guy we're looking for." He keyed the mic. "Camp Ryder to Captain Harden... This is Bus... Lee, can you copy me?"

Static. Unending and emotionless.

Bus huffed into the handset. "Lee, this is Bus... Answer the fucking radio! This is Bus!"

Behind him, Bus could hear Vicky murmuring, "I'm sorry. I'm so sorry. I had no idea..."

"Can anyone copy my radio?" Bus held the PTT button down so hard, he thought he might break the handset. "Can anyone copy me? This is urgent!"

Bus slammed the handset down and looked at Tomlin with alarm tweaking his features.

Tomlin shook his head. "Something's goin' on, Bus."

Jerry held the dangling cable in his hand with a savage grin. He could feel the energy coursing through him like his nerves were rioting, like his blood had been set on fire. He dropped the cable and watched it droop over the mounting brackets of the radio antenna posted on the roof of the Camp Ryder building. He hadn't permanently damaged it but simply unplugged it. After all, they might need to use it in the future.

He stood and put one leg up on the lip of the roof, looking out over Camp Ryder, nearly shaking with anticipation. Beside him stood Greg, holding the little orange flare gun. Jerry took a brief moment to grip his shotgun solidly in his hands and breathe in the crisp air from the rooftop. From up here, he could barely smell the latrines and the dirty, filthy smell of the people themselves.

From up here, he felt like a god.

"Do it," he said. "Give the signal."

Greg pointed the flare gun up and shot it into the sky.

At the sound of a flare gun going off, Bus bolted to the office window.

"What the hell was that?" he said.

"Was that a gunshot?" Angela asked, alarmed.

Tomlin shook his head. "I don't think so. Bus, what's going on out there?"

Staring out the window, Bus watched a column of ten men, running across The Square toward the Camp Ryder building, rifles at the ready. "Uh...I don't know..."

When he laid eyes on them, his insides flip-flopped around.

"Do you see anything?" Tomlin demanded.

"Yeah." Bus hesitated for a moment. "I think about...ten guys? Running this way. They all have guns. Shit, I don't know...It doesn't look good."

Bus's mind raced back and forth, dizzy with the possibilities and unable to settle on any particular explanation for what he was seeing. He just kept staring out the window, shaking his head and frowning as though it were some puzzle to be solved, even as the ten men drew closer to the building.

Movement from the front gate caught Bus's eyes.

"Wait a minute," he mumbled. "There's a group at the front gate. The sentry is letting them in... It looks like...I think it's Professor White." Bus suddenly snapped his head toward the radio and stared at the defunct piece of equipment, and then launched himself away from the window. "Fucking Jerry!" was all he said.

Angela covered her mouth with her hand. "Oh my God!"

"What?" Tomlin almost shouted. "What's going on?"

Bus reached to the top of the metal file cabinets that sat against the wall behind his desk and pulled down the M4 that Lee had given him and that he rarely carried. He shoved the M4 into Tomlin's arms, then reached back on top of the file cabinets and ripped down the shoulder bag with the six extra magazines. "It's Jerry! He's trying to take over!"

Tomlin didn't ask questions. He slung into the shoulder bag, checked the chamber of the rifle to make sure it was loaded, and snicked the safety off. He angled himself toward the door. "We can hold off a dozen guys or so, but I don't know for how long."

"No." Bus snatched his old Colt 1911 from his shoulder holster. "They took out our radio so we can't call for help." He grabbed Tomlin by the sleeve of his jacket, staring at him with laser-like focus. "You can't go through the front door. The only way is over the roof. Can you make it?"

"I can figure it out."

"You've gotta tell the other settlements. Get some help to us. And find Captain Harden."

Tomlin nodded.

Bus pushed him toward the door. "Not much time! Go!"

Tomlin moved without hesitation. He bolted through the office door and never even asked how to get to the roof. Bus was confident that the man could do it. He looked to Angela and Vicky. "You two get out of here while you can."

Angela put an arm around the other woman's shoulders and ushered her to the door, but then she only shoved her through and closed and locked the door behind her. She turned and produced a small black pistol from her waistband. "I'm sorry, but I left my rifle in my shack."

Bus shook his head adamantly. "You're not staying up here with me. Lee would kill me if he found out..."

Tears welled in Angela's eyes. "Bus...I don't even know if Lee is alive."

Bus's jaw worked hard underneath the thick, dark beard. "He's alive."

From below them came the sound of a door being thrown open, and people started shouting. Two shots rang out, causing both Bus and Angela to jump and stare at each other with unabashed fear.

"Alright." Bus nodded. "Too late to turn back now."

He grabbed the heavy desk with an underhanded

grip and with one great, growling effort, he heaved the desk over onto its side. Then he crouched down behind it, and Angela joined him.

"We're not gonna fight if we don't have to," Bus said. "But I'm talking face-to-face with Jerry before this is over."

Angela only nodded, her hands trembling.

They waited.

Tomlin worked his way through the shadows, his heart thrashing around inside of his chest. Wild and panicked, it belied the steady, sinewy movements of his body as he crept over the catwalk that ran along the upper level and stood like a bridge across the main open area of the Camp Ryder building, where a few people still had their shanties and most people gathered to eat their meals as a community.

To the left, the catwalk dropped over a single flimsy rail, and he could see the people below milling about in panic as five of the gunmen began to surround them, firing their rifles into the roof for effect and making Tomlin pray that he didn't catch a ricochet from one of those idiots.

To his right, the catwalk butted straight into the wall where a slew of pipes, air ducts, and electrical conduits ran horizontally along the six-foot space between the catwalk and the ceiling. Straight up ahead, Tomlin could see what appeared to be the ladder that led to the roof.

The clanging of metal rungs brought his attention straight ahead.

Someone was climbing down from the roof. He could see legs working quickly down the ladder.

Attack or hide?

Hiding gave him a narrow chance, but it was the only chance he had. Bus's plan was the only plan, and he suspected that even if he had more time to consider it, he wouldn't have come up with a better one. The only hope for Camp Ryder and Captain Harden was for Tomlin to get to one of the other settlements and sound the alarm that shit was going down.

He dove to the side, wedging himself between a row of three large pipes that sat abreast of each other, and an air duct. Panic shot through him like he'd stuck his finger in a light socket. He felt sure that he was not hidden well, that as soon as whoever was coming down from the roof passed by, the person would see him sandwiched in there, and he was crammed in so tightly that he wouldn't be able to defend himself. He pictured it, his arms pinned down to his sides, his rifle facing harmlessly in the wrong direction, as his enemies raised their weapons and pumped round after round into him, and he would be conscious as each bullet ripped into his guts and split him open.

The sound of boots struck the catwalk.

Someone shouted, "Let's go, Jerry!"

More boots banging on the catwalk, then the sound of running, pounding and reverberating harder and harder as it drew closer to him.

Yes, keep running... If they sprinted past him, their chances of noticing him wedged into all these dark-colored pipes were pretty slim. If they would just keep running.

"Wait, slow up!" a new voice said, an older voice.

Shit shit shit!

"You see that?"

"Yeah."

"Motherfucker's holed himself into the office!"

Relief flooded him so hard, he thought he might piss himself.

The footsteps picked up the pace again, and two shadowy figures passed by, only inches from him. He could have reached out and touched them, and at any point in time he feared they would suddenly stop and turn to look at him, but the office held their attention.

Tomlin waited until their footsteps had retreated off the catwalk, and then he scrambled to free himself from his hiding place. He twisted and turned and finally extricated himself and his rifle, although a sharp bit of welding took a nasty chunk out of his left forearm. With his feet under him, he moved as quickly and quietly as he could manage toward the ladder.

So close . . . so close . . .

"Hey!" someone shouted.

Maybe they're not yelling at me.

"Shoot him!"

The distinct barking sound of an M4 firing three rounds in quick succession came from below him. He wasn't sure where two of the rounds went, but he watched a section of cement wall to his right suddenly explode into fragments, and he knew that the rounds were meant for him.

All pretense of stealth immediately left him.

It was do-or-die time.

He bolted for the ladder, crossing the last dozen

480 D.J. MOLLES

yards in an instant and leaping halfway up the rungs as more rifle reports came from behind him. This time he felt the rounds, impacting close to him. He could feel the shrapnel from the cement wall stinging his face, feel the ladder lurch under him as they struck the metal. He cringed, waiting for that ricochet to find him.

He kept pulling with his arms, thrusting with his feet.

Daylight above his head.

He grabbed the lip of the roof and pulled himself up like he weighed nothing at all, then vaulted himself over the edge. He hit the ground and rolled twice, then scrambled to his hands and knees, and finally to his feet.

He ran toward the edge of the roof, but then stopped himself short.

He looked around, gasping for air.

"How do I get down? How do I get down?"

The sound of shouting, echoing up to him from the ladder.

He scanned the entire perimeter of the roof but didn't see anything that looked remotely like a ladder. Not even a drainpipe that he might scramble down. How high up was he? Two stories? Three? If he busted his ankle on the way down, he'd be screwed...

A banging noise.

Metal on metal vibrations.

Someone was shimmying up the ladder.

He crouched down, making a small target of himself, and brought up the M4.

An identical rifle to his own suddenly protruded

from the hole in the roof, and it began spitting out bright tongues of flame, the operator of the weapon blindly firing over the edge, hoping to strike something. But he'd chosen the wrong direction and was firing uselessly off to Tomlin's left.

Tomlin snapped off one round and watched the rifle fly out of its owner's grip as the bullet struck it right in the receiver. From the ladder came a yelp of surprise and pain.

Should hold them off for a second...

His options were dwindling quickly. It was either jump or eventually get waxed by an enterprising individual who chose to pop up from the ladder at just the right time when Tomlin wasn't looking. He wouldn't last on the roof forever.

He ran to the edge of the roof and looked down.

It looked more like ten stories than the two or three it was.

He'd never been a fan of heights.

Lucky for him, he was facing the backside of the building, and there before him was the very same shipping container that he had escaped from, maybe five or ten feet off the side of the building. It would cut down on the distance he would have to fall and lessen his risk of injury.

More shouting from behind him.

Now or never...

He backed up a few paces to get himself a running start, then flung himself over the edge.

He thought the drop was going to take much longer, but the top of the shipping container rushed at him with surprising speed and he didn't quite have enough time to set himself up for a good landing. He hit the top of it with an explosive noise and immediately pitched forward.

He was too close to the edge.

He tumbled off the shipping container and hit the ground on his side, the magazines in the shoulder sling jabbing mercilessly at his side and sending shooting pains through his ribs. He felt the air leave his lungs and refused to go back in, his shocked diaphragm locked in position.

Got the wind knocked out... It'll come back...

He hobbled to his feet, feeling woozy and hoping his breath came back sooner rather than later. His vision swirled just slightly, and then found its correct spot and became solid reality again. He ran straight forward, toward the fence, and all the while looked up at it with his mouth hanging open, getting small breaths into his lungs and gradually working them into larger breaths.

Barbed-wire fences.

He wasn't going to climb that shit.

He glanced behind him, saw that there were no immediate threats—yet—and then turned back to the fence he was running toward, trying to find a point where he might make it through. For the most part, the bottom of the fence touched the ground, and in some places the dirt had built up and swallowed the first few rows of links. But just to his right there was a section where erosion had carved miniature canyons into the dirt. The ground cleared the bottom of the fence by a few inches.

A few inches would have to be enough.

Tomlin knew instantly he wasn't getting under

that fence with the rifle and spare magazines, but there wasn't a chance in hell he was leaving them behind. He shucked off the shoulder bag and slung it as hard as he could over the top of the fence, and then did the same with the rifle. The two objects cleared the barbed wire and clattered down a few yards into the woods.

He dove to the ground, his hands splayed out in front of him, trying to sweep the bottom of the chain-link fence away from his head. He was only partially successful, getting most of his head through before the bottom of the fence swung back into place and gouged him from the ears to the neck and then caught on his clothes.

Tomlin writhed under the pressure of the fence, only gaining inches with each movement, feeling panic welling up and not fighting that feeling. This was no fine motor skill that required a clear head; it was not a critical decision of what was a threat and what was not a threat. This was just an animal trying to get out of a trap, and if there was any time in the world to panic, it was then.

He cleared his upper body, then dug his fingers into the soft dirt and *clawed* himself all the way free of the fence. And when he was free, he didn't stop to look back or to assess the damages. He lurched to his feet and pointed himself straight into those woods. As he ran, he scooped up the rifle and shoulder bag and flew as fast as his feet would carry him.

THIRTY-ONE

JERRY

THE POUNDING AT THE office door continued for nearly thirty seconds straight. Crouched behind the overturned desk, Bus stared at the door and wondered how long it would last once the men on the other side started kicking. The pounding now was only someone's fist. It was a big, industrial door with a metal frame and would not come down easily, but it would *eventually*.

And then what? Bus thought.

The hammering fist ceased, and a voice that was only vaguely familiar came through, slightly out of breath. "Bus! You need to come out of there before we come in and get you! Don't make this harder than it needs to be!"

Bus gritted his teeth and shook his head, but he didn't respond.

Angela watched him quietly and adjusted the grip on her pistol.

"Bus..." the voice called again—Greg? Was that his name? "Are you armed?"

"Of course I'm fucking armed!" Bus yelled at the door. "Where's Jerry? Let him speak for himself. He wants to take this place over, he can come look me in the eyes and we'll talk it out."

This time it was Jerry's voice that came through the door. Lilting, proud, bitter, engorged with his own perception of victory. "I'm here, Bus, waiting for you to open the door, if you really want to face me like a man. But there will be no talking this out. We're through with talking. You've pushed us into this position, so don't bitch now that we're taking control."

Bus hung his head for a moment, and there was silence between him and the people on the other side of the door. How many were out there? Five? Ten? All armed? And Jerry especially...wouldn't Jerry enjoy it if they had to get in a shoot-out? Because there was really only one outcome to that.

"Bus, we are trying to handle this with as little violence as possible," Jerry intoned self-righteously, as though this whole situation was Bus's fault. "But you're making it very difficult. And the longer you hole up in there, the more likely it is that someone is going to get hurt."

Bus closed his eyes, rubbed them. When he opened them, he looked at Angela with a strangely serene look on his face. "You know, Angela, when I first met you, I never would have imagined one day we'd be barricaded in this office, holding guns."

Angela looked grim. "And yet, here we are."

Bus actually laughed, as though the situation was some comedic story he was hearing about secondhand. "Yes...here we are."

"I'll tell you what," Jerry shouted through the door. "I've given you plenty of chances to handle this like an adult and face the music. I'm giving you one minute to open this fucking door before we break it down! And then whatever happens will be on your head, not mine. You hear me, Bus? It's your fault! It's always been your fucking fault, and it's gonna be your fault again! Open the fucking door!"

Bus almost winced at the sound of the man's shouts, as though his voice were a particularly ear-piercing and high-pitched noise that you could feel in the fillings of your teeth and down the skin over your spine. When the room grew quiet again, he sighed quietly.

"You've got a lot of fight, Angela." He looked at the pistol in his hands. "Probably a lot more than I ever gave you credit for."

"Bus," she said, licking her lips nervously. "Maybe we should—"

"Here." Bus held out his hand. "Let me have your gun."

She stared at him like he was nuts.

"Come on. Let me see it for a second."

Slowly, she held the pistol out to him and dropped the heavy metallic object in his out-stretched hand. Bus looked at it like some alien artifact he didn't quite comprehend, and then he stood up from behind the desk.

"What are you doing?" Angela asked, a note of apprehension coming into her voice.

Bus ejected the magazine of her gun and jacked the round from the chamber. He looked at her with a sad smile, and then tossed her weapon on the floor so that it skittered away into the other corner of the room.

"Bus!" Angela stood up like she was going to make a leap for the gun.

The big man held out one giant paw to stay her, and when she was firmly rooted behind the desk again, he retracted his hand and tossed his own weapon to the ground alongside Angela's. He shook his head. "We've survived this long. I'm certainly not going to be taken out now by this motherfucker."

"Open the door, Bus…" Jerry taunted.

Angela and Bus regarded each other for a long moment, but both knew that it was the right decision. This did not have to end in bloodshed, and Bus would do the people of Camp Ryder a disservice by making a useless sacrifice of himself.

He reached forward and unlocked the door, and then stepped back.

It took the men on the other side a moment to comprehend what he'd done, but then the door flew open and two men burst through, shouting and pointing their rifles at Angela and Bus, yelling at them to raise their hands.

The man—it was Greg after all—who pointed his rifle at Bus stepped to one side, and behind him Jerry stood in the door of the office, staring balefully at Bus from under scowling eyebrows and pointing his sawed-off shotgun at him.

For a moment, Bus's heart jumped, thinking that Jerry was just going to shoot him dead right then and there… but no. Jerry didn't have the sack for such an overt act of violence. Jerry was a politician, and he knew that even though his supporters disliked Bus, they wouldn't look at it very kindly if Jerry gunned him down for no reason.

Jerry stepped forward and raised his head so that he was looking down his nose at Bus, and he sneered, the picture of haughty defiance. "Get on your knees, Bus."

Bus shook his head. "Why are you doing this?"

Jerry leaped forward but still left about a foot between the muzzle of his shotgun and Bus's chest. "Because you fucked us over, Bus! You have us running around like lackeys for that G.I. Joe, giving everything we have to his 'mission'! You just let twenty of our group—twenty innocent people—march out of Camp Ryder on a fucking suicide run to God-knows-where, to do God-knows-what, all because The Great Captain Harden said it was a good idea!" Jerry's face was a contorted mask of rage. "You're fucking pathetic! Pathetic!"

Bus laughed in his face. "And what are you going to do, hero? What's your master plan for all of this? Run and hide? Wait for it to be over?" The smile on Bus's face dissolved abruptly into a snarl. "Because I have news for you. It's not going to be over! You're not going to be able to wait it out!"

"Shut up!" Jerry shrieked.

"You think you can just wait for them to die, but you can't. They're just getting stronger!"

"Shut the fuck up!"

"And they're breeding! They're breeding, Jerry!" Bus took a step forward and reached toward Jerry in a supplicating gesture.

The shotgun blast shook the room like an explosion had gone off underneath their feet. The twin barrels flashed bright, hot, violent smoke, and Bus toppled backward like some invisible force had yanked him to the ground.

"Bus!" Angela screamed, and shoved past the man guarding her, who stood with his eyes as wide in shock as everyone else in the room, their panic-stricken gazes crossing rapidly between Bus's figure on the ground and Jerry, who stood over him, his eyes wild and glistening like a madman.

It seemed to take Jerry a moment to realize what he had done. For a moment so fleeting that it seemed to have been only a trick of the light shifting through the cloud of gun smoke that hung in the air before him, Jerry looked terrified.

"Did you see that?" Jerry began screaming. "He tried to grab my gun! You saw that, didn't you? Greg! You saw him try to grab my gun. I had to shoot him! He was trying to grab my gun so he could shoot me! I had to do it!"

Greg stood, petrified in place. His mouth worked. Like he could find neither the courage to tell the truth—that there had been no aggressive movement on Bus's part, that Jerry had shot him in cold blood—nor the intestinal fortitude to directly affirm Jerry's lie.

Angela fell to her knees at Bus's side. "Bus! Somebody get help! Help him!"

The big man lay on his back, his eyes wide in surprise, staring at the ceiling, as his chest hitched up and down, all the brawn of it mangled under the tattered and bloody remnants of his jacket. Strange noises came from him, from his mouth and from the air seeping through his lungs and directly out of his chest. No one in the room moved or ran for help, partially because they were unsure how Jerry would react, but also because they all knew that no amount of medical help would save Bus from what was coming.

Angela put her hand on his brow and smoothed back the dark curls of his hair. Hot brine welled in her eyes and her breath was becoming ragged with sobs. "Bus, look at me! Look at me! You're not gonna die. You're gonna be okay! It's gonna be okay . . . Just fucking look at me!"

As though he had not heard her until this last pained request, his eyes focused just slightly and moved down to meet her tearful gaze. His head came up off the ground with what appeared to be every ounce of effort he had within his body and he stared at her with shocking intensity for someone so close to death. "Take it," he said. "Take it. You have to."

And then his eyes became unfocused again and he collapsed backward into unconsciousness, his face shedding its color like a tree shedding the bright autumn leaves to welcome the cold barrenness of winter. The hitching of his chest became more rapid, and then it slowed, and the last sound that came from him was a slow and beleaguered groan, like the sound of a steel structure giving way under an immense pressure.

Angela squeezed her eyes shut, felt the tears trickling down her face.

She whirled on Jerry. "You fucking murdered him!"

Jerry shouted angrily back at her. "He tried to grab my gun! What was I supposed to do?"

"You're a fucking liar!" She pointed her finger in a broad, sweeping gesture. "And you're all fucking cowards for letting him do it. Murderers and cowards!"

Jerry's sneer returned to his face like stagnant water freezing over. "Tie her up and find someplace to put her. Someplace where she won't be heard."

Moving slowly, still in shock, two men took Angela by the arms and placed them behind her back. One held them clasped there while the other began to restrain her with thin cordage that bit painfully into her skin.

The anger and disbelief were suddenly vaporized in an explosion of thoughts for her daughter, Abby, and for Sam. "Jerry! I've got children! You can't do this!"

"I'll make sure they're taken care of," he said quietly. "Perhaps when you decide to calm down, you can see them again."

Angela began to pull against her bindings, but they'd already been tied too tight. "I've got to see my daughter. You can't do this! Let me see my daughter! Let me see Abby!"

Jerry gave her one last look of disdain, strangely tainted with remorse, and then shook his head. "Get her out of my office."

Angela screamed bloody murder and thrashed wildly as they carried her out, until they managed to gag her and safely lock her in the very same shipping container that Tomlin had occupied only a day before.

When the people of Camp Ryder saw Angela being dragged past them, kicking and screaming, they averted their eyes or simply shook their heads because they knew that her loyalties were to Bus and Captain Harden, and most of them who remained supported Jerry.

They looked on, scared and unsure, and some of them thought it was shameful to see such a nice lady treated like that, but none of them lifted a finger to do anything about it, because they were sure that Jerry had his reasons for doing what he did.

This would be the new Camp Ryder, and they trusted in Jerry, that he had made the right decision, no matter what it was. Now they had hope for their future. Now, things would change for the better. No more of Captain Harden's warmongering. No more sending their people out to die for reasons they couldn't understand. No more of Bus wasting their precious resources on refugees who had no right to them.

Yes, everything would be better, now that Jerry had taken control.

LaRouche stood with his feet on the double-yellow line running down the center of the highway. He faced south, his head tilted up as though scanning the skies for evil portents of things to come. A bloody sun splattered the western sky with red, a bleeding heart viewed through an open wound. The shadow of the day covered them with a cadaverous chill, and LaRouche zipped up the collar of the microfleece sweater he wore under his jacket to cover his exposed neck.

His eyes remained affixed to some elevated object in front of him.

Jim's voice was shaky beside him. "Should we . . . take them down?"

LaRouche blinked, without words.

They stood on a section of highway just outside of Fremont. To the south, a narrow but well-traveled dirt road led away from the main highway, and presumably to the camp that the man with the convoy of two pickup trucks had escaped from.

Beginning there at the dirt road, and extending east along the highway at intervals of perhaps three hundred feet, were wooden utility poles sunken into the dirt along the shoulder. Upon these poles were hung the naked bodies of ten men, some of them young, some of them older. They were hung upon crossbeams of two-by-fours, spiked through their wrists and feet, and the crossbeams lashed to the poles with rope and wire.

It was exactly as the man had described.

The aspect of their deaths that the man had been unable to describe was the disembowelment. The executioners had not simply hung the victims and left them to die, but had slit them across the bottom of their midsections, just below their navels. Their carcasses hung hollow on the crosses, their insides piled below them at the base of the pole, tethered to them only by the pale linkage of unraveled intestine.

Hung around the neck of each body was a placard on which a single word had been printed: UNREPENTANT.

LaRouche put a fist to his mouth and swallowed hard. The air was filled with stenches unimaginable, and he could feel the acid of his stomach inching up his throat, a prodding nausea insistent that he purge himself. His gaze traveled down the road.

On the side of the road, perhaps twenty-five yards from LaRouche, lay the bodies of three infected that had been tearing at the bodies like carrion eaters before the convoy had arrived and gunned them down. The fourth of their small pack had fled into the woods, wounded in the leg.

Finally, LaRouche fought down the urge to vomit enough to speak. "No. Leave them." He turned and faced Jim, whose eyes were filled with tears, and who looked like he was struggling to contain his own stomach. "We don't have time to bury them all before dark. And they might serve to warn away anyone traveling east."

Jim nodded, trembled. "Except us."

LaRouche didn't respond.

Wilson leaned out of the lead Humvee, just a few yards behind them. "Sarge, I can't get anyone from Camp Ryder to respond."

LaRouche looked at the dark-skinned man and considered this for a moment. "I'm sure they're just missing the transmission. They're probably..." He swallowed again. "Eating dinner."

"Do you want me to keep trying?" Wilson asked, his voice sounding vacant.

"We'll try again in a little while."

LaRouche turned back toward the south, but he could not look at the crucified bodies again.

Jim spoke. "What do we do now?"

A cold wind blew from the north and buffeted against their backs. It scrubbed away the foul stenches like whitewash clearing a canvas to a blank slate. But it was only so that new and unknown horrors could be painted on it. It froze them to their cores and its soft voice whispered of an end to the things they knew and a beginning of long, dark months ahead, of changes that would not only reshape them as people but would also reshape the world around them.

"We keep going," LaRouche said quietly. "We complete the mission. Whatever it takes."

THIRTY-TWO

WHAT DOESN'T KILL YOU

IMAGES OF FLASHING SMOKE and burning sparks, conforming to roiling towers of flame that reached for him, seared his eyes and puckered his flesh, and melted into vast fields of lava flow that distorted his vision with heat like the surface of the sun. He felt the right side of his head melting, hot and tingling at first, and then cold and clammy.

A beast appeared before him, its breath hot and rank, and it gnashed its teeth at him and began to eat the melted portion of his head. He did not react to this because it did not make sense, and it could only be a part of some strange death dream.

Behind the beast that fed on him, he could see random crisscrossing patterns of light and dark, slate gray and deep navy blue. The dark shapes clawed at the corners of his vision, then the gray took the center and gave way to the flailing talons of these dark creatures. In the immensity of the gray stood a lonesome spark that burned, burned, and throbbed.

Slowly, dreamily, he reached up and pushed the beast away from him, because he could not bear the sensation of it eating his melted head any longer...

Like a series of firecrackers going off along a lit fuse, the truth began to light up his mind, beginning with the feeling of *fur*.

Fur.

Dog's fur.

Not a beast.

Deuce.

He wasn't gnashing at him; he was barking.

Lee touched the side of his head that he thought had melted and felt it was intact, save for a raised, fleshy groove that stung at the prodding of his fingertips and caused him to jerk his hand back. Deuce continued to wail and bark and whine at him, and this was not truly registering with him just yet. He was dead. He was dead.

He had been shot in the head.

This wasn't—couldn't—be real.

He forced his fingers once again to the ragged wound that ran along his scalp from the hairline of his right temple to the back of his head, behind his ear. The pain cleared his mind, but only slightly. It burned badly now, the only sensation of coolness coming from the evaporation of Deuce's saliva as he dutifully licked his master's wound.

Sometimes the bullet skips off the skull, Lee heard himself say, as though it were some fleeting memory of a past life.

The barking...

The barking...

The barking...meant there were infected nearby.

Lee blinked rapidly, trying to clear his head,

trying to organize a million thoughts that
screamed at him for his attention. No, he could
not give them his attention. He could not think
about Eddie Ramirez, or betrayal, or Abe Darabie,
or—*Shit! Where's my GPS?*

In his pack.

In the Humvee that was long gone.

Sonofabitch...

But he was here, he was now, and that GPS was
somewhere else. He had a different set of problems
that he needed to solve first. There was the present
to worry about. And presently, there were infected
nearby.

Infected.

Infected. Lee forced himself to focus.

Compartmentalize...

Deuce had turned himself so that his stiff and
fearful tail was nearly touching Lee, and he faced
into the woods, barking savagely.

Weapon?

Of course not. He leaned upward, felt dizzy for a
moment, saw sparkles at the edge of his vision and
a massive, nearly debilitating headache throbbed
through his skull. Perhaps a fracture. Perhaps a
concussion. Perhaps swelling on the brain that
would kill him momentarily anyway.

*Can you even be conscious and have brain
swelling?*

He didn't think so.

He felt around on the ground, searched it
with his eyes, but found nothing but rocks and
dirt. Then he felt his vest, still strapped to him.
His magazines remained in place, along with his

KA-BAR. Eddie Ramirez must have shot him and just kicked him out of the driver's seat and into the road. If he had bothered to take the time to search the body, maybe he would have discovered that Lee was not actually dead.

No, I'm fucking alive.

I'm ALIVE!

He felt exultant, but the feeling was quickly clouded over by pain and more confusing thoughts, like the impact of the glancing bullet strike on his skull had rearranged some wires inside his head and now things were not processing correctly.

Weapon, he repeated in his mind.

The only weapon he had was his KA-BAR.

He ripped it from its sheath and held it firmly in his right hand.

The dog at his side continued to bark ferociously at the darkening woods. The sun was setting; dusk was taking over. It was cold. Soon it would be dark, and it would be even colder. He had no food, no water, no shelter, and he was unsure how long his body would hold out. He was unsure how much damage the round had done to his head. He knew other soldiers who had caught rounds to the head and survived. Some of them were normal. Others had trouble speaking. Some were paraplegics.

As though testing that last theory, he rolled onto his hands and knees and with some effort pulled one of his feet underneath him. Everything hurt. Excruciatingly.

At least I can move.

I can move, and I have a knife.

He took a deep breath to steady himself.

If you can move, and you have a knife, you can run, and you can fight.

Deuce was backing away from the wood line, nearly in a panic.

They were close now.

It was time to run.

extras

orbit

meet the author

D.J. MOLLES is the best-selling author of The Remaining series. He published his first short story, "Darkness," while still in high school. Soon after, he won a prize for his short story "Survive." The Remaining was originally self-published in 2012 and quickly became an Internet best seller. He lives in the southeast with his wife and children.

introducing

If you enjoyed
THE REMAINING: REFUGEES,
don't miss the next book in the series

THE REMAINING: FRACTURED

by D.J. Molles

CHAPTER 1

A CAPACITY FOR VIOLENCE

Angela closes the bedroom door. Her hands are shaking and the knob rattles noisily. She stands there in the hallway and stares at the door, at the flimsy fiberboard construction of it. And she knows that it won't do her any good. It won't keep him inside if he gets loose.

It is just after eight at night and the hallway is dim. Just the barest hint of the setting sun, turning everything into blues and grays. The air is still hot and humid inside her house and it smells like sickness and the rank of her own sweat. The power has been out, and she has not showered in more than a week.

From behind the closed bedroom door comes a mongrel sound. Like a dog fighting for a scrap of meat. She steps away from the door, one hand clutching her stomach, the other pulling her frazzled blond hair out of her face. She wants to feel pity for him, but there is only dread as thick as clotted blood. She cannot stop shaking.

"Is Daddy okay?"

Angela turns. Finds Abby standing there, an image of herself thirty years ago. The girl is dressed in her jeans, sneakers, and a bright pink top, everything colorful and bejeweled with rhinestones. Twinkling in the darkness of the hall.

Angela tries to answer but chokes on her words. She rubs her sweat-slick forehead and swallows hard. "Daddy's not feeling well right now."

"But is he gonna be okay?"

"Honey..."

"Is he sick like the other people?"

Inside the bedroom, he begins to thrash. The sound of the wooden bedframe rattling. He moans now, mournfully, painfully, but it soon fades to a sound of rage. A gnawing sound. Chewing. Trying to chew through the leather belts she's used to strap him to the bed.

Tom...

Angela turns away from the door and takes her daughter by the shoulders. "Come on, honey. Stay with Mommy."

She goes to the bathroom where the last of their water lingers at the bottom of a bathtub. There are a few empty jugs piled in the corner between the clogged toilet and the bathtub wall. The bathroom smells like a sewer—they'd stupidly used it for a day after the pipes stopped producing water. She's concerned about the water being in the same room as all those germs, but what choice does she have? They need to go somewhere, and they need water to get there.

Wherever "there" might be.

Maybe a FEMA camp will still be open for them. Maybe some National Guard troops will come by soon and pick them up, take them to safety. Whatever might happen, they can't stay here in this house. Not with Tom going crazy in the next room.

I could kill him.

And she had thought about it already. Thought about it for a long, long time. Sitting there next to his bed as he sweat profusely and muttered nonsense and soiled the sheets. She had thought about it as she held the printouts of his last e-mail to Trisha, whoever the fuck *that* was, before he took the flight out to Cincinnati for a "business trip." The papers had grown damp and limp in her hands, a confrontation that would never be made, and she just kept staring at this man who was a stranger to her in more ways than one.

Thinking about just doing it.

Getting it over with.

Before he tried to hurt her.

Before he tried to hurt Abby.

But she couldn't go through with it. Or wouldn't, though it amounted to the same thing. So she had tied him to the bed with leather belts from his closet. And she wasn't going to untie him when they left. And that was as cruel as she was able to be. To leave him there to die, wallowing in his own filth.

She left the printouts on the nightstand, as though Tom might come to his senses one day and read them. Now, she doesn't know what to feel, not toward Tom or the situation or the whole goddamned world. All she knows is that she is Abby's mother. And Abby is still alive. Abby still needs her.

Angela's knees crack as she crouches down next to the tub. There are tears in her eyes now, though she is not sure when she started crying. She makes no effort to hide them from Abby, just grabs a jug, uncaps it, and dips it into the tub of water.

"Help Mommy fill a water jug," she says quietly.

Abby's blue eyes well up. "Why can't I see Daddy?"

"Because Daddy is sick, and I don't want you to catch it."

"But you were in there and you didn't get sick."

Angela feels her stomach tighten like she might vomit. Between the smell of the bathroom and the emotional vertigo, she feels nauseous. "Mommy's okay. I'm a big girl and I don't get sick very easily."

Please God, don't let me get sick.

The slopping sound of water filling the jug. She pulls it up from the tub, dripping and cool. She twists the cap on and reaches for another water jug. But then stops.

The house is quiet. Tom isn't growling or thrashing in the bed.

Angela stands, takes a firm hold of Abby's arm, and moves toward the bathroom door. She leaves the other jug where it is. She steps out into the hallway, Abby's arm in one hand, the filled jug of water in the other. The bedroom door is still closed. She turns her back to it but then realizes she has forgotten something.

Something she needs.

She turns back down the hallway and stands there. The thing that she needs is at the end of the hallway, leaning against the corner nearest to the bedroom door, seeming to mock her as she considers the distance between her and it as though it is a chasm. It is Tom's softball bat. The only decent weapon in the house, and she'd been lugging it around with her everywhere she went. But in the tumult of distractions, she'd left it there.

She stands frozen in the hall, for a moment unwilling to go to the door.

But the door remains closed. Everything beyond it is quiet.

"Abby," she says quietly, "stay right here and don't make any noise."

Abby doesn't respond. She just stands there staring at her feet with her lower lip stuck out, nostrils flaring rapidly.

Angela steps lightly to the end of the hallway and takes hold of the slim, rubberized grip of the bat. It is an aluminum one, but it still has some heft to it. From inside the bedroom there is nothing but silence. Not even the sound of his labored breathing. The center of her gut aches to look in at him, to see him, maybe even touch him one last time. And then as rapidly as the feeling appeared it is replaced with the cold, bitter truth.

He got himself sick on a trip to fuck some whore in Cincinnati.

Almost didn't make it back before they canceled all the flights.

Almost left his family to die...

Almost? He did. He's leaving us right now, and it's just Abby and me.

Just Abby and me.

She turns, takes a step.

A floorboard underneath the carpet creaks.

It is like she has stepped on a land mine. From behind the door comes the most wretched, horrifying sound she has ever heard. Some high-pitched screech of rage and hunger, and the explosive cracking of heavy wooden boards as they give way. The rhythmic slamming of furniture being lifted completely off the ground and crashing back down on its feet. And she thinks that there is no way Tom can do these things because he just isn't strong enough.

She flies down the hall, seeing nothing at all but Abby at the end with her blue eyes open so wide that they seem to encompass her entire face.

"Abby! Go!"

In the bedroom there is catastrophe. Glass breaking. Wood breaking. Walls breaking. Things are being thrown, shattering, cracking, *booming* against whatever surface they collide with. And under it all is the sound of his screams coming through clenched teeth. The kind of scream that makes the belly ache and scrapes the throat raw. The kind of scream that only comes from a madman.

She seizes Abby by the arm, hauls her along with her. They move past the laundry room, past the basement stairwell, into the kitchen. Everything is dark in the waning daylight, dreamlike and smudged together. Black around the edges. Her heart beats itself to death against the cage of her ribs. From deeper in the house, the sound of the bedroom door opening and slamming against the opposite wall. Footsteps pounding down the hall.

She bolts around the kitchen counter, ripping open the back door, and then flies out into the yard, into the overgrown grass. Outside is only slightly brighter than the darkness inside the house. The gray-green earth below, the pink-splashed sky above. She keeps going straight ahead, legs pumping, dragging Abby along with her as they move through the knee-high grass.

Shapes ahead.

Pale shapes at the edge of the gray woods.

She cannot go that way. She spins just in time to see Tom lurching out of the house, still in nothing but his soiled boxers. He stumbles into the yard, strings of drool hanging from his mouth, linking to glistening patches across his chest and down to chunks of vomit that still cling to his abdomen. His dark hair is pressed in random directions by sweat and heat. His eyes are unfocused, wild, and feverish. His right arm hangs awkwardly, the wrist crumpled into a claw and bleeding where the leather belt had bitten into his skin as he repeatedly yanked against it, eventually breaking his own bones to get free.

"You bitch!" he screams at her.

For a moment it freezes her. Is it him talking or delirium? Is he angry with her for leaving him tied to the bed, or has he just gone insane?

"Tom." Angela winds up the bat, ready to swing. "Go back to bed!"

"You bitch! You bitch! You bitch!"

Abby sobs hysterically.

Tom lurches for them. For Abby.

Angela steps into his path and swings the bat in a hard right arc. It cracks him across the temple and Angela is already moving again, this time back toward the house. Her mind is almost blank but for the imperative of flight and survival. There is no conscious thought. No decisions. Only escape.

She heads toward the big orange ladder, still leaning against the side of the house from Tom's attempt at cleaning the gutters. She latches on to it and shoves Abby up, yelling at her: "Go! Climb, Abby! Climb!"

The little girl's panic causes her arms to be unwieldy and she fumbles up the ladder, losing her grip several times. Angela realizes she is still holding the water jug and the softball bat; and for no other reason than the bat is in her strong hand and she needs it to support her child, she drops it and keeps the jug.

They hurtle over the top of the ladder and onto the roof. Angela spins, her jeans scraping on the rough grit of the shingles, and she kicks the ladder off. Below them, in the backyard, three of the shapes from the woods are still racing toward them—a man and two women. They dodge the falling ladder and crowd underneath the roof, jumping and screeching and clawing at the siding.

Angela stares down at them, holding her daughter to her chest while the little girl wails, soaking her mother's shirt. Angela is wide-eyed and feels nothing but the hammering of her own heart, and she wonders if she'll ever be able to gather all the shattered pieces of herself back together.

It seems so out of control that if it weren't for the girl in her arms, she wouldn't care at all. How can you care about something so completely incomprehensible? How can you make sense of it? How can you quantify it to a point where feeling one way or the other will do you any damn bit of good?

Below them, Tom begins to stir, hitches himself up.

The thing that was once Tom.

Was once her husband.

She scoots herself and Abby away from the ledge, up to the crown of the roof where they can't see the backyard anymore. Where Abby can't see her father go insane beneath them.

Abby cries, "What's gonna happen to us?"

Angela's voice is distant, emotionless, shell-shocked. "Somebody will come for us, honey. Somebody *has* to come for us..."

Angela opened her eyes and found herself in darkness.

The air was cold and musty with the smell of greasy engine components. She tried to fight off panic and had trouble breathing for a moment. Like she was drowning in a tub of dirty engine oil. She could picture where she was, even though she couldn't see. The rusted box of a shipping container, filled with abandoned mechanical components. A place to put things to keep them out of the way until they might be useful again.

She could hear people moving about outside, so it must've been daytime, but no light reached her in the trailer where Jerry had thrown her away. She caught her breath and calmed herself, the memories fading like storm clouds that have passed on, rumbling in the distance as they leave a path of beaten fields behind them. She listened to the pulse of her heart and eventually it was steady.

She sat for a long time in one position, then another. Her mind only wandered so far. It ran a circular groove around the same questions, like a dog on a short chain: Where was Abby? Where was Sam? Where was Lee? And was he even still alive? What was happening outside of these four rusted walls?

How long had she been locked away?

Days, she thought, but she couldn't be sure.

It was difficult to gauge the time. She slept when she wasn't tired, remained wide-awake when bone-aching weariness tried to blanket her. She'd been given water and food once, but it had been a while ago. Now she felt starved and her mouth was dry as sawdust.

How long were they going to keep her there?

How long were they going to keep her from seeing her daughter?

She jolted at the sound of the chains being drawn back from the doors of the shipping container. She rose unsteadily to her feet. Felt faint for a moment, felt her scalp tingle with light-headedness. Outside the doors she could hear murmured voices. She strained to pick out what they said, but it was like the darkness dampened her ears as well as her eyes.

The doors clanked loudly. Harsh light erupted through the shadows. She squinted against it, felt her pupils constrict painfully. A gust of wind came in with it, seeming to give the light substance, and it chilled her instantly. She shrugged her shoulders, wrapped her arms around herself.

A silhouette stood in the center of the opening. She could not see the details of it, but she knew who it was. She could see the casual coolness of his body language, the long jacket hanging down to mid-thigh. The shotgun slung from his shoulder. A sawed-off contraption of his own creation.

She took a step back, feeling exposed. Her palms were moist and clammy. Every time she thought of him, every time she thought of that damn gun, she just pictured it bursting Bus's chest open. She saw her hands sinking into the gore. The stickiness in the webbing of her fingers. The way it clotted under her fingernails. Bus looking up at her and saying, "Take it. You have to..."

She swallowed. Took a breath. "Where's my daughter?"

Jerry stepped into the trailer, regarding her blankly. His hair was combed nicely, as it seemed to always be, no matter the situation. The only thing that told her that Jerry had been under any stress at all over the course of the past few days was the pale stubble along his jaw. Usually he kept himself shaven.

She waited for him to speak. His eyes meandered unpleasantly over her. The silence became long and deliberate. Just another weapon that Jerry wielded to chip away at her.

He crossed his arms. "You're a bit of a conundrum, Angela."

She considered that for a moment, not sure how to take it. Pretty sure it wasn't a compliment.

He took another step closer. "Reminds me of that old saying about women: Can't live with 'em; can't kill 'em."

Angela wanted to hold his gaze, but she was tired and her eyes drifted off to the right, to the open doors, hoping to see someone she knew, someone who would help her, but there was only the expanse of dirt and gravel that made up the backside of the Camp Ryder building, where people rarely went. The "backyard," they called it.

"Let's just be honest, shall we?" he said flatly.

She clenched her jaw. Didn't respond.

"It would be easier for me if you were dead." He spoke thoughtfully. "And yet I didn't kill you. I had an *opportunity* to kill you, but I didn't. Which, in retrospect, was a poor decision on my part. However, now everybody knows that you're in this trailer being held captive. And there are quite a few people in Camp Ryder who still view you in a positive light. So, if I were to kill you right now then I think people would...dislike that. So now I find myself in a dilemma, Angela. A conundrum."

He ran a palm gently along the side of his hair. "If I keep you locked up, people will start to wonder why. Sure, there are only maybe a half dozen or so who think of you as a friend. But they'll talk. And then others will talk. And before I know it, everyone's beating down my door and telling me to set you free. So obviously I can't keep you locked up here indefinitely, despite how much I'd like that. On the other hand, if I let you out to see your children, then what reassurance do I have that you'll play nice?"

Angela grasped at the one hope that seemed tangible. "Please, Jerry. Just let me be with my daughter. I won't cause problems."

"Ah." Jerry smiled without pleasure. "You say that now, but when some time has passed and you're getting comfortable again, you'll talk. You'll have...unkind things to say about me. You'll be the little bad apple that spoils the whole bunch."

Angela shook her head firmly. "I won't, Jerry. I won't. Just let me be with Abby."

Jerry's eyes glimmered with a strange light. He reached out to her, speaking as he did. "I'm going to let you be with Abby. I'm going to do that for you, Angela..."

His hand touched her shoulder, glided up toward her neck.

Without thinking, Angela jerked her body away and swatted at his hand.

Jerry lurched in close, so that she had no room to run, and he reached the other arm around her shoulder and pulled her down. She wasn't sure what he was doing, but then she felt his fist slam into her stomach. Just once. But surprisingly hard.

She doubled over, wheezing, and then collapsed onto her side.

She tried to catch her breath, tried to force air into her lungs, but it just kept leaking back out of her mouth with a weird groaning noise. It shocked her, but then the pain started to grow. Dull at first, and then sharp. Made her stomach feel hollow and achy.

She finally caught a breath and coughed. She watched a gob of saliva fly out of her own mouth and hit the metal floor, still trailing a glistening strand back to her lips.

Jerry sank down to his knees over her, put his hand on her neck, squeezing hard enough to let her know that she should be very still, but not so hard that it pinched her airway. Then he leaned down close to her face so that his lips brushed her ear and his hot breath moistened it.

"You see, Angela, I would never hurt you. Not like that. Because I'm just not that kind of person. But I know men who are. And if I were to allow you this kindness, if I were to let you stay in Camp Ryder and live peacefully with your child, and if you were then to repay my kindness with disrespect... well, then those men who do things for me might find you, Angela. Maybe in the middle of the night when you're snug in your bed, cradling your daughter. They might find you there, and they might do terrible things, Angela. Things that don't heal with time. Things that fuck you up in the head. Things that might fuck Abby up in the head, because she'll see it happen. She'll see every bit of it. Do I make myself abundantly clear?"

Her face pressed against the floor, staring at the trail of her own spit across it, she nodded slowly under the pressure of his hand on her neck. "Yes, I understand."

Then Jerry stood up and brushed off the knees of his pants. He regarded her with disdain, then turned and left her lying there, apparently with nothing further to say. Behind him, the doors to the trailer remained open, and another freezing gust of wind whipped through as though it might sweep her out of the enclosure like a pile of dead leaves.

Angela coughed again and sat up, rubbing her neck. She shook all over. But there was something else to it besides plain old fear. There was a tension that spread itself across her frame. Like there was a winch in the core of her body and it was connected by steel cables to all of her limbs, and someone had just tightened it a few notches. The kind of tension that eventually breaks, and breaks violently.

She picked herself up off the floor, the throbbing in her gut making it difficult to stand up straight. She bent over, hands on her knees for a moment, staring at the ground, trying to make the pain subside. Finally she forced herself upright and stepped to the edge of the trailer.

She stood there, looking right and then left.

No guards.

No people to see her leave.

She could run right now. Escape Camp Ryder.

But where else would she go?

She wrapped her arms around herself, feeling suddenly and incredibly alone. Abandoned. Without hope. Like she was caught behind enemy lines. What was there for her now? To quietly go about her life like everything was normal? Ignore Bus's murder? Ignore Jerry's threats?

She touched her stomach again, found it tender like a bruise.

A reminder that Jerry was not all frills and politics, as he often seemed.

He was capable of violence as well.

But so am I, she thought, remembering the feel of the bat as it struck her husband's skull and toppled him. Because Abby stood right behind her. She remembered the smell of gun smoke in a dark upstairs hallway in some little abandoned house with Lee battling for his life, and she remembered how the shotgun bucked in her grip, remembered watching that lead payload as it ripped flesh and bone from human beings. And she never stopped because Abby stood right behind her.

I am violent if the right buttons are pushed. She looked up into the gray-clad sky and her mouth tightened into something harder than what it had been before. She brought her gaze back down to the dirty world she lived in, and she stepped out of the shadow of the trailer and went to find her daughter.

CHAPTER 2

ANOMALY

Jacob stood at the window to the neonatal room of the Johnston Memorial Hospital in Smithfield. The same place where parents had stood to look in at their newborns. Now, though, the light of a few halogen lamps gave the place a more severe appearance, and there was nothing good inside.

It seemed a perverse place to house one of these things, but it made the most practical sense. Concerns about infant abductions had caused the hospital to make the room somewhat of a fortress to keep people out. But it also worked to keep things in. With lockable doors and a reinforced, shatterproof window, it provided Jacob and Doc Hamilton with opportunities to watch their subject without being within arm's reach of her.

So Jacob watched her, feeling a little queasy.

She was crouched against the back wall, regarding him with unreadable eyes. She was naked and horrific. The protuberance of the thing growing inside of her seemed oddly large. Perhaps indicative of some other medical problem. She still appeared dirty, but Jacob and Doc Hamilton had cleaned the worst of it off the first time they had her sedated. Partly just to relieve themselves of the smell, though it didn't last long—she continuously defecated in the corner of the room.

The way she was crouched, Jacob could see the cause for his current concerns.

Significant vaginal bleeding.

He broke the uncomfortable eye contact with the creature inside the room and looked to his right. Doc Hamilton stood there with the ultrasound cart, gloves already on, and a syringe in his hand loaded with Propofol. A cold, nervous sweat began to break out along Doc Hamilton's heavily receding hairline. He was a staunch supporter of Jerry, and their difference of beliefs was a source of unspoken tension between the two of them. Jacob also knew that Doc Hamilton had been slipping information to Jerry. Sort of spying on Jacob and his experiments.

On the cart with the ultrasound machine was a tray from the hospital cafeteria, slopped with some canned chicken, beans, and corn. Pretty decent eating by today's standards, and it seemed sacrilegious to give it to one of these beasts. But they wanted to keep their subject's pregnancy viable as long as possible. And that meant giving her as much nutrition as they could.

Everything had to be coordinated. The giving of meals, the running of tests, the checking on any medical problems such as the bleeding. It all had to be compiled into one session, because they didn't want to keep pumping her full of drugs. Though the sedative was considered mostly safe for a pregnancy, it also wasn't intended to be given on a daily basis, so they tried to give the minimum amount and make their sessions brief and fruitful.

Beside Doc Hamilton, two other men stood. One held a riot shield and a pistol. The other held the makeshift dogcatcher's pole that Jacob had originally caught his test subject with. They looked at Jacob, seeming a little nervous even though they'd done it twice already. They were two of the regular guards, and though it seemed they didn't like what had happened at Camp Ryder, they also didn't really resist it. And when Greg and his crew came knocking, they were clearly friends.

Jacob nodded to them. "Just remember to be gentle."

"As gentle as we can be." One smirked to the other.

Jacob turned back to the window. The creature still stared at him, though she had leaned forward, one hand supporting her weight. Jacob got the distinct impression that she'd seen him look away and was going to use that opportunity to creep up closer to him. Unconsciously, he stepped back away from the window.

The sound of the doors unlocking drew her attention. But she didn't attack. She recoiled, scrambling away from them on all fours, hissing and screeching at them. This was how she had reacted each time. Defensive, until she was cornered. Then she would start lashing out.

Jacob and Doc Hamilton watched as the two men got her into the corner, using the shield to protect themselves and to pin her down while they got the dogcatcher's pole around her neck.

"We got her! Come on!"

Doc Hamilton was surprisingly quick for such a small man. He ran in and slipped quickly between the two men, sticking the writhing form in the side and squeezing the payload into her bloodstream. She became more violent at first, but that was typical. After perhaps thirty seconds, the fighting slowed, and her screeching turned into a hollow-sounding moan. And maybe ten seconds after that she was completely unconscious. Arms and legs twitching. Eyelids fluttering.

"Alright." Jacob pushed the ultrasound machine into the room. "Get her up on the bed."

There was already a bed there in the room, kicked off to the side. She didn't use it—at least not as intended. She would push it into the corner, creating a little den with it, and she would hide underneath sometimes, and often sleep there. But never on it. Like she feared being exposed.

The two guards hauled her up, one at her feet and the other at her head. As they waddled backward toward the bed, they heard the steady dribbling sound of liquid hitting the floor. The guard at the feet glanced down and grimaced.

"I think she's pissing herself."

Jacob nodded, following them with the ultrasound cart but avoiding the yellowish puddles left behind. "She's heavily sedated. Not unusual."

They hefted her onto the bed and then vacated quickly, wiping their hands off on their clothes, their noses wrinkled in disgust.

Jacob pulled the ultrasound up beside the bed. Doc Hamilton hurried over, disposing of the needle in one of the biohazard bins, and then plugging in the machine. While they waited for it to boot up, Jacob put the tray of food on the floor and slid it away from them; then he gloved up and began squeezing the tube of light-blue gel onto the pregnant belly.

"Doing good, Stacey," Jacob said softly as he worked.

Doc Hamilton regarded him with some distaste. "Why you gotta name the damn thing?"

Jacob glanced at him. They'd already been through this. "We have to call her something."

"How about Subject One?"

To Doc, the creature before them was just a science experiment. He didn't want to consider that she had once been a person, and he thought that Jacob's naming of the thing spoke of some sort of hopeful naïveté, as though Jacob thought they might coax this damaged thing back to sanity. Jacob had named her, but not because he thought she was still a person.

Jacob shrugged. "She looks like a Stacey."

"You must've had a very bad encounter with a girl named Stacey," Doc mumbled.

Jacob smiled. He'd never actually known a Stacey— at least that he could remember. But for some reason when he thought of what to call the creature lying unconscious before him, he just kept thinking of her as Stacey. No idea why. She just was.

"It's ready," Doc said, handing Jacob the ultrasound wand.

Jacob pressed it against the swollen stomach. The thing called Stacey twitched a bit, but then lay still again. She made an unpleasant gargling sound, drool coming from the corner of her mouth. The speaker on the equipment crackled like a garbled radio transmission. Fluidic sounds of something squirming through the amniotic sac inside.

The heavy, steady *thump-thump* of Stacey's heart.

Then a more rapid beat.

Jacob steadied the wand, kept it there. He eyed the screen.

Doc Hamilton leaned around to get a look at the screen. "Looks like it's still alive in there."

He almost sounded disappointed.

Maybe Jacob was too. He didn't really know how he felt about it.

Doc frowned after almost a minute passed. "That…" He made a face. "That heartbeat doesn't sound quite right."

"No?" Jacob eyed his partner. Doc Hamilton was the general practitioner. Granted, he was no OB/GYN, but Doc probably had a lot more experience with pregnant women than Jacob had, since Jacob had essentially none. Jacob knew about small things. Viruses. Bacteria. Infections.

Not reproduction.

Doc Hamilton raised his wrist and looked at the windup watch he still had strapped to it. He seemed utterly focused on it, the little second hand moving about and Doc's eyes watching it like a hawk, all the while the air in the room filled with the strange *slish-slosh* of the fetus's movements and the rapid *thip-thip-thip* of its heart.

"What's wrong with it?" Jacob asked.

"Well." Doc lowered his wrist. "I guess there's nothing wrong with it, per se."

Jacob frowned at the other man, trying to get to the meat of what he was saying.

But Doc just stared at the screen, shaking his head. "It doesn't make any sense."

Greg hated Arnie's little red Geo. In a world where you were lucky not to be walking, he still hated Arnie's little red Geo. It stank of decades of decaying fast food, tiny morsels that were lodged somewhere down in between the seats and glued there by soda. Since those glory days of overindulgence, Arnie had shrunken—all that skin that used to be stretched tight by his immense stores of fat now swung around loosely inside his clothing—but when Greg was stuck in the front seat, with Arnie driving beside him, he couldn't help but picture the man at his fattest state, driving with his knees while he double-fisted cheeseburgers.

With four men crammed into it, the smell became that much worse. With the weather hitting a cold spike over the last few days and true winter coming on, people were using the outdoor shower stalls less and less. Instead, most of them opted to give themselves a "wipe down." This consisted of wiping your armpits and crotch with a wet cloth. Or a baby wipe, if you were lucky enough to find one.

Great to make sure they didn't grow a fungus, but it didn't do much for the smell.

So Greg sat in his quiet misery while Arnie drove them down the highway.

West toward Lillington.

In the days following Jerry's movement and the deactivation of the radios at Camp Ryder, there had been no word from OP Lillington. They'd heard from Doc Hamilton and Jacob at Smithfield. They'd heard from OP Benson. But nobody had seen hide nor hair of Old Man Hughes and his group.

In Jerry's opinion, Smithfield was necessary, because it was a hospital. OP Benson kept the roads between Camp Ryder and Smithfield clear, so that anyone who needed serious medical attention could go to Smithfield and see Doc Hamilton. But OP Lillington was just a waste. Another drain on their resources. It only existed so that Captain Harden could expand his area of influence and use Lillington as a jumping-off point for his operations.

So Jerry sent Greg, Arnie, and the new guy, Kyle, to scout it out. The fourth passenger, crammed in tightly with the others, was Professor White, the leader of the group from Fuquay-Varina. He'd been curious about Lillington and had been pressuring Jerry into letting him take a group to go check it out. Greg supposed that he held some sort of attachment to Lillington, or perhaps to Old Man Hughes and his group, since they had shared Lillington for a short time.

Who knew what Professor White was thinking?

But he'd been very insistent. To the point of accusing Jerry of covering things up. Suggesting that OP Lillington *had* contacted Camp Ryder but that Jerry just refused to render any help to them. And there were other issues souring their relationship. Professor White felt he'd been promised that as soon as Captain Harden and Bus were overthrown and the supplies accessed, they would all immediately make a run for the mountains. A mass exodus to escape.

Obviously Jerry was in no hurry to do this, and each day it became more evident that it wasn't going to happen. Which left White feeling betrayed. And Professor White had never been shy in his attempt to sway the court of "public opinion," if you could call a few dozen survivors living in shanties the "public."

White's presence in the already cramped car was a result of him butting heads with Jerry for the umpteenth time in the past forty-eight hours. White wanted to know what had happened to Lillington, and Jerry assured him that he would send a group out to investigate. At which point White insisted that he be a part of it. And if he didn't get what he wanted he was going to make a stink.

So he got what he wanted.

They turned onto South Main Street and hit the bridge over the Cape Fear River. Arnie slowed them down but didn't stop. They continued rolling until they were across the river. They trundled over a set of train tracks and Greg leaned forward in his seat, motioning Arnie to a stop. He pulled out a pair of binoculars and glassed the downtown area of Lillington, the little square of buildings where the outpost had been set up.

"Why are we stopping here?" White asked, shifting abruptly in the backseat and setting the vehicle to rocking.

A look of mild irritation passed over Greg's face. He pulled the binoculars away from his eyes and waited for White to quit fidgeting so the car would be still, and then he put the binoculars back up and continued to scan, slowly, carefully.

"We're checking the area, Professor," he responded, his voice less than enthusiastic.

"So you *do* think that someone is there," White pronounced triumphantly.

Greg sighed and dropped the binoculars in his lap. "I think that if I blundered into unknown situations without checking them out from a distance, then I'd be dead by now. I can't see any movement in or around the buildings." He glanced back at White. "Hostile or otherwise."

"So…"

Greg turned fully in his seat and looked at White. The professor regarded him with that usual pinched expression that sat amid all of his snow-white hair. His head slightly inclined, looking down through his thick glasses at Greg. Like he resented being forced to converse with such a lowbrow specimen.

Greg adjusted his Yankees ball cap. "Let me explain something to you, Professor. You might be able to manipulate Jerry and get what you want out of him by threatening to trash him publicly, but I don't like you. I am not beholden to you. I don't give a fuck what you think or say. I only allowed you to come along with us today as a favor to Jerry. And given the fact that I generally regard you as an idiot, whose survival so far defies logic and probability, I'm going to need you to sit back there and shut the fuck up. Okay?"

Professor White stared back at Greg, looking somewhat shocked.

But silent, at least.

Kyle sat beside Professor White and looked tense and awkward. Which wasn't difficult for him. He was one of those guys whose awkward stage somehow lasted well into his twenties. A thin, gawky neck. Just a smattering of unsightly facial hair that clumped at his cheeks and his chin, leaving the other areas bare.

Arnie grinned, chuckled. His loose folds of empty skin quivered under his chin like a wattle.

Greg turned back around. "Go ahead and take us in, Arnie. Slow and easy."

"You got it, boss."

They rolled on, Greg and Kyle readying themselves for whatever they might find, while Professor White sulked. They rolled their windows down and laid their rifles on the doors, barrels protruding out, though it was tight to maneuver a rifle in such a small vehicle.

They stopped at the intersection of South Main Street and Front Street, kitty-corner to OP Lillington. The ring of redbrick buildings had been partially secured—most of the windows and doors were boarded or covered with some sort of barricade. A few were still open, giving it the look of an abandoned project.

Greg leaned forward again, looked up to the roof of the building, and watched it for a minute.

"No watchman?" Kyle asked.

Greg just shook his head. "Go ahead and take us around back."

Arnie took them into the entrance, a narrow alley wide enough for a single vehicle. The end of the alley was usually barricaded by a car, which the guards at OP Lillington would roll out of the way for incoming friendlies, like one might open a gate.

The barricade car was rolled away. No one around it.

They crept past, then stopped in the middle of the open space, surrounded completely by all those buildings. The other barricades still stood intact—the Dumpsters and tires and other abandoned cars still stacked up and crowned with loops of barbed wire. It was only the entrance that had been left open. Like an abandoned house with the front door hanging off its hinges.

Greg opened his door, stepped out. He took a moment to survey his surroundings while behind him the others squirmed their way out of the tiny hatchback car. It was very still there in the center of OP Lillington. Greg would still check the interiors of the buildings, just to say that he had, but he already knew that the place was abandoned. He could tell just from the immense silence of it.

"Hellooooo?" Professor White yelled. "Anybody here?"

Greg spun on the man. The professor had his hands cupped around his mouth like a megaphone and took another deep breath to continue his shouting. Greg slapped the hands away from his mouth, then stood there, glaring.

"What the fuck are you doing?"

White looked concerned. "I was trying to call out—"

"Didn't I tell you to shut the fuck up?"

"But what if there are people around?"

"And what if they're the wrong people?" Greg shook his head. "Jesus, it really is astounding that you've lived this long." He turned away from the professor, stood without moving for a moment, feeling out the ensuing silence, listening for sounds of anything that might be coming for them.

Nothing.

Greg started walking for the buildings. "Kyle, you're with me. Arnie, stay with the professor, please. Make sure he doesn't do anything stupid."

"You got it."

"I don't need a babysitter, Greg!" The professor sounded indignant.

"Oh, I think you do," Greg said without turning around.

They cleared the buildings and found nobody, just as Greg had suspected. Nor did they find any sign of somebody. Or any clue as to where they had gone. Like OP Lillington had never existed.

In the quiet darkness of one of the buildings, Kyle spoke up. "You think the infected got them?"

Greg considered it but shook his head. "No. There'd be bodies. Blood."

"You think . . ." He lowered his voice. "Maybe the *hunters* got them?"

Greg just made a face of consternation. "The who?"

Kyle glanced around uncomfortably. "Some of Harden's guys were talking about these new infected they were calling hunters. Said they were big and fast. Said they hunted like animals. Ran in a small pack. Grabbed people and carried them away, instead of tearing 'em apart right there like the normal infected. Maybe that's what happened here. Maybe the hunters got them all. Carried them away."

Greg shook his head again. "Bullshit."

"Well, what do you think happened?"

Greg shrugged nonchalantly. "I don't know, Kyle."

Before they exited the building, Greg found a good pry bar lying near one of the outer doors. He picked it up, judging its heft. He seemed satisfied and left the building. In the back parking lot, Arnie and Professor White sat on the hood of the Geo, the professor looking sour and Arnie looking amused.

Greg walked over to the professor and motioned with the pry bar. "Let me show you something, Professor."

White slid down off the hood and Greg led him toward the entrance. As he passed, he gave Arnie a small nod, and then Arnie and Kyle hopped into the Geo. As Greg and White exited the former OP Lillington, the little old car rattled to life, the fan belt squeaking loudly for a few seconds.

White looked back. "Where are they going?"

Greg rolled his eyes. "Relax, Professor. They're gonna swing around and pick us up."

"Well, what's so important out here?"

Greg just kept walking until they reached Front Street, and there on the corner, he stopped. He pointed across the street with the pry bar. "You see that, Professor?"

White squinted. "What?"

"Directly across the street. Don't act like you can't see it."

White frowned with irritation, stepped past Greg. "My eyes aren't what they were . . ."

Greg hit him in the side of his right knee with the pry bar. White cried out in pain, his leg seizing, and he stumbled, trying to grab at his knee. Greg swung again, this time catching White's hand as it gripped his knee, the impact crushing his fingers. White screamed and collapsed onto the ground, holding up his injured hand.

"What are you doing?" he screamed.

Greg ignored him. He swung the pry bar down and finally hit White's knee straight on, breaking the bone and inverting the joint. Then he went to work quickly on the other leg, getting into a sort of rhythm as he hammered down onto the kneecap while Professor White screamed on and on. He felt the second knee break and then Greg stood up straight, breathing hard.

He dropped the pry bar on the ground.

Professor White sobbed uncontrollably. "It hurts! It hurts!"

Greg raised his voice over White's blubbering. "While conducting a routine scouting operation into the disappearance of the group at OP Lillington, we were attacked by a pack of infected. Unfortunately, during the ensuing struggle, we were unable to save Professor White." He bent down and made eye contact with White. "How's that sound?"

"You bastard!" Spittle flew from White's mouth. "You fucking bastard!"

Greg just shook his head. "You should've learned when to keep your fucking mouth shut, Professor. Sometimes the squeaky wheel gets the oil. Sometimes the squeaky wheel gets gone."

"I'm sorry," White muttered. "I won't say anything else! I promise!"

But Greg had already turned his back on the professor. He walked to the Geo and sat down inside, closing his door against White's rising voice as it begged and pleaded for them not to leave him there. Greg motioned Arnie on, and they sped off, leaving the professor on the sidewalk, hollering desperately as he attempted to crawl after them, dragging his crumpled legs behind him.

Greg looked into the backseat at Kyle.

The kid's face was pale.

"You gonna be okay with this?" Greg asked.

Kyle seemed shaky, but he nodded. "Yeah. Yeah. I'm okay."

The pain in his legs was blinding. Like they were caught in a mechanical crusher, one of those big ones they used to turn cars into little cubes of scrap metal. He crawled after the vehicle, dragged himself along the sidewalk, elbows and palms scraping into bloody messes against the rough pavement.

The car made the turn onto South Main Street, heading toward the bridge over the Cape Fear River. Heading back toward Camp Ryder. And then it disappeared. White lay there, one arm outstretched after the vehicle like he might just reach out and grab it. Then he collapsed, weeping in agony and despair.

He lay there for a moment, just trying to overcome the pain. Just trying to make himself move more. He didn't want to die right there, but the pain was so bad he didn't think he had the strength to keep going. Maybe Greg would come back for him. Maybe it was all just a cruel trick, to teach him a lesson so that he wouldn't talk bad about Jerry anymore.

"I learned my lesson!" Professor White screamed in desperation. "I'm sorry!"

A scraping growl echoed off the buildings.

Fear flooded his system. He evacuated his bowels in terror.

"Oh, no! No!" He hitched himself up onto his raw and bloody elbows, trying to look behind him. All he saw was a lean, sinuous form ducking behind a building, only a block from him. "No, no, no! Somebody help me! Please! Help me!"

He looked back toward South Main Street and there,

just in front of the railroad tracks, he could see a figure. Standing there next to the woods. At first he thought it might be an infected, but it was astride a dirt bike. White didn't know whether it was friend or foe, a bandit or just a regular survivor. In that moment, it didn't matter. He would take anything over being eaten alive.

He raised his hand weakly. "Help! Help!"

The figure rolled forward on the dirt bike.

"Over here!" White yelled excitedly—someone was going to save him! "Please! Help me!"

The dirt bike worked its way around the railroad tracks, and then onto the road. And when it hit the concrete, it turned, heading away from Professor White, and the engine gunned, loud enough that he could hear it over his own cries for help. He thought maybe it was a mistake; maybe the man on the dirt bike just needed to get around a median or something.

But in the following quiet, he could hear the sound of the dirt bike's engine fading.

Fading.

And then nothing.

He stared in the direction it had disappeared to. Who the hell was it? Why wouldn't the person come help him?

A guttural noise behind him.

He looked and didn't see anything.

The same noise again, this time from above.

Professor White looked up. And screamed.